THE COCKROACH BASKETBALL LEAGUE

THE COCKROACH BASKETBALL LEAGUE

by CHARLES ROSEN

DONALD I. FINE, INC.
New York

Library of Congress Cataloging-in-Publication Data

Rosen, Charles.
    The cockroach basketball league : a novel / by Charles Rosen.
       p.   cm.
    ISBN 1-55611-289-0
    I. Title.
  PS3568.07647C6   1992
  813'.54—dc20   92-53074
                                                                              CIP

Manufactured in the United States of America
10 9 8 7 6 5 4 3 2 1

Designed by Irving Perkins Associates

DEDICATED TO:

Ken Bannister
Warren Bradley
Tico Brown
Steve Burtt
Fred Cofield
Bo Dukes
John Fox
Andre Gaddy
Darren Guest
Alvin Heggs
Royce Jeffries
Cedric Lewis
Derrick Lewis
Darryl McDonald
Pace Mannion
Gary Massey
Dwayne McClain
Ralph McPherson
Lowes Moore
Pete Myers
Orlando Phillips
Derrick Rowland
Darren Sanderlin
Jose Slaughter
Clinton Smith
Elston Turner
David Wood
Steve Woodside

Thanks for the run, guys.

FOREWORD

by **Phil Jackson**

Basketball novels have not been regular fall-featured readings like spring's counterpart, baseball. For the reader who loves the game of basketball, it is like hunting down a basketball "run" in Japan. The sport itself is not as familiar to the reader as baseball because the telling takes a level of understanding of the sport. Rosen tells us why the sport is a perfect game—one that demands as much attention to offense as defense, that requires teamwork that no other sport emulates, and that has the athleticism that is unmatched.

Nearly twenty years ago Charlie Rosen and I began a relationship, making life as real as basketball. The saying, "Basketball is a metaphor for life," has long since been reversed. Problems in life have become turnovers and picks, and the joys of life have become blocked shots and fifteen foot jumpshots. Imagination only extends to what a "hammer dunk" would be if either of us could relate to such an act.

In the mid-seventies Charlie persuaded me to tell a short-lived story of my life that became *Maverick*, a book that sure is one of a kind. We shared many moments about basketball in the flesh and in the spirit. Playing against Charlie is an experience most players remember not so much from their brain-memory but from the body blows that have etched their way into the muscle-memory. Charlie at that time was a writer/teacher who coached basketball as an avocation. He was then a devoted, tie-dyed, dedicated Dead Head and could evoke a line from any song to fit the scene. Charlie's evolution moved him out of New York City and up the Hudson River to Woodstock, New York, where he began a serious artist's life as a writer. I am at fault for taking him from his typewriter and onto a bench as a coach. When I got an opportunity to coach a Continental Basketball Association team in Albany, New York, in the early 80's, I offered Charlie a job as my assistant coach, a.k.a. "trainer." The CBA at that time didn't make any room on the team's roster for an assistant coach, so Rosen, a physical education major at Hunter College, went to a quick Red Cross program, got a certificate and joined me, as a trainer on the bench. I still have a picture of him in a white suit looking like a Good Humor man. Our relationship proved a good combination of Charlie's fire and brimstone and my appearance of reasoning and patience. We had success working together for three years and Charlie moved on to become a CBA head coach.

Minor league basketball has taken a very big role in providing players for the National Basketball Association. Coaching in the minors has made Rosen a very capable coach, and his jaundiced eye has given us a view of the multi-faceted life that a coach leads in that world. The author's choice of the cut-to-the-chase scene by placing us in the playoffs of his "CBL" cuts through the many rollercoastered games and road trips. The hope of the perfect basketball play and game has been the author's true joy of the game and *The Cockroach Basketball League* is the best hope for a true basketball junkie. The practices, with or without a full roster, the preparation for the games, and the players themselves breathe of the all-too-real-world of minor leagues. Boxscores, pregame plans and set plays drawn in longhand color the story for those who like basketball strategy.

"Basketball is a very simple game," Red Holtzman used to say. The offense is dedicated to getting a good shot everytime down the floor and the defense defends its basket. What is difficult is producing the kind of chemistry necessary for a team to share the glory of scoring on the offense and the sacrifice necessary to help one another on the defense. Charlie's novelistic rendition of the life in the minor leagues certainly gives us the litmus test of the chemistry of the CBL.

—Phil Jackson

SAVANNAH STARS
PLAYOFF ROSTER

11	Brusher, Josh	6'8"	210	Savannah State '82
8	Butler, Carl	5'9"	170	Fresno State '90
10	Cooper, Donald	6'9"	230	Utah '91
7	Franks, Sam	6'5"	180	Southern Missouri '84
12	Kennison, Nate	6'8"	225	Southeast Texas '83
24	Michaels, Richie	6'5"	205	Penn State '87
13	Morrison, Benny	6'9"	265	Rhinegold State '85
32	Patton, Earl	6'7"	210	Nevada State '84
6	Royal, Kelly	6'2"	180	Metropolitan U. '88
40	Springs, Brent	6'4"	200	UCLA '89

INJURED:

Jameson, Lem	6'10"	240	Michigan State '84

KEY

- ——————→ • cut
- ——————┤ • pick
- ++++++++▷ • pass
- ∿∿∿∿↝ • dribble

1

LOOK AT THAT lazy son of a bitch.

The most talented player I've ever coached.

If I had a gun I'd shoot him.

Samuel P. Franks—6'5", 180, Southern Missouri, '84. Runs, jumps, creates, stops and pops as good as Jerry West. Sometimes plays clawing defense but mostly takes the Great Circle Route around picks. During his all-American senior year at Southern Missouri, just plain Samuel Franks went to court and added a middle name—the P. officially stands for "Points."

Sam was subsequently drafted #1 by the Dallas Mavericks (twentieth pick overall) and received 350K guaranteed for one year, which he quickly squandered on a white Cadillac, white women and white drugs. His lifetime NBA numbers—a paltry 3.2 points per game, shooting only forty-three percent from the field. Cut by Dallas in '85, Sam lasted six weeks with the Boston Celtics, six games with the sad sack Sacramento Kings and three days in France. These days Sam earns $550 per week for scoring 24.7 ppg for the Savannah Stars of the Commercial Basketball League, in league with losers, whiners and lunatic princes of the moon.

And now look what the hell he's doing—only two precious days of practice before our first playoff game and Sam refuses to shoot the ball. Even worse, as we scrimmage, allegedly rehearsing the plays I hope will overcome the Oklahoma Rangers, Sam is

matched against Brent Springs, a hard-working defensive specialist who normally can't score with a pencil. Olé says Sam, and
Brent drives hoopward one-on-none for still another resounding
rim-jammer.

Traditionally, coaches are armed with a gleaming whistle dan-
gling from a lanyard around their necks. But I am a congenital
"pinko-liberal" and a lapsed hippie, so the shrill sound of a
whistle resonates in my soul like the howling clarion of Gestapo
wagons or the promise of gunfire from fascist referees. So I
shout into the echoing arena, "Hold it! I've seen enough! That's
horseshit, guys. Go shoot free throws. And Points, come over
here."

Always stylish, he approaches the sideline slowly with a stiff-
hipped ghetto bounce. His bright penny-colored skin yellows his
eyes while a sinister Fu Manchu beard suggests a razor concealed
in his Nikes or a gun in his jock. But Sam's smile gives him away—
above perfect shining teeth there's a glip in his upper lip and his
smile is shaped like a heart. That's why, despite his arrogance and
his cultivated menace, I'm almost convinced that the notorious
Samuel P. Franks is harmless as a bunny rabbit. Nevertheless, I'd
love to bench him, trade him or even cut his lazy ass.

That's because I'm a professional basketball coach—"minor
league," please, not "semipro"—and part of my job is to speak and
act with authority. With sixteen CBL teams and twenty-seven in
the NBA, the total is forty-three pro coaches, count 'em, in the
entire country. Staying employed is the whole idea. As Kevin
Loughery once told me, "Being a pro coach is better than working.
Being a pro coach is also better than not working."

Another reason for busting Sam's chops is that he makes my life
a lie: if I'm no longer interested in yahoos democracies, if my head
has outgrown my hair, I still pursue the Sacred Hoop, truly believ-
ing that life is a metaphor for basketball.

Hi, I'm Robert Eugene Lassner—6'8", 245, Bronx College '73.
Scouts report that I'm a banger with a good eye, heavy sneakers,
bad hands and sharp elbows. Divorced, childless, a screamer on
the bench.

My lifetime stats so far:

	G	FG%	FT%	RBS	AVG	AST	TO	BS	ST	PTS	AVG
Bronx College— '70–'73	59	50.1	72.3	779	13.2	42	99	17	7	1234	20.9
Scranton Miners— '73–'74	12	66.7	66.7	13	1.1	3	5	1	0	23	1.9

SEASON	TEAM	W	L	PCT	PLAYOFFS
'87–'88	Peoria Storm CBL	29	27	.502	2-4 Lost 1st Round
'88–'89	Peoria Storm	18	38	.311	—
'89–'90	Peoria Storm	36	20	.644	8-8 Lost Championship
'90–'91	Peoria Storm	22	34	.390	—
'91–'92	Savannah Stars	33	23	.589	????????????????????????

Along the way, I've learned that a basketball coach, especially in the CBL, has a license to act like a prick. That means, when the players play like shit, I'm suffered to scream curses in the locker room, to call them cunts and faggots, maledictions which would certainly get me whacked back home in New Yawk. During an average season I'll also dispose of at least twenty ballplayers— "Sorry, Player X, I've decided to make a change." Sending them home or on to another team—"You'll love playing for Coach Y." Ruthless or humane, it all depends on the deal.

And sometimes, inside some lonely hotel room somewhere on the road, especially after a loss, I've also learned to grieve for everybody's lost dreams.

"Coach," says Sam, showing his valentine smile. "What's goin' on?"

I usually call him "Sam," so we both understand that when I publicly hailed him as "Points" in this time, this place, I've confessed a certain weakness. In truth, should Sam decide not to exert himself against Oklahoma, we'll assuredly lose and my bullshit ass is grass.

"What the fuck's goin on out there, Points? Since when do you pass up open shots?"

"Coach, don't sweat it. I'm just savin' myself for when it counts. Just givin' the young brother some confidence. If he can stop me, he can stop anybody. If he can score on me, he can score on—"

"Sam. We don't need Brent to be scoring. Sam. We need . . ."

His eyes flinch. "Whatever," he says tightly. "You the man."

"Yeah, sure. Go shoot some free throws."

While Sam sashays into the darkness at the far basket, I retreat to the hoop at hand. It seems that whenever we're fortunate enough to practice in the cavernous Savannah Coliseum, the lights are always too dim.

Standing on the foul line is Benny Morrison—6'9", 265, Rhinegold State '85. The scouting report says this about Benny: a ferocious competitor, quick moves inside, fifteen foot range, runs well for his size, short-arms too many rebounds, takes bad shots, definitely a mistake player.

Benny played two back-up seasons with Portland and was surprisingly adequate but was released when his agent demanded a three-year package guaranteeing 2.2 million. For the next two and one-half seasons Benny wallowed around the CBL, averaging eighteen points, ten rebounds and five turnovers per game, two six-packs and two pizzas per meal. Two months ago, however, the Stars purchased his rights from the Madison (Wis.) Marauders for $3,000, and Benny arrived in Savannah with a new agent, a diet and an attitude transplant. When he comes to play, Benny is easily the most dominant big man in the CBL.

Aside from his bulging bulk, Benny Morrison's most notable feature is his head—cleanshaven and topped with a thick jagged scar. "The motherfucker conked me with a beer bottle," he explains, "so I ripped off both his ears and bit off his nose."

Benny is universally referred to as "The Beast" but I always address him as "Mister Beast."

Also shooting at the same basket are Kelly Royal—6'2", 180, a reformed point-shaver from Metropolitan U., '88; the aforementioned Brent Springs—6'4", 200, UCLA '89; as well as the Stars' most dependable player, Earl Patton—6'7", 210, Nevada State '84. The topic under discussion is injuries.

"I saw it on the news," says Kelly, talking as he shoots a brick. "Tripucka pulled a hamstring last night. They're gonna wait a few days and see how it is. It's gotta be you, Earl. A white boy for a white boy."

Earl's smile reveals a crowd of crooked teeth under a bristling brown moustache. His face is hard, his eyes blue and sere. "Don't call me bwoy, bwoy."

All the while they move clockwise, shooting two shots at a time. When Benny misses two, Earl motions for him to stay on the line. "See the basket before you shoot," I tell Benny, who nods, sets and rattles one in.

"Only two kinds of boys," Kelly says. "Cowboys and white boys." He waits for the laugh. Jesus, I wish they'd've let me trade him. With his sloping forehead and recessed chin, he looks like a monstrous bug. No wonder Earl calls him Jiminy Cricket. "But that's all right, Earl," Kelly chirps. "You still my nigger."

An exchange of daps before Kelly adds at large, "I saw Earl last night stickin' pins in that voodoo doll, doin' that mumbo jumbo."

"Hey, you Jiminy-lookin'-motherfucker," Earl says, laughing. "Whatever works. I got to get the fuck out of here and back into The League. And what the fuck you doin' peepin' through my key-hole?"

But Kelly has another bulletin: "They said on the tube they're gonna X-ray Isiah's hand again today. Please, Jesus! Let it be broken!"

In mid-season Earl Patton spent twenty days on the Pistons bench. "If it is broken," he says, "then Detroit's entire coaching staff is gonna commit suicide, drown themselves in a pool of Scotch."

"Hey," Kelly says, "do they have ten-day contracts for coaches? If they all die, maybe Rob can go up."

"Hee haw," I say. "Okay, switch baskets." Please, Jesus. Don't let any NBA big men get hurt.

Sam remains at the far end and I am joined by the team's only rookie, Donald Cooper—6'9", 230, Utah '91. Also Richie Michaels, a.k.a. "Eggplant" or "Eggs"—6'5", 205, Penn State '87. Nate Kennison is the CBL's lifetime leader in games played (558) and points scored (11,829)—6'8", 225, Southeast Texas '83—and the team's psycho-killer is Josh Brusher—6'8", 210, Savannah

State '82. Carl Butler is 5'9", 170, Fresno State '90, doubling as the team drunk and back-up point guard. Carl jiggles his crotch and points offstage right. "G'head," I say, but I know he's bound for the pay phone in the lobby instead of the toilet.

This time, the topic is pussy.

"The bitch sat on me," says Richie, a fat-assed lefty jump-shooter. "Oh, *shit*. Then she spins around slowly, does an entire three-sixty. Lordy. I shot my load and almost bounced her off the fuckin' ceiling. Tonight she says she's bringin' some strawberry jam and whipped cream."

"Why don't you take notes," says Nate, "and teach the technique to your wife?"

"Sheeit," Richie says, delighted to lead the laughter. "Home cookin' ain't nothin' but meat and potatoes."

Everybody is tickled, including Cooper, and Richie pretends to be offended. "Hey, Rook. What chu laughin' at? You the only virgin in the history of professional basketball. What chu know about fancy fuckin'?"

"Don't confuse him," says Nate. "Rook, just do like I tole you. Put flap A into slot B."

Cooper shakes his head in self-defense. "The Lord is my shepherd," he mutters beneath their laughter. When he misses his next free throw, he turns to me. "Coach Lassner, what'm I doin' wrong?"

Suddenly I am envious of the brothers' joy and, like Richie, resentful of Cooper's presumption of beatitude. Resentful too of this entire sad-assed nightmare season.

Only four players here today have been with the Stars since training camp convened late last October. Don't even remind me about Bobby Parks taking 26.7 ppg to the Philippines the week before Christmas. The crusher was a three-day span in mid-January when Gary Holten, a 6'5" rookie and demon defender, tore up a knee and another rookie, 6'11" Cleve McNeil, flunked a drug test. Among other consequences, Cooper is the only surviving rookie—a loose-jointed, hot-shooting, fearless innocent, desperate to become a player. Currently, he is my pet project. When he makes The League, I'll claim to have invented Donald Cooper.

So instead of spitting or cursing, I exhale deeply, a breath I've seemed to be holding in for days. "Player Cooper," I say, "your feet are still set too wide apart and your hips are locked. You're doing this. . .instead of this. . ."

Shortly thereafter I walk them through Oklahoma's offense. The Rangers are coached by Marty Kuback—5'7", 145, Lehigh '52—a hardheaded old hypocrite who claims personal credit for every victory and blames each loss on "those stupid assholes." A CBL lifer, Kuback is also renowned for working his players like slaves, for squeezing every last drop of sweat out of every practice and even day-of-game shootarounds.

Two seasons ago, with his wife home in Philadelphia recovering from a mastectomy, Kuback got a Ranger cheerleader pregnant and aborted. Earl Patton played briefly for Kuback in Cedar Rapids in '89 and finds hope in his ex-coach's amorous exploits. "When I'm his age," Earl always says, "I hope I'm still fuckin' cheerleaders too. You gotta love it."

As much as I despise Kuback and his methodology I've also got to give the old lecher his due—Kuback's teams are always talented, well prepared and very tough to beat. He's been in the CBL final round four times, winning championships in '77 and '79. And who knows? Maybe in my heart of hearts I secretly want to be just like him when I grow up.

Oklahoma's go-to player is Ozman Joseph—6'6", 185, Oklahoma City '86—a streak shooter and earnest defender with an all-around lively game. Rumor has it that Oz remains in the CBL only because Kuback routinely bad-mouths him to NBA coaches and scouts. Too bad for me that Oz usually eats Earl's lunch.

"Who knows what Kuback's up to," I tell the team after we review the Rangers' passing game and cross-picking box-set. "Especially with three days to prepare. He's liable to put in a whole new offense. But whatever they run, it's for certain that Oz winds up with the ball. Either here"—I assume a pivot posture on the right block—"or here." The left side now, foul line extended. "Earl and Richie? When he posts, his release is much too quick for us to double down. We tried that all season long and it never really worked. So let's do this instead, something I've been saving for the playoffs. Let's front him, then double weakside from the baseline and rotate down. Like this. . ."

We go live for fifteen minutes with moderate success, although neither Richie nor Earl can approximate Oz's quickness. For the expected foul-line isolation we'll use a variation of our normal wing-trap, our "L.A." defense. I'll show that old goat. Am I a fucking genius, or what?

Oklahoma's other prominent scorers are Sidney Hodges—6'9", 210, Mississippi '86, a three-year NBA vet and rehabbed druggie. Also a rookie, Larry Fort—7'0", 250, Kentucky '91. Hodges must be pushed left and kept off the boards. "Fort is a pussy," I say. "He's gotta be bashed."

"Business as usual," Benny grins as he slams his massive right forearm into his left hand. "I'll make his fuckin' head look like a lump of silly putty."

"The Beast speaks," says Earl.

"All right. Practice here at eleven tomorrow. In case you forgot, today's payday. Checks'll be ready at two. While you're at the office make sure to pick up your scouting reports. Magoo swears they'll also be ready by two. All right. Let's do it!"

We squeeze into the center-jump circle and pile our hands in midair, suspending them over the team's logo, a dark blue nautilus emblazoned with a yellow star. As always, Sam's left hand tops the pile while my right hand is at the bottom.

Donald Cooper is a bona fide preacher's kid, yet all the players insist that Nate lead us in the Lord's Prayer. ". . . deliver us from evil . . . the power and the glory forever amen."

Later, the usual stragglers linger for reasons of their own—Cooper to practice free throws, Sam, Nate and Kelly to match three-point shots, Mr. Beast and Richie to play pivots.

"Don't fuck with me," Sam yelps when he fills the net from the far baseline. "Watch me, motherfuckers. I'm gonna drop it like it's hot." Another swisher and Sam is ecstatic. "Don't fuck with Points. Nigger, I'll steal your free cheese."

Instead of scurrying back to the confines of my hotel room like I usually do, for lunch or a nap, to make random busybody phone calls to a small list of friends, I find myself leaning against the scorer's table, afraid that Kuback has my number.

Where is happiness if it can't be found from tip-to-buzzer within the white lines? And why doesn't my wife want to live with me anymore?

When I raise my eyes to heaven, I find only 10,000 empty seats and a huge blind scoreboard. And in lieu of salvation God sends me Earl Patton.

Earl has just run several voluntary and solitary "suicides" before perching beside me on the table. Ever the consummate pro, he produces a Hilton towel from an official Detroit Pistons workout bag. "You okay?" he asks me.

"Yeah, sure. I really want to beat Kuback."

"You know," he says as he wipes his face, "fronting Oz is a great idea. And don't worry, I really think we'll be ready. After this I'm heading out to the club to lift with The Beast, so you know he'll be pumped to the sky and foaming at the mouth. He'll knock the piss out of that big wimp. Only thing is, Points and Kelly are partying tonight and Richie is just about fucked out. Those're the only problems I can see. Just make sure I get the ball down the stretch and we'll kick their ass. Kuback beats on his players too much. He takes away their heart."

"What about Tripucka? Any chance you'll get the call?"

"Not really. I'm just bullshitting the brothers. My agent says it's doubtful. Fuck 'em, anyway. Charlotte's what? Twenty games out of the playoffs? I was in The League for most of five years anyway. I've got my pension, right? So fuck it. I'd rather be in the playoffs here than be playing out the string in Charlotte. Life in the CBL. Hey, Rob. It's reality."

2

RUNNING TO DAYLIGHT in Savannah always brings a tear to my eyes and a tickle to my throat. That's because there's a paper-bag factory eastward near the airport and whenever the wind is wrong the stench is reminiscent of cockroach spray with musky overtones of boiled cabbage. The aroma is particularly overpowering when the factory cranks up on Monday mornings, strong enough to cause foolhardy birds to drop dead from the sky. Strong enough to force the airport to reroute approach and departure patterns.

When questioned, the locals take deep, defiant breaths and claim that everything smells just fine. "We're used to it," Herm Pudleigh always says. When pressed further, native Savannians declare that the factory employs four thousand workers and lowers real-estate taxes all over town. Sure, but when I first got here last October I spent two months clearing my throat and coughing, on the verge of bronchitis.

On the upside, wonderful restaurants abound in Savannah and the seafood is forever fresh. The recently renovated waterfront area is quaint and vigorously thronged with tourists who marvel at the charms of the Southland, who studiously ignore the smell, also the oil slicks and the condoms floating on the Savannah River.

The downtown area is dotted with restored Colonial houses and lush pocket-gardens, each bracketed with wrought-iron fencing and gold-lettered historical markers. The first synagogue in America is over on Elm Street. A Revolutionary War cannon sits on the margin of Bay Street, aimed inland at The Stars and Bars Bar. There's even an oldies station on the radio, WREB. The city's main traffic artery is called Victory Drive, all shaded with gracefully drooping cypress trees, presumably named to celebrate Sherman's decision not to torch Savannah. The air is always wet and even the trees seem mildewed.

The metro population of 150,000 is fifty-two percent black and the people of color out on the streets still tend to cast their eyes to their shoes whenever they pass a white. The crime rate is high— assaults, rape, burglaries—but the average white man in the street is, I suspect, secretly thrilled that most crimes are black-on-black.

It's a fifteen-minute walk to the Stars office, where I have an appointment with Herm Pudleigh, the team's managing partner, the genius who hired me. And I need the time to ponder the whys and wherefores of my days and ways. . .

We were gastronomical Jews—fried matzohs on Passover, gefilte fish on Chanukah and chicken soup every Friday night. Momma worked in the laundry at Javits Hospital, only a short subway ride from our apartment building on Fulton Avenue and 174th Street. Apartment 9, 1775 Fulton Avenue, Bronx 57, New York, New York, New York. Our building had been ritzy when it was built in the twenties, overlooking the green rolling vistas of Crotona Park just across the street. Then came the Depression and the population changed—like us, most of my neighbors were desperately trying to avoid the dubious benefits of the welfare system. So Momma labored mightily all day collecting, cleaning, drying, sorting shitty sheets and pissy pajamas. After work she haunted the neighborhood subway station handing out Party literature. Momma was a sweet woman, always tired, long-faced and sad-eyed, and stubbornly incapable of abstract thinking. If Daddy had been a Seventh-Day Adventist, Momma would have just as zealously hawked copies of The Watchtower.

Daddy was the family intellectual—thin, spectacled, bald, forever cursing his fate. "What did I ever do to deserve this?" he'd ask his empty hands. "My life is shit." Crippled by heart disease and what he called "sugar diabetes," Daddy worked out of the apartment as bookkeeper for a local settlement house. He liked to read when he wasn't working, he also liked to argue the shape of things to come with his cronies over rye bread, bowls of borscht and pamphlets.

Daddy was a brilliant man who spent his invalid years devouring whole libraries and corresponding with novelists, political columnists and anyone else who lived "out there" and bothered to answer his letters. Nelson Algren, I remember, wrote him at least one letter. So did Max Lerner.

Next to Daddy's bed was a gray torpedo of oxygen which he gulped and sucked at whenever he breathed the smell of his own death. I used to lie in bed with my pillow stuffed over my ears trying to shut out the hissing sound that meant he would live until at least the morning.

I was the doltish son, who wasted his time playing ballgames and who was only good for ferrying books into and out of every public library within reach of public transportation. My mother's young brother, Jerome, was selected as Daddy's spiritual heir. Even though Jerome was regaled with brilliant conversation and primed with the proper reading matter, he turned out to be a beer-swilling sanitation worker who married a witless girl from Brooklyn. But all of this was after my father died.

> "Whistle while you work,
> Hitler is a jerk.
> Mussolini is a meanie,
> And the Japs are worse."

All of the apartment buildings on Fulton Avenue lay exposed to a bone-stabbing wind that honed its edges along the Bronx River and drove hard through the flatlands of Crotona Park. According to each tenant's lease, the landlord was obliged to provide heat whenever the daytime temperature dropped below sixty-five degrees. In addition, the boiler was supposed to be fired at 6:00 A.M. and not dampered until 10:00 P.M. The situation required constant attention, so each building had its own superintendent living in a grimy basement apartment adjoining the boilerroom.

At 1775 Fulton Avenue, the super's name was Karl Baumer. A short, lumpy man with blanched skin and a muscular forehead, Karl also had a wife named Margaret and a police dog we called

Hitler. All three were reputed to roam the dark corridors of the basement in search of unwary cats and children to torture.

My parents would never squander a telephone call from the third floor to the basement of the same building, so I was often sent "downstairs" to complain about a leaking radiator valve or a clogged toilet. And the basement was indeed a fearsome place—all full of ratsy-scratchy noises, cats' eyes glowing from overhead pipes and secret snares set amid a crunch of broken glass. Once a week my friends and I would follow in the footsteps of the delivery man to watch the coal come tumbling into the bin. But Jeff Korkorian was the only one among us who showed no fear of the cellars of doom.

There were two obvious accesses to the basement—a flight of slatted metal steps in the front of the building, and a creaking metal doorway in the rear alley. We also believed that Karl kept the front stoop under constant surveillance from some hidden peephole: on the first day that Karl took over the job, all the neighborhood ruffians dashed madly down the street to knock over the garbage cans that routinely flanked the stoop. But before we could race to a hiding place, Karl appeared with Hitler on a short chain. The dog snarled and pawed after us and we knew that it would kill us if it only got the chance. "I know who done it," Karl grunted at our flying backs.

Those were the only words he ever spoke to us. Then he took Hitler back into the basement and calmly cleaned the mess without even looking at us as we cowered behind a visiting Buick. Jeff Korkorian said he thought he could hear Karl singing as he worked. And none of us, not even Jeff, ever mishandled Karl's garbage cans again.

We usually caught a glimpse of Karl when he stood silently at the edge of the coal bin and inspected each delivery. Once in a while the dumbwaiter would break and Karl would go from door to door collecting garbage in a huge canvas sack. A satanic Santa bearing rotting refuse and jagged tin cans, attended by the devil's legion of flies.

Yet whenever we were moved to play stickball, Jeff always accepted the dare and slithered alone through the back alley door to steal one of Karl's brooms. There were other supers and other basements, but Karl's exotic (imported?) hardwood brooms were the equivalent of Mickey Mantle's bats. A good broom handle would last several weeks until it cracked on a long home run—and Jeff was never caught.

I never saw Hitler again, and I never actually saw Karl's wife, but Jeff would report on their activities. "I seen her dipping a dead rat in a pail of blood and eating it," said Jeff. "I seen her fuckin' the dog."

Karl was always a loyal employee, so at least two evenings every week the radiators on the top floor would begin to cool at nine o'clock. Within ten minutes the entire building would ring with a bedlam of pots banging against the silver-painted radiator pipes. Then the old women would peep out of their doors, kiss their doorjamb mezuzahs and scream down the stairwell: "Karl! Where's the steam? You Nazi!"

The landlord was a Jew, so the heat lasted until eleven on Friday nights—but the steam always rose at the same time every morning. The pipes began gurgling and clanging exactly at six on the first floor and at ten-minute intervals up to the sixth floor.

I had a tiny bedroom in the rear of the railroad flat and I always heard my mother stirring early every Saturday morning. Sometimes I even caught a whiff of frying onions, or an early savor of pot roast or stuffed cabbage. I would snuggle into a coarse brown blanket, dreaming of warmth, of love, of a boiled drumstick. But once a month, whenever my mother "did" the kitchen, I would roll out of bed at the first sound of heat.

Momma would be wearing her oldest housedress, with a kerchief tied over her head. For many years she never let me help but I was permitted to watch from the doorway. First off, she spread newspapers on the floor, the stove, the table, the top of the refrigerator and over every other naked surface in the room. Then she would creep on the floor, clamber up chairs—and use a squeaky flitgun to spray the corners, crevices and recesses of the heating pipes with a pungent roachicide. As she sprayed, the shiny black vermin would be roused from their nests to wriggle out along the pipes until their stiff, greasy bodies fell and tapped like timid gunfire against the New York *Times*, the *Compass* and the *Daily Worker*. Whenever a neighbor's apartment was newly painted and the resident roaches displaced, the "doing" required two doses.

After the fumes settled and the most stubborn victims succumbed, Momma would throw open the windows to the frigid winter wind and scrub every inch of the room with rags, steelwool and Old Dutch Cleanser. When I graduated from elementary school my mother allowed me to dispose of the newspapers.

The carnage could never be harbored overnight or until our next scheduled appointment with the dumbwaiter. So as soon as the roaches stopped falling I would gather the newspapers and lightly stuff them into several empty paper bags. I usually completed the task at a run, but I always took special care to lean the loathsome packages as precariously as possible against Karl's garbage cans— so they could be knocked over by a breeze, a passing car or a heavy footstep. Just to bust his chops.

Then, big as I was, my hands still slippery with roach slime, I would hide behind a stone railing at the top of the stoop until Karl emerged from his lair. While he muttered gutteral curses he would cram the poisonous mess deep into the garbage cans with his bare hands and stomp it down with his foot.

And I know for certain that he never saw me hiding there on the stoop. Because after the very last time I ever spilled my cockroach debris on the sidewalk, I watched him throw his hands to the sky and weep.

No surprise that my parents were staunch atheists and both sets of grandparents were long dead, but Daddy was sick and who knew how long he would live, etc., so tradition proved stronger than politics. That's why for six months previous to my thirteenth birthday—while my classmates lingered in the schoolyard playing ball, flirting with girls, sharing secrets and rumors—I had to be home every day at 3:30 and submit to an agonizing bar mitzvah lesson.

Old Rabbi Shapiro understood that Momma was still at work and Daddy was either reading or asleep, so he always commenced each lesson by reconnoitering the refrigerator for a slice rye bread, maybe a boiled chicken wing, your mother wouldn't mind, tell her it was for the rabbi.

For his services the old man charged $1.25 an hour, teaching me to translate Hebrew markings into meaningless sounds, then to croon those sounds in ancient laments. The rabbi picked his ears and teeth with the same popsicle stick he used to lead me through the sacred texts.

"Baha baha. Adonoi elo hainu."

Finally the great day arrived. Inside the synagogue, stale and dry as a crypt, the congregation intoned their mournful morning prayers with their heads nodding at each fearful *"Adonoi."* I wore my only suit (an all-purpose blue, also suitable for funerals), a blue necktie and a white prayer shawl. For the occasion, my father gave me the same black yarmulke from his own bar mitzvah and it stuck to my head like a scab. "Stand here," Rabbi Shapiro said, grizzly faced and sucking on a sardine candyball. "I'll tell you ven."

In the front gallery the old men finished first and coughed until the others caught up. Then Rabbi Shapiro grasped the podium, cleared his throat to silence the congregation and said, "We have here with us today, this morning, a bar mitzvah boy, soon to be a man." Then he turned with a loud, hoarse whisper: "Now. Don't vorry. You'll be just great."

But the script in the open golden book was much more medieval than the lean characters in my own bar mitzvah handbook. Meanwhile, the women sat unseen in a balcony behind me and I could hear Momma sobbing as I began:

"Baha baha. K'dosh. K'dosh. Elo hainu prehagofen. Baha baha."

This time, Rabbi Shapiro used his forefinger to guide me, a long yellowish bone topped with a curving yellow horn. One by one, the Hebrew symbols screamed as the fingernail scratched across the page. *"Adonoi. Adonoi."* Behind me, something was poised to do me harm, but I dare not turn from my throbbing text. *"K'dosh. K'doshes. K'doshem."*

. . .We were a desert race, living inside goatskin tents and howling at the moon. Then farmers, worshipping wooden phallix and raping vestal virgins in ecstatic rites. *Baha. Baha.* Then Lord Jehovah spake unto Abram to kill him a son. "Woe for my chosen people for they are hard-necked and brass-hearted. Yet are these among the signs of my covenant with Thee." *Baha. Baha.* But the heathens are forever clamoring at the gates—Assyrians, Babylonians, Persians, Greeks, Syrians, Romans, Arabs, Nazis, Iraqis. So the Wandering Jew goeth forth carrying the prophet Job within his heart, pretending to be a merchant, a tax collector or a mad poet.

"*Boorku est Adonoi. Ba Chaim est eeyahoo. Baha. Baha.*" And shortly thereafter, I theoretically became a man.

"*Mazel tov!*"

"*Mazel tov!*"

Yet I stood clenched, waiting for the blow from behind, when came a sudden wild shreik from the balcony and I was struck in the back of the head: a glancing blow, and I ducked behind the podium as another missile sailed past. "It's a custom from the old country," Rabbi Shapiro said as he calmly picked a small beribboned paper bag from the floor. "The women throw bags of candy to celebrate your manhood. *Mazel tov!*"

"*Mazel tov!*"

Roosevelt High School was on Fordham Road, only three stops northbound on the Third Avenue El. But school was for bozos.

Jeff Korkorian was a senior and I was merely a junior, but one fine spring day Jeff invited me to lunch with some of the guys from his gym class. "We'll meet you at the White Castle," he said. "It's easy to sneak out of school, but if you want I'll forge you a pass."

Inside a ptomaine palace, crafted of white bricks and white tile: "Hey, Marie!" Jeff shouted to one of the ladies-in-waiting. "I saw that delivery truck out back and I thought I heard some dogs barkin' inside. And I said, 'Whoa, what's in these things?' "

Marie was pug-faced, her blue eyes sharpened with mascara, each eyebrow a stark black line. Her stubby body was stuffed into a tiny white uniform and she resembled Dwarfolina, the Lady Wrestler. "Go eat in the deli," she said as she flexed her forearms and straddled the grill. The square little burgers were punched with holes to make them cook faster, and the Castle reeked of fried onions and secondhand grease. "Go eat in the toilet."

"Ooh, I heard that Marie. MA-ree, my chops you're breakin'. MA-ree, you'll soon be—"

"Five to stay wid onions! Six to stay wid onions and pickle. Somethin' to drink? Who's next?" Reluctantly, I glommed three burgers and a sweet-cola concoction.

"I know a guy," said Jeff, "can eat fifty of these things without gettin' sick."

I returned to school in time for my English class, where the subject was *King Lear*. "Nothing," quoth Miss Goldgas, "will come of nothing."

Suddenly my stomach was stabbed with cramps.

"Unhappy that I am, I cannot heave
My heart into my mouth."

Jumping to my feet, I shouted, "Miss Goldgas! Miss Goldgas! I have to leave the room, it's an emergency!"

Alas, she commanded me to sit still and behave. "Kill thy physician," she said, "and thy fee bestow upon the foul disease. . ."

Another spasm forced me out of my seat once more. "I mean it, Miss Goldgas! I have to go real bad."

After correcting my use of adverbs, she vowed to place an indelible conduct mark on my permanent record. I was left with no choice but to mutiny and leave the room without a pass.

I was also late getting to my next class: "Señor Lassner. ¿Porque está usted tarde?"

"Señora Dilda. *Yo estoy tardo* because *yo estoyed* too long in *la casa de guana*."

I was quickly dispatched to the principal's office and scolded by an angry man in a brown suit. "One thing I won't tolerate is impudence," he said, flashing his meat-colored eyes. "Wiseacres like you don't belong in school."

Always a diligent student, what else could I do but recite the noble words of the martyred Earl of Kent? "Fare thee well, King. Sith thus thou wilt appear, Freedom lives hence, and banishment is here."

Then, to the eternal credit of stomach-burgers and Shakespeare, I was forthwith suspended from school for five glorious days.

My first hoop was nailed to a tree on a dirt road in Brotherhood Acres, a "politically oriented" bungalow colony in New Hampshire. This was quickly succeeded by the only available run, a black wintertime game played on a painted stone floor in the locker room of a public swimming pool in a "Negro" neighborhood just fifteen blocks south of home. The game was presided over by "Bill," rumored to be an ex-Globie. There was no retrieving, so each missed shot turned every player into an offensive rebounder and the shooter was the only player who would ever dare admit to being fouled. The competition was fierce, the falls were hard, I was young and noticeably white, so I learned to shoot from the perimeter.

My parents were overjoyed that I was playing in an "integrated" game. But sometimes my playmates called me "Bookworm." "You got lots of book learning," they told me, "but no common sense." So I also learned to talk the talk.

Then on to hoops at Junior High School No. 44, playing in a cold, windy schoolyard in long pants and shirttails. Getting humiliated for being so big and so clumsy. Getting "the strap" from Daddy for tearing my pants.

After that, organized ball in a local community center with The Apaches, a fast-breaking ballclub of reckless fourteen-year-olds. And whenever the Apaches defeated The Jabones, a team of tough guys and troublemakers, we had to fast break all the way home.

I played varsity basketball only in my senior year at Roosevelt HS. The coach was a math teacher whose only admonition was "Bend your knees, boys. Bend your knees." My career high for the Rough Riders was five points against the sissies of Grace Dodge Vocational High School.

The freshman team at Bronx College was next. I was getting bigger and stronger but I remained somehow uninvolved. I averaged 8 ppg as a frosh and went scoreless against CCNY the night my father died.

My Daddy was forty-three going on a hundred when he finally succumbed to an attack of something quick and painful. I accompanied my mother in the ambulance, and just before we reached the hospital, Daddy opened his eyes. I remember that his gray eyes were tightly clenched and staring at a space just above my head. "Hi, kid," is what he said before he closed his eyes and then died for the last time.

At the time, I thought I hated him.

Throughout my varsity basketball career at Bronx College I was never inclined to work hard enough to get into really good shape, so I faked a limp whenever I had to run hard. My real problem was that I was too much of a spectator to play effectively—whenever someone dealt me a nice feed I'd say "good pass" even as I was missing the layup. I rebounded well because of my size and I could (and still can) shoot like a little man.

I played only one season in the semipro Eastern Professional Basketball League, the precursor of the CBL. During the playoffs a 6'8", 260-pound criminal named Tarzen Spencer crunched my nose with his elbow for no apparent reason. Three games later I kneed Spencer in the jewels just as the final buzzer announced a championship for the good guys. After that, retirement was my only option.

Sure, I played pick-up games (also knock-down games) since then: for the St. Anthony Eagles (at $15 per game), St. Claire's Crusaders (in exchange for a hurried blow job by the coach's sister), New York Bears (at $20 per), Eat at Joe's (free meals) and the Rotolo Electricians (for an illegal cable TV hookup). I've played against a one-eyed all-American, assorted drunks and playground no-names in midnight schoolyards in Harlem, in interchangeable Y's, a home for the blind, on the top of a mountain, on a parallelogram court. But the only thing I ever learned was that I played inside a deep sleep and that the buzzer was imminent.

And besides, when I thought I fell in love, my fabulous jump shot turned hairy and ugly.

Her name was Racheal and I met her at the library. I was inspecting Lawrence Durrell and she was entranced by the Doester. I was teaching fizz ed at a junior high school in the South Bronx, she was a social worker in Queens. We both believed in the perfectability of everybody, excepting ourselves. We started dating once, twice, three times per week. We went to see foreign films, we ate in French restaurants, we took midnight cruises on the Staten Island ferry, we saw the Knicks lose, the Yankees win, we went to a Czechoslovakian restaurant and Racheal had a laughing fit when I asked a Czech for a check. Racheal had curly brown hair, brown eyes, a trim body and big tits—I cried with gratitude the first time she let me fuck her. We got married a year later.

Then we started picking at each other. Why did she squeeze the toothpaste from the middle of the tube? Why didn't I make the bed if I was the last one up? How could I go to the store and not get milk? I liked Chinese food, she liked Italian. She wanted to watch a

Bette Davis movie, I had to watch a football game. She'd scream whenever I'd stick the jelly knife into the peanut butter jar. I liked life rare, she liked it well-done.

Before long Racheal began eating too much. In the spirit of "togetherness" I used to follow her around the A&P, pushing a shopping cart through the aisles. Her brown hair in curlers, her rapidly swelling thighs colliding beneath a red-striped house-dress. As we cruised along, she fondled jars of pickled artichoke hearts. Then she danced her fingers across the frosty covering of a frozen pizza. She paused to breathe deeply at the bakery counter.

"Bread," she announced. "I love bread. It's so filling."

"Yeah, sure."

Then she caressed the length of a large Italian loaf. "Look at all the sesame seeds on this one," she said. "Too much bread makes you fat. It's my ruination."

"Yeah, sure. Do what you want." I felt as though we'd been married for fifty years.

She cradled three loaves in her arms before stacking them in the shopping cart. "I'll make some spaghetti tonight," she said, "and some garlic bread."

Still, I guess I loved her. I had to, didn't I? I was a retired hoop-o-maniac in those days. So if love wasn't real, what was left?

My mother died, Racheal miscarried after four months, there were cockroaches in our love nest in Queens. Then one morning, just a week before school was to start, I got a call from an old college teammate, Jack Phillips. It seems that Jack was coaching in something called the Commercial Basketball League. The Peoria Storm was the team, and he wanted me to be his assistant coach— $300 per week, a free hotel room, free car, playoff bonuses plus $25 per diem on the road. Racheal didn't want to give up her job, so she stayed in Queens.

The Peoria Storm won some games and lost some games. At season's end I returned to Queens and our renewed honeymoon lasted about a week. Then I started getting annoyed at the half-filled coffee cups she left all over the apartment. She began com-plaining that I left the dishes greasy when it was my turn to wash. "You're doing it on purpose," she said, "so's I'll get pissed off and wash them myself. Well, I won't!"

One day I overheard her talking on the telephone to another

social worker. "It sounds like the answer to all my prayers, Sheila. I even went out and bought a small container on my way to work this morning. Sixty-two cents a pint at Waldbaum's. I'm telling you, Sheila. I can see the difference already. It's just like they said on TV. The smaller the curds, the fewer the calories. It stands to reason. No matter what it tastes like, Sheila, it's a breakthrough."

Two years later Jack Phillips accepted a coaching job in Belgium for 65K, a house and car, and I accepted the Peoria job—for 35K, the same hotel room, the same car, the same per diem. Racheal still wouldn't leave her job. "I owe it to my clients," she insisted.

As before, the Storm won some games and lost some. But suddenly my anger blossomed after all those years and I became involved, passionately involved, a warrior of the black rose. Even as a rookie coach I yelled at the referees and paid a total of $1,750 in technical fouls. "You fuckin' asshole," I told an official whose dad reffed in the NBA when he called a charge instead of a block. "If it weren't for your father you'd be drivin' a fuckin' elevator." Oh, I ranted and raved and the hometown fans loved me. The Storm's owner was a real-estate tycoon named George Pullman and he also liked what he called my "spunk." When George was busted last year by the IRS, his nerd-ass son fired me because my benchside manner "set a bad example for children."

No matter.

While in Peoria I spent whatever free time I had reading, and I was proud to remain monogamous. Perhaps I was simply too embarrassed to show Mandrake the Magician to strange women. Yet I persisted in convincing myself that I still loved Racheal. After all, she was still the only woman kind enough to fuck me. She also did my laundry, cooked my meals, vacuumed the rugs, and whenever I misplaced my car keys, Racheal would always find them for me. If that ain't love. . . .

Last summer, Racheal and Sheila enrolled in an aerobics course at the Y. Racheal proceeded to lose twenty-three pounds and began complaining about my breath, my belches.

Then one night last November I returned to my hotel room in Savannah after the Stars lost a ballbuster of a ballgame to Oklahoma— we were up by nineteen to start the fourth quarter, only to lose by one on an offensive rebound at the buzzer. Naturally, I had just finished crashing a chair against a wall when the phone rang.

"We can't go on like this," Racheal told me. "We're more like roommates than lovers. It's not my fault we can't have children. You're selfish and lost in your own world. I want a divorce."

Nineteen fuckin' points. Play great defense on the last sequence and Sam doesn't box out. "But, Racheal. I love you."

"That's always been easy for you to say."

Nineteen fuckin' points. Kuback beats me again. "Yeah? Well, this is even easier . . . Fuck you and the horse you rode in on."

3

ACROSS THE STREET from the county-court building, the Stars office is situated on the ground floor of a cedar-shingled Cape built just after World War II. A bail bondsman works the upstairs office and the Stars staff is frequently visited by wandering felons, rapists and extortionists looking for low cost dollars. The lawn is unkempt, overgrown and littered with empty beer bottles. Since the building is owned by one of the team's minority stockholders, a notorious slumlord hereabouts, the Stars office space is gratis, a considerable tax write-off.

There used to be a yellow star on the blue front door but last Halloween somebody painted JEWS AND NIGGARS DIE in red over the team logo. The local newspaper, the Savannah *Gazette*, subsequently ran an editorial explaining the difference between "a regular American star" and "a Jewish star." Nothing was said about a "niggar" star. Afterward, the front door was painted in red, white and blue stripes.

Inside, through a low-slung doorway, is a reception area presided over by Mona Sutherland, a brazen, boom-bosomed redhead with a country accent. "They's some may-sayges here for y'all," she tells me.

"Okay, I'll get them later. Any chance Magoo was in to copy some scouting reports?"

"Nope. Ain' seen'm no how."

The Stars public-relations person, Chet Jeffries, maintains his headquarters in what used to be the dining room. At age thirty-four, Chet is too old to be such an ass-licking puppydog, to be so easily amazed and so provincial. Like most Savannians, the pint-sized Chet believes that football is played by war heroes, roundball by mutants.

Sharing Chet's office (but never his precious computer) is Tom Blanks, the sales manager, along with a rotating crew of sales temps working strictly on commission. A renovated broom closet now houses Wilma Mae Kirkus, the team's bookkeeper. The whole joint is furnished in postbellum folding chairs, tubular desks and bridge tables in matching shades of gray.

The living-room suite belongs to Herm Pudleigh, the Stars managing partner, the snakeoil salesman who brought pro hoops to Savannah. Herm's official designation is President, but as a Christmas bonus last year he rewarded himself with another title—President and Founder.

The ballclub is owned by approximately fifty local businessmen and I am still being introduced to innumerable minority owners with glad hands and forgettable names and faces. Each minimum share amounts to $15,000, but three real-estate biggies control fifty-one percent of the club. The entire bankroll includes 650K to buy into the CBL last year as an expansion team, plus an 800K annual operating budget, plus last year's loss of 200K. Herm is in for the minimum and no one really knows how he sweet-talked and tap-danced his way into his present employment. Earl suggests that Herm "must have a photograph of somebody important fuckin' a sheep."

Before the Stars came to town, Herm was an insurance salesman, and before that, an unsuccessful candidate at the University of Georgia Law School. Twenty years ago Herm was an all-state half-back for East Savannah High School before ripping his knee to shreds in his senior year. Like me, Herm affects a limp whenever the pace gets too swift.

He's still trim at 5'9" and 170 pounds, but now his hair is terminally thinning and his habit of combing and plastering the few remaining strands across his gleaming pate is a source of constant amusement to the players. "Ass Head," they call him. I wonder what they call me.

Herm has a manly cleft in his chin that he's fond of thrusting—

he also shows a moony face supported by a perpetual shit-eating grin. His eyes are blue, close-set and forever asquint. I've caught him sneaking admiring glances at his own reflections in mirrors, windows, silverware, even puddles in the street. Herm is married to a no-runs-no-tits-no-errors blondie named Gloria, who's gloriously pregnant with their first. And sure, Herm hired me when I desperately needed a job, but all in all he's still a prick with ears.

Sharing lazy greetings with my coworkers, I pick my way toward Herm's office. As I pass the erstwhile dining room, Chet pokes his shiny face into the hall. "What d'ya say, Chester?" is my usual greeting. "I'd love to stop and chat but the Flounder is expecting me."

Instead of smiling, Chet invariably sucks his teeth and blushes. "Shh," he warns me in a hoarse whisper. "Don't say that so loud. Hey, I've got a crazy story to tell you later. Y'all had lunch yet? Be careful, he's in a shit mood."

Herm's office is luxuriously burnished in woods and leathers. The carpet is plush and the biggest picture hanging on the wall shows a teen-aged Herm in full regalia, swivelhipping and stiff-arming an imaginary tackler. He points to a vacant chair on the nether side of his huge walnut desk, then grimaces for my benefit as he says "I understand" into the telephone. "Of course," he says, now he's winking, see what he has to put up with?

Suddenly I feel like taking a shower.

"Let's have lunch next week," Herm tells the telephone. "One of them power lunches," he sniggers.

When he's finished, Herm aims his cleft and his smile at me. Also his hand as he says, "Coach, my coach. How was practice?"

His grip is momentarily firm, then just as quickly his hand slides away and disappears under the desktop. Herm knows from shit about basketball, yet he has gradually usurped my contractual prerogatives and currently functions as the Stars director of player personnel. Over the course of the season:

1) He wouldn't let me trade Sam.
2) He had to be tricked into approving the purchase of Mr. Beast's rights.
3) He forced me to trade for Josh Brusher.
4) And worse.

For Herm, basketball reality can be measured only in numbers. He dismisses Xs and Os as an occult science akin to astrology. He jokingly calls my magnetic playboard a Ouija board. Team chemistry is alchemy. Motivation is a coach's voodoo. His catechism is comprised of points per game, asses in seats and sound bites on TV.

"Practice was okay. We put in a new defensive scheme, doubling down with the four-man across the baseline and rotating down with the three-man from the weakside to cover. Hopefully, this will force somebody other than Oz and Hodges to make decisions they don't normally make. But I'm sure that Kuback has some—"

"Coach," Herm says, showing his hands again. "In layman's terms, are we ready to win?" His smile flickers. . . Last year, in the Stars expansion season, Artie "Mr. Nice Guy" Barfield coached them into last place with a record of 17–39. Even though Artie was fired one week after the season ended, Herm was almost fond of him. That's because Artie was quiet, inarticulate, self-effacing, and Herm was the darling of the local media muppets. Despite my success here, I'm always good for a controversial quote, so Herm would love to manufacture any excuse to fire me.

Now, do I tell him we're not ready to win, thereby promoting myself if/when we do win? Or do I tell him yes (which is what he wants to hear), thereby immolating myself should we lose?

"Yeah, sure. We're definitely ready to win."

"Good." He beams. "Good." But he squirms in his chair. "How's Points? How's he shooting the ol' ball?"

"Sam? He's a pain in the ass. What else is new?"

We stare blankly at each other until I fake a cough and look away. It was as early as training camp last October when I knew I had to trade Sam Franks. I thought my reasons were conclusive—no defense, too selfish, no defense, detrimental to team unity, no defense, probably using drugs. But Herm absolutely refused. He regretted that "a layman" had to "temporarily" supersede my authority, and he subjected me to a recital of Sam's numbers for last season—29.2 ppg, 52% FG, 83% FT, etc. Besides, the fans love Sam's style (the word Herm used was "panachee"). Besides, opening night was at hand—November 5th at home versus the Paloma Palominos—which was also "Points Franks Poster Nite" sponsored by Hygrade Hot Dogs. And what would Herm do with five thousand 36″ × 24″ four-color posters if we traded that "bad boy"?

That was the first time I was overruled. Now, five months later, Herm serves up the same advice he did then: "*Make* Points play defense. *Make* him be unselfish. Bring him into the corral with everyone else. That's why y'all're my coach. I know y'all can do it."

Yeah, sure.

Now he's randomly rearranging several notepads and pencils scattered on top of his desk. Perhaps the shit is about to hit the coach. "Let me ask you one more thing," he says with the same crisp grin, "but don't take this the wrong way. Don't get your nuts in an uproar. I'm asking you this as a Stars fan, not as your boss. . . Everyone 'round here remembers when Josh Brusher led East Savannah High to three straight triple-A championships. We also remember him as a star at Savannah State right here in town and also the one season he played with Sacramento in the NBA. Now, I understand he's thirty-two and not what he used to be. But a lot of fans have been complaining about his lack of playing time. Like I say, y'all're the coach and I'm just asking as a fan. But how come he doesn't play more?"

"Herm," I say, surprisingly calm, "when Josh first got here two months ago he had this attitude—I'm the veteran on this club and I'm gonna show everybody what it takes to win. He had advice for everybody, including me. Meanwhile, all of his fuckups were always someone else's fault. After seeing his song-and-dance routine one time too many, everybody just started ignoring him. Now he's off somewhere by himself. He's useless, Herm. All he does is piss and moan into his beard."

"But," Herm insists, "remember that game against Fort Myers when he first got here? When he blocked three shots in the last minute of the game? I think the more you play him the more he produces. Sure, he can't play forty minutes anymore. But what about fifteen minutes? And he absolutely swore to me that he's not drinking any more. Coach, you know what this business is all about. All's I'm saying is that everybody in the living world knows that the more Josh plays the more we draw."

"Herm. . ." Watch yourself, schmuck. ". . . he's a play-buster. All he wants to do is shoot the ball. And whose time can I give him? Cooper's? That kid works his ass off and he's so unselfish even Sam likes playing with him. No, Herm. I can't. . ."

"All right, all right. Hold your horses, Coach. This isn't anything to get all fired up about. All's I'm saying is a lot of us would sure appreciate it if you'd try to work him in whenever you can. Maybe Josh just needs to know you believe in him, even though maybe you really don't. You know what I'm saying?"

"Yeah."

"Anyway," he says, looking at his watch. "I've got a plane to catch. There's an emergency league meeting tonight in Chicago, but don't worry, I'll be back in plenty of time for the game tomorrow. Ask Mona for my number if you need to find me."

I am hereby dismissed and I long to escape, but I'm paralyzed by any chance of being refired, of being rejected once more. Am I prepared to argue, to grovel, to make threats? "Uhm," I mutter. "There is one thing, Herm. We touched on this briefly last week. It's about next year. I've had several feelers from other teams in the league." *A lie.* "But I do have a sense of loyalty to you and to the Stars." Gasp.

"Rob," he says, his smile more benevolent than ever. "Like I told you last week, when the season's over I'm gonna sit down and evaluate every aspect of the organization. Nothing's changed since we spoke about it. As you well know, we only finished seventh in the league in attendance and it's crucial that we draw better for the playoffs. Crucial. It costs us about sixteen thou to open the arena for each home game. It's nothing personal, Rob, just dollars and cents. So everything is subject to review. Who knows? I may even have to fire myself." Smile. "And as far as the feelers from other teams. . . well, you know that I consider you to be a friend, a good friend, so I would never stand in your way if you think you can improve your position. All I can say right now is that as of right now you're my coach."

The phone rings, again, again, even again. "Fuck!" says Herm, pointing his cleft out the door. "Where is everybody?" Another ring and Herm lifts the receiver. "Good afternoon," he chimes. "The Stars come out in Savannah. How may I help you?. . . *George*, why I was just looking up y'all's number. . ."

He looks up and salutes me, the Pope blessing an axe murderer. "Have a nice trip," I actually say.

Chet is the office gossip, and as he drives his dented '88 Yugo across town to Wong's he fills me in on the latest news:

ITEM: All season long Wilma Mae has been depositing gate re-
ceipts into the wrong checking account. "There are two
different accounts," Chet explains, "one is interest-
bearing but costs two dollars for every check we write
against it. The other generates no interest but allows the
teams to write free checks." According to Chet, Wilma
Mae's mistake cost the Stars a total of $3,250 in check fees
until the error was discovered. Since she earns a mere
$15,000 per annum, why doesn't Herm fire her? After all,
she's forty plus and hefty with a sort of clownish face and
paper-bag tits. "Herm can't fire her," Chet reports, "because he's fuckin' her."

ITEM: Tom Blanks, the sales rep, has a booze problem and has
been dipping into the petty-cash box. He's sure to be
canned after the season.

ITEM: Mona has moved in with Josh. "I can't believe it," Chet
says.

ITEM: This morning Chet handed Herm the preview copy of an
article about me that will appear in the magazine section
of Sunday's *Gazette*. "How many times is my name men-
tioned?" Herm wanted to know. "Once." Herm's response
was: "I don't want to read it."

ITEM: The Oklahoma Rangers PR guy says that Kuback says
they're gonna kick our ass.

ITEM: There is no emergency league meeting tonight in Chicago.

Along with the menus a waiter places a basket of white bread on
the table. I order hot-and-sour soup and moo shu shrimp. Chet
doesn't like Chinese food. He complains about "cats' tails" and
"American pilots' fingernails left over from the war," then he orders
"a plate of Chinks."

And this is the story he's been saving up to tell me: Last night
Chet and his girlfriend Sandra went to the Riverfront for a late-
night drink. "She was getting well-awled, hot and bothered," Chet
says, "just like I planned. We were just about to leave, it was after
midnight, when lo and behold, Herm wanders in, already drunk as
a skunk. He starts buying us drinks. Then he starts whining that
he's so horny 'cause Gloria is in her eighth month and won't give
him any."

After a while Sandra excuses herself and heads for the ladies room. Shortly thereafter Herm announces that he too must make "a pit stop, ha ha." There's Chet, waiting and waiting, all by his lonesome. After waiting too long, he goes to the mens room, only to find it empty. "So then I go into the ladies room and what do I see? Herm and Sandra fuckin' on the floor."

"God bless America."

"And guess who he's takin' to Chicago tonight? That's right. Sandra."

"Bust him," is my advice. "Call Gloria."

Here's my moo shu. Chet gets a combination plate—egg roll, fried rice and chicken chow mein.

"I can't. He's my boss. I like this job. It's the only one like it in Savannah."

Nodding in agreement, in sympathy, all I can say is: "Herm Pudleigh reminds me of Moses."

"What?"

"Sure, just like Moses he turns his staff into snakes."

"What? Y'all're one crazy fuckin' Yankee."

There's only lint in my wallet, so I have to return to the office to collect my check. As I follow Chet through the door, Mona pushes a handful of paper in my face. "Coach, y'all forgot y'all's may-sayges." I have no office to call my own, not even a desk, so I squeeze the messages into a ball and stuff them into my pocket.

The office is swarming with players—Richie, Kelly, Nate, Mr. Beast and Josh have commandeered all the available phones, calling agents, family, girlfriends, buddies, coast-to-coast and across the waters. Mr. Beast looks up from Tom Blanks' phone and gives me the high sign. "Definitely a veteran move," he says.

There's a stack of scouting reports near Mona's desk but Magoo has come and gone. Quickly I inspect my assistant's handiwork—instead of sketching the bad guys' offense by position (1–the point guard, 2–the shooting guard, 3–the small forward, 4–the power forward and 5–the center), Magoo insists on using their uniform numbers. I know who Oklahoma's point guard is but who's Number 25? 32? 43? We've only been over this a dozen times already but

Magoo is spaced on the far side of sixty, rapidly approaching the outer rings of senility.

Suddenly Earl bolts out of Herm's office shaking his head, laughing, and says, "Points is a crazy motherfucker. Check this out. . . I'm in there with him and Ass Head, right? And Points wants to call his wife. He's all the time gotta be a big shot, right? So he puts the call on the speaker phone. Right away his wife starts screamin' at him. What's her name? Salina? She says some bitch's been callin' the room all day just lookin' for Points. So Salina says she kept tellin' the bitch to fuck off. Points, well he freaks out for real. He says to his wife, 'What that bitch's name, bitch?' She says she don't know. So Points, he says, 'Well, next time you better get her name.' Then he looks at me and Ass Head with that goofy smile on his face, right? Then he says to his wife, 'I'm warnin' you. Don't fuck with my pussy!' "

Herm's door is ajar, and before I leave, I venture a peek inside. While the boys are blissfully dialing for dollars, Herm sits like a schoolboy in his dunce chair, nodding his head in eager agreement, and there's Sam, jabbering away, sitting in the command chair with his feet on Herm's desk.

4

AND ANOTHER THING—Herm arranged a trade-out deal (courtside tickets, banners hanging from the rafters) with a local Jolly Cholly for two courtesy cars, one for him, one for me. Herm's car is a spanking new Lincoln Continental and he rattles around inside it like a dried bean in a gourd. Mine is a three-year-old Honda, in which I fit like the proverbial two-pounds of shit in a one-pound can.

In any case, I never park my car in front of my room (#197) at the less-than-luxurious Swedish Inn. Nor do I ever park it in the same spot twice. That's because the players also reside at the Swedish Inn and it's none of their business when I'm out (rarely) and when I'm safely ensconced.

My room is way out back, fortuitously situated near a soda machine, but also commanding a view of a dentist's office and the adjoining parking lot. When the weather permits and the stench blows out to sea, I like to open my only window. Too bad that my reading, my schmoozing and my snoozing are thereby violated by occasional muffled screams and by the whine of Dr. Dento's drills.

Inside, the beige wallpaper is textured to resemble burlap. The furniture is fashioned from artificial wood—a sturdy double bed, two blocky chairs, a matching dresser and table. My mattress is too rigid and too short but it's functional. I sleep on it and hide my money under it. Put my hard-earned cash in a bank? In the bastion of capitalism? My parents would do 360s in their graves. Besides,

Savannah's largest savings-and-loan corporation went bust last summer.

By special arrangement with the management I am also allowed a minifridge and a hotplate. Every room at the Inn has the identical picture hanging above the bed, a snowcapped undifferentiated alp. The only other Swedish motif I can find is a steam attachment to the shower that's always on the fritz. And a shower seems like a good idea right about now.

I see no good reason for taking a shower the first thing in the morning, unless I'm fortunate enough to have a wet dream. It's like another ridiculous cultural imperative, washing my hands after pissing. The implication being that my public hands are cleaner than poor sequestered Mandrake. Unless I piss on my hands unawares.

Hot, nearly scalding showers are my delight, more stimulating, more convenient and much more sanitary than wearing a hair shirt. On the other hand, opened pores plus a balding dome equal a nasty cold. Here's another factor . . . showers always make me sleepy, but if I nap now I'll never get to sleep tonight.

That's me, fussing over my own workaday trivia like a monk savoring his beads.

So, I'll make a witch doctor's compromise with myself—a shower but no shave. If I can allow my incipient beard to grow for another day I'll surely get a close pregame shave tomorrow afternoon at about 4:30. As though I really do believe we'll win if I'm smooth-of-cheek and lose should I bleed.

In lieu of a nap, I read my messages.

—Coach Tom "T-Bone" Donaldson of the Winnebago Willies called. I am requested to call him tonight at his home.

—I'm to be a featured guest tonight at 6:10 on Al Sandman's popular "Sports Talk" show on WSAV, 1130 on your everlovin' dial. The producer will call here at 6:09.

—Joe Patterson, the basketball writer for the *Gazette*, wants me to call him ASAP at his office.

Patterson, a good enough Joe, helped bring Mr. Beast here to Savannah. . . Early in January, K.C. Moon, the general manager of the Madison (Wis.) Marauders, called to say his team was conducting a fire sale because of a successful halftime promotion they held the night before. Say what? Moon went on to say that, in cahoots with a local Ford dealer, he drove a 1992 Galaxy to the center jump circle and opened only the sunroof. Each of the 2,429 fans in attendance were encouraged to write a name on the front page of the official Marauders program (at three dollars), make a paper airplane of same and launch it toward the car. The first such missile to land inside the sunroof would win the car. K.C. Moon had been instructed by the CBL's director of promotions to turn on the arena's ventilation system full-blast just as the shootout began. Moon was also assured that the odds were 1,000,000–1 in his favor. Too bad somebody had been practicing for two weeks and won the car. The Ford dealer was contractually obliged to pay only $2,000 in such an eventuality and Moon needed to raise $12,000 in a hurry.

From the shopping list he offered I was definitely interested in Mr. Beast at $3,000. It's not my money—and Mr. B. is a bona fide 6'9" NBA vet who'd had some good-to-middling games against us. But Herm said, "No way in the living world will I do that. Morrison's too fat and lazy. He's washed up and his contract is for seven-hundred bucks a week, which is way too much. The only way I'll okay the deal is if you can totally guarantee that we'll win the championship with him."

Hmm. . . I knew that Joe Patterson liked Mr. Beast so I called the *Gazette* and explained the situation. Joe understood totally—in a flash he called Herm and said, "What the Stars need is an experienced big man. I hear that Benny Morrison is available."

HERM: You really like him?

JOE: I love him. If you can get him, whatever the cost, it's a steal. You'd also have my vote for Executive of the Year.

And presto chango, Herm called me immediately, saying, "I thought it over and I've changed my mind about Morrison. What the Stars need is an experienced big man. Whatever the cost, it's a steal."

For tomorrow's column Joe wants to know anything I can tell him. To wit, my "sources" indicate that Earl is a long shot to replace Tripucka. Also, practice today was "inspired." Mr. Beast is especially focused, *baha baha*. Joe picks us to beat Oklahoma three games to two.

*   *   *

My next decision is perhaps the most pivotal of the evening—what to eat for supper. Too bad I've already had Chinese. That leaves Bugger King? The Kernel? Perhaps a bag of shit from Mickey D?. . . But of course! It's pizza tonight. Delivered. With extra cheese and, as a sure sign of my emancipation, green peppers.

That's because peppers always give me gas in a hurry. And what could be more mortifying than farting in public?

> *And, spite of pride, in erring reason's spite,*
> *One truth is clear, 'Whatever IS, is RIGHT.'*

So let's see, I'll read until the radio show. . . I favor long historical novels that make me appreciate indoor plumbing. After yakking with Al Sandman I'll eat my pizza and watch hoops on the tube, enjoying my last evening as a civilian.

"Hi, coach. Hang on. Al'll be with y'all in thirty seconds."

". . . tell it as it is, talkin' the way I'm walkin'. . . arright. And we're havin' so much fun down here at the Magnolia Cafe. So come on down. That's at twenty-one-thirty-eight Northwest Twenty-fifth Place, right near the Piggly Wiggly Market. We got prizes and celebrities. We got gorgeous waitresses. We're havin' a ball, right, gang? Arright! Arright! This is Mrs. Sandman's little Al from Joisey City comin' atchu from the Magnolia Cafe right here at twenty-one-thirty-eight Northwest Twenty-fifth Place. Arright! Right now we got the coach of the Savannah Stars right here on the phone, coach Robert Lassner. . . Coach, how are ya?"

"Fine, Al."

"That's great! Arright. I betcha can't wait to get the playoffs started. Don't forget. That's tomorra night at seven-thirty, down-town at the Coliseum. Come see the Stars play the Oklahoma Rangers to open a best-of-five series. Arright! How we lookin', coach?"

"Well, if we play our game and maintain our focus, we'll be fine, Al."

"Arright. Love to hear it. Let's go to the phones. . . Hello, you're on Sports Talk so start talkin'."

"Hi, Al. My name is Jepthah and I'm from the West Side and, and I've got a question for the coach."

"Shoot."

"Coach? I've been a basketball fan for a long, long time. I can remember a long, long time ago before the Big One when everybody shot with two hands. I can remember playin' basketball inside a cage. That's why they're called cagers. This was maybe fifty-sixty years back. . ."

"Arright, Jaspar or whatever your name is. This ain't war and remembrance, so just ask what you got to ask."

"Hunh?"

"Have a nice day, arright?. . . Okay. You're on Sports Talk so start talkin'."

"Coach? This here's John from over by East Savannah? And I want to know how come you ain't hardly playin' that boy from the high school over here. Whatsiz name?"

"Josh Brusher? Well, John from East Savannah, it's just a question of chemistry. Right now Josh has got to get more into the flow. He's got to learn his role. It's a question of platitudes, John. When the going gets tough, the tough gets going. It's like America and apple pie. You do like apple pie, John, don't you?"

"Hot damn, I surely do!"

"Arright! Arright! This is little Al Sandperson talkin' and squawkin' atchu. Here at WSAV, eleven-three-oh on your everlovin' dial. Start talkin' sports, sport."

"Coach. I'm Gus from Sugar Island? And I been noticin' the low attendance y'all's been drawin' this year and 'specially last year. How come y'all think y'all can make it a go here? This here's football country, boy."

"Actually, that's a very good question, Gus, and not being from Savannah I don't really know how to answer it. I will confess that I was disappointed to find that there are only two wooden basketball courts in the entire city. One in the Coliseum, the other out at a mental hospital near the mall. All the other gyms have either tile or plastic floors. Apparently there are some old-time fans around here like Jepthah from the West Side who just called. But aside from Purvis Ellison and maybe Josh Brusher, there's never been any high-level basketball talent from this area, so the tradition is weak, I agree. Then why do I think we can make it? Because basketball is such a great sport, the ultimate team sport, the kind of competition everyone can enjoy. Because on this level, the coaches and the players are so accessible. There's no elitism in this league. Because—"

"Arright! Let's take one more quick call before goin' to commercial. Hi, this is little Al down here at the Magnolia Cafe. Who are you and what do you want?"

"I want to know why there's so many damn nigras on your team, that's what I want."

"Hey, bozo," I snap. "You racist half-wit. Put your hood back on and crawl back underneath your rock. It's morons like you who give morons a bad name."

"Arright! Arright! Thanks for bein' our guest tonight, Coach. I know you got game tapes to watch and miles to go before you sleep. . ."

Lying on my bed, playing TV roulette with the remote. The pizza is late. According to the weather channel, there's a cold front on the way. Low tonight in the low fifties. So . . . do I turn the heat on and wake up every time the system clangs on and off? Or do I sleep in my sweats?

Meanwhile, there are two TV games on tap—Metropolitan U. versus Pilsner University, and later a pro contest, San Antonio against the Lakers. In the Swedish Inn, a special channel always shows the indoor pool, so that worried mothers can observe their children frolicking unattended. Right now, channel 21 is black and white and grainy as ever, showing a family of four, Mom, Dad, Sis and Junior. Dad shotputs Junior ten feet and they all laugh and splash, oblivious to the fortunes and misfortunes of all the bullshit basketball alphabet. Just together. Having fun.

There's a knock at the door. "Coach," a black kid says, pizza in hand, "I recognize you from TV." He wears a green Pizza Hut parka, also gloves, earmuffs and a scarf.

"What's it, snowing out there?"

"It's cold, Coach." He laughs. "We got thin blood down here. That's twelve dollars and seventy-nine cents. And, Coach? Could I bother you for your autograph? I'm a big fan of yours. I love the way you go after the refs."

"What's your name?"

"Jeff."

On a slice of hotel stationery, I write my customary inscription:

> *To Jeff,*
> *Happy hooping—*
> *Best wishes,*
> *Rob Lassner*

I give him fifteen dollars and we both say "thanks" at the same time. I switch on the college game.

What's wrong with college basketball? Zone defenses, for one. Pass, pass, pass, stand around, then somebody casts a twenty-footer anyway. Zoners rarely learn how to play pro defense. Red Holzman used to say, "Zone, schmone, sooner or later somebody's got to guard somebody." But not any more.

I also detest the forty-five-second shot-clock. The pro clock is twenty-four diurnal seconds, a natural number. It was even Bill Bradley's number with Princeton and the Nix. Forty-five is too long, too ungodly. Bob Rule wore Number 45, a lefty who played no defense. With a forty-five-second clock, college coaches can coach in a rocking chair.

The average fan thinks that undergraduate coaches are the best in the business, thanks mainly to the yocks and puffery of TV commentators like Dick Meat and Gilly Slacker. Truth is, pro coaches can coach rings around college coaches. Look what college coaches have done in Olympic and Pan-American competitions. They were overwhelmed by the international style of play. They were inflexible in their preparation and incapable of making the kinds of game-time adjustments that pro coaches consider routine. Sure, sure, I do love Dean Smith. . .

Q: Who's the only one who can hold Michael Jordan under twenty-five points?

A: Dean Smith.

Yeah, yeah, I also like Mike Whatever-his-name-is at Duke, Roy Williams at Kansas, Gene Gillen at Xavier and several others. But I never judge a college coach on the basis of his Xs and Os, his Ws and Ls. More important is, what are his players like after a certain coach has directed them for four formative seasons?

With few exceptions, Big Ten players are assholes who think that the NBA is only this much better than the likes of, say, Indiana and Iowa. Snark's players admit to taking a pay cut to play in the CBL—they also turn their heads in defense of backdoor cuts, and on offense, all they want to do is follow the bouncing ball. I'd rather watch Butch van Breda Kolff's teams at Hofstra (and his disciple, Pete Carill's at Princeton) work their recognition combinations on offense and defense.

And look at Metropolitan U. There are no dorms at Metro, so the players are stationed in fancy apartments paid for by rich alums, then the players are given legal allowances to pay their nonexistent rent. Insiders also swear that not long ago the Metro athletic department provided free drugs for a seven-foot all-American addict. And the media treats the coach like he's a saint.

So what else is wrong with college basketball? Recruiting eighteen-year-old kids who have already been stroked by parents, friends, high-school coaches and sometimes agents. The coach as hooker: "It'll be just great, kid. You'll love State U. You'll start for me your freshman year. I'll get you ready for the pros. The boosters will give you whatever boost you need." Then you play zone, sit his ass on the pines and placate him with baubles, passing grades and pussy.

Like I said, I'll take pro ball—more talent, better coaches, and if a player turns out to be a knucklehead, you can trade him.

And what's wrong with pro ball? Mostly the referees. But fuck me. Tomorrow's soon enough to be thinking about them.

More obviously, it's the media hype that's hurting the pro game. Athletic competition has been changed into primetime entertainment. Look at the caliber of NBAers the media has elevated into the status of culture heroes: okay, MJ is super legit. But consider the well-known chokers. They play ten outstanding sequences in a game of 200-plus sequences, then play invisible. But buy their sneakers, kids. Drink what they drink. And if you can't be them, it's still cool to look like them and do like them.

God bless America.

Arright. Let's look at those numbers that Herm loves so much. Games Played, Minutes Played—in my mind the only pure, unadulterated statistics on the books. Everything else—FG, FGA, FG%, FT, FTA, FT%, PPG, REB, BS, AST, TO, ST—measures what happens when a player is in direct contact with the basketball. Of course, Magic had the ball more and Kurt Rambis less, but given ten players, one ball and 48 minutes, a theoretical player theoretically touches the ball 4.8 minutes per game. What's he doing the other 43.2 minutes? Where's the camera, where are the stats to register picks and set-up passes that lead to assists? Who tallies backdoor cuts, defensive switches, crunching box-outs that discourage offensive rebounds? Only the coaches and some of the players know what goes on without the ball, and hardly anybody else knows enough even to ask a sensible question.

What should b-ball be? What's the right attitude? Certainly not US versus the ENEMY, five-on-five. It should be ten players playing one game. A total communion. The flow subsuming us all—players, coaches, refs and fans. When the final buzzer sounds, we should all have to look at the scoreboard to discover who won. . . Ah, hoopness were paradise enow. Ah. Do I wake or do I dream?

The phone rings. "Bo Bo, wake up." It's Coach T-Bone from Winnebago, a one-time NBA assistant with the Washington Bullets and the only CBL coach who's never lied to me (I think). "What chu doin', Bo Bo. Watchin' those dang game filems?"

"Naw. Just lazing around. Reading, eating pizza, watching the Spurs–Lakers game. Basically waiting around to take a dump so's I can go to sleep."

"That's important," T-Bone says. "Don't ever underestimate the value of a good shit, especially on the road."

"What do you hear?"

"Nuthin'. Everybody's nervous about Tripucka bein' hurt and they say Isiah's maybe messed up too. But nobody knows who's gonna replace either of them. SOS. Same Old Shit."

"Yeah. Earl says his agent says it's not gonna be him."

"That's good for you. Bad for Kuback."

"Fuckin' Kuback. You know, I'm pissed off at this series even before it's begun. We were five-and-three against Kuback in the regular season and we finished, what, two games ahead of him? So by every measure we should have the home-court advantage for the playoffs. The first two games should be in Oklahoma and the last three games should be here."

"That's correct," says T-Bone.

"But Herm is worried sick that if we play the first two games in Oklahoma, we might get swept. Then we might only get to play one game here in Savannah. So Herm switches it all around with the league so that Savannah's guaranteed to have at least two home games. Now if Kuback can split down here, I'm fucked."

"That's also correct," he says, "but hey, you're still playing, I'm not. My season's over. The only thing I'm playing is golf tomorrow morning with the two owners, Bud and Lou. That's when I'll find out if I have a job next year. So I don't want to hear you complain."

"I hear you."

"Oops. There's a call on the other line. Be right back. . . Bo, I've gotta take the call. One of my players left a five-hundred-dollar phone bill at the hotel and everybody's goin' nuts. I'll call you tomorrow night. Good luck."

Now, should I map out tomorrow's pregame practice? No, it'll just give me nightmares. Should I rereview the last game we played against Oklahoma? No, we lost by seventeen at our house and it'll give me nightmares.

So I read myself to sleep, hoping to disremember my dreams.

5

I SLEEP LATE, finally wakening to yearn after a retreating tail-feather of some elusive eagle dream.

Outside, the sun is already banging on the city like a hot, yellow drum. The air stinks and I belch peppers.

Magoo is waiting for me at the Coliseum. "Good morning," he says brightly. His real name is George Robertson and for twenty-five years he was a moderately respected practitioner of the fast-break at Southeastern Georgia State, a small NAIA college only twenty miles east of Savannah. He's been retired for five years, leaving a lifetime legacy at SGS of 487–332. Since then, he's been the manager and part-owner of a sporting goods store downtown on Jefferson Davis Boulevard. Still brisk and wiry at age sixty-seven, George jumped at the chance last fall to get back into "the game I love so well." It was all Herm's idea and George's new part-time job pays $100 every week. George's duties are restricted to sitting on the bench at home games, wandering the court during home-court practice sessions and deciphering game tapes. The old man is friendly and eager, but, frankly, useless. When I speak of George's shortcomings, Herm says, "He gives us credibility in the community."

George has a round, hairless face equipped with a bulbous nose. His small brown eyes are surrounded by fleshy folds and wrinkles so that he appears to be constantly squinting, hence "Magoo."

45

He asks if I liked his scouting report and I insist that I do. No sense making a fuss at this point. Next time I'll do it myself.

The players arrive in clusters of twos and threes for the pregame "shootaround." The concept of the shootaround was devised by Bill Sharman when he coached the Los Angeles Lakers in the midsixties. Originally intended simply to force the players out of bed, to prevent the loggy feeling that lazing around all day can create, the shoot has become a strategic necessity.

There's still ten minutes before we officially begin and everybody's here excepting Sam. The rest sit along the sidelines unlacing their street sneakers and climbing into their game boots. Chatting, jabbering, getting ready for work.

"That chick is driving me nuts," says Richie with a weary smile. "Tonight after the game she's talking about hot oil and a cold knotted rope."

And despite myself, I'm glad to be among them, glad to be part of their juice, their vitality.

While the others filter onto the court and begin fondling the basketballs and sighting the hoops, Kelly sidles over with some bad news...As a schoolboy at Nazarene HS in East St. Louis, Kelly Royal was quicker than a wish, sporting the most deceptive right-to-left crossover dribble in the history of Western civilization. Sure, he was also wild as a storm, the kind of player who kept both teams in the ballgame. But what a talent! What a physical specimen! Recruited by every Top Twenty powerhouse, Kelly was ultimately seduced by Carl O'Reilly at Metro U. The longtime tradition at Metro was "seniors come first," and Kelly was willing to accept a three-year apprenticeship as the price for a showcase senior year and subsequent entry into the NBA's millionaire club.

However, shortly after Kelly's junior season, Coach O'Reilly outbid the world to keep Brooklyn Catholic HS's ace playmaker, Joe Hennessey, in New York. "A player like Hennessey," O'Reilly told the media, "comes along once every decade." For sure, Hennessey was a jump-shooting machine, also tough and savvy—but at Metro U. freshmen hoopers had a time-honored nickname—"Scumbags." Even so, O'Reilly suspended Metro's senior-first tradition and awarded Kelly's starting spot to Hennessey.

As a result Kelly suffered what Metro's public-relations department called "stress-related anxieties." But after some "expert counseling" Kelly accepted his backup role and had a "successful senior year." The streetwise guys had a different version: Kelly was so enraged, so bitter, that he colluded with a certain well-known gambler to shave points and perhaps to throw ballgames.

Two years ago an ambitious Brooklyn district attorney subpoenaed Kelly and questioned him about the sinister rumors. Witnesses were produced, including a notorious gambler (who had another problem pending with the IRS). Sources indicated the gambler was willing to make a deal implicating Kelly and who knew who else.

At the same time New York City was enflamed by a race-hate serial killer, caught and brought to justice after raping and dismembering five black beauty queens. The ambitious DA decided there were more headlines to be garnered by prosecuting the killer, so Kelly skated.

Now, Kelly's arachnoid brow is beetled with worry. "Coach," he says. "My agent called early this morning. He said the DA is reopening the point-shaving investigation."

"Kelly . . ."

"I didn't do nothin', Coach. I swear it. If I'm lyin', I'm dyin'. I swear on my mother. It's a setup. It was Ladell Farquar that was doin' the point shavin' but he's in the NBA now, so they won't go after him."

"Kelly . . ."

"My agent says they'll probably subpoena me and I'm gonna have to go to New York sometime next week. My agent, he says the best he can do is try to get me immunity. Shit, Coach. What'm I gonna do?"

By now his eyes are leaking. "Where's DiGennaro, is that his name? The gambler?"

"In jail on tax evasion."

"Kelly . . . take it easy. I believe you." Not really true, although I'd like to. "Here's what we'll do. . .I can speak to Herm and see what the Stars lawyer has to say, then I'll have the lawyer call your agent. Maybe we can delay the subpoena until the season's over and there won't be as much publicity. So try and put it out of your mind. Just concentrate on tonight's game and let us take care of this."

And just like that, Kelly is smiling. "Thanks, Coach," he says, his eyes bright and dry, his brow smooth and innocent. Sixty seconds later and he's trading insults with Mr. Beast.

The session is to begin promptly at 11:00 A.M. Any latecomers are subject to fines, the minimum amount being ten dollars, with a dollar added for each late minute over five. Since shoots generally last one hour, the maximum fine amounts to sixty-five dollars. Most other CBL teams simply confiscate and recirculate the players' fine money. Earl maintains that Kuback stuffs it into his own pockets. My practice is to allow the players to compete for any fine money—foul shots, three-pointers, we have a menu of shooting games.

"Time," Nate announces. "Fine the fucker! Let's shoot for Points's money."

But Sam Franks appears just ten seconds before the curtain goes up. "No sweat," he says as he jumps onto the floor and begins to stretch. "It's all about timing, baby."

Accompanying Sam is none other than Lem Jameson—6'10", 240, Michigan State '84—as always, looking sloe-eyed and slightly paunched. Jameson is a CBL lifer, an eight-year veteran and three-time CBL All-Star. Lem has all the skills to be an excellent NBA benchman—he can shoot, run, rebound, post-up and he's one of the finest passing big men ever. Lem's lifetime NBA numbers consist of one game played with the Philadelphia '76ers, three minutes, and donuts across the board. That's because he's even lazier than Sam Franks. And he smokes more reefer than a Dead Head.

Before breaking his left hand in late January, Jameson was scoring 23.4 ppg and rebounding 10.4 for the Stars, stats that undoubtedly impressed Herm. What Herm doesn't understand is that Jameson is a forty-five-minute player—i.e., one who turns into Casper the Friendly Ghost whenever a ballgame is up for grabs. It was Lem's injury that necessitated the purchase of Mr. Beast, and since the fracture I've seen nothing of Jameson.

"Coach," Lem says with an easy grin. He shows a short, wooly hairdo to match his moustache, also high cheekbones and half-shut purple eyelids. He wears sneakers and a sweatsuit. "I'm ready to go."

"Go where?"

"To play. I'm ready to play."

"Have you gotten clearance from the doctor? You look heavy. Have you run, ridden the bike, done anything?"

"I'm fine," he swears. "I spoke to Herm this morning and he said if it's okay with you, it's okay with him."

"If what's okay. What's this, a riddle?"

"If it's okay to activate me. To put me on the roster."

We exchange blank stares. I know he's much more intelligent than he lets on, but we've never really connected. The only way I've ever been able to motivate him was to threaten to trade him to Kuback. "First off," I say, letting my annoyance rise, "I don't know if you're ready or not. I'm sure you've been sitting on your ass for, what is it now, ten weeks? And even if you are physically okay, if you are healed, who should I cut to make room for you?"

"Him." He points his chin at Donald Cooper, my project, my pet.

"I'm happy you've got it all figured out. I don't know, Lem. I don't think it's such a good idea. Speak to me afterwards."

The players are lying on the court stretching their hamstrings and Kelly is providing the floor show. "Eggplant," he says to Richie. "You're so black your teeth are brown. You're so black your momma was never marked present when she went to night school. You're so fuckin' black—"

"Arright," I actually say. "Let's get it started. Let's go. I've already seen this movie."

Still laughing, they jog up and downcourt in our prescribed routines. Next, we dummy through our entire offense—three distinct sets totalling over seventy-five plays, a process that usually takes about fifteen to twenty minutes. I work with the starters— Kelly, Sam, Earl, Nate and Mr. Beast, while Magoo choreographs the subs. On my end, Nate mumbles every time someone else's play is run: "I'm not getting enough shots, Coach. How can I keep my stroke if I don't get enough shots?"

"Four-Up!" Kelly calls, and Nate misses his assigned twenty-footer. "That's why," Kelly says.

As always, Magoo's crew is finished before we are halfway through. "What's going on down there?" I shout. "Did you do the side out-of-bounds? The underneath out-of-bounds?"

"Magoo doesn't know the plays," says Earl. "You should be down there with them and send him here with us. That's why Richie and Josh bust plays all the time, because Magoo fucks them up."

With the offense completed, we're walking through Oklahoma's offense and our defensive responses, when Sam suddenly calls out, "Oh, shit, here she fuckin' comes. Coach, please . . . tell her I called in sick." He runs off-court and vanishes underneath the stands.

It's his long-suffering wife Sharina and their two-year-old daughter LaSheel. Timidly they approach, as we all stand transfixed, uncertain. Sharina is a sweet-natured woman as far as I can tell, light-skinned, shy, all the requisite curves. They've been married for ten months.

"Excuse me," she says, painfully embarrassed. "I . . ."

"That's okay," I say with my best bedside manner.

"It's just that Points didn't come home last night and I . . . I'm just worried sick. I'm scared something might've happened to him, you know? I mean, when he didn't get back by three A.M., I called the police, I called the hospital. I . . ." Now she starts crying and I don't know what the hell to do.

Then Nate moves to the rescue. "He's over at my place, Sharina. At the hotel. See, we were out having a few drinks last night. And we . . . ah . . . we had more than a few. A friend of mine gave us a lift back to the hotel. It was about midnight, maybe earlier. So Sam kinda passed out on the couch and I kinda passed out on the bed. I got up when the alarm went off this morning but he didn't. I tried to wake him but he just wouldn't come up for air, see? So I left him there. He's alright. I mean, he was just too drunk to wake up. Now I'm sure Coach here will fine him, but other than that . . . I'll get him up when we're done here and send him home. It's alright, Sharina. Boys will be boys."

Sharina ponders her situation. She and Sam are legally married, Sam has a job and a bad temper. She seems actually relieved to discover that he's not dead or maimed in a car accident. Sam will never change, so why hassle him? Of course, Nate's story is preposterous but it gives Sharina an excuse to say, "Thank you," then to leave as quickly as she can.

Meanwhile Lem Jameson has neatly stepped onto the court as though nothing is amiss. He knows our offense and our defense and he's smart enough to fake whatever new stuff we've added since he's been gone. As we resume I watch Lem, noting that he runs around his left hand, that he hides his left hand on defense. Obviously, he's still hurting.

After Sharina is long gone Sam peeps out from behind the bleachers and Jameson yields the court to him. "You owe me, motherfucker," Nate tells him. "I saved your black ass."

Sam bows deeply. "Whatever you want, my brother, you got."

Nate eyes me carefully and says, "Points, all's I want is halfa your shots."

The mood is light as we concentrate on our baseline trap aimed at defusing Oz Joseph, also our buttonhooks against Oklahoma's fullcourt press. As the players shoot free throws, I see Tim Packman, local sportscaster, and a cameraman setting up their gear beyond the far basket. At the same time I can see the Oklahoma players in their sweats milling around in the foyer near the visiting team's locker room. To complete the trifecta, here comes Lem Jameson wearing a puppydog smile.

"What you think?" he asks. "I'm ready to play tonight, right?"

"I don't think so. It looks like your hand's still sensitive, still sore."

"I'm ready," he insists, up on his toes as his irritation mounts.

I know Lem needs the money. Injured players only get Workman's Compensation, which in Georgia comes to sixty-six percent of Jameson's salary. "You say yes, I say no. You have one vote, I have a vote-and-a-half. That's the way it is." Then I turn and walk toward the camera, leaving Jameson to fume and fuss.

"Fuck you," he mutters, just loud enough for me to hear. "Fuckin' asshole."

The wheel keeps on spinning and now I'm face to face with another of my least favorite people, Tim Packman, the top-rated TV sportscaster in town. He's a square-jawed 6'4", 220-pounder who played college ball in some obscure midwest Division III school and still fancies himself a player. It seems that last year's coach, Artie ("What a nice guy!") Barfield, allowed Tim actually to practice with the Stars. For some reason Tim thought that I'd do the same. He's been on my ass ever since I turned him down. At midseason, when Earl Patton was gone for his twenty-day stint with Detroit, we lost five consecutive ballgames and Packman suggested on the air that I be replaced by Magoo.

"Got a few minutes, Coach?" Packman asks, his capped teeth agleam, his smile frozen.

In fact, I've walked toward him only to get away from Jameson. "Sure. Let me finish up here." Packman flashes me another cold smile. We don't exactly trust each other.

I convene the team at centercourt, planning to talk about focusing, about playing hard, but Kelly is still bouncing around, laughing at Sam's marital dilemma, goosing Richie's protruding butt, happy as a pig in shit. Before I can curse Kelly into silence, Mr. Beast reaches out to smack Kelly's forehead with a meaty hand and says, "Yo, boy. Shut the fuck up before I flatten your Jiminy Cricket head."

So I unfold my rap to an attentive audience. *Baha. Baha.* Then Nate says a quick prayer, pleading with the Lord to keep us injuryfree, to feed the poor, to save the sinners . . . "And one more thing, Lord," says Nate. "I need more shots."

The Rangers file onto the court and all the players mingle, each team joking, complaining about their respective coaches, or else comparing pussy posses.

"This here is Savannah," Points says to Oz Joseph. "Ain't no nigger getting no white pussy down here."

Here comes Kuback—short, limping, his gray hair pomaded and slicked back. His blue eyes are limp and moist and a slight twitch pulls up the right corner of his mouth.

"Hi, Marty." I beam, ever the gracious host. "How was your trip?"

He cuts right to the chase. "I hear it's a sure thing that Earl is going up to replace Tripucka," he says with a quivering smile. "Might even happen as early as tomorrow. Sure puts some pressure on you to win tonight, doesn't it?"

"Yeah, sure."

"Boy, I'd hate to be in your shoes if you lose tonight. Herm will be on you like stink on shit. Listen, Robert, I've been around this league for more years than I'd care to admit and my suggestion is this . . . Don't let Herm push you around. Stand up to him."

"Umm. Thanks, Marty. I really appreciate your advice." Yeah, sure. Fuck you very much.

Tim Packman and I never shake hands; instead, he proffers the clip-on microphone and tells me where to stand. "Big one tonight, Coach," he says as the camera blinks its red eye. "With two at home and three on the road there's a lot of pressure for you to win the opener."

"Tim," I say slowly, "is this one of them true-or-false questions?"

"Ha ha," he quips. Under pressure himself, he shows his teeth. "Seriously, Coach. Tell us about the pressure of the playoffs."

"Pressure? That's a media term." I turn my head slightly, hoping to angle into the arena and see what the Rangers are doing. Seems to be some sort of a passing game. ". . . I just coach the way I coach and hope for the best."

"What about the rumor that Earl Patton will shortly be called up to Charlotte to replace the injured Kelly Tripucka?"

"Yes, Tim. What about the rumor?"

"Is it true?"

"If it's true, then it wouldn't be a rumor."

He sneers, then gives up. "Okay, Coach. Good luck tonight."

On my way out of the arena I stop at a pay phone and call Chet in the office. "What's up, Chester?"

"Nothing," he says. "It's dead here. The Stars' first playoff game ever and Herm isn't even in town. Ain't that a bitch? I just hope we can three-thousand tonight. If we do any worse he'll sure as shit be blaming me. Oh, yeah, the commissioner will be at the Coliseum tonight to talk to the players before the game."

Cy Rose is the commissioner's name nowadays. He's an old sportswriter out of Philly who worked in public relations for the '76ers when his newspaper folded. His real name used to be Seymour Rosenbloom.

"What a treat," I say.

"Be good, Coach," Chet cautions. "Don't get yourself into any trouble. The season's almost over."

"What's that mean? You think we're gonna lose to Oklahoma?"

"Well, I'd rather not talk about it. But they did kick y'all's ass the last three times we played."

I hang up in disgust and drive over to Savannah State for a workout.

As always, the Nautilus room is uninhabited during lunchtime, which suits me fine. Most of the players frequent a fancy health club downtown—wall-to-wall mirrors, beautiful women prancing around in ass-sucking metallic Danskins, everybody flexing with all their might. Here, there are no reflective surfaces and no company. Here I can grunt and push and try to make my head stop talking to me. "Fucking Kuback," I say to the leg extension apparatus. "Shut up," I say to the biceps machine.

There's a kinesiology class in session next door and through the thin walls I can hear muted discussions of clavicles and tibias. The dick-bone connected to the hand-bone.

I add five pounds to each station, forcing myself to suffer. Purification through pain. "What bullshit," I confess to myself.

Truth is, I am afraid of tonight's game, as I am afraid of every game. I work out for two reasons only: to try and force some heat into my cold limbs, and to exhaust myself, to insure a long nap that will eat up the afternoon.

I bring Chinese takeout back to my room. Eating shrimps with black bean sauce while reading a gory Civil War novel by Don Robertson. A confusion of succulent sauce and coagulated puddles of blood, slivers of garlic and oozing pieces of brain.

All in a trance I nap, shower and shave, a clean bloodless shave, no cuts or nicks. Gray slacks, blue blazer, my lucky red-striped tie. The fool in the mirror smiles at me, and for a moment I am calm, self-assured, eager for combat.

Then I recall my midafternoon's dream, smoky visions of a ten-foot-high gallows with a peach basket nailed to the crossbar.

6

NINETY MINUTES BEFORE game time the vacant dressing room is peaceful as a shrine. The Brotherhood of the Sacred Hoop.

There are ten cubicles for the players, each space equipped with appropriate hooks and shelves and separated by latticed wire panels. Before each stall is a bare gray folding chair, cousins to the furniture in the Stars "executive" offices. The plastic rug is a darker gray, the walls and ceiling are whitely enameled but grayly peeling from a season's worth of postgame steam spilled from the adjacent shower room. On the longest wall, the unscriven blackboard looms and pulses like a huge, living stone.

The trainer's room is off to the left, a tiny chamber cluttered with a white plastic-and-leatherette taping table, an old clanking refrigerator, a hotbox to keep the hydoculator pads boiling and a neat row of gray supply cabinets.

Another of Herm's suspicious bargains involves the "Savannah Rehab Lab." According to Chet, the Stars supply an 8' × 10' advertising banner suspended from the Coliseum's rafters, plus ten season tickets in exchange for a game-day student trainer (apparently a different one every game), a season's worth of tapes, gauzes, unguents and free medical care for Herm and his family.

Tonight's trainer-trainee is dressed in home whites like a Good Humor Man. He shows blotchy cheeks under thick glasses as he scurries about the alcove arranging and rearranging his sterile materials. He looks up suddenly from a stack of stretchtape and is startled to see me. "Hello," he says. "My name is Gary." But I invoke my pregame priesthood and ignore him.

Since we won our last regular season home game (117–109 against the Madison Marauders), I'll gladly use the same stub of chalk as I used them. (Last week? Last month?) And in my childish block letters I print our game plan, a fantastic construction that never ever quite comes to life:

MCDONALD—quick–pressure in backcourt then loosen–great X-over rt → left–contain–make him shoot–will pressure ball—KELLY

FERGUSON—shooter–3 pt range–crowd–deny–pulls left–goes rt–no D–handle?—SAM

JOSEPH—quick–shoots 3 pts–does everything–push baseline– posts → TAJ both ways–BOX–plays passing lanes—EARL

HODGES—runs–15′ range–posts → TAJ left, jump hook rt–BOX–shot blocker—NATE

FORT—slow–posts → TAJ right, pump fakes and steps thru left–BOX– soft–bang him—MR. BEAST

COLLINS—#1–great defense–no shoot–penetrator–keep him in front of you → push left–BIGS → show and recover

HAYES—#2–streak shooter–needs pick–18′ range–no D–iso him– runs out–leaper– → BOX–deny–send → hoop

KRAMER—#3 & #4–physical–10′ range–posts strong–tricky moves–stay down–push baseline–BOX

LEDERMAN—#4 & #5–role player–sets moving picks–rebounds– physical–cheap shot artist–gets shots off boards–slow

PALMER—#5–3 pt shooter–thin–runs–shot blocker–rarely plays

DEFENSE

Box Set

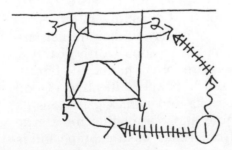

- top baseline pick
- front Joseph in post
- 5 rotate down
- bump pickers
- chase Ferguson over double
- pressure entry pass

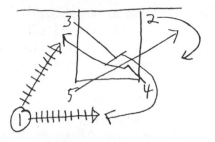

- to post Fort or Hodges
- to pop Joseph for jumper
- chase Joseph thru back pick
- or shoot gap if possible
- weakside–bigs–→don't let Ferguson curl

Passing Game

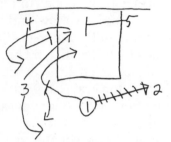

- switch #1, #2 & #3
- open up on weak side
- bang guards setting picks

- BOX–no 2nd shots
- get back on D–Hayes runs out
- LA Joseph on wing or elbow from McD or Collins
- pressure ball
- bigs–step out on picks
- talk
- rotate

OFFENSE

- start with Flex 12 40L 33 44B 5
- execute–set picks
- watch point guard poaching post pass—go back door
- 1-3-1 ½-court trap–use FIST offense–move ball quickly
- be unselfish–make extra pass
- be patient

GET GEEKED !!

As always, Donald Cooper is the first player to arrive. Since he's the lone rookie, his stall is the one nearest the blackboard, subjecting his clothing and uniform to pregame and halftime clouds of chalkdust. "Hi, Coach Lassner," he says brightly. "Jesus told me we're going to win tonight."

"Hi, Player Cooper. What else did Jesus tell you?"

"He told me to tell you that I deserve more playing time."

Carl Butler and Brent Springs arrive together. All three dress quickly and run out to the court to shoot. Mr. Beast and Nate Kennison are the next to enter, the former resplendent in a black pin-striped suit, the latter wearing a gaudy yellow-and-black sweatsuit. The two veterans sit before their stalls and majestically begin their pregame rituals. Here comes Josh Brusher, by himself, clad in new jeans and a crumpled Miller High Life sweatshirt. Richie Michaels, Kelly Royal and Earl Patton travel together and Sam is always last, toting his weathered Boston Celtics gym sack as well as a greasy brown paper bag.

"Hey, Beastman," Kelly shrills, "where'd you get that gangster zoot suit from? Robert Hall? And where'd you get those pointy-ass Puerto Rican shoes from? They look just right for climbing back-alley fences. And for squashing cockroaches in the corner."

"Shut the fuck up," is the Beast's retort. "Bug-eyed, bug-headed, flibber-lipped, Planet of the Apes motherfucker."

The brothers are perpetually sensitive about the size and shape of each other's heads. So when Nate emerges from the trainer's room Kelly greets him with, "Yo, Headley, wassup?"

"Yo, peanut head."

"Yo, popcorn head."

Then Nate looks at me and says, "This here brother's crazy."

My pregame instructions will commence at thirty minutes prior to tipoff and will last for fifteen minutes. Until then every player has his own routine:

Cooper will reenter the dressing room at 6:45, already sweating from his pregame workout. Then he'll towel off, pee, tighten up his sneaker laces and pray until I'm ready to begin. There's Cooper mumbling and crossing himself like a man scratching after fleas.

Sam won't mount the court until he must. Meanwhile he sits

quietly and fidgets with his socks. Because of Sam's thin legs (Kelly calls them "bird legs") he wears six pairs of socks, three short and three calf-length. "You look like an old man," Kelly always says, "wearing Supphose." Furthermore, when Sam is satisfied that his threads are in order he opens the paper bag and slowly eats his favorite pregame meal—a large Coke and two chili dogs. "It gets me fired up," he says.

My practice is to hide in the dressing room until the last possible moment. Meanwhile, Coach Magoo is outside patrolling the sidelines and chatting with his cronies. When Magoo comes back inside, perhaps he'll tell me that Kelly has "the stroke tonight" or that Cooper "can't piss in the ocean."

Beast goes outside to practice his free throws—during the season he shot only fifty-eight percent from the line, making it difficult for me to play him in the endgame. The big man will come back inside just after Cooper, then he'll sit solemnly on his chair, absently picking at the ingrown hairs on his neck.

Earl and Nate are outside under the lights playing one-on-one, while Kelly only wants to practice shooting three-pointers. Richie Michaels is having his usual pregame problems: the tape job is either too loose or too tight and must be redone; a sneaker lace broke; the drawstring of his uniform shorts is lost inside the waistband; he's constipated; he has the runs.

In the far corner Josh Brusher leans his chair against the wall, his head back, his mouth open, asleep.

At 6:55, Jeff Bradley, the Stars public-address announcer, pokes his head into the room to notify me of the visitors starting lineup—McDonald, Ferguson, Joseph, Hodges and Fort—and to ask for mine. "The same." Then Bradley identifies tonight's officials—two young black men, Stevie Stephenson and Archie Fathers.

"Fuck me!" I say.

As part of the NBA-CBL contract the NBA is responsible for paying, scheduling and supervising all the CBL's refs, but the difference between the two leagues' officials is profound. In the NBA the refs determine the outcome of approximately ten percent of the ballgames, while in the CBL the proportion approaches two-thirds. Why is this so? Because nobody in the NBA really cares about us. Because Barret Smith, the NBA's supervisor of officials, believes that the CBL has only one narrow function—to develop refs for The League.

Refs, lawyers and cops. Whistles, writs and guns. Even in the best of circumstances I consider basketball officials of any ilk to be a necessary evil.

There are three categories of CBL refs: the first being those who have been promoted into the sunlight and work a mere handful of CBL games to inspire their purblind brethren. These veteran officials have nothing to prove and no reputations to establish. For the most part they are confident and easy going, unafraid to let CBL coaches voice calm, reasoned objections. Since the NBA employs three refs per game and the CBL only two, many of the more senior officials actually enjoy the extra freedom of working a CBL contest.

Archie Fathers belongs to the second category, the half-timers who work about thirty-five games in the CBL and thirty-five in the NBA. These are the bozos on the bubble, with one foot in heaven and one in hell, with their balls in an uproar. Two nights ago Fathers worked a Lakers–Celtics game on the illustrious parquet floor in the Boston Garden. Tonight he's in Palookaville and he's pissed. Arrogant and arbitrary, he'll take no guff from any CBL player or coach. He's the big pointy shoe and we're the cockroaches.

And this is Fathers's specific grudge against me: two years ago in a game at the Fairgrounds Arena in Waco, Texas, it was obvious to me that Fathers was constantly out of position and late on every call, so I yelled, "Hey, Archie! Get in the game." He was at the other end of the court and immediately double-bammed me, thereby banishing me to the locker room. Later, he told one of my players that he T-eed me because he thought I called him "gay."

The last group of refs are the tadpoles who only officiate CBL games. These are the mechanics and plumbers who have no feel for the game. I've always contended that all refs, college and pro, should be required to play in five-on-five tournaments so they'll know what a pick feels like, what is and isn't incidental contact. But as always, the most ignorant lawkeepers are the most self-righteous.

Stephenson has been a CBL ref for three seasons. A tadpole

without a tail, he is only 5'5" and just can't see around the big bodies. The players say he's "light in the ass," that he has "big ears and a short fuse." Earlier this season Stephenson ran me at home because I called him "a standing blow job."

At six o'clock Magoo shepherds the on-court players inside and we gather in the middle of the locker room to pile our hands. Just as Nate is about to call for a blessing, the door opens and Commissioner Cy Rose bustles into the room.

He is a round-faced man in his early fifties with thick glasses perched stolidly on a sharply crooked nose. His squat body is stuffed into a fat gray suit and he's obviously very proud of himself. Too bad his public-relations background and his newspaper experience have left him spectacularly unprepared for his current employment.

In the CBL technical fouls cost twenty-five dollars each, and for years the standard procedure was to deduct the fines from any offending player's or coach's paycheck. However, Rose's first official act upon assuming office last October was to require that the CBL collect its fine money exactly as the NBA does. To wit, fines were to be sent to league headquarters in the form of cashier's check by each finee within seven days of the infraction or else face further fines and suspensions. The truth is that none of the players live permanently in the CBL cities in which they play, precious few have local bank accounts and even fewer have any notion what a cashier's check is. The result was a confusion of sudden suspensions, bookkeeping errors and ballgames lost for twenty-five dollars. The board of directors forthwith rescinded Rose's resolution and ever since then the commissioner asks permission to pee.

"Hello, Coach," he says to me, then without waiting for a response, turns to the players and says, "Hello, men." The commissioner of us all next reaches into his coat pocket, extracts several sheets of paper and begins to read in a dull flat tone:

"Gentlemen. As duly elected commissioner of the Commercial Basketball League it behooves me to make this visit to each of the teams currently involved in the CBL playoffs. This past season has been a landmark season for the league. Indeed, since our humble beginnings . . ."

"Fuck this," Sam says.

"What?" Rose blinks, needing time to wrest his focus from his speech to reality. "Who said that?"

"Me," Sam says. "Lookit, we got a game to play, man. We ain't got time for no history lesson. What if there's an NBA scout out in the stands looking to check me out and I ain't loose because of this bullshit? You're fucking with my future, man. Why didn't you come this afternoon during the shootaround?"

Rose looks wide-eyed at me but I shrug, saying, "Right on, Sam," then look away.

"Ahem," Rose says, rustling his pages. "What I mean to say is . . . there is a certain logic . . . ah, here it is . . . the heart of the matter . . . so . . . Be it understood that the league will tolerate no outburst of violence in any circumstances. Be it understood that fisticuffs of any nature, whether offensive or defensive, will be severely punished with fines and suspensions. And be it—"

"Yeah," says Sam. "We be understanding all that. What else you got?"

"Drugs. The drug policy of the CBL is strict and unyielding—"

"Okay," Sam says. "We promise not to fight and not to do drugs. Right, fellas?" Everybody grunts. "That it?"

By now, Rose desperately needs a joke, an anecdote, a surefire punch line. "Here it is," he says aloud, "at the bottom of the page . . . let me leave you with one pertinent thought . . . as Al Davis says, 'Just *win*, baby!' "

The players laugh as Rose scampers toward the door. On his way out Rose glares at me. "Lassner, I'm holding you responsible for this."

After the laughter simmers we reform our circle and Nate prepares once more to address the Master of the Universe. "Wait a minute," Earl says, annoyed, his first words since his arrival. "Who's not here? There's only nine of us."

"It's Richie," says Kelly. "He's in the bathroom taking a shit. Hey, he didn't get to hear the commissioner's rap. Maybe we should go get him and bring him back. Richie! Eggplant! You midnight nigger! Get on out here!"

Standing quietly on the fringe of the group, Cooper overlaps his index fingers to shape a cross and points them at the back of Sam's head. "All right," I say. "Enough of this. We've got a game to play. To win."

Finally, we circle-up and Nate appeals to God Almighty in Jesus' blessed name for a victory, free of injuries.

By now I'm forced to condense my pregame message into a scant five minutes, mostly reiterating and emphasizing what's already on the blackboard. Another quick circle, a rapid chant of "one, two, three, DO IT!" and they race from the room, leaving me, already sweating, to stare at Magoo.

"Crisp passes," Magoo says (to me? to himself?). "Crisp passes and defensive intensity."

Ignoring him, I sequester myself in the shitter, lid down, pants up, head in my hands. Right now I don't care if we win or lose. I just want it to be over.

7

In TRUTH, I am a pagan, subject to foolish liturgies and idle superstitions. Anything to discover the unknowable.

Whoever wins the opening tip will win the game. Better yet, whoever scores the first basket will win . . .

During the "Star-Spangled Banner" (sung tonight by the G.I. Joes, a barbershop quartet sponsored by the American Legion) I always stand behind the players along the sidelines parallel to the bench. My eyes are tightly closed as I listen hopefully for the gurgling of my competitive juices.

As part of my routine my eyes snap open at "the rockets' red glare." For an instant my interior darkness is blasted with light and time seems to be another casualty of war . . . There's a good crowd on hand, perhaps 5,000—Chet will be happy, win or lose. There's a little boy in section BB caught with his finger in his nose. And the satin-clad cheerleaders, standing at attention and saluting, even their satinized nipples erect. At the press table Herm is talking sideways to Chet and the little feller can't nod his agreement fast enough. In front of me, Sam is blowing kisses and waggling his tongue at a big-breasted blonde in section D. There's Cy Rose, further down the press table, his eyes closed, singing along with the G.I. Joes.

Then another informal huddle, full of frantic advice and enthusiasms. "DO IT!"

The ball looks like a massive pumpkin in Stephenson's tiny hand and his toss is at least thirty degrees off-center, easily backtapped from Hodges to McDonald, and the game is underway.

"Rejump it!" I yell.

Immediately the Rangers show a new offensive set and my brain is suddenly engorged with blood. I must loosen my tie and undo the neck button of my shirt. Yes, my chops are up and I'm ready to kill.

First off, it's a UCLA set with the two big men out of the way on the weakside. In a flash I can see several possibilities:

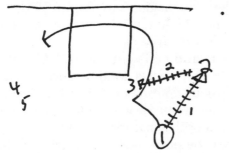

• to iso Joseph

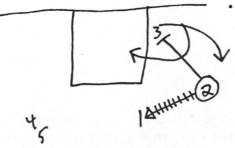

• or, #3 picks down–to post Joseph
• or, #1 backpicks up–to post Joseph

• or, #2 picks down–to pop Joseph or to curl Joseph

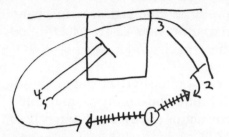

• or, #3 backpicks for #2—to iso Joseph or to pop Ferguson

But Earl scraps and scratches and Joseph misses a seventeen-footer under pressure. Then, alas, Nate neglects to box out Hodges, who dunks the offensive rebound. *They win!?! Better make that two-out-of-three, perhaps three-out-of-five . . .*

Kelly walks the ball downcourt and calls out, "Flex!" All told, we operate with three offensive sets and a total of seventy-five different plays (not including inbound situations). But for no discernible reason, Nate decides to abort our very first play. Nate is an eight-year CBL vet, a bitcher and a bellyacher for sure, but a stolid, tax-paying citizen. Nate receives the entry pass from Kelly at the left elbow, then, instead of reversing to Beast, he hoists a twenty-footer. "No!" I shout, but the shot is true.

Next time down, the Rangers present a new variation of their Box Set, also designed to iso Joseph,

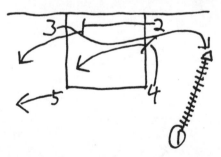

who easily beats Earl to the baskét.

OKL—4   STARS—2

As the game wears on, Kuback's strategy comes clearer. The Rangers will hold their deadly 1-3-1 trap in abeyance and, instead, collapse their defense into the paint, challenging us to beat them with perimeter shots.

Also, every time Sam touches the ball he is doubled. To counter this, Sam is supposed to pass quickly to Kelly, who in turn will swing the ball to Earl on the weakside. But Sam has his own game plan—to accumulate "numbers." Unlike hockey, basketball offers no statistical reward for the pass that leads to the assist pass. That's why Sam holds the ball and shouts for Kelly to cut through. It seems that Kelly sports a notoriously unreliable jumper and Sam will most likely remain assistless (an important number for a guard) unless Kelly can convert his passes into layups. Trouble is, Kelly is much more comfortable dribbling through traffic than catching in a crowd, so he hangs suspended above the key. Add all the factors and vectors, and Sam is stubbornly resolved to launch his shots one-on-two.

Nate now has an excuse to force two more bad shots, making the second one. And at both ends, Oz Joseph is schooling Earl. The first mandatory timeout comes at 6:37.

OKL–19   STARS–11

Nate is my immediate priority in the huddle. "What's going on, Nate? This isn't like you. Run the offense."

"Fuck," he says. "I'm two-for-three."

"And nobody else is involved. That's why we're already down by eight."

"I'm getting mine," he says. "Let them get theirs."

"Well, fuck that. Coop, go in for Nate."

Sam is next on the triage list. "Reverse the ball, Sam. You're holding it too long and all your shots are forced."

"Tell Kelly to cut," Sam says. "He ain't gonna hit no jump shot."

"Go to me," Earl puts in. "If I can hit a couple maybe they'll come double me, then we can swing it to Sam and get him started."

"Arright!" I say. "Arright!" Where did I pick that up from? "Let's do this . . ." I diagram a play for Earl on my Ouija board, then one for Beast. "This's twelve . . . this's fifty-six." Earl is having no luck fronting Joseph and my brilliant scheme never comes to life. Instead, I start illustrating our "White-move" sequence, a double-down from the top.

"No," says Earl, his blue eyes flashing. "I can handle him by myself. Don't worry about me. But, Beast, you've gotta hit somebody. Coop, keep that fucking Hodges off the boards. Let's show some teamwork out there. Some heart. We're supposed to be professionals."

"Exactly," is my lame refrain.

"DO IT!"

Cooper makes a difference: The offense runs like a clock and Hodges is stifled. Beast converts a quick turnaround jumper to the middle before the defense can collapse. Then while Earl inbounds a made free throw and both refs are turned downcourt, Beast detonates an elbow into Fort's chest, sending the rookie sprawling. But Earl continues shooting blanks and Joseph runs amok... Bang! a three-pointer. Snatch! an offensive rebound.

Just before the quarterbreak I substitute Richie for Earl ... no use, another three-pointer for Joseph, now he rips Richie and breaks away for a roundhouse dunk.

OKL–36   STARS–23

Carl for Kelly. Brent for Richie. The fans chant, "We want Josh." I glance down the bench and catch Josh furiously chewing on his fingernails. He sees me and his face slides into a maniacal grin.

Carl steals the ball from Collins twice but misses both layups. Brent does bother Joseph for a time, chasing him around picks, Bogarting him off the block, until Oz scores twice on offensive rebounds. Apparently Kuback will play Joseph the full forty-eight minutes.

OKL–44   STARS–35

Cooper always plays confrontational defense, chest-to-chest, hand-on-hip, forever flopping and trying to draw a charge. But Fathers won't be fooled, calling the block on Cooper and later also whistling the rookie for an overly aggressive hand-check. Yet when Cooper drives to the cup, his shooting arm is clearly smacked by Hodges, a flesh-on-flesh impact that can be heard in the upper balcony.

"A blind man could call that one," I shout.

"All ball," says Fathers.

OKL–49   STARS–41

Earl for Sam. "Fuck," Sam blurts as he approaches the bench. "I can't score nothing sitting here."

Beast and Fort are standing together when Kuback calls timeout. Suddenly Beast steps on Fort's front foot, throwing the rookie off-balance, making him stumble forward. Beast then chests Fort to a rude stop. "Get off me, boy," Beast threatens before turning toward the bench.

During the timeout Sam perches on the nearest edge of the press table. Picking up the telephone, he dials an outside line. "Fatso," he says loudly. "You're my fucking agent, right? Well, get me the fuck out of here. Like tonight. Spain. Italy. Bongo-Bongo Land. I don't care."

At halftime, the Rangers lead by 58–53.

The players slump forward in their chairs and only Cooper looks up as I work the blackboard. "Way to come back," I say, "let's do this against their UCLA . . . Switch this. Bump this. Deny this. Okay? Everybody got it? Now, let's post Earl and put some defensive pressure on Joseph. Like this . . . okay? We'll run the Thumb Up three-ten to iso Sam in the middle of the court. Also let's do this. This. And this."

Neither Nate nor Sam will join our circle and the locker room enforcer, Mr. Beast, is too distracted to notice. "Sam!" I shout. "Nate! Are you on this team or not?"

Nate reluctantly strolls over and barely touches his fingertips to Earl's shoulder, but Sam says, "Fuck it," and leaves the room.

"DO IT!"

On the first play of the second half Stephenson calls Cooper for a phantom foul, his fourth. Nate apparently gets his feet tangled up in his warmup pants, missing the dead ball and the immediate chance to replace Cooper. The next opportunity presents itself forty-six seconds later upon the occasion of Cooper's fifth foul.

Kuback, that wily bastard, has begun the third quarter with the passing game, an offense we were ostensibly prepared to defend at the beginning of the game. By now, few of my players can remember to switch #1, #2 and #3, to open up on the weak side, or to bang the guards setting picks. So I must burn a twenty-second TO to remind them.

OKL–67   STARS–59

Next, Kuback switches to his accustomed box-set and I must wait until the six-minute mandatory TO to remind my team of the defenses we've been practicing for two days.

"We want Josh," the crowd chants.

Meanwhile, the Beast stands at the foul line, twitches mightily before he shoots, then laughs as the first shot bangs high off the board and rattles through the rim. He flashes double-handed victory signs until Fathers reloads him. This time, his shot is three feet short.

On the very next sequence, when Fort tries to swing a hook shot over the Beast, the rookie is clubbed to the floor. After Fort flubs both free throws, Beast gallops downcourt blowing on his right elbow as though it were a smoking gun.

OKL–73   STARS–64

Joseph has not cooled off but Earl starts finding the range. This forces Kuback to play us straight up, and Sam suddenly gets the feeling . . . two in a row! Three! Four! As he passes the bench, Sam yells at me, "It's my world, motherfucka!"

Entering the last quarter the score is

OKL–81   STARS–77

By this time we've adjusted to the Rangers' passing game and also their box, so Kuback reinstates his UCLA offense. "Hunh?" says Kelly.

Nate is back in the corral, but Sam misfires again and won't stop shooting. "Give me the ball," Sam commands Carl. "And get the fuck outta my way."

OKL–90   STARS–83

Following his own personal agenda, Sam decides to post-up Ferguson, never mind that the call is 55B, a post-up for Beast. "No," I yell. "Get outta there!" Too late. Fathers tweets his whistle, says, "Three," and signals us for a lane violation.

"Three?" asks Magoo. "A foul on three? There's no number three out there." Before I can stop him, Magoo has left the bench to inquire at the scorer's table.

OKL–96   STARS–90

With 7:52 remaining we have already been tooted for five team fouls, while the Rangers have none. Cooper has replaced Nate and I am anxious for Carl Butler to implement a 50, a high-post isolation against a lead-footed Kramer. But Carl can't hear me.

"Carl! Run a fifty! Carl! Cee Bee! Five oh!"

Apparently "Stee-vee" Stephenson believes I am ragging him about the unfair discrepancy in team fouls, so he presents me with a T.

OKL–104   STARS–100

Timeout at 2:43—"Let me play power forward," says Earl. "Put Brent on Oz." What a great idea!

The Rangers finally unleash their fearsome 1-3-1 half-court trap. Our offense quickly turns to stone but Earl and Sam nail desperation jumpers as the game rushes to a conclusion.

OKL–109   STARS–107

Beast rams home a rebound and, despite his embarrassing performance at the FT line, I will let him finish. Joseph drills a twenty-footer with Brent in his jock. Earl finds Sam alone under the basket.

OKL–111   STARS–111

"We want Josh!"

Finally, we get a call from Fathers—Earl tumbling backward to draw a dubious charge against Joseph. Then Sam misses, Joseph makes and Sam misses again.

OKL–113   STARS–111

The game clock reads 00:32.7, their ball, their TO. We have a solitary TO remaining, they have two plus their :20. Both teams have surpassed the foul limit.

Now, if they score we certainly need a TO. But if they don't score and we rebound, consider this—if we call our last TO Kuback can trap, double, prepare some kind of sinister scrambling defense. In this scenario we'll have maybe ten to twelve seconds left to find something for Sam or Earl. For Earl.

Q: Do I trust us (them) to be poised and unselfish under maximum defensive pressure?

A: No.

But, if we can stop them and then push the ball downcourt, perhaps we can catch them unawares and find an easy shot. Okay.

"Listen up. Good defense everywhere. White-move if Joseph posts. Everybody to the boards. If they score we want a timeout. If they don't and the ball is still alive, let's do this . . . whoever rebounds look to outlet to Earl or Kelly. If we can get it across midcourt quickly, then go! But . . . But . . . Earl or Kelly, if you have to back up with the ball, then call the timeout. Okay? Timeout if they score. Good dee. Double Joseph on the block. Five to the board. Outlet to Earl or Kelly. Take it if the floor is open. Timeout if you're challenged. Everybody understand? Okay! DO IT!"

The Rangers run a safety inbounds

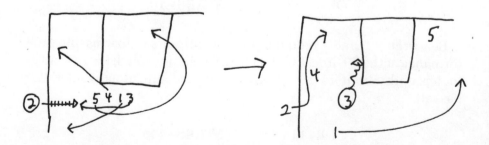

and Joseph holds the ball, waiting to create a shot against Earl. This time Earl is on him like stink on shit. With :14 on the game clock, Joseph's shot is a potato that wobbles off the front rim to be rebounded by the Beast.

Quickly, Beast outlets to Kelly, who rushes downcourt. The Rangers expect us to stop the clock and are slow reacting. Only McDonald understands our ploy, but his angle is askew and Kelly has an open lane to the basket! Then . . . for reasons known only to himself, Kelly pulls up his dribble when he crosses the time-line.

"Timeout!" I yell, jumping, waving. "Timeout!"

The defense recovers and just before the clock expires, Kelly passes to the Beast, who misses a thirty-foot heave by five feet.

BZZZZZT!

8

My POST-MORTEM must be forceful and meaningful. But there's not been sufficient time to digest the ballgame, to understand what really happened out there. In any case I must start off angry before soothing them and offering encouragement. After all, there is another game Saturday night.

And, no, I'm not relieved that it's over. I want the game to continue into overtime, quadruple overtime, all night, if necessary, until we win.

"That was horseshit, guys. A fucking playoff game and we weren't ready to play. So we had to play the entire game climbing out of a fucking hole. There's no possible excuse. And where was our execution? We were selfish, impatient, stupid . . . Nate, Sam . . . like a buncha fucking rookies. And I'm telling you this right now . . . if you break a play on Saturday, wham. Your ass'll be riding the pines. That goes for everybody. It's impossible for a team to win in the playoffs unless they run their offense. No matter how talented they are. And the fucking kicker is this . . . as bad as we played, we could have won the game. We were right there." I must fake a cough to avoid looking at Kelly. "Well, fuck it. Tomorrow's another day and we'll make some adjustments at practice. But we've got to hang together, guys. We've got to learn from this game. We've got to be ready to fucking play. All right! Let's bring it up here."

Nate clears his throat. "Thank you for this day, Heavenly Father. Thank you for letting us play with no serious injuries. Help each one of us to accept whatever blame is ours. And help us in Jesus' blessed name to kick their butts next time. Amen."

My custom is to work the room softly, pausing before each player's space to reestablish contact, to give advice, to hear confessions. Cooper is distraught. "Why won't they let me play?" he asks.

"It's simple," I say. "They're not used to your style of play. Even refs need a scapegoat. That's why God created rookies. It's nothing personal."

"I don't know, Coach. A foul is a foul."

"I wish that were true. Hey, Coop. Just keep playing hard. It'll come around."

"I don't know, Coach. I think it's the devil's work."

Nate is slicing the tape off his ankles with a specially crafted one-edged scissor and looks up when he feels me hovering. "Tough game," I say, letting him make the first move.

"My bad," he admits. "I had a fucked-up attitude to start with. Ya know? Just last night my wife told me she was pregnant. Right? With two kids still in diapers. Don't make love without a glove, right? Anyways, we just bought that new car and I'm already up to my ass in bills. It's all fucked up. So I started getting crazy behind all this. I started thinking that I'm gonna be thirty-one next month. I been eight fucking years in the CBL and not even one lousy ten-day contract. Not nothing. So I'm thinking this is it, my last chance to make The League, to make the dough. Stupid shit, ain't it?"

"Nate. It's okay. Everybody in this league is frustrated. Nobody wants to be here."

"No, it ain't okay. Lookit. I fucked up the game. I'm the one who started shortcircuiting the offense. I'm the one who made Points so horny to shoot. That's why we never got into any kind of rhythm. It's my fault."

"Nate. It takes five to win and five to lose."

He ignores my wonderful aphorism. "And deep in my heart," he says, "I know I'm not an NBA player. Never was to begin with. Shit. I'm six-foot-eight, two-twenty-five and all's I can do is shoot. I can't post-up, I can't bound and I can't really defend."

"Nate. Lighten up."

"No, no. Don't be bullshitting me, Rob. I know the fucking score. I'm a fucking loser. That's what it comes down to."

"I don't even want to hear that shit. If you were a loser, you wouldn't be suffering so much. Losers always hold back when they play, they always save something to hold on to. Losers blame everybody else for everything that goes wrong. Winners hold nothing back. They leave their hearts on the floor. That's why winners hurt so much when they do lose. And after every loss, winners have to rebuild themselves back up from nothing. Like you have to do now. No, Nate. You're not a loser."

"Well," he says softly. "Maybe. But tell me this, if you can . . . what the fuck am I gonna do with the rest of my life? The meter's ticking, Rob."

"I can't answer that. Hey, maybe when this is all over the two of us can open up a bowling alley or something."

"Nah," he says, showing his teeth in paltry imitation of a smile. "Brothers don't bowl."

"For real, though, if we can win this series, the CBL pays each of us an extra five-hundred bucks. If we can somehow win the championship, the bonus is two thousand."

"Yeah," he sighs. "I know. I'll be fine, Rob. Just let me get over this my own way."

The upper shelf in the Beast's cubicle is loaded with assorted lotions, pomades and colognes. On the shelf's edge is a handy three-pack of lubricated, ribbed, lambskin condoms.

I tell him that he played well but he's unimpressed. "We lost," he says with a grim smile. "That's all that ever matters."

Sam, Carl and Josh are in the shower. I can hear their laughter booming off the tiled walls. And I manage to intercept Richie on his way to join them.

Richie wears a blue terrycloth robe and matching plastic thongs. "It's not your fault," he tells me. Who said it was? "I just couldn't get started."

"Are you staying out too late?" I ask. "Not getting enough sleep? Savannah's a small town. I hear you're out clubbing every night. Richie, we need you playing well for us to win."

"Thanks, Coach," he says.

Thanks?

Earl is always devastated by defeat. "I sucked," he says as I move Richie's chair beside his. "I couldn't hit a shot. I couldn't guard my own fucking shadow."

"Take it easy. Joseph is a stone bitch. He doesn't belong in this league."

Earl looks up, his eyes soft and empty. "It's true. He kicked the piss outta me, didn't he? What can I do with him?"

"Knock him down next time. Be physical. Go to war. See how big his nuts are."

Earl nods, then picks at his sneaker laces. "Rob," he says, "you gotta do something about Points. He's killing us. All he does is yell for the ball. He's totally out of control and some of the guys are upset. Like, the Beast is on the verge of seriously kicking his ass."

"What can I do? We need his scoring. And besides, Herm loves his dirty drawers."

"Fuck Herm," Earl snaps. "And fuck Points. Just bench the cocksucker. Play Brent. At least the kid is hungry and wants to play defense. Believe me, we can win without Sam."

I don't believe him.

The door swings open, admitting Chet and Lem Jameson. No doubt the media is waiting for me outside in the corridor. Joe Patterson and Tim Packman. My plan is to tell them that I should have stopped the clock, that there was some avoidable confusion on the court. I'll take Kelly off the hook and hang myself.

"Tell me this, Earl. The real deal. Should I have called the timeout?"

"Fuck no. You did the right thing. If the Beast'd given me the ball we would've won. Kelly just choked. Plain and simple."

"I think so too."

"And, Rob. Really bust our ass in practice tomorrow."

Like Earl, Kelly hasn't even begun to unpeel his uniform. He looks like a boy whose puppy has just been mashed by a truck.

"Coach," he says. "I'm sorry."

"Bullshit. You played a good game."

"Yeah. Except for that last play. I don't know what happened out there. Maybe I thought there was more time left. Maybe I thought McDonald had the angle on me. Shit. I don't know what I thought."

"Kelly. Everybody makes mistakes."

"Yeah, but mine costed us the ballgame."

"Not so. There's forty-eight minutes in a game. What happens in the first minute is just as important as what happens last. If Carl makes one of those layups, if Beast hits a free throw . . . you never know. At least we wouldn't've been in such a tight spot at the end."

"You really think so?"

"Of course." Jesus! How can I live with myself? Forget about plays and replays, forget about who plays and misplays. My most pertinent talent is being able to lie without laughing, without crying. "And, Kelly, I should have called that timeout. Just to make sure we were all on the same page."

"You really think so?"

Carl is toweling off—only 5'9", he has the physique of a lifelong weightlifter. It's Kelly who insists that Carl has spent considerable time in some prison or other, pumping his body parts in the yard. A notorious boozer, Carl has bounced around the CBL for years, destined to be a backup forever. But I like his toughness, his defense, and his gold tooth. I don't like the fact that he seems to be hanging out with Sam.

"Two fucking layups," Carl says. "My bad."

"But you played good defense."

"Shit," he says, waving me away.

Lem Jameson is in conference with Sam. When he sees me, Lem toasts me with a can of beer raised high in his left hand. Smiling broadly, he rotates his left wrist, then chug-a-lugs the beer. "I'm ready," he calls across the room.

Chet sidles up beside me to deliver his own postgame report. "A tough one to lose and Herm is bugged that you didn't play Josh, but otherwise he's happy as a pig in shit. Herm says since y'all lost at home, y'all would've lost anyways in Oklahoma City. He says y'all'll probably lose again on Saturday and then get swept on the road. He says he's a genius because he's getting two home games instead of only one. He's a fucking asshole is what he is."

"Chester. What time can we practice here tomorrow?"

"It's all fucked up, Rob. There's a regional competition for high-school cheerleaders going on in the Coliseum all day long. I'll bet that's where Herm's gonna be. Y'all can't get on the floor until eight o'clock. But you can have Savannah State at noon if you want. From noon to two."

There's Josh at his cubicle, sucking on the fingernails of his right hand to stem the bleeding. Sam and Lem are laughing in a loud conspiracy. Kelly has finally dragged himself into the shower. Earl still hasn't budged from his chair. Magoo wanders aimlessly around the room, shaking his head and wringing his hands, looking for something to do. Chet goes into the trainer's room, withdraws two cans of beer from the refrigerator and hands me one. "I'll go see what's holding up the stat sheet," he says.

I summon Magoo: tomorrow after practice I want to review the game tape with the players. Can Magoo arrange for an empty classroom at Savannah State at about 2:00? How about a VCR and a TV? We'll also need a trainer.

"No problem," he says.

Then I call the team to order and announce the practice time and place. "We'll look at the game afterwards," I add.

"Should we get taped?" Sam wants to know.

"Yes. We're going hard tomorrow."

"That's fucking bullshit," Sam mutters to Lem.

Chet reenters the room and distributes a stack of stat sheets. The players crowd around him like he's giving away money.

"Fuck," says the Beast. "I had more than eleven rebounds. Who's responsible for this shit?"

Before Beast leaves in cahoots with Lem, Sam also pauses to peruse his official numbers. "Say what?" he shouts. "I got fucked out of an assist." Then he suddenly turns and points a menacing finger at Kelly. "And you, you can't shoot for shit! And I don't care what anybody says, you fucking choked."

In the trainer's room Josh is busily stuffing his gym bag with cans of beer.

COMMERCIAL BASKETBALL LEAGUE
Official Scorer's Report

Date: March 15, 1992   Game #: 01   Arena: Savannah Coliseum   Attendance: 5634
Visitors: Ok. City Rangers   Home: Savannah Stars   Length of Game: 2:05

No	Visitors Rangers	Min.	Field Goals M	A	Free Throws M	A	3 Pt Field Goals M	A	Pts.	Rebounds O	D	TOT	AST	PF	TO	BS	ST
2	McDonald (G)	40	4	10	2	2	0	0	10	0	2	2	10	4	3	0	2
4	Collins	8	0	2	0	0	0	0	0	0	0	0	2	1	2	0	1
10	Hayes	14	2	4	1	1	0	1	5	1	1	2	1	3	1	0	0
11	Joseph (F)	48	16	23	9	10	2	3	43	4	5	9	6	4	2	1	3
12	Kramer	18	2	3	0	0	0	0	4	1	4	5	0	4	1	1	0
14	Ferguson (G)	34	8	15	6	6	0	2	22	0	4	0	1	4	1	0	1
15	Palmer	DNP	Coach's Decision														
20	Fort (c)	35	4	15	1	3	0	0	9	2	6	8	0	5	2	2	0
21	Hodges (F)	39	9	16	2	3	0	0	20	5	7	12	1	5	1	0	0
23	Lederman	4	0	1	0	0	0	0	0	0	0	0	0	2	0	1	1
	TOTALS	240	45	84	21	25	2	6	113	13	29	42	21	32	13	5	8
	Pct.		50.6		84.0		33.3			Team 9				0			

No	Home Stars	Min	Field Goals M	A	Free Throws M	A	3 Pt Field Goals M	A	Pts.	Rebounds O	D	TOT	AST	PF	TO	BS	ST
6	Royal (G)	37	3	7	2	4	0	0	8	1	3	4	7	3	4	1	2
7	Franks (G)	42	8	21	9	9	2	5	27	0	2	2	2	2	3	0	0
8	Butler	11	0	3	0	0	0	0	0	1	1	2	1	1	2	0	2
10	Cooper	25	5	8	4	5	0	0	14	2	5	7	3	5	2	1	1
11	Brusher	DNP	Coach's Decision														
12	Kennison (F)	23	5	13	3	4	0	0	13	1	3	4	0	4	3	0	0
13	Morrison (c)	40	8	13	2	6	0	1	18	3	8	11	1	4	2	1	0
24	Michaels	6	0	3	0	0	0	0	0	0	0	0	0	2	1	0	0
32	Patton (F)	45	10	23	8	11	0	3	28	3	6	9	4	4	3	1	3
40	Springs	11	1	2	2	2	0	0	3	0	2	2	1	0	1	0	1
	TOTALS	240	40	95	29	41	2	9	111	11	30	41	19	26	21	4	9
	Pct.		42.1		70.9		22.2			Team 4				2			

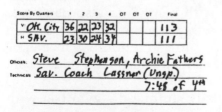

Score By Quarters	1	2	3	4	OT	OT	OT	Final
V OK. City	36	22	23	32				113
H SAV.	23	30	24	34				111

Officials: Steve Stephenson, Archie Fathers
Technicals: Sav. Coach Lassner (Unsp.)
7:48 of 4th

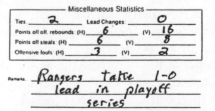

Miscellaneous Statistics
Ties 2   Lead Changes 0
Points off off. rebounds (H) 6   (V) 16
Points off steals (H) 6   (V) 8
Offensive fouls (H) 3   (V) 2

Remarks: Rangers take 1-0 lead in playoff series

9

BACK INSIDE MY cave, I can only study the entrails of the game. The same damn game with the same damn ending, back and forth, watching, cringing, as Kelly kills his dribble again and again.

So I take notes. Yes, yes. When Sam is doubled on the wing, Kelly must cut to the basket. Yes, yes. Then Earl will rotate to the middle in place of Kelly, and Nate will assume Earl's place on the weakside wing. Naturally, Sam will gladly pass to Earl, who will gladly shoot or pass to Nate, who will rain glorious jump shots from the sky.

Here's what it looks like inside my head:

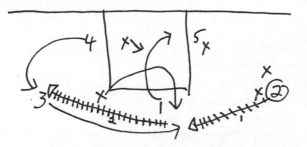

On the screen, tiny, flickering images, the heat and passion of a ballgame reduced by a factor of ten thousand. And, God-like, I am in control of the past, the present and the fast-forward, but still impotent, still unable to change the result.

Is there a Rob Lassner game tape somewhere? Is God watching a tape of me watching a tape? Is he likewise helpless to change the final score? Thank you for this lost day, for this secondhand ball-game.

Supper is a bag of chicken sandwiches from Wendy's drive-in, but it remains unopened, and I am overjoyed when the phone rings.

Sidney Dryer is a full-time scout for the Charlotte Hornets, whose beat includes the CBL. Sidney was a member of the original expansionist Hornets back in 1987 until a severe stress fracture ended his career after only twenty games. He's 6'5", still 190 pounds. He claims his jumper is still alive but his legs are dead. Sidney's a decent guy and we've been acquainted for three years, ever since I led him to Chang's Restaurant in Peoria.

Sidney now asks about tonight's game and I go into more detail than he probably wants to hear. "Sounds like you made the right call," he says. "Now you've got to take the loss and turn it into something positive. That's why you get paid." Then I wait for him to ask about Earl, but he says, "Tell me more about how Oz Joseph played."

So I recite Joseph's line from the stat sheet and I embroider the numbers—he shoots with range, he handles, runs, defends, passes, plays hard and plays smart. He helps old ladies to cross the street.

"Kuback tells me the kid is a pussy," Sidney says.

"I haven't seen it. I mean, Joseph takes it into a crowd, he bodies up and he's not afraid to draw the charge against the big guys. You know, of course, that Kuback has a history of putting his players down?"

"I've heard that. Kuback also says something about the kid having problems off the court."

We both know that "off-court problems" are a euphemism for drug abuse. "I haven't heard word one," I say. "I can ask Sam Franks at practice tomorrow. I'm sure he'll know."

We both laugh. Nervously, I ask, "Is it Joseph you're looking at?"

"Yep. Tripucka's out for the season and we like Joseph's athleticism. By the way, how's Earl Patton doing? I remember you were high on him."

"Earl had a mediocre game tonight but he has played well for me. He's usually at the top of his form when our backs are to the wall.

Trouble is, that kind of attitude means that we always have our backs to the wall. Actually, Earl's spent so much time in the NBA that he tends to get bored down here. Not that he doesn't play hard . . ."

"Rob, don't worry. We're not interested in your boy."

"I just don't want to stand in his way if—"

"I think we'll wind up taking Joseph."

"When? We play them Saturday. How about I go help him pack and then drive him to the airport?"

Sidney laughs. "I'll give you our Fed-Ex number," he says. "Do us both a favor. Send me tonight's tape. Kuback claims his copy is blank."

Back to reality—yes, yes. Kelly is indeed three dribbles away from an uncontested layup. Fuck and double fuck. But I am a professional, so I carefully rewind the tape and review my notes. Then I dial the CBL's 800 number to confirm my sanity:

"Thank you for calling the CBL Scorephone for Thursday, March 15, brought to you by Bartlett's Computer-Sports, Incorporated. This is the final update of the evening . . . In Savannah, the Oklahoma Rangers beat the homestanding Stars one-hundred-and-thirteen to one-hundred-and-eleven, taking a one-to-nothing lead in their playoff series . . ."

Also, the Capital City Cosmos over the Twin-Cities Fog, 137–133. In the other conference, Manchester beat Williamsport and Waco downed Santa Fe. Yes, yes. I am not alone in the universe.

Now that I'm up to date, whom else can I call? Let's see, it's only half-past-midnight in Wisconsin . . . "T-Bone! Wake up, It's Rob."

"Coaches never sleep," he says. "Especially unemployed ones."

"Whoops. They fired you?"

"Not yet. I think they're waiting for someone else to turn them down before they ask me back."

"Who?"

"I wish I knew . . . Tell me about your ballgame."

I do and he sighs. "What a business," he says. "The entire future, our family, our mortgage payments all depend on a bunch of knuckleheads. But it's where the action is, ain't that right?"

I agree, then I press him to decide if my last call was the correct one.

"From what you tell me," he says cautiously, "it sounds like it was. But there's one thing I've learned in twenty-seven years of coaching . . . if the call you make is the right one and it doesn't work, then it's the wrong call."

To lighten my mood, T-Bone relates a bizarre episode that happened at tonight's Twin-Cities game. It seems that in the locker room prior to the game the Fogs' diminutive coach, 5'7" Paul Lyons, had a "disagreement" with one of his benchwarmers, a 6'10" airhead named Bobby LeFester. After a vehement exchange of curses LeFester proceeded to lift Lyons off the floor, flip him ass over teakettle, then stuff him headfirst into the nearest toilet bowl, flushing and flushing, until a security cop interrupted the attempted coachicide. Later, when the Fogs' starting center was tossed for bumping a ref, LeFester wound up playing thirty-five minutes and scoring twenty-three points! After the game Lyons and LeFester "kissed and made up."

I stay away so late that I'm afraid to look at my watch. My eyes ache but I'm also afraid to stop reading . . . The rebels charge the stone wall and the Union troops hold fast. Whizzing minié balls, shrieking horses and, outside the hospital tent, fly-smothered piles of amputated limbs. "The poor brave boys," says the general . . . Finally I sit up, fling my book against the far wall and scream into the night, "Fucking Kelly. You fucking choke bastard."

Then, to calm myself, I phone the front desk and ring up Kuback's room. After three rings Kuback emerges from a deep dream of peace and croaks, "Hello?" I hang up and try to laugh myself to sleep.

It is 3:27 A.M.

10

FOR BREAKFAST I gulp down last night's chicken sandwiches. Then I climb into a plain gray sweatsuit, the old-fashioned kind, sans glitz, sans logo, and set out for Savannah State College on the other side of town.

Whatever the route, whatever the time of day, Savannah traffic is always congested. Reckless too, horns being preferred to brakes. Even in cooler weather everybody drives with their car windows closed and their air conditioners blowing hard. That's because the regional odor dissipates only when iced.

There's the usual jam-up at the turnoff into the Oglethorpe Mall, and there's some kind of confabulation in progress one mile northward at the national Boy Scout Headquarters, a boxy brown-shingled building that looks prefabricated. And no one excepting tourists ever walks the streets of Savannah.

Situated twenty-five minutes northwest of the Swedish Inn, Savannah State is a private liberal-arts school comprising 2,500 full-time students and (ever since the glory days of Josh Brusher faded ten years ago) a pitiful Division III basketball program. Nursing and computer programs are the in-house specialties. The spacious campus is landscaped with crumbling fieldstone buildings (somebody's prebellum estate sold for back taxes), with renovated stables and slave quarters transformed into classrooms. Near the main entrance numerous trailers have been marooned and gutted to serve as computer labs. The lawn sprinklers are forever in full spritz, yet the grass remains brown and brittle. Occasionally the view is enlivened by wandering students, the boys clipped in crew cuts, the coeds in helmet-shaped doos. Otherwise the immediate horizon shimmers with rising heatwaves and sinuous mirages.

Out near the north-forty the basketball court lies helpless under a huge inflated plastic bubble. The bubble's back entrance blows open once the door handle is properly turned, and to enter the structure I have to plunge headlong through a rushing of coolish air. Closing the door against the pressurized windstorm requires a two-handed grunt and pull. Inside, the air is heavy, relatively odorless and mechanically reduced to maybe ten degrees cooler than outside. The playing surface is rubberized and the baskets are attached to cuddly half-moon backboards. There are sufficient bare-boned bleacher seats to accommodate some 300 onlookers. The showers and locker rooms are in a separate building.

Most of the players are dressed and shooting, and the innocent sound of basketballs bouncing boomerangs throughout the plastic rotunda, returning sevenfold and ominous. The natural sunlight diffuses through the thick chemical skin and from time to time the shadow of a sea gull flits between the bubble and the sun.

All of the basketballs are either egg-shaped, patched or worn smooth. Of course. I've neglected to instruct Magoo to transport the ballbag from the Coliseum, and here he comes smiling, nevertheless. "You'll never guess what you forgot to tell me," he says and beams, "and what I forgot to do."

Too late now. What about the trainer? The VCR? The TV? The empty classroom?

The trainer's here but the machines are superfluous because, even though Magoo yanked every available string, there are no unoccupied classrooms. He's already taken the liberty of reserving a conference room in the bowels of the Coliseum for two-thirty. Then his wrinkles furrow and his eyes dim. "Morrison won't be at practice," Magoo says with gravity. "He called me early and I know you sleep late the morning after so I didn't want to wake you. He said he's got an appointment at the dentist for some minor oral surgery. He said he made the appointment several weeks back. He knows the timing is bad and he'll pay whatever fine you say. I think he's being truthful, but if you want, I'll call the dentist and check up on him."

"No, forget it." Magoo is so naturally cheerful, so eager to please that I ask him for his impressions of last night's game.

"You made the right call, no question about it. Kelly just made a poor decision. I guess that's one of the reasons why Kelly's still playing here in the CBL."

And what would Magoo's game plan be for tomorrow night?

"I always like to press and trap. Run the pants off them. Force them to make quicker decisions than they're used to making. Make it a full court game."

Yes? Perhaps? . . . but, no. Earl doesn't have the energy. Nate doesn't have the wheels. The Beast would be useless in an up-tempo game. We lack depth and character. And we'd wilt under Oklahoma's pressure before they'd give in to ours. "I'll think about it," I say. "Thanks for the input."

On the court the players are casually shooting in a more subdued mood than usual, especially Kelly. Are they serious, repentant, focused, ready to play? Or just partied-out?

Their chatter centers around an entry in the "Transactions" column of today's *Gazette*. I never read newspapers, so I ask Earl to explain.

"It's drugs," he says.

Each of the CBL's playoffbound teams was drug tested before their last regular season game. Waco and Twin-Cities completed their schedule three days before we did—and what happened is that two of Waco's starters have been suspended by the CBL for violating the league's drug policy. As such, they are banned from CBL competition for one calendar year and cannot be reinstated until they a) complete an accredited drug-rehabilitation program at their own expense and b) petition Commissioner Rose for a personal hearing. Barely one of ten drug offenders gets invited by the CBL to Come Back Later. The rest get gigs overseas or else find employment stocking the high-flying shelves in their hometown A & P.

In the NBA, druggies are permitted three dirty tests before being booted "for life" (they can apply for readmission after two years) and all rehab expenses are provided by the Players Association.

But even after three strikes, the NBA's druggies are still valuable commodities and are encouraged to play in the CBL. This, so the NBA can avoid any possible litigation charging them with monopolistic labor practices that deprive players of the chance to earn their livelihood. On the other hand, the CBL's own in camera druggies are treated like child molesters.

With the Beast getting his incisors sharpened and Lem nowhere in sight, I am nominated to lace them up and pretend I can still play. What a disaster this practice is. While I sit on the bench, fussing with my socks and jock, I cordially invite Sam over for a heart-to-heart.

"What the fuck, Points?"

"So it's Points now, hunh? That means you want something from me."

"Points. Sam. What's the difference? What does your mother call you?"

"Her bastard."

We glare at each other, suddenly defiant, aching for some kind of showdown. But Sam backs off. "I just want to win," he says, smiling and oh so charming. "It's frustrating for all of us. And for us to win I've got to get more shots."

"You had twenty-one last night."

"I mean better shots," he says. "And in my opinion, that'll only happen if you bench Kelly. Rob, I promise you, the boy ain't shit. He can't score with a pencil. He can't play dead. All he has is that crossover which don't fool nobody no more."

"And who plays the point? Carl?"

"Fuck no. I'd put Earl at the point. Listen, hear me out. Earl is the best passer on the team, you can't deny that. No contest. When his shit is in-hand he's also a dangerous shooter. And I'll admit it to you and to nobody else, he's even smarter than me out there. Okay, he's slow but he plays good team defense. And McDonald's not gonna hurt us anyway. Listen, we can still run the break. We can run on the pass instead of the carry."

He flexes his kissy-faced grin, warming to his outlandish thesis. "Know what else I'd do? I'd play Josh instead of Nate. That's right. Me and Earl could take up the scoring slack and we'd have a legit shot-blocker out there. Our defense would be so much better. Now, I know Cooper played okay last night, but watch out. The playoff pressure will shrink his jock sooner or later and then it'll be too late. What I'd do is cut somebody . . . Cooper, Carl . . . or suspend them, or make up a phony injury. See? I'm thinking like a coach already. And then I'd have a spot open for Lem—"

"I'm glad that you're so worried about everybody else," I say. "But I haven't heard anything about what you'd do about yourself. Okay, Mr. Coach. What do you do if your leading scorer is a selfish pig?"

He winces but his smile remains intact. "A team's leading scorer has to be selfish," he says calmly. "That's his job."

We're back to staring at each other. If I had a gun . . . But this time I'm the one who looks away.

"Okay, guys. Let's get it started."

Somebody outside throws a handful of stones to the top of the bubble. As they bounce toward the ground, the pebbles thunder like an avalanche.

We will do 10-and-2s to get our running done. This is an arithmetically increasing sequence of three-man weaves—two full-court weaves with a layup at each end, then four, six, eight, ten, with each set being repeated, should a layup be missed. The concluding "2s" are two consecutive full-court sprints requiring flawless weaves, perfect airborne passes and topped by a resounding dunk at each end. Normally it is a training camp conditioning drill, which players detest. But the running is clean, accomplished with no contact, no advocacy and little chance of injury.

Running in three groups of three, the players are quiet and efficient. "Push it!" Earl shouts when Josh lags. "Work!" says Nate. Occasionally I admonish somebody or other to "turn the corner." Otherwise, I'll clap my hands, saying, "You gotta love it or else you'll hate it!"

Midway through his squad's penultimate set of eight full-court dashes, Sam starts hobbling. I don't believe him, even as the latest trainer (whose name I was never offered and don't care to know) bares and pokes Sam's left ankle. The trainer aims a bland glance at me from across the court before shrugging and retaping Sam's thin thoroughbred ankle. "I'm okay," Sam announces at large.

"Whoopee do do," says Earl.

Sam rejoins us as we dummy our offense, run through a shoot-ing drill (in which every miss is blamed on the funky balls) and undertake a controlled half-court scrimmage: Kelly, Sam, Richie, Cooper and Josh versus Carl, Brent, Earl, Nate and me. Their ball to start and we need three consecutive defensive stops to play offense. Fouls are do-overs and any out-of-bounds is considered a stop.

Their first offensive play is a 40L to isolate Josh against me. In my dotage I can no longer run nor jump and my meager skills have long since eroded—but I can still foul hard enough to hurt some-one. And from similar emergencies in the past, the players are well aware that I will zealously wield the Elbow of Experience. Too bad I can only get close enough to Josh to smell his boozy breath. If I struck a match I could explode his face.

My presence makes the competition decidedly uneven and we are forced to double-team Josh, thereby opening jumpers for Sam and Cooper. The dented balls, however, make every easy jump shot an adventure. Even so, they have the ball for ten minutes before we can gain possession. Despite the competitive imbalance, my pres-ence also adds a certain interest to the game and even Sam has forgotten to limp.

On offense we mostly run isolations for Earl or Nate, reducing me to an almost immobile picking post. And when Kelly is careless in my vicinity, I attack him with a vicious, albeit moving, pick. Kelly merely shakes his head, laughs and patronizingly pats my rump. But, try as I might, I just can't nail Sam, who always knows where I am and blithely circles my stalking, awkward attempts to punish him.

I miss the only shot I attempt and, besides blasting Kelly, my most gratifying play is tossing a deft lob-pass that Earl has the pleasure of dunking.

While I impersonate Mr. Beast, Magoo must oversee the action—adjudicating fouls and lane violations, correcting imprecise cuts and passes. Too bad Magoo calls fouls only after the players com-plain and appeal to him and he can't correct what he doesn't comprehend. Before long, everybody's more concerned about bitching and moaning than in playing. Kelly and Carl have to be pried apart when they angrily dispute each other's penchant for dangerous defense. " 'Bow me one more time," Kelly shouts, "I'll break your ugly face."

Like all coaches, I love to see players fight during practice. It shows intensity, a will to win. Let there be blood.

At this point we might as well break for water. Next up, I demonstrate all the adjustments I've gleaned from the game tape. Sam is especially delighted when I order Kelly through the middle and replace him with Earl, etc. We conclude with a free-throw drill.

At the epicenter of our circle I explain the foul-up over the empty classroom, careful to avoid pinning the rap on Magoo. After Nate's prayer we will adjourn to the Coliseum to watch the game tape. Conference Room G at 2:30.

We don't get underway until three o'clock because:

—Sam and Carl have stopped along the way to buy sandwiches and sodas.

—Richie, Kelly, Nate and Josh arrive with two buckets of chicken wings from KFC.

—Cooper and Earl bring a pizza.

I decide not to fuss. I load the VCR and the game lives again. What follows is mostly a monologue:

"It started from the jump ball. Look at that fucking toss. That little dickhead is too short to live . . . Good defense, Earl."

"That's right," Earl agrees. "But only on the first play of the game and the next to last play."

"Nate? That's a real bad choice . . . See there, Sam? He's wide open. Give him the fucking ball . . . Carl? There's that two-foot takeoff we've been talking about. Let's see that again . . . See that? You lose all your power, all your hops, and you get no extension . . . Anybody see a foul there? What a bullshit call . . . Nate? Another questionable move . . . Sam. Look inside when you catch the ball. What if Coop's man has a sudden heart attack and dies on the spot? Give it up . . . Look how much your head is turned, Richie. Just a little more and you'd strangle yourself . . . Good pick, Nate . . . And he calls *that* a foul. Look at that again . . . Here's that curl move Joseph likes. One more time . . . See? The Beast's gotta step out and bump him . . . Good help there, Coop . . . Nice pass, Kelly . . ."

The players love to see themselves in action and they yelp unashamedly at each acrobatic move and dunk.

Eventually, we watch Kelly's freeze in total silence.

Still grimy under my sweats, my next stop is the Stars office. Mona has no messages for me. As I hand her the game tape and the Hornets Fed-Ex number, I reappraise her wondrous breasts and her pizza-face. Is Josh really shacking up with her? Could I have had Mona if I had made a move? And why am I still sleeping alone?

Chet waylays me as I pass his always opened door. "Oh, shit," he blurts while he clears off the only other chair, "Herm's been goggle-eyeing the cheerleaders all day. Actually patting some of them on their tight little asses and saying, 'Good job.' I saw him do it. I swear, he makes a total fool of himself. Everybody laughs at him behind his back but he still swears his shit smells like Old Spice. Hell, Herm honestly believes he could get elected mayor of Savannah by unanimous vote."

Clearing my throat, I recite the following:

> O wad some Pow'r the giftie gie us
> To see oursels as others see us!
> It wad frae monie a blunder free us
>   An' foolish notion:
> What airs in dress an' gait wad lea'e us,
>   And ev'n Devotion!

"*What* is that?" Chet is astounded.

"It's Jewish."

"I swear, y'all're nuttier than a nut cake. Say, did you read the *Gazette*? Patterson roasted you up, down and sideways."

"Fuck him."

"I don't know about that, Rob. I think y'all might want him on your side when the spit hits the fan . . . because I think Herm's gonna want to fire you if y'all don't win this series."

"Who told you? Where did you hear that? Did Herm say something to somebody?"

"It's just a feeling I have. The only clue is that Herm got a call early this morning, before he went to horn the cheerleaders."

"From who?"

"From your ol' buddy, T-Bone Donaldson. All's I know's that Herm closed the office door and they talked for a half-hour."

There's a sudden lump high in my stomach. "Donaldson hasn't had a winning record in three years," I say. "He can't coach his way out of a paper bag."

"Don't matter. He's from Mississippi and he's got those down-home, hog-drawling, shit-kicking ways. Whatever he's done, he for sure don't speak Jewish."

Here I am, sitting in Chet's office like a delinquent schoolboy waiting to face a reprimand from the principal. But where else can I go? What else can I do? How about solitary confinement? How about coaching a nice little Division III school near a beach, a lake, a mountain? With a lifetime contract worth $40,000 per, why be greedy? With a special assistant to recruit and another assistant in charge of zone defenses.

The door to Herm's office opens and he's so happy to see me! Come on in. What an exciting game that was. Hadn't had so much fun since he copped Eulila May's tittie at a pep rally the night before the Bishop Marley game. Come to think on it, he lost that game too. Well, come in, come in. Coach, mine coach. Let's have a long talk.

Herm sinks into his executive chair, then pushes a button on a desk console. "Hold my balls, Mona," he says with a wink, "I mean my calls, for, oh, five minutes."

Before he can get rolling I tell him about Kelly's problem with the ambitious district attorney in Brooklyn. "Really?" he says. Then he scribbles on a note pad and promises to consult the Stars legal counsel, another minority-owner.

He also mentions Patterson's story in the *Gazette*. "It's not good," he warns. "Public opinion is important in this town. Did y'all really tell him that? Did he quote you accurately?"

Of course. Why not? It's already too late, isn't it?

Herm is "disturbed" that Josh never got off the bench. Maybe we could've-would've-should've won "the darn game" had he played. Maybe not. I'm the coach and Herm is the loco-motive. Hee. Haw. Small joke. But seriously. What am I planning to do with Lem Jameson?

"He was at practice day before last," I say. "It was obvious that his hand is still tender. He's not ready."

"What if he gets medical clearance?"

"Impossible."

"What if?"

"His hand would still hurt and he still wouldn't be ready to play. And I'd report the quack to the AMA."

Herm wants me to "reconsider." His latest brainstorm is to activate Lem and cut Richie Michaels. After all, Richie had only six minutes last night, oh-for-three, two fouls and one turnover.

Making that move would give us five big men and no scoring off the bench behind Earl and Sam.

He defers to me, the "expert." He's merely a "layman," trying to "lay women." Hee. Haw. He's certainly given me enough "longitude" and he hopes that I "don't fail to succeed."

The phone rings and our "long talk" is over. Manfully, we shake hands. "Just *win*, baby!" is what he says.

I eat three Big Smacks and a bellyful of cold fries. "No calls," I instruct the front desk. "Don't even blink the red light on the phone."

Then I fall asleep, even before the twilight screaming stops in the dentist's office.

11

My introduction to consciousness this morning is a keen awareness that the Savannah Stars will indeed win tonight's ballgame. The Oklahoma Rangers will be overly confident, satisfied already with a split on the road. Kuback will hound them, of course, threatening fines and suspensions for lackluster play, and their practice yesterday (in the bubble from three to five) must have been fierce. But Kuback's players won't respond. Most likely they were out late last night, partying with Sam, Lem and Richie. If we can get out of the chute quickly, we can control the ballgame.

Is there a war brewing somewhere in the world? Then all I need to know is the draft status of my players. Is there pestilence? Just tell me who's been vaccinated. Is there famine? Are snakes and frogs raining from the heavens? Are the moldy dead scrabbling from their graves? I just want to know when Oz Joseph is leaving for Charlotte.

The Beast materializes at the shootaround, minus two wisdom teeth. His gums are still oozing and while he practices he must chomp down on a folded gauze pad. "I'll be ready," he says. "I'm just a little dumber than I was yesterday." I am justified in fining him ninety-three dollars, one-seventh of his weekly salary, but I ask for fifty dollars and he says, "Whatever."

Once again we review our offensive stuff and walk through our battle plan. The guys are unusually attentive. "Everybody is committed to winning tonight," Earl tells me.

Even so, Richie informs his teammates that he "threw the bitch out" last night. "She pulled out a whip and some handcuffs," he elaborates. "At first I thought she was some kind of freaky cop. Then she starts talking something about a bandage. I thought she was gonna kill me!"

The players divide themselves into four teams for a spot-shot game—medium-range jumpers, fifteen from the baseline, fifteen from the foul line extended, then fifteen from the foul line. Rebound your own shot, first team to total forty-five makes will win. The two winning teams down here, the losers go with Magoo. I front the Beast's fifty bucks and the bank pays win, place and show. Nate and Richie split thirty dollars. Sam, Coop and Brent neatly share fifteen dollars. Earl and Kelly argue over five dollars, while Josh, Carl and Beast each runs a suicide for finishing last.

Chet shows up just as the session is ending. "I'll bet y'all don't know what today is."

"Saturday. The Ides of March."

"No, sir. Ain't no Jewish holidays down here. This here is Saint Patrick's Day, ever hear of it? The highlight of the social season in Savannah. Let's go down to the waterfront and have lunch outdoors."

Surprise! Every year, some 60,000 pilgrims make their way to Savannah to honor the saint who chased the snakes out of Ireland. According to Chet, most of the celebrants are college students from Atlanta, some from South Carolina and some from Florida. Traveling hundreds of miles for the opportunity to puke on each other, to yell and get drunk in public.

And the crush of riotous communicants is impressive. We must walk single file through the mob—and with me running interference there is little chance for us to talk.

It's barely 1:30 and the celebrants are already deep in their cups. Some wear emerald green leprechaun hats fashioned of cardboard or silk. There's someone in a green satin tuxedo. T-shirts proclaim collegiate affiliations—Georgia's Bulldogs, Florida's Gators. One shirt reads: MY DICK IS PAINTED GREEN. INQUIRE WITHIN. Another says: BEER IS GOOD FOOD. An old man totters atop the sea wall, toasting one and all with a long plastic horn filled with green beer. The colleens hang on the arms of their dates or else travel in pasty-faced packs. In a small clearing, a string band called The Rovers plays a plaintive tune, "The Wild Colonial Boy," while a group of old-timers weep and slosh beer on passers-by. We stop at a food booth to lunch on beer and (vot den?) corned beef sandwiches.

One sip of beer and I am lost. Are Jews allowed to be here? My heart may be pinko but my money is green.

Another sip of beer and I want to shout, "Hey, I didn't do it! I can't even use a hammer without smashing my fingers. It wasn't me. The Romans did it!" Another beer and I'm not so sure.

Who are these children? How can they all be so happy and carefree? So uninhibited? And why do I feel so guilty? Lord knows, on a game day I should be sleeping in my cave to be well rested and alert for tonight's confrontation with the forces of evil.

Chet is oblivious. "Sure gonna be a wild crowd at the game tonight," he enthuses. "I can't hardly wait. Can you?"

Soon enough, the dressing room, the players, the preparation. The trainer of the evening is a young girl, apparently fragile and shy. Her name is Amy and her face is a pale map of Ireland. Has she been to the festivities at the waterfront? No, she's been at the rehab lab all day nervously practicing her taping techniques.

Beast's gums are still leaking and he will play with his mouth clenched on his gauze pads. Richie appears to be dazed, his eyes like whirling pinwheels. "I'm ready," he says. Kelly's face is clenched like a fist. "I'm ready," he says. Nate is calm and smiling. "Everything's under control."

Sam enters the trainer's room to get taped. "What have we here?" he says when he sees Amy. The Big Bad Wolf meets Little Red Riding Hood. Sam looks at me behind her line of vision and wags his tongue against his upper lip. "Have you ever been with a black man?" he asks her.

Then shy, innocent Amy says, "No. I hear they're very selfish."

"Not me," Sam boasts. "I'll lick your thang all night long."

"DO IT!"

As anticipated, the Rangers are less intense than in game one. They seem content to remain within striking distance, confident they can play hard and win down the stretch.

OKL–8   STARS–15

Kuback has ordered the 1-3-1 half-court press to start the game, hoping to get his charges involved right away. But their explosive trap is easily defused as Earl smartly swings the ball to Nate, who calmly scorches the net. "Drop it like it's hot!" Sam yells at Nate.

OKL–14   STARS–23

Nate gets all his shots within the parameters of the offense. He seals Hodges off the boards and even rebounds on his own . . . "We want Josh! We want Josh!"

OKL–19   STARS–27

The pressure is looser on Sam and he manages to dribble through a double-team. When Sam hits a corkscrew fadeaway, his momentum carries him toward the Rangers bench. Sam points wildly at Kuback. "Hey, old man. Get somebody out here who can fucking guard me!"

OKL–28   ·   STARS–37

Earl is steady as she goes. His jumper is falling and, to Magoo's delight, his passes are crisp.

OKL–37   STARS–44

Joseph is still scoring in bunches but Earl makes him struggle for every shot. Near the end of the half Joseph inbounds the ball directly in front of me. Leaning forward, I tug gently on his pants, saying, "Don't tell Kuback, but I know for sure that the Charlotte Hornets are bringing you up tomorrow. I swear it!" He looks back at me and the return pass bounces off his leg.

OKL—46   STARS—58

"We haven't won anything," I remind them during the intermission. "Keep playing hard."
"DO IT!"

Kuback abandons his pressure tactics and comes out in a straight man-to-man. Our offense momentarily falters until we get adjusted, but some sharpshooting by Nate and Earl keeps us in control.

OKL—58   STARS—67

Kelly is somewhat cautious on offense, content to facilitate the plays, but he defenses the shit out of McDonald.
Carl and Coop get into quick foul trouble. Richie remains in a funk but he buries a pair of three-pointers.

OKL—67   STARS—74

I insert Josh for Nate at 2:39 of the third quarter. First shot he takes, he misses badly. Then he comes from nowhere to block Joseph's layup but the ref calls a foul. On the first play of the fourth quarter Earl makes a nifty pass that finds Josh alone under the ring. The ball grazes Josh's fingertips before he can gather himself. Josh recoils in pain and the ball glances harmlessly out of bounds.

OKL—82   STARS—90

Brent's defense is savage. He flattens Joseph and even hits a long three-pointer.

OKL–90   STARS–99

The Rangers' big center, Larry Fort, asks Kuback to remove him from the game after the Beast casually spits a gob of blood on the rookie's jersey.

OKL–96   STARS–102

The Rangers make their run with two minutes to go, trailing by six. Since Sam has five fouls, my strategy is to try and keep him in the game only when we have the ball and let Brent play defense. "Sit next to me, Sam. You're going right back in."

OKL–99   STARS–103

After two such switches, Sam speaks up: "Let me play, man! You're fucking me up. You're telling everybody in the house that I can't play defense."

OKL–101   STARS–104

I ignore him, but with forty-seven seconds remaining, we have the ball coming out of a twenty-second timeout. "Sam," I call, but he is sitting on the bench with his left sneaker unlaced. "Sam, go in for Brent."

"I can't, man. My ankle hurts. I'm through for the night."

"Your ankle? That's bullshit. Get in the fucking game!"

"Well, fuck you! It ain't your ankle that hurts."

Earl notches two free throws and we pull it out by 108–105.

In the dressing room the celebration is joyful yet restrained. Sam has "dissed" me in front of the team and something has to be done. Magoo distributes the itineraries and everybody has an excuse to mumble quietly.

Sunday 3/18   Van leaves Swedish Inn at 5:00 A.M.
                   Flight 1340 AMERICAN
                     Departs 6:05 A.M.
                     Arrives Atlanta 6:54 A.M. (Eastern)

Flight 67 AMERICAN
Departs 8:07 A.M.
Arrives Oklahoma City 10:21 A.M. (Central)

Van leaves hotel 3:45 P.M.
Practice at Downtown YMCA 4:00

Monday 3/19   Van leaves hotel 10:45 A.M.
Shootaround at Myriad Arena 11:00

Van leaves hotel 5:15 P.M.
Game at Myriad—7:00

Tuesday 3/20   Van leaves hotel 10:45 A.M.
Shootaround at Myriad 11:00

Van leaves hotel 5:15 P.M.
Game at Myriad 7:00

Wednesday 3/21   Van leaves hotel 1:45 P.M.
Practice at Myriad 2:00

IF SERIES IS OVER   Van leaves hotel 5:15 A.M.
Flight 709 AMERICAN
Departs 6:20 A.M. (Central)
Arrives Atlanta 10:10 A.M. (Eastern)

Flight 461 AMERICAN
Departs 10:56 A.M.
Arrives Savannah 11:43 A.M. (Eastern)

Thursday 3/22   Van leaves hotel 10:45 A.M.
Shootaround at Myriad 11:00

Van leaves hotel 5:15 P.M.
Game at Myriad 7:00

Friday 3/23   Van leaves hotel 5:15 A.M.
Flight 819 AMERICAN
Departs 6:24 A.M. (Central)
Arrives Atlanta 10:15 (Eastern)

Flight 32 AMERICAN
Departs 11:00 A.M.
Arrives Savannah 12:07 P.M. (Eastern)

Oklahoma City Best Western
355 SW Babbit Street
(405)555–3459

As I make my rounds I discover that:

—Cooper is upset. He wants to go home, or to Europe, or to the NBA. He wants to play more and sin less.

—Kelly is jubilant. As far as he's concerned, game one never happened.

—Nate is in control of his destiny. He thinks he'll try to get a job coaching at a high school back home in Baltimore.

—Sam is conversing privately with Amy. He looks over his shoulder in my direction and laughs.

—Josh sits quietly and sucks his fingertips.

—Carl is speechless with frustration.

—Richie is shouting too loudly and too often: "We kicked 'em! We kicked 'em! We kicked 'em!"

—Brent is ecstatic, especially proud of his three-pointer. He tells me that he wants more playing time.

—Earl warns me that I will lose the team's respect if I don't stifle Sam. "In a hurry!" he says. My sentiments exactly.

Back in my cave I review the game tape, then study the CBL's Operations Manual and Bylaws:

Upon his suspension, a suspended player is ineligible to play for at least one (1) ballgame, after which he may be activated at the team's discretion.

With the exceptions noted below, a suspended player may not be replaced on a team's active roster for ten (10) days or five (5) games, whichever comes first. A suspended player may be immediately replaced on a team's active roster if the player leaves the country, abuses drugs or is signed by an NBA team.

If the suspended player feels he has been treated unfairly he may submit a written appeal to the Commissioner within 48 hours of his suspension. The Commissioner may then order a conference call to investigate the suspension within 24 hours of receipt of the player's appeal (said call to be at the expense of the team in question). If the Commissioner finds for the player, the team must immediately re-

COMMERCIAL BASKETBALL LEAGUE

Official Scorer's Report

Date: March 17, 1992 Game #: 02 Arena: Savannah Coliseum Attendance: 4967

Visitors: Ok. City Rangers Home: Savannah Stars Length of Game: 1:55

Visitors: Rangers

No	Visitors	Min.	FG M	FG A	FT M	FT A	3Pt M	3Pt A	Pts.	Reb O	Reb D	Reb TOT	AST	PF	TO	BS	ST
2	McDonald (G)	42	3	7	0	1	0	0	6	1	1	2	5	2	4	0	1
4	Collins	6	1	2	0	0	0	0	2	0	0	0	1	0	1	0	1
10	Hayes	8	0	2	2	2	0	0	2	0	1	1	0	3	0	0	0
11	Joseph (F)	48	13	29	8	8	2	5	36	2	8	10	3	3	4	1	2
12	Kramer	24	4	6	2	4	0	0	10	2	7	9	0	4	3	4	1
14	Ferguson (G)	40	10	16	5	7	0	3	25	1	5	6	4	4	3	0	0
15	Palmer	DNP – Coach's Decision															
20	Fort (C)	30	3	8	0	3	0	0	6	1	3	4	1	4	2	1	0
21	Hodges (F)	42	9	18	0	2	0	0	18	2	10	12	3	3	3	2	2
23	Lederman	DNP – Coach's Decision															
	TOTALS	240	43	90	17	27	2	8	105	9	35	44	17	23	20	8	7
	Pct.		47.8		62.9		25.0			Team 5					3			

Home: Stars

No	Home	Min.	FG M	FG A	FT M	FT A	3Pt M	3Pt A	Pts.	Reb O	Reb D	Reb TOT	AST	PF	TO	BS	ST
6	Royal (G)	35	2	5	3	5	0	0	7	1	2	3	8	2	2	0	3
7	Franks (G)	39	11	18	5	6	1	2	28	0	2	2	3	5	3	0	1
8	Butler	13	1	1	0	0	0	0	2	0	1	1	2	4	0	0	2
10	Cooper	16	2	6	1	1	0	0	5	1	4	5	0	4	2	1	1
11	Brusher	6	0	2	0	0	0	0	0	0	2	2	0	1	1	0	0
12	Hennison (F)	32	8	15	1	1	0	0	17	3	6	9	3	1	1	1	0
13	Morrison (C)	37	4	11	0	4	0	0	8	2	8	10	1	1	3	2	1
24	Michaels	18	2	5	0	0	2	2	6	0	1	1	0	0	1	0	0
32	Patton (F)	44	12	20	6	8	1	4	31	4	8	12	7	4	2	1	4
40	Springs	9	2	4	0	0	0	0	4	2	1	3	1	0	0	1	2
	TOTALS	240	44	87	16	25	4	8	108	13	35	48	25	22	15	6	14
	Pct.		50.6		64.0		50.0			Team 7					2			

Score By Quarters	1	2	3	4	OT	OT	OT	Final
V Ok.City	31	25	36	23				105
H Sav	27	31	32	18				108

Officials: Steve Warshaw, Greg Dodge

Technical:

Miscellaneous Statistics

Ties 2 Lead Changes 2
Points off rebounds (H) 12 (V) 4
Points off steals (H) 10 (V) 8
Offensive fouls (H) 2 (V) 3

Remarks: Stars even series 1-1

store the player to the active roster, paying him in full for the time he was under suspension. Should the Commissioner find for the team, the player's suspension shall proceed according to the CBL guidelines.

Then I call the CBL's after-hours transaction line and record my message: "This is Bo Lassner of the Savannah Stars. It's Saturday night, eleven-fifty P.M. The Stars suspend Sam Franks for conduct detrimental to the team."

I dream of a tombstone looming through a foggy, rain-swept cemetery. And I dream of the inscription on that tombstone:

> HERE LIES ROBT. E. LASSNER
> 3/25/52—St. Paddy's Day
> "We can win without him."

12

THE MOTEL LOBBY features the same blocky, woodlike furniture as the rooms. All the chairs and sofas are angled to face a red-brick fireplace, wherein a black ceramic log is set aglow by gas-jetted flames whenever the outside temperature dips below fifty-five degrees. Like now.

Most of the players will be here soon, preferring to ride the team van to the airport and avoid the daily eight dollar parking fee. Also, the security at the airport parking lot is notoriously negligent— during our first road trip last October, Earl's Mercedes-Benz (an eight-year-old model, purchased with his signing bonus as Utah's #1 draft pick) had a window smashed and the cassette-deck gouged out of the dashboard.

I am never late for meetings, for practices, for van departures. It's my job to be early, so after snatching perhaps two hours of exhausting sleep I enter the lobby at 4:50 A.M., only to find Brent Springs already waiting there. Whereas I am dressed in sneax, jeans and another generic sweatshirt, Brent wears gray slacks, a blue blazer with gold buttons and a hi-fashion red floral tie. He stands when I come through the front door. "Coach," he says, "I'm sorry for what I said last night."

In the off-season Brent lives with his widowed mother in a rural township in West Virginia called Parsons Crossing. To contact him one must telephone his cousin and leave a number for Brent to call back collect. Whatever the weather, the cousin will walk half a mile

105

down a dirt road and return with Brent or news of his where-abouts.

At a husky 6′4″, Brent played center for his high-school team, undefeated in his senior year, the West Virginia Class-C champions. Brent was a unanimous all-state selection and he accepted a scholarship from the most distant college that recruited him, UCLA. Unfortunately, he could not make the transition to the backcourt and became a benchwarmer with the Bruins.

Seventeen months after his collegiate career ended (he never graduated), Brent was one of 100 hopefuls who paid seventy-five dollars each to attend the Savannah Stars' second annual free-agent camp. Most of the applicants were locals, some were flown in by their agents from places like Houston, Baton Rouge and Miami. Brent was the only free agent who came in by bus. He paid his tuition in wrinkled bills.

I hate free-agent camps—ripping off minitalented kids who think they're as good as Michael Jordan and just as deserving of his multimillion-dollar contract. Sure, some of the free agents are simply high-school coaches and hoop-o-maniacs out to scratch a chronic itch. But most are lost souls looking for someone new to blame for their cramped lives. FA camps are mostly a cruel deception—but Herm claims that the Stars cleared $5,000 on the last one.

Brent spent his post-UCLA season delivering kegs for a local beer distributor and working on his game in a bar league. His jumper remains suspect and his right-to-left handle is somewhat exposed—but Brent's defense and desire convinced me.

Now he's apologizing for something he said last night. With all the tension in the postgame dressing room, I can't rightly recall what he said that needs amending, so I ask him to refresh my memory.

"I told you I wanted more playing time," he says, so ashamed that he jams his hands into his pants pockets. "That was out of line. I'm just glad to be here. Glad just to sit on the bench. You know, Coach, if you decide to play me for one single minute, I'm gonna give you all I got. It's just that I been listening to the wrong people . . ."

The front door opens and several other players walk in from the darkened morning—Earl, Beast, Kelly, all lurching like zombies. Here come Nate, Coop and Richie. And whatever the occasion,

Josh always comes alone. Nobody knows where he lives and nobody knows his unlisted phone number. He drives an old Buick
and he wears old Nike sweats, both left over from his one glorious
season in The League. Carl is close behind, slowly blinking, hung
over. Sam's wife usually drives him to the airport. And at 4:58, just
two minutes shy of a fine, young and foolish Steve Collins makes
his usual dramatic entrance.

Steve is the play-by-play man for WRDK, known in basketball
parlance as the "RG," the radio guy. He is twenty-three, a recent
graduate of the drama department of some artsy college in Atlanta.
His ambition is to be rich and famous—even now he wears a
maroon sharkskin suit with his jacket sleeves rolled up to his
forearms. A white T-shirt and brown loafers (but no socks) complete his wardrobe.

"Here's a new one," Steve says brightly to no one in particular.
"Kennison shoots! It's up! It's in! I kinda like it. I'm gonna use it
tomorrow night . . . It's up! It's in!"

Steve gets fifty dollars per game plus the standard twenty-five
dollars food stipend on the road. Besides relaying the ballgames to
Savannah's shut-ins, his duties also require him to handle the
airplane tickets, the luggage and to drive the van.

In total darkness, in total silence, Steve chauffeurs us to the
airport. The Rangers are flying through Dallas and won't depart
until 7:15 A.M. How did Kuback manage that?

As part of his rookie dues Cooper must drive the van to the parking
lot while the rest of us dump our bags near the American Airlines
counter and Steve gets on line. We fly about 30,000 miles per
season, yet I am the only member of our traveling party who gets
credit for frequent-flyer mileage. That's because, instead of the
players' names, the CBL's official travel agency in Chicago arranges
for their tickets to be issued under the following names: Cy Rose,
John Smiley, Herm Pudleigh, several of the Stars majority stockholders, plus other numeraries in the league office.

Everybody flops nearby, ready to collect their per diem envelopes when Steve is through checking us in. We will be paid only
through Wednesday, and Chet will wire us more money should the
series last the full five games. Since we are scheduled to arrive just

after noon on Wednesday (or Thursday), Herm has opted to pay us only a half-day's per diem for our last travel day. Subsequently, each of our envelopes contains two chintzy quarters.

I sit where I can command a view of the main entrance, waiting for Sam. Earl plunks down beside me. "Why the fuck do we always leave so early? It's not like we have a game tonight."

"The first flight out is always the cheapest for group rates." I start to tell him about the suspension, but here comes Sam . . . Slick in a black leather jacket with matching pants, alligator shoes, leather-framed sunglasses and even a black leather porkpie hat. He is barechested under his jacket, showing only a heavy-duty cross of gold.

There's no suggestion of an injury as he strides over to the counter and drops his bag. He only begins to limp when he turns and approaches us. "Wassup?" Richie says from somewhere behind me. For Sam to respond he must look through me. "I got my rocks off"—Sam smiles—"then I sent the ho home. Whole thing took me about a twenty-second timeout."

I push myself to my feet and stare into Sam's reflective shades. All I can see is myself, rumpled, balding, disgusted. "Sam," I say, "let's go have a talk."

He follows me to a quiet area near the USAir counter and I turn to him. "Sam, I've put you on the suspended list."

"Say what?"

"You're suspended. Your season's over."

"What you talking about? Suspended for what?"

"For refusing to go into the game last night."

He smiles, pretty certain it's just a joke, something he can sweet-talk his way around. "My ankle was hurt. I told you that last night. Rob, don't be fucking around."

"This is for real, Sam. And I don't want to hear about your ankle. You pulled up lame at practice because you didn't want to run. You used your ankle as an excuse last night because you didn't like the offense-defense substitutions. We both know there's nothing wrong with your fucking ankle. Grow up, Sam."

"You can't do this," he says, ripping off his shades. "Herm swings on my dick and he won't let you get away with this."

"It's already done, Sam. It has nothing to do with Herm. This is between you and me."

His eyes register my resolve and the need for new tactics. "Rob," he says, softer than before, "don't be doing this to me."

"You did it to yourself, Sam."

"Rob. Rob. Let me explain . . . All right, so maybe my ankle doesn't hurt all that much. Hey, I always play hard for you, don't I? I give you numbers night after night. Rob, I haven't missed a game all year."

I dismiss his argument with a wave of my hand.

"Rob. Please. I have nothing. I have no life without this bullshit league. Please. Don't do it."

Yes, yes. He's genuinely hurt. Isn't that enough? Look, his eyes are wet. Shouldn't I just phone the league office and say that last night's call was a mistake? "Maybe," I say, "it's time for you to find a real life in the real world. I'm sorry—"

Then he actually drops to his knees and clasps his hands together. "Please, I beg you, don't do it, Rob. I beg you in Jesus' name."

"Get up, Sam. Don't make it worse. Just go home. I'll call you tonight and we'll talk about it."

He leaps to his feet like a gymnast. Now his eyes overflow with menace and his next question is a threat. "Does Herm know about this?"

"Not yet."

With that, he replaces his sunglasses, turns and walks away, headed, no doubt, to the nearest telephone. By the time I pass through the security checkpoint and reach the departure gate, I hear my name being paged over the public-address system. There is "an important message" for me and I am urged to check in at the nearest yellow courtesy phone.

Not a chance. Let Herm squirm until we reach Oklahoma City.

Earl moves in beside me as we line up to board the plane. "You did the right thing, Rob. It's a gutsy move, but it was either him or the rest of us. I'm proud of you."

I always like to sit toward the tail end of the plane because airplanes very rarely back into mountains. Also because I want to see all my players, who's asleep, who's playing cards, who's hassling who. It's part of my job. As I pass Brent's seat he touches my arm. "I know what you're doing, Coach," he says. "Thank you. I

won't let you down. And I want you to know that I'm with you
through thick and through thin."

They've all got earphones plugged into their heads. Rap, jazz, rock,
hip-hop, Al Jolson, who knows what they listen to. Anything to
keep from thinking. Cooper, Brent and Nate will sometimes read
their Bibles. Everybody else reads newspapers (sports sections
only) or selected magazines (Sports Ill., Jet or Ebony). Most
hoopers' idea of highbrow is The Sporting News. Steve Collins
reads biographies of movie stars.

We're barely off the ground and already they're all asleep—
nestled against the miniature airline pillows and under the see-
through blankets, sprawled across all three seats or curled in foetal
positions as the space permits. "Fellas," I always advise them, "get
a good night's sleep in your own bed before we travel. You can't get
any rest sleeping on a plane. All you can do is pass the time."

Me? The only way I can sleep on a flight is to take off my
sneakers, stretch my legs as far as possible, fold my hands on my
lap (taking care not to arouse Mandrake), then drop my chin to my
chest. The hangman's position.

In the airport in Atlanta with nearly an hour to kill. Once again I
am paged but I don't respond.

The players are slowly coming to life—except for Carl, who
stretches out on the floor under a vacant row of seats and sleeps
with his mouth wide open. "How about this one?" Steve Collins
says to Earl. "Patton shoots his patented jump shot! Count it! . . .
Get it? Patton? Patented?" For the others, food has become a priority. Yogurt, sausage on a bun, gyros.

Kelly returns from his perambulations with a banana and a mis-
chievous grin. As he approaches Carl, the players gather around
anticipating some sort of sideshow. First, Kelly peels the banana,
then he kneels down beside his still slumbering teammate and
unzips his own fly. Kelly gently eases the bald banana into Carl's
open mouth, until Carl stirs, vaguely aware that his mouth is occu-
pied by something that shouldn't be there. Coughing, "Whazzit,"
Carl asks. Just as Carl approaches full alertness, Kelly withdraws

and hides the banana. Then Kelly piddles with his fly and says to Carl, "Man, that was great! The best head I've had in a long time!"

Carl jumps to his feet, clamping his hand to his mouth, staring at the bulge in Kelly's pants. "What! What'd you do, mothafucker?"

Explanations are made amid much laughter. Even the civilians assembled to board the same plane are entertained.

And somehow, I get the feeling that the players are avoiding me. I've shown my power with Points and they are reminded that I can do the same to them.

The airport, too early on a Sunday morning . . . Children crying and running loose. A businessman in a hurry, his briefcase flapping against his thigh. A visiting grandmother about to depart for her home back in San Diego, weeping softly as her grandchild is taken from her arms. Flights departing, arriving, changing gates, delayed, canceled. "Will Robert Lassner please pick up a yellow courtesy phone?" No. Dogs in cages. A Swedish gymnastic team on tour. Two muscular he-men with bleached-blond tresses must be professional wrestlers. Stewardesses walking in small groups, their luggage-on-wheels following on plastic leashes. Honeymooners. Old ladies in wheelchairs.

As our flight is called, Josh stands up and makes a sudden announcement in my general direction: "I'm not getting on this plane. No, sir. I'm gonna take a different flight. Even if I have to pay for it myself. See y'all later and God bless your immortal souls." Whereupon he walks quickly toward the main terminal.

The rest of us are left to shuffle on board, nervously laughing at Josh's antics. "What's his problem?" I ask Earl.

"There's only one explanation," Earl says. "Josh is just a downright, straightup crazy motherfucker."

After that, none of us dares to sleep on the flight to Oklahoma City, but we land safely and on time at the Will Rogers International Airport—the only airport in America named after a man who died in a plane crash.

The motel sits at the crossroads of Route 66 and Interstate 40, and there's something afoot as we check in. Weird signs are posted on pillars and walls scattered throughout the lobby: INTER-GALACTIC GATHERING—9:00 TONIGHT—ROOM 237. RODDENBERRY LIVES! SPECIAL SEANCE! MIDNIGHT! ROOM 666! And there are people walking around in costumes—ridged foreheads and pointy ears are the rage. Dozens of robust young women in gossamer gowns. Dogs on leashes. Here and there, middle-aged men clad in red-and-black futuristic uniforms.

What could be better—it's a Trekkie convention.

Nate gets the single room as reward for his seniority in the CBL. As per instructions, my room is always on a different floor than the players. And there are five messages waiting for me at the front desk: ASAP call Herm, Chet, the CBL office, Joe Patterson at the *Gazette* and Tim Packman at Channel 17. But before I can face the music, I find my room, lift the phone from its cradle and fall asleep as quickly as a stone sinking in a well.

Later, I call the CBL office and am directed to John Smiley, Rose's assistant, who wants to know the whys and wherefores of Sam's suspension. After I relate what happened he says, "No problem," then repeats the pertinent bylaws. Roster moves called into the after-hours transaction line by "accredited persons" are "irrevocable." Smiley also tells me that Herm called earlier trying to rescind the suspension but he, Smiley, refused. "What does he think this is?" Smiley says with an appropriate edge of indignation. "Some kind of bush league?"

"Chester. What's the latest?" I say.

"Rob! You crazy bastard! Why haven't you called? All hell's busting loose here. Why'd you do it?"

After he hears my reasons Chet says, "Well, Herm ain't gonna like it . . . Say, did you hear the rest of the news? Oz Joseph got called up . . ."

"By Charlotte."

"Oh, yeah, Mister Wiseguy? Have you heard this one? Richie Michaels failed his drug test."

"Don't fuck with me, Chet."

"Honest to God. He's already on his way back to Savannah. And tomorrow we're flying him back home to Philadelphia. That means you've got eight players for tomorrow's game—Hold on, that's my other line ... It's Herm, madder than shit. You better call him pronto."

Good-bye Richie. You fat-assed hot-shooting pussy-loving son of a bitch. Poof! Presto-change-o! And we'll never see each other again.

"Herm, it's Rob."

"Well, lookee here," he says, his salutation sounding carefully rehearsed. "If it isn't the wandering ... coach? I guess you'd better fill me in on the details. Don't forget to tell me exactly how y'all have the gall to make that kind of decision on your own. It's totally irresponsible."

I tell him what Sam did. By the time I came to a decision on Friday night it was too late to call Herm. I didn't want to wake up his wife. Then it was too early. Say what? Yes, I heard about Richie. Bad timing, eh wot?

Still, Herm remains incredibly rational. It seems that the Stars face another $200,000 deficit this season. This is a business, he points out, not a game. He doesn't care if the players respect me, so long as they win. Any other consideration is "supercilious." Why, look at the old St. Louis Cardinals of the late 30s, the "Gas House Gang." Look at the Oakland A's of the 70s. What are the lessons that these teams prove?

That ballplayers and coaches can hate each other off the field and still win. For my information, this is not "Father Shennanigan's Home for Boys." We are not here to make a solid citizen out of Samuel P. Franks. Bo Lassner is here to win. Herm Pudleigh is here to make money for the stockholders. Hopefully we can both succeed. Do I understand?

Anyway, our job now is damage control. Herm will handle the media. If anyone should ask about Richie, I'm to say that I am not his babysitter, etc. As for Sam, the good news is that he accepts "the lion's share of the blame." Sam swears he'll apologize to me, to the team. Whatever it takes, he'll do with "no hard feelings." As it stands now, Sam will only miss one game. Herm has also taken the liberty of activating Lem Jameson "effective immediately." Both Sam and Lem will be flying into Oklahoma City tonight at 10:47, flight such-and-such. Have Steve pick them up. "And Rob? I'm going through a lot of trouble to protect you because, after all, I'm a team player. I'm also the guy who hired you so my ass is on the line too. But hear this. If we win this series, we're both heroes. If you lose, you're an ex-coach."

13

THE COURT AT the Downtown YMCA turns out to be a slippery-floored, bent-rimmed relic of the days when basketballs had raised laces. One long side of the court is bounded by a set of rusting steel bleachers that rattle and tremble when mounted. The remaining three walls are hung with heavy leather padding and the available balls seem to be fashioned of the same dense material.

"These balls weigh ten pounds," Nate complains. And I wonder where the Rangers are practicing today.

As the players tighten their laces and adjust their straps, they can't stop speculating about the gathering of Star Trek aficionados. "You know they're fucking those dogs," Kelly says. "No question. And did you see that guy dressed up like Mister Spark? And that seance at midnight? That's ghosts and shit. Man, I know I'm staying in tonight."

"It's in room six-sixty-six," Cooper notes. "That's the devil's number."

"Yo, rookie," I say. "All of those people are nothing more than a bunch of misfits looking for a fantasy that won't bite back. Believe me, Coop. They're harmless."

But Nate agrees with the majority opinion. "Un, uh," he grunts. "All them Star Track mothafuckers roaming the hallways. Gonna be a whole lot of niggers reading their Bibles tonight."

Before we get started, it's time for a brief meeting. I tell them that
Sam is suspended for one game only, that he reportedly is flying in
tonight with a brand-new attitude. I tell them that Herm is squeezing my nuts, but that Sam's arrival doesn't guarantee he'll get off
the bench. "In my mind," I say, "we're a far better team without
Sam than they are without Joseph." I tell them that Herm has
activated Lem, that the big man is still hurting, that there's no
available playing time for him anyhow. Then I say *kaddish* for
Richie, warning them to avoid the same pitfalls. In conclusion, I
exhort them to stay focused, get plenty of rest, eat green leafy
vegetables, baha, baha.

Today's practice is loosey-goosey. After stretching, we go full-
court four-on-four with an imaginary fifteen-second shot clock,
five baskets wins, best four-games-out-of-seven. The shoot-and-
scoot scrimmage minimizes contact yet maintains their competitive edge.

For the series so far, we're shooting sixty-eight percent from the
foul line. True, if Beast's 2-10 is subtracted, everybody else is
seventy-six percent efficient (about the norm for a pro team). However, free-throw shooting is always a concern in the playoffs. I call
Beast and Kelly down to one end while the others practice FT's on
their own. Kelly just needs to slow down his stroke and sight the
basket before he begins his shooting motion. Beast needs me to
remind him of the proper checkpoints—foot position, eye contact
with the rim, hand position on the ball, keeping his elbow tucked,
coming down straight, going up straight, being aware of his release
point and his follow through. "Limp wristed," I say, "like a faggot."
Beast shoots fifty-plus free throws and when he finally makes five
in succession, I tell him to quit.

On our way to the van I pull on Earl's sleeve. "Let me buy you
dinner tonight."

There's a BBQ joint, Fat Albert's, across the road and we ren-
dezvous there round about 7:00. "That was a good practice today,"
Earl says. "Just the right light touch."

The decor seems to be the great outdoors—lacquered picnic
tables, plastic trees and sprightly green carpeting. The "Bill of

Fair" is posted on the wall behind the counter—ribs, chicken, sausage, brisket of beef (flanken!), fried okra, cole slaw, plus a local specialty, BBQ bologna, as well as Fat Albert's deluxe baked beans, a sweet, gummy mess of undifferentiated fart pods. We both order double-combo platters and too much beer.

"Did you ever see such a fucked-up team as this?" I ask, and Earl shakes his head. "Poor Richie," I add. "I guess I'll miss him. He's just a happy-go-lucky kid who could score like a man with a fistful of pardons in a womens prison."

"I'm glad he's gone," Earl says, gnawing on a bone. "He was high all the time. He was selling weed to Sam and Carl. To Lem, too, when he was around."

"But not to Josh?"

"As far as I know, Josh just drinks. Rob, I really think you should be playing Josh more."

"The guy's had it. His wheels are falling off. Besides, I think he's a potential ax-murderer. One dark and stormy night he's gonna knock on everybody's door and hack us all to pieces."

"Play him six minutes at a time," Earl persists. "Press and trap whenever he's in there. Scramble up the game and let the crazy motherfucker block shots. It gives us a different look."

"Yeah. Sure."

From here on, as the empty beer bottles multiply, we find ourselves reviewing the Stars roster and comparing our personal scouting reports of all the players.

What about Benny the Beast? I think he's strong enough to power us to a championship. Earl claims that every player in the CBL is afraid of the Beast, "and so are the refs." The only problem is his free-throw shooting. Will he get called up during our playoffs? Possibly.

Kelly, the point-shaver? . . . I love his talent and oh, that crossover dribble. All Kelly needs is playing time and confidence and he'll become an acceptable shooter. Can we win with Kelly holding the reins? Earl thinks not. "Kelly's got no heart," Earl says. "He's too silly, too frivolous, too damn young. Kelly will always find a way to lose."

Carl the inebriated? . . . In my opinion he can't score and plays scared. That makes him a limited-time performer. Earl believes that with our personnel our point guard is not required to score. Let Carl run himself into scoring opportunities (still another reason to press and trap). Earl admires Carl's heart, his intensity, and would rather play with Carl than with Kelly. "Trouble is," Earl says, "Carl really thinks he should be playing in the NBA right now, even as we speak. He swears he's light-years better than Kelly and he's pissed at you for making him Kelly's caddy." In any event, the sauce makes Carl's production problematical.

Brent the Schwarzenegro? . . . We both like him better than Sam. But Carl, Kelly and Brent are all unreliable shooters—playing any two of them together will prohibit us from executing an effective setup half-court offense. (Shit on a hard roll. One more reason to trap, press and let the players play. Why haven't I realized this on my own? Am I too tight-assed to relinquish whatever control I *think* I have?) Also, since Carl and Brent have essentially the same game at different positions, we must pair Brent with Kelly and supplement them with at least two scorers—Nate and Earl. "Plug Josh into that unit," Earl says. "Press and trap. There you go. You can't escape it."

What about the late great Nate? . . . My view is that he's limited, a scorer who's very effective handling the ball in the flex offense. But Nate is also a moody CBL lifer who needs constant prodding to maintain his interest. Earl agrees, adding, "Nate goes with the flow. He's more of a follower than a leader." Earl further claims that Nate is out carousing every night and that come playoff time, "Nate is all fucked out."

Coop the true believer? . . . An interesting player. I think he has the fire and the raw skills to someday be an NBAer. Earl agrees but can't get past "the religious trip." Nor does Earl like playing with the rookie: "The refs don't like Cooper flopping and falling all over the court because he puts too much pressure on them. None of us get the marginal call when Cooper's in the game."

Sam the Shaman? A wastrel. And I'm aggravated with the way I let Herm bulldoze me into accepting the wolf back into the fold. Earl shrugs. "A job's a job." Lately I've also been toying with the idea of simplifying the offense and running more iso's for Sam. Clear a side and let him do his thing. Earl likes the concept. He's also enthusiastic about the adjustments I made to handle the

Rangers' "hard double on Sam." Both of us hope we can win tomorrow without him.

Lem the chicken-hearted? Another wasted talent. Behind his hooded eyes, Lem's intelligence slumbers like a poisonous snake in hibernation. But there's chicken shit in his veins. If I ever need him, if he ever gets in game-shape, my plan is to go to Lem early. If he wants the ball in the last six minutes of a game he'll have to fetch it off the boards. "I can deal with Lem," Earl promises. "The trick is to keep him away from Sam and to keep him away from drugs. Which is a redundancy. Yes, I'm a college graduate."

And finally, Earl the whirl? "I could have played with Utah forever. The Mormons loved my white ass. Remember Toady McGraw? The worst coach in the history of the NBA? Remember when he fined Damone Bradley thirty dimes for griping to the press about his playing time? Thirty pieces of silver. A shitty thing to do to anyone. Anyway, I sided with Bradley, and McGraw got rid of us both."

The rap against Earl is that he can't shoot well enough to play guard and he's too frail to play #3. "That shit doesn't really matter," he says. "On an NBA team most of the eleventh and twelfth guys down the bench are political appointees anyway. I'm sick of all that crap. Next year I'm gonna play in Europe."

Earl's agent promises six-figures in Italy, plus a complimentary villa, car and live-in teenage maid. In Europe the basketball teams are owned and operated by industrial monoliths—Shell Oil, Lotto Athletic Shoes, Pepsi-Cola, Einchem Inc. The bucks are so bountiful that thirty-nine-year-olds like, say, Bob McAdoo can still command $600,000 per. "And the European game sucks," says Earl. "It's one team's two Americans against the other team's two Americans. Except for an occasional exhibition game, you only play once a week. A breeze. They allow zone defenses, which also reduces the physical wear and tear, and the guards can avoid contact by taking an extra step to the basket. Playing over there is like stealing money. But the coaches? A joke. When I played in France two years ago I had this one coach who made us run up and down the court bouncing balloons off our fingertips. We did this for fifteen minutes every day. He said it would help our shooting touch! So I don't care what anybody says, the competition in the CBL is a helluva lot better than anywhere in Europe. Guys who play over the waters for too long get too soft to ever play in the NBA. On the upside, you can extend your career overseas for an extra five years. So screw the NBA. And after the playoffs I'm out of this rinky-dink league too."

We order more beer and share another rack of ribs. "What about you?" Earl asks. "Where are you when this is over?"

The same place as the CBL . . . nowhere.

That's because the CBL is governed by jackasses who are willing to absorb annual losses of $100,000 to $600,000 in hopes that the NBA will some sweet day bail them out. Their plan is for the CBL to become the official farm system of the NBA, with one-to-one affiliations similar to major- and minor-league baseball. In this scenario each NBA team will subsidize a CBL franchise with dollars, front-office personnel and even leftover players. It's a pipe dream, the NBA Players Association will never let any NBA team control more than fourteen players (twelve active and two injured). The NBA Players Association is a powerful organization constantly lobbying for more legislated free agency. In recent years the NBA's collegiate draft has dwindled from eight rounds down to two, and if the Players Association has its way (and it will), the draft will be abolished in our lifetime. Their idea is to have as many players as possible able to sell their services to the highest bidder.

And what does the NBA connection actually do for the CBL? Sure, it pays the freight for the refs, not much of an advantage. Why not have CBL refs who are responsible only to the CBL? Okay, the NBA–CBL contract also pays each CBL franchise approximately $40,000 per year, which just about covers league dues. Moreover, the CBL teams are permitted to use the NBA logo (a white-out silhouette of Jerry West dribbling with his *left* hand!) in certain promotions. But the primary function of the interleague agreement simply allows the NBA to override the CBL's player contracts. A CBL franchise gets $1,000 whenever one of its players (usually the team's best) gets a ten-day contract, another $500 if the ten-day is extended to twenty, and an additional $500 if the player is signed for the duration of the season. Terrific for the player (who earns about $7,500 for each ten-day pact). Lousy for the CBL coaches, who must trade, connive and/or wheedle to replace their stars with players not as good.

If I did the talking the CBL would tell the NBA to fuck off. Let Barret Smith train his referees in schoolyards for the YMCA leagues. Let NBA teams pay CBL teams $25,000 per player—or else let the NBA try to steal overpriced players from the marsh-mallow European leagues.

But the CBL's bigwigs love the NBA connection. It lets them maintain delusions of being big-timers instead of piss ants. They're too cowardly to challenge the NBA and secure financial advantages for themselves.

So the CBL plays musical franchises, ten relocations in the last three years. And teams continue to go bust—the CBL has either folded or bailed out (to the tune of $60,000 assessed to each surviving franchise) three teams in the last four years. And a once-upon-a-time chairman of the CBL's Expansion Committee was amenable to accepting inducements in lieu of bona fide letters of credit. Worse, the CBL must ante up nearly $750,000 every year just to keep pace with its ongoing litigations.

And as for me? I hate most college ball and, more to the point, I can count no collegiate coach or athletic director among my acquaintances. Similarly, to become an assistant coach in the NBA you must be well-connected to an NBA coach or general manager. I have none of the above. So, like the CBL that spawned me, I have rocks in my pockets while I tread water in Shit Creek.

"You read too many books," Earl advises as we exit the BBQ. "What you need to do is get laid."

Which is precisely why I find myself approaching Room 237 shortly before ten o'clock. The Inter-Galactic Get-Together has overflowed into the hall, where a dozen or so alien princesses, Star Fleet officers and shabbily dressed otherworlders seem amused at my height. "What a great disguise!" says a fat lady wrapped in aluminum foil. "It's the Predator!"

At least fifty more Inter-Galactitioners are crowded inside a two-room suite. There's a female midget in a string bikini, her body tattooed with white stars, varicolored planets, moon slices and fiery comets. Slumped on the floor against a wall is a sleeping beauty wearing a Grateful Dead T-shirt, the familiar smiling skull biting on a rose. The TV is activated and the fate of the entire universe is at stake as Captain Kirk battles hand-to-claw against a lizardman. The reefer lamp is also lit and everyone turns to stare as I bend through the open doorway.

I hold my right hand open above my right shoulder as though I were swearing to tell the whole truth in a court of law. Then I part my ring and middle fingers and utter the Vulcan's customary greeting. "Live long and prosper."

"Hear! Hear!" says a fat man in a Klingon mask, who then points me toward the bathroom. "There! There!" The bathtub is filled to the brim with ice cubes and beer cans. I pop the tab on a salty, fizzy Bud and reenter the main room. I actually recognize the food piled high on a table set before the TV—BBQ ribs, chicken, beef and Fat Albert's own baked beans.

A vampire dips his hand into the cole slaw, then sneaks up behind the midget. "Ahchoo!" says the vampire as he flings his handful against the little one's back. And I am reminded of Kelly's banana blow job.

There's another fat man wearing somebody's pink prom dress, which is bursting at the seams. He also wears pink angel wings and, from a black vertical stick, a golden halo hangs over his head. "Here's a riddle," he says. "What did Mrs. Kirk find in the toilet bowl? Give up? She found the Captain's log."

Hoo! Ha!

"Here's another one," says a Mr. Spock lookalike. "What's the similarity between the Starship Enterprise and a piece of toilet paper? . . . They both circle Uranus looking for Klingons!"

The Dead Head has revived and offers me a pipe and a burning match. "Eurithium crystals, man. Like, it's warp-nine time."

"No, thanks. Drugs are highly illogical."

A youngish woman overhears us and approaches me when the Dead Head leaves. She has red hair and green eyes. She wears an "ordinary" blue cocktail dress that enhances her slim hips and statuesque bosom. Her hair is brushed back and secured with two large golden clips, and from each clip there protrudes a long, bouncy, insectizoid antenna. "Hi," she says, and her smile is comely. "Didn't I see you in the lobby this afternoon with all those tall Negro men? What are you? A basketball team?"

"No, elephant jockeys."

Her antennae bob and weave when she laughs. "Are you a closet Trekkie?"

"Yes. I love 'Star Trek' because truth and justice always prevail. Because the good guys always win."

She samples the beans, then leads me to a recently vacated love seat near the window. I introduce myself, coming clean about my profession, "an itinerant basketball coach," and my players' fearful reaction to the convention.

Her name is Sharon Maxwell, she's thirty-one-years-old, recently divorced and living in Dallas. Hubby was an English professor at Southern Methodist University, "a snob" who believed that his sacred duty was to preserve the "cultural continuum of Western Civilization." When Sharon balked at reading Shakespeare or Milton (the latter the subject of his dissertation) he scolded her for being "a functional illiterate." Hubby's idea of a good time was watching arcane cable programs that featured thirty-minute closeups of Ming vases. When he wasn't home, Sharon eagerly read Agatha Christie mysteries and enjoyed reruns of "The Beverly Hillbillies." It wasn't until after the divorce ("Thank God there were no children") that she discovered the wonders of Star Trekking.

"I'm a secretary for a real-estate broker," she says. "A boring job that I hate with a *passion*."

She swears me to secrecy before confessing that she prefers "Star Trek: The Next Generation" to the original version. "Kirk and the boys are too hammy," she says. "There's less violence in the new series. 'The Next Generation' is also less sexist and the technology is more believable. To be completely frank, I must admit that I find Mr. Spock to be infinitely sexier than Data."

She then extracts a joint and a book of matches from the soft valley between her breasts. She lights up, puffs and offers me a toke. I refuse, citing the random drug tests to which I am subject. She tells me she has a fifth of Jack Daniel's back in her room.

"Well," I say, "why don't we activate the negative-matter ion chamber and turn on the platitudium energizer rod?"

"I think I can do it, Captain."

*   *   *

In her room we sip the booze and fumble on her bed until we're both naked and ready for atomic fusion. Then, just as she is priming poor Mandrake, Sharon Maxwell unlooses a resounding flatulation. Mandrake immediately falls on the field of battle, leaving me to mutter, "Baha, baha," to grab my clothes and quickly transport myself to a safer, more theoretical universe.

14

As soon as I wake up, my head comes loose and some vast, mighty hand starts dribbling it around the room. Ouch. Now I'm slam-dunked. Ooch. Then passed crosscourt and downcourt until I'm dizzy. Intercepted, rejected, pinned to the backboard. Get that shit outta here . . .

The Myriad is enormous, seating 15,000, much too large a venue for the CBL, where the average game attendance approaches 2,500. At gametime (any game, any time) there are always plenty of good seats for sale, leaving no convincing reason for the Ranger fans to purchase season tickets. Subsequently, any forecast of bad weather—which in Okie country means frequent and severe thunderstorms, hailstorms, flash floods and tornadoes—will keep the house under 1,000. That's why the Rangers lose $150,000 every year.

In fact, the only CBL franchise that regularly turns a profit is the Tennessee Studs, who play in a 3,700 seat civic auditorium in Knoxville. Every seat for every game is a hot ticket, and the Studs lead the CBL in season tickets and corporate sales.

Sam had missed the hotel van and is a no-show for the shoot-around. Lem is punctual, his left wrist swathed in an elastic bandage, his only greeting is a nod.

Everybody is relieved that the Trekkies have blasted off. Nate reports strange interstellar nightmares, "women with three tits and a cunt under each armpit." Kelly and Carl, roommates, slept with their lights on.

The lighting is poor inside the Myriad—with so much space to illuminate, the light-banks are too low and, from certain angles, lofty passes and high rebounds are lost in the glare.

On the court itself something else is amiss. We are a better outside shooting club than the Rangers, depending more on three-pointers than any other team in the CBL. Accordingly, Kuback has encouraged the Myriad's maintenance crew to tighten the rims, a manuever designed to repel any shot that catches even the slightest curve of the ring. Which is an indication that Kuback will replace Joseph with Kramer (a physical post-up player) instead of Hayes (a perimeter shooter who needs a pick).

Kuback also wants to run tonight—the nets have also been tampered with; they've been shortened and stretched to only briefly detain any successful shots. Which, in turn, promotes an uptempo pace, facilitating quicker inbound passes after a score. What a trickster the old man is. What else has he in store for us?

We review our 1-2-1-1 traps (code name "Diamond"), both half- and full-court, neither of which we've used in weeks. I doubt whether Kuback is even aware that the Diamond is part of our defensive repertoire.

And even without the pinched rims, good shooting teams rarely shoot as well on the road as they do at home. For the season we converted 52.7% of our field goal attempts in the Coliseum, only 48.9% elsewhere. The difference is the lighting, the rims and the variances in depth perception created by the different back-grounds behind each basket. So tonight (especially without Sam) we'll change our tactics. Yes, yes, we might as well trap and press. But we'll continue stuffing the ball inside to the Beast, and we'll also post Brent, letting him revert to his glory days at Parsons Crossing. Does Ferguson have the will to bang heads with Brent in the paint?

*   *   *

I make a serious attempt to eat lunch back at the hotel. The restaurant off the lobby is called Boomers and features paintings and miniature replicas of oil rigs and gas pumps. There is a salad bar set up inside a long, narrow reconstructed prairie schooner. But, all the veggies are limp and some appear to be melting. I'll sleep instead.

Later . . . the locker room is too hot, an old trick that presumably makes the visitors drowsy. The only countermeasure, turning on the cold water taps in the showers and washbasins, is mostly ineffective. But at least the players think I know what I'm doing.

Our hosts have thoughtfully provided us with a cooler full of Cokes, another ploy by Kuback. The "high" induced by the caffeine and the sugar will quickly burn away, tending to leave the players listless. To explain the biochemical process to the likes of Kelly is too exhausting. I just tell them to shun the Cokes because the local bottlers are on strike. Nobody cares.

One of the corners that Herm has sliced from the Stars budget prohibits us from having a trainer travel with the team. Instead, Steve Collins has three separate $150 checks for the Rangers trainer, who has agreed to rent his time and his expertise, and to sell the necessary materials to us. But the resident trainer doesn't get around to our locker room until 6:10 when he's finished doing the Rangers. This throws off our entire pregame routine—neither Nate, Lem, Earl, the Beast nor Kelly is able to get out on the court until 6:45, after my pregame spiel. Also, since the taping table is situated near the blackboard, the trainer can reconnoiter our game plan while he works. Soon as he leaves, I change the sequence of our opening plays, but he will certainly tell Kuback of our 1-2-1-1 press.

Despite the distractions, the players seem up. There are no practical jokes, no playful insults. Just grim game faces.

"DO IT!"

The officials are little Stevie Stephenson (ugh) and Larry Fontana, an NBA regular who only works in the CBL during the playoffs. Fontana is lazy, sensitive and favors the charge over the block.

The Rangers have instituted a new seating arrangement especially for the postseason. Picture this, there are twenty padded
folding chairs aligned along the sideline on each side of the scorer's
table. In our previous appearances at the Myriad, the first ten chairs
to the left of the table constituted the visitors' "bench." But now our
seating area has been moved down ten spaces so that my new seat
is astride the endline. What used to be our bench has been peddled
as "Jack Nicholson Seats" for fifty dollars each.

Worse, there is a 300-pound Rangers fanatic sitting immediately
to my right, body-to-body, breath-to-face. He wears a tan cowboy
hat, blue jeans, a green plaid shirt with matching string tie, and
fancy lizard-skin boots. His neck is so red it must glow in the dark.
His jowls sag and his features are porcine. "We gonna kick y'all's
ass," he says, as some of his beer splashes on my pants.

As the teams gather for the center-jump (once again presided
over by the short-armed Stephenson), Earl is upset about the game
ball. "There's way too much air in it!" he shouts over to the bench.
An overinflated ball is difficult to shoot and to handle. Kuback
strikes again. But Fontana will not be moved by Earl's distress. "It's
round and it bounces," the ref declares. "Let's play ball!"

Now I'm forced to get involved, reminding Fontana that basketball tradition requires the visiting team to approve the choice of
game balls. I also cite Section II, paragraph f (1) of the NBA rules,
which stipulates that the interior pressure of the ball must be
somewhere between $7\frac{1}{2}$ and $8\frac{1}{2}$ pounds. Fontana is furious but he
must return to the referees' locker room and retrieve his gauge. Nor
is he mollified when the ball registers $9\frac{1}{4}$ pounds. After the adjust-
ment is made Fontana says, "Let's get this *fucking* game started."
Meanwhile, Kuback shrugs and pretends ignorance.

The tradition in these here parts is for the loyal fans to rise up
and scream until the Rangers score. When Piggly Wiggly stands I
cannot see the court and must stand beside him, jockeying for the
best sightlines. Both of us remain standing for nearly two minutes
because the Stars come out like gangbusters.

Despite the fruits of the trainer's espionage, the ferocity of our
Diamond pressure forces the Rangers into committing bad shots
and errant passes. Brent and Kelly are dervishes—stealing, deflect-
ing, creating layups for themselves and their mates. When we must

play half-court, Beast has his way with Fort. The Rangers are
unprepared when Brent takes Ferguson into the pivot. Kuback
calls a quick twenty-second and then a full timeout but he can't
prevent us from jumping out to a 25–9 advantage.

Can it really be this easy? Is my job saved? Is Sam so readily
rendered superfluous? Am I indeed a genius? A hero?

The only ominous sign is the fact that we are the undeserving
beneficiaries of every close call. From past experience I know that
this is inevitably a prelude to getting screwed later on. But after
twelve minutes we've had ten free throws, they have four—and our
lead is 36–18.

Their big rookie, Larry Fort, has quit on Kuback and is replaced
by LaShon Lederman. I send Josh and Cooper in for Beast and Nate.

Our lead has stretched to 40–21, when the game turns against us:

—Josh nabs a rebound, then dribbles coast-to-coast and dis-
patches a wild off-balance jumper that Ferguson retrieves and
turns into a layup at the other end.

—Brent's nervous energy (caffeine and sugar?) suddenly dissipates and he forgets who he is. Rather than sticking to his hard-ass
defense and post-up offense, he starts impersonating Sam. The
only difference is that Brent's twisting jump shots make thudding
noises as they carom off the back of the ring.

—When Earl carries the ball to the basket he is whacked by
Kramer. "Tweet," says Fontana. "Foul on number twelve. White."
The foul is blatant, out in the open, just a normal workaday hack.
But Kuback erupts with epithets I can't quite hear, until Stephen-
son T's him with pleasure.

—With that, the refs remember that the visitors are not supposed to blow out the good guys, especially in postseason play.

—Ferguson finds the range.

—Carl is useless.

—The ballboys have vanished and we must get our own water,
lining up to fill our paper cups one at a time before the cooler.
Half the timeout is gone before we can get down to business.
When Piggly Wiggly tries to push his way into our huddle, Beast
shrinks him with an ominous stare. And after the players step

back into the ballgame the fat man says to me, "That little ol' bullshit play you tol' them wouldn't work against a bunch of blind chinks."

—Cooper plays well but every flop is called a foul.

—Every time I stand up, Piggly Wiggly hollers, "Sit down, *boy*."

In the second quarter we shoot three free throws (Kramer's foul on Earl plus the resultant technical), while the Rangers are awarded fifteen.

We are still ahead at the half, 52–50, but as we convene in the locker room we feel doomed. I try to pump them. "We had our run and they had theirs. Now the game is up for grabs. Hey, guys, who the fuck died around here? Wake *up*." It's no use. "DO IT!" convinces nobody.

The Rangers' press finally catches up with us and the refs are unmerciful . . . Earl is shoved out of bounds and called for walking. Cooper gets his nose bloodied by a stray elbow and the foul is whistled on the rookie. "What'd he do?" I yell at Fontana. "Foul the guy's elbow with his face?"

Piggly Wiggly nudges me and says, "Stop crying, *boy*."

So I wheel on him. "Shut the fuck up, you fat prick."

He is, of course, outraged. He paid a lot of money for his seat and he "won't abide" my cussing.

"Listen, you fucking lump. Do I come down to Burger King and bother you when you're working?"

Cooper dribbles hard to the basket and collides with McDonald. They both crash to the floor and the ball bounces to Kramer, who passes upcourt to Hayes and the Rangers have an easy score.

"Make a damn call," I shout at Fontana. "Any call will do!"

"Shut up, Coach," he says. "You're lucky I didn't call a charge."

"If you see a fucking charge, then *call* a fucking charge. Don't do me any fucking favors—"

"Boom," says Fontana. "That'll cost ya."

In the third quarter the Rangers shoot fifteen free throws, we shoot two. Oklahoma's lead is 87–51. The game is over.

"Sit down, *asshole*," growls Piggly Wiggly.

Oh, well, at least here's a chance to play Lem—who needs more time than usual to load his jumper and who tiptoes around the boards but whose overall court-awareness is a pleasure to watch.

Beast and Cooper foul out. With no subs lurking at the scorer's table, Josh actually settles down and does some good things. Kelly and Earl are still battling for loose balls, playing with abandon. Nate has read the tenor of the game and has long since settled into cruise control.

With 2:10 on the game clock Oklahoma's free-throw edge for this quarter is 12–0! And with the game out of reach, both refs will call touch fouls on the Rangers to make the final statistics look more compatible.

"Sit down, *asshole*."

Yeah, sure . . . I stand up with my ass aimed at Piggly Wiggly's face. Then I put my hands on my hips and flare out my jacket to block his view of the court. Piggly retaliates by pushing his foot up between my legs, his intent being to deliver a kick to my balls. I flex my Nautilus-trained abductors and lock his foot long enough for me to escape. When Piggly stands up to challenge me I turn and bump him back into his seat. His next move is to reach out an expensive high-heeled boot and stomp hard on my left foot. The game continues behind me while I direct rude reproaches into his face.

BUZZZT

STARS–91   OKL–110

Exploding, I trash the locker room, hurling cans of Coke at the blackboard until a longitudinal crack appears, throwing a trash can into a mirror, smashing every chair within reach (four of them) into the nearest wall. The players duck and shield their faces behind crossed arms.

"I treat you like men and you play like cunts. Pussies. Pieces of shit."

They sit motionless while I stomp around the room. When my anger has abated I tell them there will be no shootaround tomorrow. Instead we'll have a meeting and a tape session in my room at eleven o'clock. Don't be late."

We even dispense with the postgame prayer.

Because of the broken mirror everybody must wear sneakers or thongs to and from the shower. And as I study the stat sheet I can hear Lem telling Kelly that he'll quit the team if he doesn't start tomorrow night.

The cleaning crews are already at work, mostly people from skid row paid a minimum wage to sweep and shovel used popcorn boxes, candy wrappers, cups empty of beer and soda. A sad group of men wearing blood-red MYRIAD MAINTENANCE T-shirts over their sad clothes.

The casual fans are long gone, only close friends and freeloaders are left to wait for the players. Here come Stephenson and Fontana over to the scorer's table for their copies of the statistics. They both wear blue bar mitzvah suits and their referee duds are stashed in identical black overnight bags. We nod cautiously at each other. Should I say something inflammatory they are liable to "write" me up and I'll be fined by Commissioner Rose.

Players on both teams mill about under the far basket. Where's the party? The hottest women? The best food? The free drugs?

Kuback is nowhere in sight, but here comes the man I'm looking for, Mack Cummings, Oklahoma's general manager . . . For most CBL teams (like the Rangers) the coach is totally responsible for all player-personnel moves—trades, cuts, suspensions, free-agent signings. The GM keeps tabs on the salary cap ($120,000 divided by seventeen weeks divided by ten players). He also tries to curb the number of players his coach will bring in and send out, since each transaction means expenditures for airfare, cab rides and sometimes rental cars. (So far, the Rangers have used thirty players this season. Savannah's body count is twenty-three.) Otherwise, the CBL's general managers deal with game promotions, group sales, merchandise and service trade-outs, corporate sponsorships and everything else nobody else wants to do. Only a handful, like Herm, interfere with roster decisions.

Mack is an old-time CBLer who, during his tenure as GM for several teams, has washed uniforms, driven vans to distant ball-games, mopped floors, swept and shoveled other people's post-game garbage. He vividly recalls the eighteen-hour van rides from Altoona to Montreal. "The secret of a successful long-distance drive," he always says, "was to turn the heat way up so the players

COMMERCIAL BASKETBALL LEAGUE
Official Scorer's Report

Date March 19, 1992   Game # 03   Arena Myriad   Attendance: 4134
Visitors Savannah Stars   Home OK City Rangers   Length of Game: 2:05

No	Visitors: Stars	Min	FG M	FG A	FT M	FT A	3Pt M	3Pt A	Pts	Reb O	D	TOT	AST	PF	TO	BS	ST
6	Royal (G)	31	5	11	4	4	0	0	14	2	2	4	7	2	3	1	4
8	Butler	17	1	5	2	2	0	2	4	0	1	1	1	3	4	0	1
10	Cooper	27	2	4	3	3	0	0	7	2	6	8	1	6	2	1	0
11	Brusher	16	2	8	1	2	0	1	5	0	3	3	0	2	4	2	0
12	Kennison (F)	30	5	13	1	1	0	1	11	0	3	3	2	1	0	0	0
13	Morrison (C)	30	3	6	2	6	0	0	8	2	9	11	0	6	1	1	0
24	Jameson	12	2	5	2	2	0	0	6	0	2	2	3	2	3	0	0
32	Patton (F)	42	9	19	5	6	2	5	25	2	9	11	3	3	2	0	2
40	Springs (G)	35	4	14	3	4	0	2	11	1	2	3	4	4	4	0	3
	TOTALS	240	33	84	23	30	2	11	91	9	37	46	21	29	23	5	10
	Pct.		39.3		76.6		18.2			Team 2					4			

No	Home: Rangers	Min	FG M	FG A	FT M	FT A	3Pt M	3Pt A	Pts	Reb O	D	TOT	AST	PF	TO	BS	ST
2	McDonald (G)	37	2	7	4	6	0	1	8	1	2	3	10	2	3	0	3
4	Collins	11	3	7	2	2	0	0	8	0	0	0	2	1	1	1	2
10	Hayes	8	1	8	1	1	0	0	3	0	1	1	2	1	0	0	1
12	Kramer (F)	35	8	13	5	8	0	0	21	4	10	14	4	5	2	2	2
14	Ferguson (G)	40	12	18	10	11	0	2	34	0	4	4	5	3	2	0	4
15	Palmer	14	0	5	2	2	0	2	2	0	4	0	3	3	1	1	0
20	Fort (C)	25	0	5	2	2	0	0	2	1	6	7	0	4	3	1	0
21	Hodges (F)	45	9	14	9	14	0	0	27	4	12	16	3	4	2	3	1
23	Lederman	25	1	5	3	3	0	0	5	2	2	4	0	2	0	2	2
	TOTALS	240	36	83	38	48	0	5	110	12	41	53	29	25	13	10	15
	Pct.		43.4		79.1		0			Team 7					1			

Score By Quarters	1	2	3	4	OT	OT	OT	Final
V Sav	36	16	19	20				91
H OC	18	32	37	23				110

Officials: Steve Stephenson, Larry Fontana
Technicals: OK coach Kuback (Unsp.) 10:21 of 2nd
Sav coach Lassner (Unsp.) 10:14 of 3rd

Miscellaneous Statistics
Ties 2   Lead Changes 2
Points off off. rebounds (H) 10   (V) 4
Points off steals (H) 14   (V) 10
Offensive fouls (H) 2   (V) 4

Remarks: Rangers take 2-1 lead in playoff series

133

can only escape by falling asleep." His humor is legendary—upon crossing the border into Canada, a customs agent peered into the van, saw the sleeping players and asked Mack about his cargo. "I'm smuggling slaves," Mack explained.

He is a large, round man with a surprisingly bony face. In post-game bars around the CBL, one question is posed more often than any other—can Mack Cummings touch his nose to his chin?

Mack knows all but tells little. "Hi there, big fella," he says to me. "Tough to win playing five against seven."

"You noticed." Then I complain about the unreasonable prox-imity of Piggly Wiggly. "How can I concentrate with stuff like that going on?"

Mack had heard there was "some kind of fracas" and he sympa-thizes, even apologizes, but there's not much he can do. Perhaps he can persuade a security cop to hang around in the vicinity. Sorry.

Good enough.

Mack informs me that the Capital City Cosmos won tonight to sweep their series against Twin-Cities. The Cosmos owner, a reclu-sive billionaire named Jason Duffy, cares not how much money he spends (and loses) in his passionate pursuit of a CBL champion-ship. Since the Cosmos will play the winner of this series, Capital City's infamous director of player personnel will be here to scout tomorrow's game. Dave Fishwick is his name, a.k.a. "The Assas-sin."

The hotel van arrives thirty minutes late. Cooper and I are the only passengers, everyone else having made their own arrangements for the evening. The rookie apologizes for "stinking up the court." I nod in silence, in the dark.

I pause at the hotel bar to hear The Rodgers Family play some C & W. Ray and Gayle Rodgers are an attractive middle-aged couple, ac-companying themselves on guitars. They wear matching blue cow-person suits replete with white fringes. Their modest sound is artificially enhanced by a bass machine and a drum machine.

At a small corner table for one, I nurse a ginger ale while they play "The Streets of Baltimore," an offbeat tune from Gram Parsons's last album. They do "San Antone," by Charlie Pride. Then "Easy Chair," by Bob Dylan. Their playlist also includes songs by Doug Sahm, John Cooper and Dave Clark. Tasty. Tuneful. I'm almost enjoying myself, on the verge of forgetting the game, my job, my life, when I see Sam passing my table with a broad-bottomed white woman hanging onto his arm. He motions her to another table, then turns to me.

"Whatd'ya say, boss?"

"Nothing much, Sam."

"You can't fight city hall."

"I guess not."

"I'll be at the meeting tomorrow. Don't worry, Rob. I'll make everything come out right."

"Yeah. Sure."

He inclines his head toward his date. "Whatd 'ya think?"

"Too fat-assed for my taste."

He laughs before he leaves. "The bigger the cushion, the better the push-in."

I watch the game tape on the VCR that Steve totes with him on the road. Every painful play. Every lousy call. Torturing myself until who knows what time.

I am still awake at 2:47 when the phone rings. "Hello?" I ask, but no one answers.

15

I JUMP OUT of bed at 8:28, just spoiling for a fight. Line 'em up—Kuback, Sam, Josh, Herm, T-Bone, Rose, the entire blasted race of zebras. Even Racheal. It almost feels good to be angry. It does feel good to feel.

But I'm frightened, because last night's postgame tantrum was genuine, not some theatrical trick to impress the team. So . . . more than sleep, more than breakfast, I need a workout, something physical to take the boil out of my blood.

The front desk recommends a nearby gym, just show my room key for free access. The cab ride is five dollars each way.

The gym is housed in an erector-set building, auxiliary to one of Oklahoma City's largest hospitals. Inside, the Nautilus machines are gleaming and the pads are plump with apparent disuse, the gym's clientele tending to be dehydrated seniors pushing minimum weights. Although they shuffle from station to station armed with towels and plastic bottles of cleaning fluid, none of them sweat. Yet they laboriously disinfect each pad, each hand grip, only one step away from Godliness.

Several of the oldsters also carry portable oxygen units slung over their shoulders like brief cases. Long plastic tubes feed the gas directly into the patients' gasping nostrils.

In addition to the Nautilus equipment, the gym shows a fleet of stationary bikes, treadmills, stair-masters and rowing machines. The entire workout area is encircled by a four-lane track and the walkers proceed with care.

I have no interest in the track, the locker rooms, the whirlpools or the saunas. But at the far end of the building, behind a floor-to-ceiling fishnet curtain, an aerobics class slowly waltzes to the strains of a thousand strings playing "Moon River." And the very surface beneath their dancing feet is a small wooden basketball court. Better yet, three wrinkled hoopsters sit patiently on nearby chairs waiting for the next *danse*.

Let's see . . . 3 + 1 = 4 = 2-on-2. So I rush through the Nautilus stations, completing my biceps exercises just in time to hear the bouncing ball.

"Mind if I join you?"

"Why?" asks a tall thin man in a HEALTHY HEART T-shirt. "Are we falling apart?"

They are in their mid-fifties, two cardiologists and a proctologist, we determine after brief introductions. Before the game begins, I catch on to the house rules—strictly half-court, game to eleven straight, make-it-take-it and the ball must be "retrieved" past the foul line after every change of possession. The wooden floor is old and bouncy, the rim is a yawning thing and the brand-new ball is wonderfully tactile. I stay outside near the key, mostly passing and shooting, going to the hole only when a game is on the line.

The ball moves quickly, the players cut slowly, the sneakers squeak sweetly on the worn floor. Running one-handers abound, so too the old give'n'-go. Good plays draw praise from everybody. The defenders call the fouls and they never lie!

Both cardiologists played college hoops, one at Johns Hopkins, the other at McGill University in Toronto. The proctologist barely made his high-school JV team back home in Rockford, Illinois. My team wins 11–7, loses 11–10, wins 11–5.

"Dr. Bassett," the Canadian says between games, "is it true that you had to use two fingers during an examination this morning because your patient wanted a second opinion?"

We decide that the most competitive teams will pair me and Dr. Bassett against the cardiologists and we play without keeping score. Sweating, grunting, joyful, I play hard enough to keep the game even.

Forget about the CBL and the NBA. Forget about Captain Kirk playing one-on-one with a lizardman. This is what counts. No winners, no losers. No fans, no refs. No money, no egos. No stat sheets, no complications. THE GAME. By itself, symbolic of nothing with nothing at stake.

Back at the hotel I barely have time enough to shower and shave when the players arrive for the meeting. They quickly fill the room. Cooper sits on the floor. The Beast and Nate have commandeered the only available chairs. Sam stretches out on the bed, his sneakers on the blanket, his head on my pillow. Lem stands sullenly in a corner, slouching against the wall.

My strategy is to remove all restraints, a risky procedure. In the past I've mustered similar assemblies that have brought a contentious team into close communion, others that have produced violent arguments and long losing streaks. You never really know.

"Say whatever's on your minds, guys. Anything goes. The only rule is that nothing gets repeated outside of this room."

I tell them we can indeed win a championship if we stay together. For the grillionth time this season I discuss roles and role-players: Kelly and Carl are supposed to initiate the offense and play defense. The Beast rebounds, picks, posts and scares people. Nate's job is to score and open the flex cuts for everyone else. Cooper runs, bounds, defends and executes the offense. Josh rebounds and blocks shots. Brent is our defensive stopper. Earl's job is to do whatever is necessary in any given ballgame. Sam is the finisher whose ultimate purpose is to fill the basket. Lem's priority is to heal. Everybody's job is to run the plays and play better defense than they're playing now.

Admittedly, this is not a classically well-balanced team—such things are hard to find in the hodgepodge world of the CBL. We need a point guard who can shoot and we need another scorer off the bench (alas, poor Richie!).

Like a fool, I go on to describe this morning's game with the three doctors. But their eyes are glazed (even Earl's) and they are impatient for the main attraction.

"Okay. I've been led to believe that Sam here has something important to tell us."

Sam gets off my bed and steps slowly to the front of the room. He wears a lightweight, crinkly sweatsuit courtesy of Adidas, and his sunglasses are in place. He smiles and puts his hands on his hips in a muted gesture of defiance. I get a sudden, unmistakable flash that Sam is an unholy martyr about to exact his revenge.

"If anybody thinks I'm here to apologize," he says, "then you mothafuckers are crazy. Listen up, niggers. I'm the most talented player on this sorry-ass team. My name is Points and my name's my game. Lookit what you mothafuckers did without me last night! Got crushed! And Oz Joseph wasn't even there! And if any of you fucking guys ever even think you're as good as me, wake up, man, you're having a wet dream . . . And another thing . . . Rob? You been fucking with my game all season long. And your offense sucks, man. Everybody knows it. Big men handling the ball at the foul line? Be fucking real. Then you put me in and pull me out like I'm a fucking yo-yo. That's boolshit, man. And I always get the blame whenever we lose. Fuck that shit. I ain't gonna be nobody's scrapegoat. That's all I got to say."

Lem, slouching in his corner, is quick to pick up the baton. "I agree with Sam," he says. "Rob's been fucking with me too. I average twenty points and ten rebounds. I make the All-Star team two years in a row. It ain't my fault I broke my wrist. Now I'm healthy and this mothafucker won't start me. And fuck all this rahrah bullshit. What the fuck do I care about a CBA championship? I just want to win this here series so's I'll get paid for at least another week. That's what counts. Money, honey."

Everybody's quiet for a heartbeat. Kelly glances around the room, ready to laugh, ready to cry. Cooper's eyes are tightly sealed and his lips are moving. The Beast grinds his teeth.

Finally, Earl speaks up. "Fuck the both of you," he says from his perch on the edge of the bed. "I've played in more NBA games than the rest of you put together. And I say the flex offense will work. But we've gotta want it to work. If we break plays, then the best offense in the world ain't worth dick. And you, Sam? Who the fuck do you think you are? You talk like you're Michael Jordan. God-damn! Have a look around you, sucker. This ain't the fucking Hilton. This ain't the fucking Plaza. This is shit city, bro. And there ain't no prima donnas in the fucking CBL . . ."

Sam eyes Earl coolly. "Fuck . . . you . . . cowboy," he say, savoring each word. "Don't be telling me 'bout no NBA 'cause you ain't shit. You a fucking has-been. Man, I'll tell you what. I'm gonna put my money where my mouth is. I'll play you one-on-one for a thousand dollars. Winner take all."

Earl laughs. "You ain't got nothing but chump change in your pocket. The drugs man got all your money."

"I'll bet on Sam," Lem pipes in.

"Tomorrow," says Sam. "At practice. Me and you."

Earl laughs again. "Sure. But we gotta win tonight or there ain't no practice tomorrow."

"Just give me the ball," Sam says, "and get out my way."

Nate buries his head in his hands. "This is fucking crazy."

Josh is sitting on the far corner of the bed and raises his hand like a schoolboy seeking permission to visit the bathroom. When I nod at him, he stands and says, "I agree with Sam." Then he sits back down.

"Agree about what?" says Nate. "You dumb field nigger."

Josh stands up once more. "About Rob fucking with my game too," he says. "I'm the best thing to ever hit Savannah and this coach treats me like a scrub."

"Yeah," Carl says. "Me too."

Suddenly the Beast jumps out of his chair and slams a huge fist against a dresser top. "Shut the fuck up! Everybody. I'm sick of all this complaining! I just want to win. I'll kick *alla* your fucking asses. One at a time or all at once. *You*, Sam. How many times do I bust my ass getting position down low and you look right through me like I'm fucking invisible? I should tear you a new asshole right now."

Sam pushes his back against the wall and everybody else also retreats, clearing a path between the Beast and Sam. Kelly scrabbles into the bathroom and locks the door behind him.

"Rob gives us everything we need to win," the Beast continues. "We just ain't performing. And if you ain't playing enough to suit yourself it's 'cause you don't fucking deserve to play. I swear on my mother's grave, if we don't win this series I'm gonna rip off your dicks and stuff them down your throats. Test me. See if I'm lying."

Earl laughs and so does the Beast. "This fucking meeting," says the Beast, "is fucking adjourned."

Yes, yes. It hurts to the core. But I've been called worse by worse players. When I cut them or trade them they sometimes look to even the score. I remember cutting a player named Mo Morton, a seven-footer who played like a point guard. It was during my rookie season at Peoria and he was a mean-looking hombre from Harlem, USA. I was afraid he'd beat me up so I cut him over the phone. "You're a bullshit mothafucker," he said, "and a shitty coach. And if I ever get you alone somewhere, anywhere, I'll fucking kill you with my bare hands."

Yes. It always hurts.

Soon after the room empties the phone starts ringing . . . It's my buddy T-Bone Donaldson wanting to know the gory details of last night's fiasco. After hearing my summary he says that his "own job is also up for grabs." The Winnebago Willies owners now want to postpone any decision until the CBL season runs its course. T-Bone says nothing about his call to Herm.

"Just keep this in mind," T-Bone says in parting. "Y'all don't have to beat a tough team twice on the road. If y'all look at it that way it seems almost impossible. All y'all got to do is beat them tonight."

The next caller is Dave Fishwick, "The Assassin." Two years ago Fishwick was a high-school coach at Capital City HS, a position he'd held for twenty-three seasons. But there was some kind of scandal, some rumored misappropriation of funds, and Fishwick was allowed to resign. Because of Fishwick's deep roots in the sporting community, the Cosmos owner gave him a sinecure job as assistant to the Assistant Director of Player Personnel. (Whereas the Stars basketball staff consists of me and Magoo, at one time the Cosmos employed a head coach, two full-time assistant coaches and three player-personnel specialists.)

During his first season with the Cosmos, Fishwick was assigned all the scumbag duties—making preliminary calls to agents, arranging practice sites and times on the road and at home, scheduling flights for incoming and outgoing players, making sure the uniforms were cleaned. He also worked hard at getting his immediate superior fired, thereby earning himself a promotion to Assistant Director of Player Personnel. Last year, Fishwick climbed over another body. Nowadays, all the assistantships have been abolished and he is the one and only Director of Player Personnel, a position earning him $25,000 per annum.

What's his *modus operandi*? Spreading rumors of alcoholism or drug abuse, of thievery or debauchery, of genital infections, deviations of the septum . . . whatever works. Ingratiating himself with the players, ownership, agents, season-ticket holders and the media. Claiming credit for everything positive and blaming someone else's incompetence for the rest.

To his credit, Fishwick does work hard. There's a callus on his dialing finger. He has a cauliflower ear that can damn near grip a telephone receiver all by itself. His eyes are red and veiny from watching game tapes. And his lips are brown.

Fishwick's next objective is to become a head coach in the CBL, replacing Barry Millhouse (the Cosmos incumbent) or anybody else who's vulnerable to back-stabbing and/or character assassination.

For example, me.

"Yes, sir," he says, his usual dick-lapping salutation. "I went over to the Myriad to watch your shootaround, and guess what? You weren't there."

When I tell him that we had a meeting instead, he asks to see our game tape. "Kuback says his came out blank," Fishwick tells me. "How about I'll trade you our last game against Twin-Cities for this one?"

Sure. What the hell. Then I tell him that I've a luncheon appointment, that someone's knocking on my door, that I've a sudden attack of diarrhea. "See you tonight," he says.

The last call is from Chet, advising me that T-Bone and The Assassin both called Herm at the office this morning. "The vultures are circling," Chet sighs. Also, the Savannah media says that the Stars are "done for." In last night's sportscast, Packman called the team "an embarrassment to the storied city of Savannah," and referred to me as "a carpetbagger coach." Patterson in today's *Gazette* adds that T-Bone is available and "perhaps the Stars powers-that-be should turn to a native Son of the South."

Chet says that Sam will give us a "boost" tonight and that the game is "winnable."

Do I hope it ends tonight? Yes. Or do I hope the season will extend for two more series beyond this one? Yes, yes.

The players' lighthearted bantering in the pregame locker room fills me with foreboding. Sam has unaccountably made amends with Earl, calling him "my nig." Kelly is back to sniping at Nate's hair ("look at Uncle Nappy"), at Cooper's clothing ("Salvation Army standard issue"), at Brent's skin ("what you got there? Cherries growing outta your neck?"), at Josh's head ("looks like somebody done hit an eight-ball with a hammer"), and he cuts me too ("Coach got such a big nose 'cause air is free").

They are frisky and rebellious. But I will remain faithful to my system. My only concession is to use adhesive tape and towels to cover the blackboard until the Rangers trainer leaves the room. The scouting reports have undergone minor changes, incorporating certain tendencies I've noted from watching the tapes. Ferguson will only pass while going left. Hodges dips his right shoulder before going right, his left shoulder before going left. Kramer head-fakes and steps through whenever he moves to his left. Their 1-3-1 traps can be compromised by certain diagonal passes. Our defense must rotate thusly . . . Down picks have been changed to back picks.

"DO IT!"

The visitors are always introduced first and when Sam's name is announced, he dashes over to the edge of the Rangers huddle. He stands there, pointing an admonishing finger, shouting, "We're gonna whip your fucking asses tonight. I'm back and you mothafuckers are dog meat!" All this before joining his teammates at center court.

The officials are Wayne Casey, a CBA dead-ender, and John Travis, an arrogant type who worked at Dallas last night. And Kuback is all over them, claiming that Sam's antics call for a full-blown T for unsportsmanlike conduct, or at least a delay-of-game warning. Both officials laugh and turn their backs.

Oklahoma captures the opening tip and the first play is a pick-and-roll involving Ferguson and Hodges. When Ferguson splits the defense, the Beast bounds to the rescue and assaults the Rangers guard, one fist to the chest, then a forearm to the head. BONG. Casey calls a flagrant foul (the proper call), which gives Ferguson two free throws and the Rangers the ball out of bounds. The Beast thumps his own chest like a King Kong and says to the Rangers, "Anybody else want some?" Kuback yells bloody murder while the refs laugh some more.

At the other end Sam dominates—shooting, passing, even rebounding. Then Sam steals a careless pass and runs ahead of the pack, a monster-dunk on his mind. The dispirited Rangers have already given up the chase and Sam veers toward the home team's bench, pausing there long enough to say, "Fuck you, old man," and poking his middle finger into Kuback's startled face before resuming his solo run upcourt and dunking with a flourish.

The Beast controls the middle like a traffic cop and Nate rebounds like there's a $100 bill taped to every missed shot. Kelly and Earl are content to direct the ball to Sam. When a woman in the Nicholson Seats yells something uncomplimentary, Sam grins and points between his legs.

It's a blowout. Even the refs can't turn the game.

At the half our lead is 67–45 and we're still not satisfied. "Kill 'em," the players shout. "Kill the mothafuckers."

"DO IT!"

By now, the refs have jumped on the bandwagon and every call belongs to us. Even so, they never see the first foul and always punish the retaliation . . . because they get suckered by ball-fakes and call walking from the waist up, because they'll blow their whistles whenever a play doesn't look right, because, like bad judges, their justice is selective.

Kuback gets a T but no relief. Sam is unconscious, filling it, drilling it from every conceivable angle. Lem is awful and Cooper seems confused. Josh shoots too often. Every time they make a mistake, Brent and Carl look fearfully at the Beast.

By the start of the fourth quarter, Kuback is shouting insults at his players as they pass his bench. "You stupid fuck," he yells when Ferguson fouls Carl thirty feet from the basket. Cooper bumps Fort off a loose ball and Kuback calls his big man "a fucking wimp."

Beside me, Piggly Wiggly is quiet throughout, but his beady red eyes broadcast his belligerence. Finally, as the game winds down, he whispers that he knows the hotel and the room I'm in.

Hayes tries to guard Sam unaided and Sam is contemptuous. "Gonna fuck with you, white boy," he says, "until your ass bleeds." Sam then shakes, shivers and nets a fallaway jumper.

"Hurt him," Earl advises.

The final score is 137–105.

Whooping and hollering in the locker room, Sam gives me a hug. "I told you!" he shouts. "Didn't I?"

"Tomorrow," Earl reminds him. "After practice. For a grand."

"It's a bet, cowboy."

The Oklahoma press invades the locker room. Where were they last night? The hot news is that Kuback is using Joseph's departure as an alibi. Kuback says that the NBA should be prohibited from calling up CBL players during the CBL playoffs. What do I think?

"If that ever comes to pass," I say, "there won't be any CBL playoffs. Once the regular season is over, most everybody'll go to Europe, to South America, to Australia or the Philippines. NBA contracts are why most of the players even bother with this league."

While I scan the stat sheet I hear Lem telling Carl that he'll leave the team if he doesn't start Thursday night.

Back at the hotel I order in a pizza with extra green peppers and sup while reviewing the game. It's all Sam's show, no strategy, no Xs or Os that matter.

There comes a knock at my door at 11:15. Oh, shit, here's Piggly Wiggly with a shotgun. But it's only Cooper with a problem.

He really is a nice wholesome kid, always looking like he's just showered. "I can't deal with all this madness," he says. "My agent called. He says there's a good chance I can go to Spain the day after

COMMERCIAL BASKETBALL LEAGUE
Official Scorer's Report

Date March 20, 199_ Game 04 Arena Myriad Attendance 3704
Visitors Savannah Stars Home OK. City Rangers Length of Game 1:55

No	Visitors Stars	Min	Field Goals M	A	Free Throws M	A	3 Pt Field Goals M	A	Pts	Rebounds O	D	TOT	AST	PF	TO	BS	ST
6	Royal (G)	31	4	9	1	2	0	0	9	0	2	2	11	1	2	0	4
7	Franks (G)	40	14	27	8	9	2	6	38	2	5	7	3	2	1	1	2
8	Butler	17	2	4	0	0	0	1	4	1	0	1	2	1	1	0	1
10	Cooper	20	7	11	0	0	2	2	16	3	7	10	1	3	1	2	0
11	Brusher	14	0	5	0	0	0	0	0	0	3	3	0	0	3	2	0
12	Kennison (F)	28	8	16	2	2	0	2	18	1	8	9	2	2	1	1	0
13	Morrison (c)	30	7	13	3	6	0	0	17	2	12	14	0	3	2	1	0
24	Jameson	14	4	9	0	0	0	0	8	1	5	6	2	3	0	1	2
32	Patton (F)	38	8	17	4	4	2	4	22	2	7	9	4	2	3	0	4
40	Springs	8	2	6	1	4	0	0	5	1	1	2	1	0	0	1	1
	TOTALS	240	56	112	19	27	6	15	137	13	50	63	26	17	14	9	14
	Pct.		50.0		70.4		40.0			Team 7				3			

No	Home Rangers	Min	Field Goals M	A	Free Throws M	A	3 Pt Field Goals M	A	Pts	Rebounds O	D	TOT	AST	PF	TO	BS	ST
2	McDonald (G)	35	3	7	2	3	0	0	8	0	1	1	4	2	5	0	2
4	Collins	13	1	2	1	1	0	1	3	1	1	2	1	1	2	0	0
10	Hayes	4	0	2	0	0	0	1	0	0	1	0	0	0	0	1	0
12	Kramer (F)	40	8	14	7	10	0	0	23	4	11	15	1	4	2	2	1
14	Ferguson (G)	44	10	24	5	6	2	6	27	0	6	6	2	1	4	0	1
15	Palmer	8	2	2	0	0	0	0	4	0	3	3	2	4	0	1	0
20	Fort (c)	20	4	9	0	0	0	0	8	1	4	5	0	3	4	1	0
21	Hodges (F)	48	12	19	0	2	0	0	24	3	10	13	1	5	3	2	1
23	Lederman	28	4	8	0	0	0	0	8	1	2	3	2	3	3	2	1
	TOTALS	240	44	87	15	22	2	8	105	10	39	49	13	23	23	9	6
	Pct.		50.6		68.2		25.0			Team 2				5			

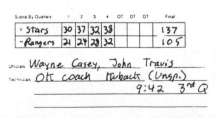

Score By Quarters	1	2	3	4	OT	OT	OT	Final
v Stars	30	37	32	38				137
h Rangers	21	24	28	32				105

Officials Wayne Casey, John Travis
Technicals OK coach Hubach (Unsp.)
9:42 3rd Q

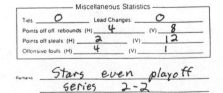

— Miscellaneous Statistics —
Ties 0 Lead Changes 0
Points off off rebounds (H) 4 (V) 8
Points off steals (H) 2 (V) 12
Offensive fouls (H) 4 (V) 1

Remarks Stars even playoff series 2-2
Franks 38 pts is Stars playoff record

146

tomorrow. Thursday. The deal is for ten thousand dollars when I get off the plane, then five thousand a game. The team is in Barcelona and they have six games left and they're on the bubble for the playoffs. That's a minimum of forty grand for six weeks. Free house, free car, all that. I don't really want to go because I don't want to let you down, Coach. The guys either. Some of the guys. I like Earl, Nate, Kelly, Brent and Benny. The others are the devil's tools. Tell me what to do, Coach."

According to the standard CBL contract, any player who bolts to Europe can be sued for $10,000 by the league. The CBL is currently negotiating with FIBA, the agency governing international basket-ball, and by next season any jumpers will be denied access to the European leagues until they pay whatever penalty the abandoned CBL team imposes. For now, the $10,000 fine is an empty threat that will never survive judicial scrutiny because the fine is worth more than the player's contract with the CBL. But is Cooper pre-pared to hire a lawyer should the CBL move to sue him? He doesn't think so.

Does he need the money? Not really. Dad teaches history and mom teaches health in the same high school in Provo, Utah. "They're not Mormons," he says, "but they're financially comfort-able." On the other hand, Cooper is engaged to his high-school sweetheart so any "extra money" would be appreciated.

The rookie is also frustrated by his playing time. Not since elementary school has he been asked to come off the bench.

"What if you do this, Coach . . . only play me in combination with Earl, Brent, Nate, Kelly or Benny? That might make things at least tolerable."

We'll see. Meanwhile, he'll call his agent in the morning and get back to me. "God bless you, Coach Lassner."

Same to you.

Earl calls shortly thereafter to report that Larry Fort attacked Kuback in the locker room after the game. "He grabbed the old man's necktie," Earl says, "and tried to choke him. None of the players made a move to break it up but the assistant coach finally called in the security police. They're done, Rob. Finished."

In the aftermath, Kuback announced that Fort would be suspended. Also, that every Ranger would be fined $100 for "lack of effort tonight." Kuback has put a bounty on Sam—$500 for the Ranger player who takes him out. Earl swears that Ferguson is leaving in the morning and that Hodges has been offered a deal in Spain, 10K up front and 5K per game.

"Meanwhile," he says, "I'm gonna kill Sam tomorrow."

"Yes. I see you two have kissed and made up."

"Strictly bidness," Earl says. "Lem is backing him, Carl and Kelly too. Sam's agent is supposed to be sending him some money. Who are you betting on?"

"I've got a bulletin for both of you. I'm not letting you two go through with this."

"Too late now," he says. "If not tomorrow at practice, then at the Y or a schoolyard. Wherever, I'm gonna fuck him over. Bloody his face. Chop on his legs. But don't worry, Rob. We can win without him."

Sure.

16

THERE'S A WAKE-UP call scheduled for 8:30 A.M. but the telephone detonates at 7:28. It's Mack Cummings, the sage Rangers GM, delivering a warning. "Watch out for Dave Fishwick," he says. "He was sniffing around the arena last night trying to find out about your hassle with that fan. By the way, the guy's name is Buddy Hastings and I did speak to him before the game. He swore to me that he'd behave himself. How'd he do?"

"No problem, except for a veiled threat to come to the hotel and do me bodily harm."

"Really. Well, after I spoke to him, I think Fishwick got around to him too. The word I get is that Fishwick's encouraging this guy to sue you for assault."

"That's insane, he's the one who tried to deball me. I'm the one with the black-and-blue toes. Why does anybody listen to a snake like Fishwick?"

Cummings laughs lightly. "Most people love to hear dirt about somebody else. It makes them feel cleaner about themselves. This is such a vicious business, I don't know how you coaches survive."

"Say, look . . . what's the deal with Kuback? I heard he's having trouble with his players. Is he solid here?"

"Personally, I hate the bastard. He has no communication skills and he acts like he invented the game. But as far as the owner is concerned, Kuback can do no wrong."

He's talking about Estelle Vandermark, a wealthy widow whose

149

late, unlamented husband made his fortune selling Cadillacs during the last oil boom. With all her facelifts, it's nigh impossible to guess her age (anywhere from fifty to sixty-five?) but she's almost attractive in a pinched sort of way. She's also renowned as a lush, using the first two weeks of every October to dry out in a fashionable Palm Springs spa in preparation for the upcoming CBL season. According to Earl, the real skinny is that Kuback's "pronging the old bitch."

"What am I going to do," I ask Cummings, "when Herm fires me?" Please tell me that he wouldn't dare. Or if it's sayonara to Savannah, please tell me about all the other teams who want me.

"I don't know," Cummings says. "You'll find something—excuse me, there's my other line. Let's have a beer after the game."

Real reassuring.

Practice isn't till two o'clock so I have time enough to grab a cab over to the gym and hoop again with the merry sawbones. Because I like to hide out in the locker room before and after ballgames, I never connected with them last night (assuming they showed).

And this time I'm prepared to play—the right shorts, a sleeveless jersey, so the shoulder action of my "jay" will be unencumbered, three pairs of socks to keep the sweat away from my feet. I also scrub my hands with a bar of Lava soap, a fixture in my dop bag, to keep my fingers sensitive.

But when I reach the gym the aerobics class has already been dismissed and the court is empty. I inquire at the desk, where a wiry, lacquered brunette tells me that the doctors often abort their game for medical emergencies, surgeries, conferences and such. Instead of communion, I sign out the only basketball and settle for a meditation.

Shooting alone, one-on-none, rebounding my misses. Rick Mount, a Purdue all-American who played in the defunct American Basketball Association and then briefly with the Lakers, had such an enlightened touch that he could shoot from anywhere on the court and adjust his rotation so that the ball always bounced back within his reach.

Jumpers, hooks, moving right, spinning left. Trying to extend my consciousness until the bright, shiny ball is part of me. Yes. It fits against my hand just so, my fingers filling the seams. Swish! Swish! Clunk!

Moving a step back, until I can retain an ethereal link with the ball even as it rolls through the air, its soaring arc a fulfillment of man's wish to fly. Swish.

Now there's a conjunction between my corporeal body and the mystic hoop itself. The ball is a flashing synapse between my outstretched fingers and the roundness of the world, of our path around the sun, of beginnings and endings, of the congress of all things.

Swish. Swish. I can't miss . . . until I do miss, remembering that missing shots is possible, inevitable.

Practice is at the Myriad and Dave Fishwick is on the court shooting free throws with a swooping, underhanded stroke. How appropriate.

He is stooped and sag-assed but his blue eyes are firm, even relentless. "Yes, sir," he says, his crooked yellow teeth gleaming under the harsh lights. "Thought I'd stop by and watch your practice." Every word is lubricated with saliva, and Fishwick pauses after each sentence to suck his teeth dry. "If that's okay with you," he adds casually.

Not a chance. Should we beat Oklahoma, we'll next play the Cosmos, who achieved the CBL's best regular season record, 40–16. Besides, we don't need any eyewitnesses when Earl and Sam resolve their differences.

Fishwick is steamed when I turn him down. He mumbles moistly about "professional courtesy" and "paranoia" before leaving under extreme duress.

Normally I enjoy conducting practice sessions during the playoffs. Facing the same team in a short series allows a coach to tinker with his offense and his defense, to get deeper into the workings of the game, to make sophisticated adjustments and subtle counteradjustments. Changing the angle on certain picks or cuts, adding an

option to a play, realigning a press, compressing his vision like a
master watchmaker. But, with Richie gone, with Earl and Sam
anxious to destroy each other, everything's fucked up.

Earl dutifully discloses that Larry Fort has indeed been suspended and has already undertaken the long drive home to Des
Moines, Iowa. Ferguson has decided to stick it out, afraid that
Kuback would poison any chance he might have for an invite into
an NBA free-agent camp. Hodges and his agent are still exploring
the offer from Spain.

"Don't work us too hard," Earl adds. "Sam's a year older but I've
got more mileage on my legs."

So we only run 6-and-2s, then we dummy our offense, rotating
everybody in, and we review both sides of every trap and press. We
have a desultory shooting contest for no prize money.

We've already wasted an hour, and like grade-schoolers just before
recess, their attention is shot. So I gather them around me at
centercourt and establish the rules: two-out-of-three games to
eleven straight, make-it-take-it, retrieving past the three-point line.
Sam and Earl are further instructed to call their own fouls, with
Cooper being empowered to approve or reject each call. Cooper
also holds the money—Sam's supporters have produced only
$650. "My agent fucked me," Sam explains. Earl covers the bet on
his own. It's hit or miss for first possession and Earl's twenty-footer
twirls around the ring before kicking out.

(What's that shadow flitting in the upper reaches of the balcony?
Fishwick?)

The confrontation is underway and the spectators cheer and yell
for their favorites, just like the ones who buy tickets. Steve Collins
is on hand attempting a play-by-play: "Earl pulls and shoots. He
misses . . ." Until the Beast tells him to "shut the fuck up."

Earl's tactic is to back Sam in as close to the basket as possible,
utilizing his two-inch and thirty-pound advantage. Once he's
there, Earl looks either way for a TAJ or jump hook. Sam wants to
jab-step and fake from the perimeter, looking to plunk his magic
twanger.

To call a questionable foul will brand the foulee as a pussy, so the game is increasingly physical. Earl uses his hands to try and knock Sam off-balance, while Sam bangs away at Earl's back with his forearms to keep the bigger man at bay. And every foul called is called in anger. "That's a foul, mothafucker," Sam shouts, and Cooper sustains the call. "Foul!" Earl says when his opponent hips him to the floor. "Don't be fucking with me, Sam."

Later, when Cooper overrules another claim by Sam, the ref is threatened: "Call it right or I'll break your teeth! Hey! How come we have a white ref? Where's the jury of my peers?"

Sam wins the first game, 11–7. Then Earl turns savage, bloodying Sam's lip en route to the hoop. "That's a charge!" Sam yells. But before Cooper can deliver his ruling the Beast says, "Where I come from only faggots call a charge. Basket counts. Play ball."

Earl's jumper heats up and he wins the second game, 11–10.

On the sidelines the players watch the final game in silence, awed by its passion, its brutality. Sam has humped up on defense . . . with no picks to circumvent, with his edge in quickness he forces Earl to rely more and more on his outside shooting.

Still, Earl leads 10–9 and the ball belongs to Sam, who shimmies and quickly spins to the baseline. Earl, caught off-balance, lunges as Sam releases his shot. Swish. And Earl yowls as the ring finger on his left hand catches in Sam's jersey.

"Pull it! Pull it!" Earl says as he runs toward me, his finger bent backward at the middle joint, quivering perpendicular to the back of his hand. "Rob! *Pull* it."

I grab the finger and yank hard but the digit is too slippery. I use my sweatshirt to get a firm grip, then pull again. This time there's a loud pop as the finger snaps into place. The pain drives Earl to his knees.

"Tie, game," I say. "It's a wash."

Sam protests and Earl agrees, saying, "Just give me a minute." Nate produces some tape from his bag, Earl administers to his wounded finger, the game resumes.

Needing only one score to win, Sam changes tactics, backing in on Earl, spinning left, daring Earl to block the shot with his throbbing hand. Swish.

Sam laughs, grabbing the money from Cooper. Then Sam and Earl hug each other. Afterward, Earl refuses to get the finger

X-rayed and on the ride back to the hotel the players are unusually quiet. Only Sam has something to say. "That's a tough white boy. You sure you ain't no octoroon or nothing?"

A free evening in a strange town means that most of the players are eager to visit a mall, perhaps see a movie. For two dollars each the hotel van will deposit Cooper, Kelly, the Beast, Brent, Earl, Nate and me at the Penn Square Mall. The others, Sam, Lem and Carl, are headed to a club on the other side of the tracks under the auspices of Sidney Hodges and Royce Ferguson. Josh is happy to sit in the hotel lobby fiddling with his Fega, a portable computer game designed to eat batteries and brain cells. Earl's injured finger is taped at the offending joint and he carries a thick zip-locked plastic bag loaded with ice. "Don't even ask," he says when we board the van. "You know I'm gonna play no matter what."

I am ideologically opposed to malls (but I've miscalculated and finished my book too soon). When I was a kid, we'd hang out in the park during the day, and at night we'd gather on somebody's stoop. We'd play punchball, stickball, boxball, stoopball, off-the-wall, off-the-curb, off-the-bench, off-the-stoop, single-doubletriple*HOME-RUN!* We talked, we bullied each other, we played poker for nickels or for comic books. A major event occurred twice each day when the Good Humor truck drove slowly down Fulton Avenue. Tinkle. Tinkle. "Hey, loan me a dime, I'll pay ya back." If you said "Haggies" before he said "No haggies," then he'd have to give you a bite of his ice cream.

But at these newfangled malls neon signs flash and blink, bells ring, buzzers sound, children cry and the fluorescent lighting gives me a headache. Total, unrelenting stimulation.

Brent disappears into the flickering darkness of the "Vidiot Arcade," to be retrieved later when the movie starts, a Japanese porno flick entitled *Nippon These*. Left to his own resources, Brent will easily spend his entire per diem simulating submarine warfare, big-game hunting, the Indy 500, spaceship invasions and games of laser basketball.

The players gravitate to record stores, clothiers and unaccompanied women while I search out a regular bookstore. There's one quick way to evaluate a bookstore—proceed to the beginning of the paperback fiction section, and if the first author is *not* Edward Abbey, then find another store.

Dalton's and Bookmasters are my only options, both of them initiating their collection of novels with Richard Adams! Fuck General Lee and the horse he rode in on . . . After much ado I am thrilled to find *The Succession* by George Garrett, his sequel to *Death of the Fox*, the most accomplished American novel since the heyday of Faulkner.

By prior agreement, we meet at the food court at 6:00. Coop, Earl and Kelly are munching Philadelphia cheese-steak sandwiches. The Beast treats himself to a bucket of chicken. Nate has pizza and I have a Greek salad from a gyro stand.

Everybody displays what they've purchased—Cooper has a cassette of Richard Burton reading *The Book of Revelations*. Kelly has the tape of a rap group, NWA, i.e., "Niggas With Attitudes." For the Beast, a T-shirt that reads, IT'S A BLACK THANG. Earl has a University of Oklahoma baseball cap. Nate has gotten a pair of black leather gloves.

"Gloves?" Earl prods. "It's seventy degrees outside."

"Man, it's cold in that arena," Nate says. "The Monad or whatever the fuck it's called. Besides, shooters have sensitive hands."

The movie starts at 7:10, Coop and I will pass. Like a sport, I stand for the cab ride back to the hotel. Cooper says his agent reports a delay in negotiations. "Looks like I'm staying here with you, Coach. Here, listen to this . . ."

> Here is wisdom. Let him that hath
> understanding count the number of
> the beast: for it is the number of
> a man; and his number is Six hundred
> threescore and six."

There's a message waiting for me—call Rod Chando, "an emergency."

Chando is an assistant coach with the Dallas Mavericks, only recently retired from a solid twelve-year career with Milwaukee-Boston-Portland-Phoenix-Dallas. A scoring guard, Rod was known as "Ro" because his D was silent.

I've met Chando at various CBL games and at the Chicago Pre-Draft camp, an annual shindig where select college seniors are evaluated three weeks prior to the NBA draft. CBL coaches are admitted to the premises (the fieldhouse at the U. of Ill.-Chicago) but are treated like stowaways. Ignored even by each other as we sniff about looking for an NBA assistant's job.

Chando's urgent message is that the Mavs want to sign Benny Morrison to a ten-day contract starting tomorrow. Herb Williams has a wrenched back and they need a "big body" to challenge second-year center Joe Stillwell in practice.

"Rod, you're in last place, about twenty games out of the playoffs. You have what? Ten games left? Why bother?"

Chando says the Mavericks are also attempting to "flesh out" a roster for their summer league team in Los Angeles. Morrison does have NBA experience, Dallas plans on drafting guards in June, and Stillwell's agent won't allow "his boy" to play in L.A. "Morrison has maybe an outside chance of making our veteran's camp in the fall," says Chando. "We see him primarily as a camper. Here's my number. Have him call me collect. We want to fly him out tonight so we can practice him tomorrow."

There's nothing I can say that won't sound self-serving, so I tell Chando that the Beast is at a movie. "I'll try to contact him there."

"Thanks."

Sure. Any time. Sure.

I have the Beast paged at the movie and he is overjoyed with the news. He'll be sure to come up to my room before he leaves.

The CBL bylaws state that a player must have dressed in eight regular season games for any one team in order to be eligible for that team's playoffs. Exceptions . . . any player cut from an NBA team is instantly eligible for the CBL playoffs, even if he has never previously played in the CBL. This is to avoid any restraint-of-trade litigation. Also, when a CBL player is called up to the NBA during the playoffs, he can be replaced by any warm body. If the player who went to the NBA returns to the CBL, both the new and the former player are eligible.

In addition:

Any player suspended for breach of contract (for drugs or going overseas) may be replaced by a player who was in the team's training camp and/or on the team's active roster at any point during the season.

Any player replacing an injured player during the playoffs must meet all playoff eligibility criteria. However, if a team's roster drops below eight (8) players due to injury during the playoffs, the commissioner may allow a team to replace one of the injured players, providing no other eligible players exist. However, the injured player is ineligible for the rest of the playoffs.

Whew. The CBL's trading deadline expired five weeks ago; therefore, I must find a free agent or else resurrect someone I've already cut who has remained unclaimed.

So I spend the rest of the evening consulting a CBL coach's most valuable possession—his telephone book. The biggest favor I ever did for T-Bone Donaldson was to Xerox my phone book and send the pages to him when he lost his own book last year. That means T-Bone still has access to my "secret" lists—semiretired players, recent NBA cuts and/or free agents now in Europe who might be sent home at any time. He also has the means of telephoning girlfriends, mothers, in-laws of players who are otherwise hard to locate. T-Bone now knows the agents I rely on for privileged information—who's going overseas, who's coming back, who's getting cut by which NBA teams.

Now, do I want another big man to replace the Beast? Or can Lem and Josh fill his slot? My other choice is to find a swingman who can score. Let's see who's out there.

First, I call Salvatore Giambalvo. An honest man, Giambalvo represents five NBA players, twelve in the CBL (from whom he collects no percentage), fifteen in Europe and one sitting home with a stress fracture. No help here.

I call John Dunn, a retired Division-I college coach who works out of Kansas City, Missouri. Does he have any spare bodies in the freezer? Well, Clifford Webster might be coming home from Belgium in two weeks. Dunn also offers a list of players who were previously waived by various CBA teams earlier in the season. No thanks.

I call eighteen more agents, including the notorious Richard Finger, who represents rehabbed junkies and thugs with outstanding debts (telephone bills, electric, car payments, tabs in restaurants and clothing stores), which must be assumed by any team foolish enough to sign them.

Nothing. Nobody anywhere any better than what I already have.

I rummage through my phone book from A to Z . . . Dennis Awtry is almost fifty, Ricky Brown is playing in Portugal, Reggie King is playing in France, Bobby Parks is in Brazil, Peter Thiebaux is in Japan, Norm White is coaching high-school ball in Nashville, Michael Young is in Italy, Danny Zahn is currently a social worker in Seattle. Nothing.

I call Herm with all the news. "That's great," he says. Really? How so? Just look at Morrison's numbers in the playoffs. Fifty-one percent from the field, thirty-two percent from the foul line, 12.7 ppg, 11.5 rebounds. "Hell's bells," says Herm. "Lem Jameson can easily do better than that."

"Why don't I take him over to Tulsa tomorrow? It's only a two-hour drive. Maybe Oral Roberts can personally heal him by game time." I'm such a card. Herm can't hardly wait to tell the Savannah media the "good news."

What's the use? I might as well go to sleep. There is no balm in the CBL.

The phone rings and John Smiley, the CBL's Assistant Commissioner, tells me that he is "perturbed." It seems that the CBL office in Chicago is routinely FAXed the relevant sports pages of every daily newspaper in every CBL city. And the Ass. Comm. wants to "verify the veracity" of a quote attributed to me in today's Oklahoma *Plain Dealer*. Did I say, "NBA contracts are why most of the players (in the CBL) even bother with this league"?

Guilty as charged.

Commissioner Rose feels that the phrase "even bother with this league" is damaging to the public image of the CBL. As such (see Section IV, eighth paragraph of my contract with the Stars), I am in jeopardy of incurring a fine and/or suspension at the Commissioner's discretion.

There have also been "disturbing" reports that I "beat up" a fan near the conclusion of last night's game. The game tape is being Fed-Exed to Chicago to see if there is any visual evidence.

To make matters worse, the CBL office has been informed that several of my players have been "betting on the outcome of ball-games." Money was seen "changing hands."

Fishwick.

Smiley listens without comment as I explain the true nature of the betting and the altercation with Piggly Wiggly. Smiley will advise the commissioner and get back to me tomorrow.

By now it's nearly 2:00 A.M. in Savannah, but I call Herm with a synopsis of Smiley's accusations. Herm is also noncommital and promises to "plead" my case to Rose.

There's one more call, from Earl, recently returned from the movie. "Good for the Beast," he says. "He deserves another shot. Now you'll need a whip and a chair to control Sam and his gang. Who are you bringing in?"

Nobody.

"Lem and Josh put together can't replace the Beast," says Earl. "You're gonna have to go with Cooper. Jeez. The fucking Beast. I'm not sure we can win without him."

17

Dreaming of death. An eternal sequence of Nautilus machines surrounded by a track of hot, glowing coals.

Where am I?

I must be on death row, waking up too early on the last day of my life.

The sunlight has turned gray as it seeps through the window. The mirror opposite my bed reflecting the rough gray texture of the ceiling. My soiled sweats piled on the dresser, my lifeless sneakers crossed on the floor.

Will it be death by hanging? By gas? By injection? By zapper? No. I long to die the way that Pete Maravich did. A sudden heart attack in the middle of a game, in mid-shot. "He shoots . . ." Gasp. Thud. And after the final buzzer, swish.

No, no. I'm just tired. I wake up tired. Worn out. I can't even bear the thought of tonight's game. The game. The game.

Why, then, am I up so early? I can't remember. Oh, yes. The other game. The reality game. Really? Would the doctors revive me? Ah, but all three of them are probably in surgery right now, ventricular and anal bypasses.

It's easier to close my eyes and sleep.

The shootaround. Sam's lip is swollen and he's cranky as an infant with shit in his diaper. When I name Cooper to replace the

Beast, Lem's perpetual sulk turns into an active glower. Cooper balls his fists and says, "Yesss!" Carl is hungover again, wading in imaginary floodwaters. I can read Earl's silent pain in the darkness beneath his eyes.

We're down to nine players again, so I must dummy through our offense along with the nonstarters—Carl, Brent, Josh and Lem. Brent hasn't spoken to me since the flight out of Atlanta. He feels I've betrayed him by reinstating Sam.

I assume the small forward's spot by default and whenever my assignment requires a pass to Lem, I purposely throw it hard to his left hand. "Don't baby it," I tell him. "Either you can do it or you can't."

Finally, instead of reaching across his body with his right hand, Lem cringes in anticipation and stabs at the ball with his left. The ball bounces loose but he smiles with self-awareness like he's suddenly snapped out of a ten-year coma. The next pass he catches left-handed. Then he tries a soft lefty hook.

"It's a little weak," he admits. "And it's stiff. But I think I can deal with it."

"Hallelujah," I shout. Cooper hears me at the other end and looks up just as a pass hits him in the head.

Lem says that he wants to start tonight, that he "deserves to start," but I wave him off. I'm getting good at that.

The flex will lose effectiveness without the Beast's ornery picks. The defense can now top the cuts, shoot the gaps and swarm the paint with impunity. So, when we must set-up we'll emphasize the box-set tonight and use double picks. But we have absolutely no post-up game. And what will we do for rebounds? Send five to the boards, that means you too, Sam.

On his part, Kuback has to pound the ball inside to Hodge and Kramer. I'll bet he's kicking himself for banishing Fort. So we revive our "black" trap, doubling the post from the baseline. Exactly the way the Chicago Bulls defensed the L.A. Lakers in the 1991 NBA championship series. It's also a variation of what we originally intended doing against Oz Joseph. The weakside rotation is vital and I try to demonstrate the nuances.

What else can Kuback be planning? With Cooper at the center spot (he can easily anticipate this), we now have another runner and passer on the court, so Kuback has to abandon his press and play half-court basketball. It's our turn to accelerate the pace.

Despite the appealing run-and-gun proposal, the players show little enthusiasm. Good. They're saving everything for tonight.

"Thank you Lord for . . ."

I get some takeout chicken from Fat Albert's and retreat to my room, then review the last two game tapes, looking for a clue. He's had one whole day of practice, what new plot will he throw at us?

Smiley calls to say that the commissioner doesn't want to "distract" me from concentrating on tonight's game. The tape of game four is inconclusive and further "fact-finding" is already underway. The commissioner himself will call me "win or lose" when I return to Savannah. "Good luck," Smiley says in his official capacity as spokeman for the wonderful wizard.

I read and try to sleep. In the CBL, home teams win 68.7% of the time. It seems to me that, whatever the sport, teams should play better on the road than they do. In a hotel, a player can control his environment better than at home. The switchboard can hold his calls and he can nap without interruption. With two to a room, there's also more basketball talk on the road, more immediate support. And teams travel like wolf packs, banding together in hostile circumstances. Okay, a new bed takes getting used to and the available food (BBQ) may be limited. But the sense of community is much more intense away from home. The real difference is the refs, everyone's a homer at heart.

So it's later for Kuback and his mysterious stratagems. The real question is, will the homer refs allow us to win tonight?

The players are somber as the van conveys us to the Myriad, and I figure their silence is a good omen. While they dress, and before I do my blackboard work, I inspect the field of battle. The floor is somewhat dusty and the rims remain tight. But there are new nets hanging from the rims, longer and tighter than before, to slow the transition from defense to offense. Yes, Kuback will grind it out tonight.

Elementary, dear Kuback.

In the locker room, our meeting is delayed while Sam lingers in one of the bathroom stalls. When he joins us without flushing the toilet, Earl and I trade suspicious glances.

I rehash the scouting report and inform them of Kuback's probable game plan. I tell them about the nets. "We want to run on every possible possession," I say. "When they score we have to reach up and pull the ball out of the net, then giddyap. Don't wait to pick the ball off the floor. And we must rebound our asses off!"

Finally it's time for inspiration: "We're all of us very lucky to be able to participate in a game like this. The ultimate pressure game. NBA, NCAA, CBL. It doesn't matter. It's the game at hand. An opportunity for each one of us to prove our true worth. No excuses. No second chances. It's been a long, gruelling season and we've come too far to fuck up now. It's a voyage of self-discovery, fellas. Let's give it all we have and do it together."

"DO IT!"

As before, when Sam is introduced, he runs over to challenge the Rangers. "Fuck you!" is all he can come up with. Once the game is underway, Sam reasserts himself as the dominant force. But Kuback's grind-it-out pace limits the number of times that Sam touches the ball.

The refs are John Hoyt and Pete Cantine, both capable NBA vets, who surprise me by letting both teams play.

Our defense is sincere, our rotation adequate, but the Rangers are beating us to death on both boards.

STARS–19   OKL–23

It's no surprise when Kuback unveils a new offensive series:

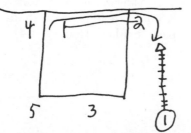

- FIRST OPTION—Ferguson (#2) backpicks for Hodges (#4), a maneuver that enables the big man to grab prime post-up position against Nate.

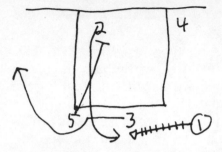

- SECOND OPTION—Kramer (#3) fans to the far corner, available for a skip pass and a quick shot—then Lederman (#5) picks down for Ferguson (#2)—this is the shot they want.

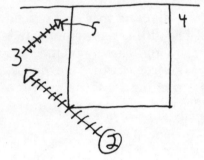

- THIRD OPTION—Ferguson (#2) passes to Kramer (#3), who passes to Lederman (#5) in the post.

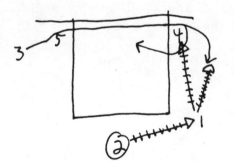

- FOURTH OPTION—Ferguson (#2) returns to McDonald (#1) —Kramer (#3) gets two staggered picks, then pops or curls —McDonald (#1) passes to Kramer (#3) or to Hodges (#4)

—if McDonald (#1) passes to Kramer (#3) he can shoot or pass inside to Hodges (#4).

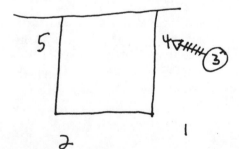

When Hayes replaces Kramer, the Rangers have two jump shooters coming hard off picks. How the hell does Kuback get his players to execute new offenses so well with such limited practice time?

STARS–27   OKL–30

Earl is out of sync and having difficulty keeping Kramer off the boards. We run 40L three times, allowing Earl to isolate his slower, bigger opponent, but Earl misses two layups and an uncontested jumper.

Nate is shooting selectively and well. Cooper is a dynamo, our only effective rebounder. We steal a few easy shots by pushing the ball. But without control of the boards we really can't crank up our running game.

STARS–36   OKL–42

Sam carries us, hitting three stop-and-go jumpers under heavy pressure from Ferguson. Josh gives us nothing off the bench but Lem is active around the basket.

STARS 42   OKL–47

As Sam lofts a step-back jumper along the baseline, Ferguson tips his elbow and the ball falls short. "Airball!" shouts Piggly Wiggly. When no foul is forthcoming, Sam screams in Hoyt's face, "You fucking homer," and gets T-eed. Earl must physically restrain Sam to keep him in the game.

Carl comes off the bench to shut down McDonald, forcing Kuback to play Collins more than he wants do.

Every substitution, every call, every matchup could swing the ballgame. When Palmer replaces Lederman, we run 44 and 55B to post Lem, who responds by netting short jumpers.

Running past the bench, Earl pulls at the front of his shirt, the universal signal that he needs a blow. It's the first time all year that Earl has asked out of a game. On a whim I send Cooper in to guard Kramer, and the Rangers forward doesn't touch the ball. Eureka.

We trail at the half by 56–51.

The Xs and Os dance on the blackboard, sending chalk dust all over Cooper's clothing. The Rangers know our plays and (except for their new series) we know theirs. During the regular season, teams can normally find good shots on the first or second options of whatever plays they run. In the playoffs, with the increased familiarity, teams are forced to their third or fourth options to produce the shots they need. Since all the players know each other's routes, the games are more and more physical as a series advances.

We want to force the Rangers to exercise the third and fourth options of their new offense, the theory being that after only one practice (could Kuback have run them twice yesterday?) their continuity will disintegrate if their primary options are denied.

"This is what we'll do . . . Sam, you have to step out and bang Hodges as he crosses the lane, then shoot the gap past Lederman's pick to deny Ferguson. Kelly, you've got to pressure the ball up top. Cooper, bump Lederman's down-pick. Earl, top the baseline picks."

Then I give them time to pee, guzzle cola, whatever. As we huddle-up, Sam is once more delayed in the bathroom and he joins us again without flushing. Earl looks at me and rubs his thumb and forefinger against his nostrils.

"DO IT!"

Our defense works like a clock, forcing Kramer, a mediocre shooter, to take too many shots, and we finally catch them early in the third quarter when Nate has a run. But Cooper gets into his usual foul difficulties and fades quickly. It's Lem, do or die.

STARS–65   OKL–64

As the game rushes on, I am unable to sit on the bench. Piggly Wiggly has been quiet, yet insulting: "Y'all's a loser, Coach. Your kind never wins." But I leave him behind, pacing the sidelines, crouching at the restraining line, kneeling on a towel.

I WANT TO PLAY! Coaching isn't enough at a time like this.

We trap Ferguson directly in front of our bench, Kelly and Sam pinning him against the sideline, waving their arms. So I edge right up to the sideline, barely out of bounds, and likewise wave my hands trying to confuse him. Flustered, Ferguson makes a bad pass that Earl runs down.

STARS–76   OKL–74

Brent throws a bag over Ferguson early in the fourth quarter and I am reluctant to reinsert Sam. Lem rebounds like a madman.

For the Rangers, Hodge is increasingly tentative. The latest word is that he's going to Spain mañana and an injury could cost him forty Gs.

STARS–82   OKL–77

I give Earl a short respite on the bench, and Cooper cages Kramer again. During a twenty-second timeout Sam hawks up a lunger and deposits it on the court. "What the *fuck* are you doing?" I ask. "Do you spit in your living room? Do you spit in church? If you gotta spit, spit down the front of your damned shirt."

STARS–92   OKL–87

Slowly, inevitably, the Rangers begin to lose heart. When it's aces up, they don't want to play for Kuback, to bleed for Kuback. They'd rather go home defeated than endure another series under his obnoxious leadership.

Our lead is merely 99–95 with 1:47 remaining when Hodges pauses at our bench during a dead ball to wish me "good luck against the Cosmos."

Just before the final buzzer bleats, Piggly Wiggly extends his hand, palms up and showing no weapons. "Congratulations," he says. "Y'all did a great job, Coach."

Earl cashes two treys and my Stars emerge triumphant, 108–101.

In the locker room, the mood is restrained yet festive. Only Sam remains hyper, and in the absence of champagne, he begins dousing everybody with Coke. It's funny, until Sam in his exuberance spills some soda on Lem's fancy civilian clothes. "Hey, mothafucker," Lem says.

There's more handshaking than hugging, more workmanlike satisfaction. We finished three games ahead of the Rangers, and although they came on strong late in the season, all we've done so far is beat a team we were theoretically *supposed* to beat.

But, oh yes. I am happy. Nearly ecstatic. Possibly vindicated. Even so, as soon as I heard the final buzzer I began to fret about the Cosmos. Our next game is Sunday afternoon in Savannah.

Kuback enters the room, still wearing his favorite smug grin. "Congratulations," he says and we shake hands. "Good job, kid. You did your homework. But I still believe we would have won in four games if Joseph hadn't of gone up. I know that's easy to say and impossible to prove. But it's the only thing that's gonna keep me afloat until the pain goes away. Here, maybe this will help you against Capital City. Beat those bastards, will you? Everybody hates that organization."

He hands me the tape of tonight's game plus a large, bulging manila envelope. I tell him what a superlative coach, husband, father, citizen and all-around human he is, and we shake hands again.

Mack Cummings pokes his head in the door. Good luck, etc. He can't make it tonight, but his opinion is that Herm can't fire me now.

A reporter sticks his face into my chest. What would have been different if Joseph had stayed with the Rangers? "That's a stupid question," I snap, and he moves away.

Even Fishwick appears to offer his congrats and to exchange tapes as per our previous agreement. Feeling magnanimous, ready to forgive, I ask him why he holds a grudge against me. Why is he out to get me? What did I ever do to him? "What're you talking about?" he says, and leaves in a mild huff. Well, fuck him. He can't hurt me anymore.

Right?

Cooper, Earl, Nate and I ride back to the hotel in the van, all of us somewhat subdued, knowing that the Cosmos are expected to sweep us. Otherwise, the rookie is oblivious. But the experienced players, the coach, also know that the joy is in the game, in the

COMMERCIAL BASKETBALL LEAGUE

Official Scorer's Report

Date: **March 22, 1992**   Game #: **05**   Arena: **Myriad**   Attendance: **5413**

Visitors: **Savannah Stars**   Home: **Ok. City Rangers**   Length of Game: **1:56**

No	Visitors Stars	Min	Field Goals M	Field Goals A	Free Throws M	Free Throws A	3 Pt Field Goals M	3 Pt Field Goals A	Pts	Rebounds O	Rebounds D	Rebounds TOT	AST	PF	TO	BS	ST
6	Royal (G)	35	3	8	3	4	0	0	9	0	1	1	5	2	1	0	3
7	Franks (G)	37	11	18	6	7	2	3	30	0	2	2	1	2	3	0	1
8	Butler	13	2	5	0	0	0	0	4	1	0	1	1	1	0	0	2
10	Cooper (c)	34	5	11	2	3	0	0	12	2	9	11	0	5	1	1	0
11	Brusher	18	1	6	0	1	0	0	2	0	1	1	0	2	2	1	0
12	Kennison (F)	34	7	14	4	4	0	0	18	1	4	5	1	2	2	0	0
24	Jameson	23	6	13	2	2	0	0	14	1	6	7	3	4	2	0	1
32	Patton (F)	36	6	15	3	6	2	2	17	1	2	3	4	4	5	0	2
40	Springs	11	1	4	0	0	0	0	2	0	1	1	1	0	1	1	1
	TOTALS	240	42	94	20	26	4	5	108	6	26	32	16	22	17	3	10
	Pct		44.2		76.9		80.0			Team	3				1		

No	Home Rangers	Min	Field Goals M	Field Goals A	Free Throws M	Free Throws A	3 Pt Field Goals M	3 Pt Field Goals A	Pts	Rebounds O	Rebounds D	Rebounds TOT	AST	PF	TO	BS	ST
2	McDonald (G)	34	2	6	4	4	0	0	8	0	1	1	7	2	4	1	2
4	Collins	14	1	4	0	1	0	1	2	1	2	3	2	2	3	0	1
10	Hayes	14	3	5	1	3	1	1	8	0	2	2	0	1	2	0	0
12	Kramer (F)	40	9	21	3	3	0	0	21	5	10	15	0	3	5	2	0
14	Ferguson (G)	48	10	19	6	8	2	5	28	2	5	7	2	4	4	0	1
15	Palmer	8	0	1	0	0	0	1	0	0	1	1	2	2	0	0	0
21	Hodges (F)	48	12	25	2	2	0	0	26	4	12	16	0	4	3	2	2
23	Lederman (c)	34	4	8	0	2	0	0	8	2	7	9	2	2	4	1	1
	TOTALS	240	41	89	16	24	3	8	101	14	40	54	15	20	25	6	7
	Pct		46.1		66.7		37.5			Team	5				3		

Score By Quarters	1	2	3	4	OT	OT	OT	Final
V Stars	23	28	25	32				108
H Rangers	27	29	18	27				101

Officials: **John Hoyt, Pete Cantine**

Technicals: **Sav. 7 Franks (Ump.) 1:47 2nd Q**

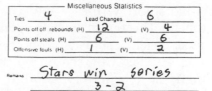

Miscellaneous Statistics

Ties: **4**   Lead Changes: **6**

Points off rebounds (H): **12**   (V): **4**

Points off steals (H): **6**   (V): **6**

Offensive fouls (H): **1**   (V): **2**

Remarks: **Stars win series 3-2**

169

competing. After the buzzer, win or lose, there is always a letdown. We can totally celebrate only one victory, the game that clinches the championship.

Cooper is early to bed. The rest of us will meet in the hotel bar in fifteen minutes. I call Herm and get his answering machine—he and his wife singing a rousing chorus of "Dixie," then BEEP. But I leave no message for him. Chet's machine has also seized control of his phone—"Hello? Who are you and what do you want?" BEEP.

Nate drinks Long Island Iced Tea, Earl has vodka with grapefruit juice and I drink too much beer. Thirty minutes later the three of us are well greased and exchanging CBL war stories.

"Remember Darryl Stevens?" Nate says. "He was the coach when I played for the Fort Worth Scouts. He was this fat dude, a black guy, who always had something cooking. Whenever he'd answer the phone, he'd disguise his voice until he knew who was calling, because somebody dangerous was always hunting him down. Anyhow, Darryl, he was married to this real nice lady, a school teacher or something. And whenever we'd go on the road, Darryl would pack his bags and his wife would drive him to the airport. 'Goodbye, sweetie,' and all that. Soon as she left, he'd take a cab back to town and shack up with some bitch. Al Smith used to be player-coach on the road, remember him? The three-point special- ist? He'd average about ten points at home and over twenty on the road, 'cause he'd always call his own number. Then Darryl would meet us at the airport when we got back and his suitcase would be full of dirty clothes. 'Hi, sweetie. I missed you.' He did it for two seasons and she never caught on."

Where is he now? He's dead of a heart attack, fell face-first into a plate of spaghetti three years ago.

"I've got a coach story," I say. "Newt Johnson? Coached the Williamsport Willies a few years back? Well, Newt had a drug problem. He couldn't coach a game until he smoked a joint. He was a great coach, a screecher, and he'd get a technical just about every game. His last CBL season he was fired and rehired three times. Finally he gets fired for good. It was in the playoffs with his team leading two-to-one in a best of five. The owner just couldn't ignore all the rumors. But Newt can't get another job and he's freaking out.

So Mack Cummings calls him and says, 'Newt, everybody in the CBL is afraid to hire you because you're supposed to be a pothead.' Right? So Cummings sets up a drug test in a hospital in New York, where Newt was living. And this drug test is gonna clear his name once and for all and make him employable again. I mean, Cummings really goes out of his way to hook him up. So Newt goes and takes the test and Cummings calls him a few days later with the results. Which show the highest level of cannabis that medical science has ever seen. What the fuck, Newt? 'I couldn't help it.' Newt says. 'I got so nervous in the cab ride over to the hospital that I had to smoke a joint!' "

Last I heard, Newt is coaching the national team in Libya, making $125,000 tax-free . . . I buy the next round while Earl conjures up another chapter of the coaches' follies. What tales do they tell about me?

"The coach's name was Ryne Erickson," says Earl, "and the team was the old Camden Aces. He was an old guy, another yeller and screamer. I forgot who we were playing but I was on the bench when a call goes the other way. Up jumps Erickson to yell at the ref, when splat, his fucking false teeth fall out of his mouth and land on the court. He snatches them up on the second bounce and shoves them back into his mouth. Then he turns to us and says, 'If any of you fuckers laugh, I'll fine you fifty dollars.' I mean, we were fucking rolling on the floor. Guys were stuffing towels into their mouths. Pulling their shirts up over their heads. One guy just got up and ran into the locker room. For the rest of the season, every time anybody laughed in front of him, he wanted to fine the guy."

Where is he now? Nobody knows.

We laugh and bullshit until nearly 2:00 A.M. The van departs for the airport in about three hours and Earl and Nate plan to stay awake till then. But I must grab whatever sleep I can. Tomorrow's a long day of traveling and then watching game tapes.

There are no messages awaiting me back in my room. Thanks Herm. Chet. Happy playoffs to you too. And just before switching off the light, I take notice of the envelope Kuback gave me.

It's twenty pages long. Kuback's scouting report on the mighty Capital City Cosmos.

18

WHILE STEVE SEES to the tickets and the baggage, the players scatter throughout the airport looking for vacant horizontal spaces large enough to accommodate them. But the civilian travelers are too numerous this Friday morning, leaving no long rows of empty seats, so most of the players simply flop on the floor.

Brent, in tie and jacket, sits erect, wedged between two hefty matrons and reading the local sports section. Cooper is also too dignified to sleep on the floor like a derelict. He's found a seat beside a nun and he encourages her to listen to his Richard Burton tape. Lem and Earl have discovered single seats near the departure gate, both of them suffering too much to sleep in public.

"It hurts like a mothafucker," Lem moans, holding a plastic bag of ice against his aching wrist. "Maybe you were right all along. I'll go see the doctor when we get back."

Earl is seated nearby, a smaller bag of ice smothering his finger. "I spoke to Sam," he tells me. "He swears he's straight as an arrow but he's fucking lying. I asked him about the toilet not flushing and he says that he's constipated."

On the flight to Atlanta I pore over Kuback's scouting report, an impressive document:

OKLAHOMA RANGERS OPPONENT SCOUTING REPORT
AND GAME PLAN FOR *Capital City Cosmos*

GENERAL TENDENCIES:

Offense:

	Yes	No
Fast Break	X	
Half Court	X	
Post-up		X
Perimeter	X	
Penetrating	X	

Basic Philosophy: Run passing game, isolations and pick and roll. Spread floor to create driving and passing lanes. Push ball quickly. Good medium- and long-range shooters. Unselfish. Will make the extra pass. Excellent scorers. Superior offensive execution.

Defense:

	Yes	No
Overplay Aggressively	X	
Pressing ½ Court (Man)	X	
Trapping ½ Court (Zone)		X
Pressing Full Court (M)	X	
Trapping Full Court (Z)		X

Basic Philosophy: Will switch most picks. Will deny wings. Very physical, bump all cutters through the middle. Pressure ball in backcourt. Box out but not good rebounders. Will double post from foul line. Will double wing from top like we do. Their man-to-man traps are loose, just looking to clean up on any careless passes. *They enjoy playing defense.*

PERSONNEL

Player: Thomas James   Ht: 6'1"   Pos: #1
Push baseline and jump him. Set shooter with 3-pt range. Pressure hard—left hand is ?? Not great passer under pressure. Works hard on D.

Player: Shawnell Wagman   Ht: 6'5"   Pos: #2
Great shooter. When he dribbles left on right side of court he will *always* spin back right for shot. Crowd, deny and push left. Poor handle. Can't guard a telephone pole.

Player: Brian Hollander   Ht: 6'6"   Pos. #2 & #3

Push *right* and jump him. Great crossover dribble right to left. 16' range. Shooting well. BOX. On left box will turn baseline for shot. Runs out on defense.

Player: Charles Henderson   Ht: 7'0"   Pos. #5

Always push him left. Wants to turn right for shot. BOX. Poor lateral movement on D. Excellent passer. 15' range.

Player: Kennedy Andrews   Ht: 6'7"   Pos. #3 playing #4

BOX. 17' range. Shooting well. On right box dribbles *left* to middle, fakes then pulls up. Push *right*, stay on floor. Deny. Not working as hard on D as he used to.

Player: Mitchell Miller   Ht: 6'7"   Pos. #4 & #5

Set shooter with 20' range. Push baseline. When dribbles left will come back with right hand. Physical. BOX.

Player: Kevin Smith   Ht: 6'1"   Pos. #1 & #2

Push left and pressure. Jump his dribble. No shooter. When he's in game, leave him to double others.

Player: Wayne Toggins   Ht: 6'3"   Pos. #2 & #3

Most dangerous offensive threat. Always wants to go baseline. Push to middle and jump him. Be *physical* with him. Can't pass going left. Will pass out of trap if he hasn't dribbled. Once he puts ball on floor he will rarely pass. Great in open field. Erratic shooter. We want him to go left and pull up. Works hard on D. Can be posted. BOX. Be careful when you change on him—he'll reach over and snatch lazy dribble.

Player: Jason Jerome   Ht: 6'11"   Pos. #5

Thin and weak. Active near basket. Shooter and shot blocker. Only plays in blow-outs.

Player: Eric Mann   Ht: 6'5"   Pos. #2 & #3

Defensive specialist with no offensive skills. Used sparingly as stopper. Denies ball well. Physical. BOX. Double off him on offense.

SUMMARY

Strengths: A veteran team. All but the rookies (Jerome and Mann) have NBA experience. Make few mistakes. Potent scorers. Very well-coached.

Weaknesses: James's handle is major weakness. No big man behind Henderson. Have no shot blockers. Team speed is slightly below average. Do not rebound well. Maybe too cocky.

Keys to Winning: Shoot a good %. Need good ball movement. Reverse ball to weak side. Cut down on turnovers. Make them play

half-court game. Be aggressive defensively. Make their scorers
play defense. REBOUND.

Game Plan: Get ball inside to Hodges and Fort. Pressure James all
over court. Open middle for Joseph to penetrate and dish to
Ferguson. Post Fort early to get Henderson in foul trouble. Trap
wings. Keep ball in #1's hands.

PLAYS AND SETS:

Passing Game I

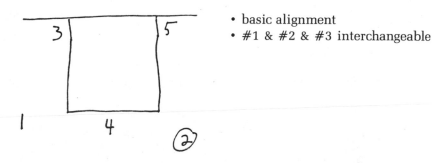

- basic alignment
- #1 & #2 & #3 interchangeable

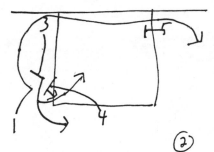

- #3 pops or curls
- sometimes #4 pops—can also
  dive
- if #1 catches, #5 posts

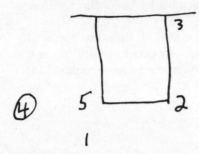

- basic alignment
- #1 & #2 interchangeable

- will look to post #1 against smaller defenders
- if #1 posts, #5 stays high
- if #2 denied he goes backdoor
- #2 passes to #3 to initiate next sequence

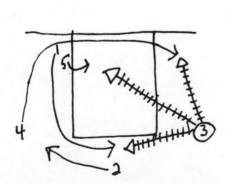

- #3 shoots or penetrates
- #4 posts
- #5 steps in
- #1 pops for shot—#2 fans
- #1 has open middle—can penetrate
- #1 passes to #2 for shot—or #2 passes to #5 in post

Pick and Roll

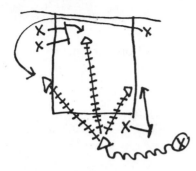

- use any combo of pickers and rollers
- good action on weak side
- bottom man on double-pick steps in

Isos

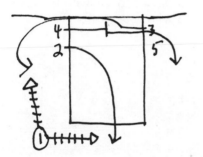

- #2 & #3 interchangeable
- will use this play most in end-game
- #2 or #3 catches and goes

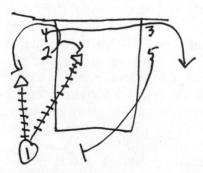

- #2 & #3 interchangeable
- #5 offers pick & roll if #2 denied

Under-out-of-Bounds

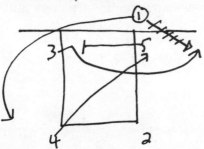

- #2 & #3 interchangeable
- iso for #3
- next option—#4 posts

Side-out-of-Bounds

- looking for defensive switch, they post #4
- #2 passes to #1 who passes to #3 who goes

And how do the Cosmos get all these wondrous players? By astute trading—exchanging draft choices and spare players for blue-chippers whom everybody else believes are in Europe for good (Fishwick's telephone book is twice as thick as mine). By enticing free agents with sizable amounts of cash ($250–$500 weekly) paid tax-free, under the table and never debited against the Cosmos salary cap. And by the arts and chicanery of their coach, Barry Millhouse.

The only CBL coach taller than me, the 6'10" Millhouse matriculated at Metropolitan University and went on to play for seven productive years in the NBA with Cleveland, New Jersey, and earning a championship ring with the Atlanta Hawks. Metro U.'s legendary coach, Carl O'Reilly, was always willing to make persuasive phone calls to secure sundry coaching jobs for Millhouse, starting with an assistantship at Southwest Florida State.

Millhouse was a recruiting specialist at SWFS, a well-groomed, articulate black man welcomed into the ghetto, a flimflammer who talked in terms of "them and us," of "whitey" and of "black pride." As part of his recruiting paraphernalia, Millhouse routinely carried a suitcase full of unmarked twenty-dollar bills. He was the laughing stock of the Division I bagmen several years back when one of his potential recruits swore allegience to SWFS, accepted Millhouse's $10,000, then enrolled at archrival Florida Baptist College. Millhouse has been a successful CBL coach for five years, winning a championship for Capital City in 1989.

Then, as now, Millhouse has maintained a reputation as an insatiable womanizer. His come-on is famous from Capital City to Gainesville, from Waco to Winnebago—"Hi, honey. I'm Barry Millhouse and I can go all night long." Then there's the time when Millhouse and one of his players had a bloody fight (the player won) in the lobby of a hotel in Manchester, New Hampshire, over the fucking rights to a young lady who turned out to be a hooker with the pox. In his time Millhouse has propositioned players' wives, female sportswriters, waitresses, nurses, quite literally hundreds of stewardesses, also the wives and daughters of owners, casual fans and season-ticket holders (both at home and on the road). The fact that Millhouse has a wife and six kids living in San Francisco doesn't seem to cramp his appetite, or style.

Millhouse is a shameless hypocrite who will do anything to win a ballgame. He has at least two faces and so many sides that Fishwick will be hard pressed to stab him in the back.

Every year for the last three seasons Millhouse has made a public announcement that he has been "born again in Christ." When seen with a floozy, he invariably claims to be giving her "Christian instruction." And the last time the Cosmos visited Savannah, Millhouse was interviewed by Joe Patterson and the following quote appeared in the *Gazette*: "God," said Millhouse, "will not let me make a bad trade."

> *"Adhuc sub iudice lis est."*
> —Horace, *Ars Poetica*, 78

In Atlanta, I search the American Airlines terminal for Carl Butler, hoping to have a heart-to-heart. Carl was a high-school all-American who had the profound misfortune to sit behind a future NBA lottery pick at Fresno State. Why, then, did Carl go to Fresno

State? "I thought I could beat him out," he's said more than once. "I still think I'm better than him."

Two years ago Carl was plucked in the fourth round of the CBL college draft by the Santa Cruz Californians, where, as a rookie, he backed up David Rivers, one-time point guard for the L.A. Lakers.

Ah, yes. The CBL college draft. Mostly much ado about not much.

The CBL's draft consists of nine rounds and is conducted by conference call sometime in mid-August. CBL teams retain the rights to drafted players for one calendar year. Since no CBL franchise has the budget to scout players during the collegiate season, most teams send their coaches to the Chicago Pre-Draft camp and/ or to the other preview camps annually assembled by the NBA in Portsmouth, Virginia, and Orlando, Florida. That covers the most elite college seniors. For rounds three through nine, however, we're at the mercy of whatever scraps of information we can grub from cooperative NBA scouts and assistant coaches. Additionally, there are several dubious rating systems published at exhorbitant prices by otherwise unemployed experts.

Those players drafted in the CBL's first or second rounds are prime candidates for spots in the NBA or overseas. There were thirty-two such players selected last summer and only five started and ended the season in the CBL. I'd rather have a ninth-round pick who reports to training camp than a first-rounder who goes to Europe.

For the Stars, Cooper was a sixth-rounder, Nate was a third-round pick of Waco's in 1983 and Kelly was chosen in the fifth round by Twin-Cities in 1988. Lem, Sam, Josh and Earl are one-time NBA draftees. During the '91–'92 regular season, a total of 337 players wore CBL uniforms, but only seventy-three of them are survivors of last year's or any other CBL draft.

That's why the CBL draft is such a crapshoot. That's why, two seasons back, I traded Peoria's #6 pick to Kuback for a Ranger sweatsuit (the one I finally received was too small). That's why every year my aim is to trade all nine of my team's draft picks by draft day.

So where do we get our players? The best ones are the NBA cuts, assigned to CBL teams through an affiliation system. In Savannah, for example, we are entitled to the Atlanta Hawks training-camp and varsity rejects. That's where Earl came from, cut by Atlanta on

the third day of their training camp last October. CBL lifers like
Nate, Lem and Sam get traded and retraded through the years. In
fact, five years ago Lem played for the Madison Marauders and
their rookie coach, Barry Millhouse. Rarely do players (like Brent)
graduate from a CBL free-agent camp. Otherwise, CBL players can
be draftees whose rights have lapsed after lengthy sojourns overseas. Or else European dropouts who managed to elude both the
CBL and the NBA drafts.

Savannah obtained Carl Butler in a special dispersal draft late
last summer after Santa Cruz's letter of credit proved to be fraudu-
lent and the CBL declared the franchise null and void. Going head-
to-head with Kelly in the Stars training camp (limited to fourteen
days' duration by the CBL bylaws), Carl Butler came out second
best and he's been bitching ever since. Carl has no understanding
that he's destined to be a perpetual backup.

I catch up with him in the vicinity of the departure gate, where
he sits on the floor, leaning against a wall, just about to nod off.
"Carl," I say cheerfully enough, "what's going on?"

"Just chillin'," he says. His skin is dull, his hair is tangled in
knots. He's twenty-five years old and his eyes have the vacant cast
of oncoming senility.

"Are you taking care of yourself? Getting enough sleep?"

"Sure."

"Hey, man. What's the real deal? You look like shit. Are you
drunk? Are you stoned? There's like this black cloud always hanging over your head."

"I want to play more," he says, his eyes suddenly gleaming. "Of
course, I'm fucking drunk. It's the only way I know how to handle
my frustration. So either play me or leave me the fuck alone. And,
Coach, even black clouds are beautiful."

Then he closes his eyes, flips some internal switch and instantly
falls asleep.

As always, Magoo meets us at the Savannah airport, smiling, a
beacon of genuine good will. He has an encouraging word, a personal salute for each one of us. Great job! Good work! Way to go!

After he pumps my hand so hard I need to pee, he advises me
that we are scheduled for a practice tonight, six o'clock at Savannah State. "After the practice," he adds, "Herm wants you and the
guys to stay there and conduct a clinic for about fifty kids. It's

Herm's doing," Magoo apologizes. "I didn't find out myself until this morning. The kids all belong to Herm's buddies."

Sam's got a split lip, Lem's wrist is sore and Earl's nursing a broken finger. No way. We need a respite, from basketball and from each other.

"You'd better call Herm," Magoo says darkly.

But when I return to my cave, my first call is to Chet. "Great game, Coach," he says.

"Yeah, sure. Now, tell me. What's going on around here?"

Turns out that Chet and Herm went to the Hoot 'n' Holler Sports Bar last night to "pussy-hunt" and ostensibly watch a Bulls–Pistons game on the big-screen TV. "It was Herm's idea," says Chet. "Without Morrison he thought y'all'd get murdered and he couldn't bear the pain and embarrassment of listening to the game."

In addition to today's unexpected practice-cum-clinic, I've been newly scheduled to speak at a "Lunch with the Coach" tomorrow at noon at the aforementioned H 'n' H Sports Bar.

And here's the schedule for the Cosmos series:

Sunday	1:30	@ Savannah
Monday	7:05	@ Savannah
Wednesday	7:05	@ Capital City
Friday	7:35	@ Capital City (if necessary)
Saturday	7:35	@ Capital City (if necessary)

Chet further informs me that Sunday afternoon's game will be televised live by SportsChannel America. "Wait," says Chet. "There's more." Commissioner Rose is accusing me of various high crimes and misdemeanors. Herm is waffling in my defense, obviously keeping the exit door open should he opt to fire me. Like Magoo, Chet says I'd better call Herm.

As I sort through my accumulated messages (one from T-Bone, one from Rose), I see that Salvatore Giambalvo, agent extraordinaire, called me this morning. My pal Sal has found a player for me— Darwin Spencer, 6'8", 215, Alcorn A & M '87. A scorer and a boardman who can play #3 and #4, Spencer is best known for having spent much of the '87–'88 season on the Washington Bullets injured list. His career NBA numbers, 1.2 ppg and 1.4 rebounds per game, are entirely misleading. Projected to forty-eight minutes, Spencer would theoretically have averaged nineteen points and twenty-two rebounds.

Yes! Yes!

"He was playing in France," says Sal, "leading the first division in scoring and rebounding, and they tried to cheat the kid out of some of his bonus money. You know how they are over there. By the time those French lawyers work over your contract, you owe them money. The kid got back late last night. He's sitting home in St. Louis feeling antsy. He's in great shape and just wants to play. Give him, let's say, six-hundred-fifty bucks a week and a free hotel room, and he'll take the first flight out tomorrow morning. I'm giving you first crack at him. The Cosmos want him badly but I don't really want him playing for that asshole Millhouse. Manchester and Santa Fe also want him. Right now, you're the only club that can squeeze him on to your roster because Morrison got called up. Check with the brass and call me later."

"Herm. It's Rob."

"Coach, my coach. Welcome home. Great win!"

"Did you enjoy the broadcast?"

"Loved it. Steve did a great job."

I tell him when it was that I first learned about today's proposed practice, and why said practice is ill advised. Herm is adamant. "There'll be fifty kids," he says, "who'll be mighty disappointed. To say nothing of their parents, some of the heaviest hitters in the business community. We're on national TV Sunday and we need an impressive turnout. Canceling the clinic would be a major disaster for the Stars."

Weary, burned-out and careless, I say, "I'm not gonna risk losing a playoff game because of some dumb public-relations stunt—"

"Dumb" is the wrong word and Herm jumps on me. What do I know about public relations in Savannah? Herm is pissed anyway because Saturday night is unavailable due to a "fucking tractor pull" at the Coliseum. Perhaps he also regrets having switched the first two games of the Oklahoma series to Savannah. And on Sunday afternoon we'll be going up against the regional finals of the NCAA tournament on network TV. So we *cannot* afford to alienate even one small portion of the community. And I "won't risk losing a play-off game?" he says. To a team that's already beaten us six-out-of-six? A playoff game we'll probably lose anyway? "Rob. Be reasonable."

Logic, he wants. On three hours sleep. "No. I can't do it."

"I hate to pull rank," he says tightly.

Then silence. Just the crackling of the wires between my cave and his ritzy trilevel mansion on Tybee Island . . . "Do it tomorrow," he says. "Give me an out."

Yes, I say, but under protest.

"*Okay.*" He laughs. "By the way, the lawyer says that Kelly has to be in Brooklyn on Monday afternoon to testify before a sealed grand jury. We couldn't get a postponement. That means he'll miss the second game. We'll have to concoct a story to explain his absence. The last thing we need is some flap about Kelly shaving points. We'll say his grandmother died."

Has Herm received any word from Rose?

"Yes. He's very upset. I got him to withhold any action until after the season but I'm sure he's got something punitive in mind."

I tell him about Darwin Spencer, his background, his capabilities, his projected NBA stats. "We desperately need another player, another scorer. Lem, Sam and Earl are hurting. Actually, Lem might even be through. And Josh is a hole in space."

Can I personally guarantee we'll beat the Cosmos if we have Spencer? he asks.

"Hell, no," I say, "but I'll personally be happier than a blind faggot in a frankfurter factory."

Where is Spencer now? St. Louis? Why, on such short notice, that's about a $600 plane ticket. No can do. Money is tight. Besides, an emergency has cropped up. "The dance team," says Herm, "needs new bras."

I order a pan pizza packed with pepperoni and peppers. Then I watch Fishwick's tape, awed by the Cosmos firepower.

My only solace is that in the event of a timely nuclear holocaust the Stars and the Cosmos will be declared the cochampions of the CBL's Eastern Division.

19

I AM TRAPPED inside my own skull. My teeth are shut and grinding. My nose is tornado alley and, just like Oklahoma City, to be avoided. There is a painting of a snowcapped mountain hanging from my uvula. I take my meals from scraps of food lodged in the fleshy folds at the base of my tongue. My source of water is a chronic postnasal drip.

Sometimes I hear dim voices coming from my brain. Maybe it's some other poor wretch trapped inside here too. So tonight, while I am asleep, I crawl through my sinuses to investigate. As I approach my brain cavity, the voice becomes intelligible. "I'm holding you responsible for this," it says. Again and again. "I'm holding you responsible for this."

As my antennae grow accustomed to the redly glowing darkness, I can discern a boxish shape perched on some kind of bony prominence where my brain is supposed to be. Upon closer inspection, the box isn't really a box. It's an old-fashioned voting booth, enclosed on four sides by black curtains, and the voice seems to be emanating from inside. "I'm holding you responsible for this." Crawling even closer, I wriggle underneath the hem of the nearest curtain, and there, speaking into a large bullhorn ("I'm holding you responsible for this."), is Commissioner Rose.

I've got to get out of here!

Yes, yes. I've heard all the rumors. There's supposed to be another opening at the very top of my skull, where a flowering lotus

*blossom grows and reaches into heaven. But the walls are slick
with blood.*

*Suddenly, I hear another strange sound, a whining, buzzing
machine. Then I hear a scream of pain. Unmistakable. A human
scream.*

Is it me? Is it the Commissioner?

No. It's only one of Dr. Dento's patients.

I call to invite Chet for breakfast and we meet at The Butternut
Diner on Victory Drive and 122nd Street. We both order "country"
ham, "country" fried eggs and "country" grits. To my humble pal-
ate, the grits taste like chewable sand. I try mine with butter, salt
and pepper, while Chet drowns his with "country gravy," a white,
viscid fluid.

As we sip our juice, Chet relates the morning's news. The Coliseum's management has demanded a fee of $1,000 to set up the
basketball court in time for the TV game tomorrow afternoon.
Twenty tons of "country dirt" must be removed overnight and the
Coliseum insists that the Stars assume the overtime incurred by
the maintenance crews. Herm, of course, is furious.

But I must interrupt his recital. "Chet. Tell me, please. What are
you getting out of all this? What's your goal? Your dream? Where do
you go from here?"

His little round face turns red. The roots of his sparse, curly
black hair quickly dampen. But he takes my interest seriously. "My
ultimate dream," he says, "is to someday be the sports information
director at the University of Georgia. They have a dozen people
working in media relations, most of them covering the football
team. I do have something of an 'in' there. My father knows the
current SID's accountant. There's a slight chance that as early as
next fall I'll be hired to cover some of the minor sports. Specifi-
cally, the men's and the women's gymnastic teams, the women's
field hockey team and the men's golf team. Not much, but it would
be a start. What I'm working on right now is getting a writer I know
from the Atlanta *Constitution* to come up to Savannah and do a
story on the playoffs, on the CBA, on you. That would look real
good on my résumé."

"And what if your dream comes true? What then? Get married? Have kids? Mow the lawn?"

"I have no urge to get married," he says while slurping his grits. "My parents were divorced when I was a kid. It was a bad situation, very mean and angry. So . . . you know? I'd just get a cozy apartment off-campus with a waterbed and indulge my one true urge, to fuck young, moist coeds until my dick turned blue." Said while still slurping his grits.

"What happens until then? What about the Savannah Stars?"

"The basketball is good, better than I anticipated. But the Stars, the CBL, it's all small-time crapola. Herm doesn't know how to manage people. There's too much wheel-spinning in the organization. He spends too much of his time on insignificant details. Like the color of the sequins on the dance team's new uniforms. Like redesigning his business card. He also spends too much time playing golf. Herm is a great salesman, a superb bullshitter. But the only thing he's out there selling is himself. I give the Stars one more year here in Savannah. Then the ownership will bail out and Herm will have to find another buyer here or in another city. The only thing that can save the franchise is if y'all win the championship. Which I don't think is gonna happen this year."

Neither do I, truth to tell.

"The people in Savannah have a massive inferiority complex. The South lost the War Between the States and it's just like it happened yesterday. So, winning the battles don't count. The Stars have to win the war."

Chet uses a fork to pierce the yolks on his fried eggs, then smushes together the yellow egg-blood, the white gravy and the grits, shoveling the mix into his face, wiping his plate clean with chunks of "country" biscuits.

"If the team was predominantly white it'd draw better for a while but then y'all'd never even win a skirmish. Or if the blacks in Savannah were filthy rich the Stars would be here forever. But I'd say the Stars are doomed."

I always eat my yolks whole, shaving off slivers of white until the yokes are totally isolated, then, without breaking the skin, carefully slide each yoke into my mouth. First the whites, then the yellows, the grits and the biscuits—like all my meals, a neat, linear succession to savor the fullness of each taste, each texture. All that's left is to drink my orange juice and be merry.

Then Chet asks the same questions of me. What are my goals? What benefits am *I* deriving here and now?

"I escaped from my life," I tell him eye-to-eye, "from my marriage, from New York. I escaped into the CBL almost by accident. My real goal is to keep my job or find a better one. My dream? It used to be coaching the perfect team to a perfect season. Harmony, communion, all that. After a while my dream was to coach the perfect game. Now, I'd settle for the perfect play. Or better yet, an imperfect win tomorrow afternoon."

I pay the bill, he pays the tip.

In the safety of my cave, I reexamine the most recent Cosmos–Stars games: a 116–97 runaway in Capital City late last month, and a 127–106 laugher on March 3rd in Savannah. Even *with* the Beast. Even with Richie scoring 10 ppg in relief of Earl. But I *will* find a way to beat them.

The Hoot 'n' Holler Sports Bar features sawdust-strewn floors and barrels of free peanuts. Also, mounted in strategic places on the oak-paneled walls are ten regulation and five oversized TVs. Other diversions include a mini hoop-shoot, a putting strip, pool tables, two long and smooth table-top shuffleboards, plus various arcade-type computer games. There's Herm's picture on the wall, still trying to evade the same phantom tackler. At least thirty photos of Herschel Walker are scattered on the walls throughout the spacious room. And four large shots of Josh Brusher: one as a skinny high-schooler smiling broadly under an afro; another action shot showing Josh in a Savannah State uniform blocking a frightened cowboy's timid layup; next in line, Josh wearing a Sacramento Kings uniform; and, lastly, Josh with the Stars.

A 15′ × 15′ boxing ring is set up against the far wall near the rest rooms. The ring is two steps above an intimate grouping of perhaps fifty people clustered around twenty tables. Two bar stools and a standing microphone occupy the middle of the ring. And lo, Herm sits delicately atop one of the stools, purring into the microphone.

"Ah, here he is," Herm says when he sees me, his right hand curled around a hefty stein of beer. "The star of the show. Grab yourself some lunch, Coach. I'm almost finished here."

He points to a long table off to the far side of the ring. Up close, the table is laden with tuna and ham sandwiches, both on white bread and cut into thrifty triangles. The feast includes plastic packets of mayonnaise, mustard and sweet relish. Looking savory are mini-bags of Mister Salty's Country Style Potato Chips. Plastic cups are stacked alongside large plastic pitchers of iced tea, the pitchers labeled "Sweet" or "Unsweet." I settle for chips and a cup of "Sweet," then find an empty table on the periphery. There's a bright spotlight on the ring and I can't recognize any of the luncheoneers in the darkness surrounding.

Inside the ring, Herm is promoting tomorrow's game. "It's a chance for the rest of the country to see what we're all about," he says. "We've got a college fraternity from over to Savannah State who're gonna shave their heads and paint big stars on their chests. We've got fabulous giveaways and free airline tickets to be won. There's a full-page ad in this morning's *Gazette* and we're running spots on TV all day long. It's a good, fun time for the whole family."

The stool wobbles as Herm shifts his weight. Is he drunk?

"And frankly," he says, "we need y'all's support. For the Stars to continue shining in Savannah, we've got to show the owners that the people of this glorious and historical city will come out and root for the good guys when crunch comes to punch. Now don't y'all get me wrong. I'm not threatening to move the Stars out of town. No. All's I'm saying is that the people, the hometown people, who lost over two hundred thousand dollars last year in their attempt to establish big-time professional sports here in Savannah, to upgrade the quality of our lives, yours and mine, by offering us another attractive option for our leisure time . . . these people have to start turning a buck. It's the American way . . ."

From the darkness, somebody yells out, "Enough, Herm! I'll sure as hell vote for you!"

Everybody laughs and Herm slides off the stool, saying, "Without further ado, let's hear from a special guest . . ." (I clear my throat quietly and rinse my mouth with warm iced tea.) ". . . One of Savannah's own prodigal sons, Josh Brusher!"

Josh gets a standing ovation as he sits himself next to Herm, then speaks for ten minutes, extolling the "gracious city of my birth," praising the CBL, his teammates and "the best coach" he's ever had. "Sure, Coach and I've had our differences," Josh says, "because any player worth his sugar wants more playing time all the time. But Coach's plan was to play me limited minutes all season long to keep me as fresh as possible, to preserve these old legs here so I can be at my best when it counts the most."

Then he promises to "kick butt" tomorrow. And before he leaves ("Got to get mentally prepared for practice."), he touts a week-long instructional camp for boys and girls he will be operating early in May. At last he's gone.

Now it's my turn. Herm introduces me and I duck through the ropes to reluctant applause. Since the locals have paid five dollars a pop for Wonder Bread sandwiches, I try to be informative. So I discuss the implications of playoff basketball. The game-to-game cycle of adjustments and counteradjustments. How familiarity breeds physicality. Then I mention how proud we should be that Benny Morrison is now "representing the Savannah Stars in the NBA."

Any questions?

The man who endorsed Herm's candidacy wants to know about Richie. "If we're supposed to be proud of Morrison," he says, and I still can't see his face, "why shouldn't we be ashamed of Michaels? How can you, as a coach, allow a drug user to be on a team that represents us, the fans?"

I tell him that during the three previous seasons Richie has played in the CBL he has taken, and passed, at least a dozen drug tests. Nor have I ever seen Richie exhibit any symptoms of drug abuse, moodswings, unusual irritability, so there's never been any reason to suspect him. "I'm sure that Richie has no addictive problem," I say. "He was just at the wrong party at the wrong time. It's an unfortunate situation for all of us. But the responsibility is Richie's. I'm not a babysitter. And as for being ashamed? Well, I don't believe it's my place to be judging him."

A woman stands up, then steps forward into the light. "My name is Sally Desmond," she says. She looks to be fortyish, perhaps a housewife. "I know I'm kind of conservative in my thinking and, like my daughter always says, not 'with it.' But I wonder if you could tell me why so many of our prominent athletes have drug problems? They seem to have so much going for them. Fame and fortune. Why do they do it?"

"That's a great question and I think the answer has to do with the nature of athletic competition itself. Being so competitive is a rush. You get all adrenalized and you're at the peak of awareness. In a way, playing in a ballgame gets you high. Then the game is over and the bottom drops out. And sometimes, some athletes just don't want to come down, or don't want to come down so fast. Or can't. There's also the matter of sex. Let me put it this way . . . cocaine and other drugs are alleged to have an aphrodisiac effect. Let's leave it at that."

"Thank you," Sally Desmond says. "That's the first time anybody's ever given me a straight answer."

"Hey, Coach!" It's the voter. "How come y'all knows so much about this here stuff? Sounds suspicious to me."

"To tell the truth, I did some experimenting with drugs when I was a kid. Didn't you?"

Sex. Drugs. Herm's had enough. He's so sorry to "break this up," but I do have a practice session to oversee and it's time for me to go earn my "keep."

Exit, stage left.

It's been near 100 degrees all day and the familiar smell hangs around like a ground-fog, making me gasp and sneeze. Inside the bubble the air is odorless, somewhat cooler but especially dense today. The bleachers are thronged with proud poppas and their clamorous offspring. The private conversations, the laughter, the shouts are all amplified by the twisted physics of air under pressure and curved plastic.

The players are listless as they brace and lace up on the sidelines. I've decided to teach them Capital City's offense, the passing games, the isos, the Side-out and the Under-out. Then we will scrimmage half-court, their offense against our defense.

I must shout to make myself heard as we gather at center court. And even though we stand shoulder to shoulder, no one can hear Nate mumble the prayer. "Amen." Later, as the players stretch, Earl waves me over for a private conference. "We've got trouble," he says.

The trouble is . . . Earl and Lem went bar-hopping last night, and happened to meet up with Barry Millhouse at The Rebel's Roost near the mall. At which time several beers were consumed and Millhouse told Lem there was a three-for-one trade already agreed to between Savannah and Capital City. The deal would be consummated as soon as trading is legal again, the day after the new CBL champs are crowned. The Cosmos have sworn to relinquish their number-one draft pick, the rights to Kennedy Andrews and any one player from their suspended list. In exchange, Savannah has allegedly promised to return Lem Jameson to his favorite ex-coach.

"Lem is fucked up in his head about this," Earl says. "The doctor told him this morning that his wrist is okay. The soreness is normal because he hasn't played in so long. But he wants to know why he should bust his ass for you if you're planning on trading him to the team he's supposed to beat? So look out, Rob. Millhouse convinced Lem that you were using him, forcing him to play in pain. Which even Lem knows is a lie. Then, when Lem's all used up, when his wrist breaks or something, you're gonna throw him into the gutter. And Lem's so confused he bought it. I don't think Lem is gonna be worth shit this series. I think he's gonna do something real crazy. All he needs is an excuse to lie down anyway, right? Millhouse did a total number on him. I've been trying to talk sense to Lem but he's too upset to listen. I told him that I'd finesse you and see if you really are going to trade him."

"I wasn't planning anything. But, you know, it sounds sort of intriguing. I'll have to take a look at the Cosmos suspended list."

Earl warns me not to say a word to Lem about "the trade," or else Lem will know that Earl is my "snitch." So unless Millhouse confesses or Lem complains to the CBL office, the Cosmos' crafty coach has perpetrated the perfect crime.

No team may attempt to sign, talk to, negotiate with, or attempt to unduly influence a player that is the property of another CBL club. A team is subject to a $5,000.00 fine for tampering. Additional penalties may be imposed by the commissioner.

Despite the noise, the heat, the players' disinclination to work and the injuries (physical and mental), the practice is surprisingly productive. With so many spectators on hand, the players feel compelled "to perform." Sure, I have to goad Sam, prod Lem and mildly chastize Carl, but they enjoy learning and executing the subtleties of Capital City's offenses. "Fuck the flex," Sam says, "let's run their own shit against them tomorrow. That ought to fuck them up." Throughout the practice, Josh works as hard as a lowly, splinter-assed rookie.

In the stands the kids are bored with all the talking, the demonstrating and standing around. They get excited twice: when I hit a jumper and when Josh stuffs an offensive rebound.

"That was a good one," I say as we huddle at center-court, directly under the plastic bubble's plastic navel. When I tell them about the forthcoming clinic, Sam starts limping. "I also got a tooth knocked loose the other night," he says, then glances at an invisible watch on his bare left wrist. "I got a dentist's appointment in fifteen minutes."

I also excuse Lem for his sore wrist, and Carl, because all the spectators under the age of twelve would instantly be intoxicated by his breath. I pardon Earl, even though he still refuses to be X-rayed. "If the finger is broken," he explains, "some jackass doctor will order me not to play." Can't argue with that kind of logic.

The injured group leaves quickly before I change my mind, then Nate speaks up. "We've done a thousand of these things," he says. "Sit down and relax, Rob. We'll take care of the whole business."

After calling the kids to order, Nate splits them into five groups and sets up five stations: Kelly does dribbling, Brent passing, Nate shooting, Cooper the defensive stance and Josh conducts the rebounding drills.

While I sit in the relatively cool shadow of the air pump, blissfully ignored, all of them work gently with the children, supportive of the fat and awkward ones, more pointed with the good athletes. Meanwhile, Herm canvasses his constituents, flexing his cleft, smiling, glad-handing.

One adult does approach me, a thick-waisted middle-aged man wearing madras Bermuda shorts, a white T-shirt, red suspenders and sockless snow boots. "Howdy there, Coach," he says, shaking my hand. "Just want to let you know that a lot of us understand what you're trying to do here. And we think you're doing it damn well. Good luck to you, son."

He leaves me squatting there with an empty, yearning, outstretched hand. What exactly is it that I'm "trying to do here"?

After an hour the players volunteer to put on a dunking exhibition, then linger to sign autographs. And despite myself, I admire their patience, their honesty and their goodwill. And I fully appreciate their gift to me.

Some NBA teams have videotape specialists. The Houston Rockets have someone who sits in a small electronic room during the first half of their home games and prepares strategic highlights for the coaches to scrutinize at halftime. NBA game-tapes are routinely edited so that a ballgame can be digested in sections: here's all the sequences when the opponent used their passing game; here's all their under-outs in succession; here's all the different ways they defended our stack offense.

In the CBL we can't afford any technology more advanced than a VCR and TV. What we have are the raw game tapes only, and I watch at least 200 of these during a normal season. I've already studied the Cosmos—Fog playoff tape four times but I can't improve on Kuback's scouting report.

And when I suddenly realize that I've forgotten to eat supper, I'm no longer hungry. So I pull my cave around me like a shawl and try to sleep.

20

Happy birthday to me. Forty is sporty.

I owe myself a meal, a big breakfast, but as I'm steering past the Swedish Inn's office on my way out of the parking lot, I see the Capital City ballplayers climbing out of a Savannah Hilton van. Making a U-turn, I park near the office and investigate.

The Cosmos players, with their luggage, are gathered around the front desk. Millhouse is nowhere in sight, but Brian Hollander comes over to greet me. The New Jersey Nets originally drafted Brian in 1987, a second-round pick out of Cheyney State, a Division II all-black school near Philadelphia, but he never survived the Nets training camp. Brian reported to the Peoria Storm the day after he cleared NBA waivers and we were rookies together.

At 6'6" and 220 pounds, Brian was tough enough, a dominant CBL player whose only flaw was his limited shooting range. Brian played at Peoria for twenty-eight games, averaging 26.8 ppg, until the Miami Heat picked him up. He remained with the Heat for a season and a half, before accepting a deal in Italy worth $175,000, plus the usual perks. Everybody in the CBL figured he'd play in Europe until his wheels fell off. Last summer Peoria finally got tired of waiting for him and traded Brian's rights to Capital City for two draft picks (#2 and #4) and an undisclosed amount of cash ($1,500). Then, surprise, Brian returned to the States three weeks ago, just in time to boost the Cosmos in the playoffs.

I haven't seen him in four years. Always a personable young

195

man, bright and sensible, Brian has the same strong features, the broad nose and assertive chin. His face is still unshaven, but his "doo" is shorter and his warm brown eyes seem more withdrawn than I remember. He always played hard for me and we enjoyed each other's company.

Greeting and hugging, we edge away from his teammates to revive our friendship without an audience. "You look great," he says. "A little grayer on top and a little thinner up there, too."

His laughter is melodic and I try to laugh along with him, but a long-term case of "coach's throat" can only produce a hoarse, braying sound. My voice won't recover its natural tone until the season's been dead for a month. "Ten gray hairs for every lost ballgame," I say, "and ten fall out for every bad call. Jeez. I never thought I'd see you again. At least not in the CB-fucking-L."

He snorts a half-laugh this time. "Rob, have you eaten? Let's get out of here. I'll let you buy me breakfast."

Sure.

He puts a rookie, Jason Jerome, in charge of his bags and we're off.

"I thought all the visiting teams stayed at the Hilton," I say en route to The Rebel's Roost. "What're you guys doing at the Swedish Inn?"

Brian blows another stifled laugh through his nose and tells me the story. Millhouse was eating dinner alone last night in the Hilton's restaurant, when he decided to make a pass at his waitress. The restaurant was crowded, the waitress busy, so a personal note would have to do. Along with a big tip, Millhouse left a message written on a paper napkin. "My name is Barry Millhouse. I'm in Room 1137 and I want to eat your pussy." The waitress, also the daughter of a prominent local minister, was highly offended. The note was quickly brought to the attention of the Hilton's manager, who called Herm to rescind their trade-out agreement—and the Cosmos were booted from the premises. "Millhouse is a piece of work," Brian says as we settle into a booth.

He politely asks the waitress if the blueberries are fresh before ordering blueberry pancakes, home fries, sausage, whole wheat toast and orange juice. Ditto for me. Then we catch up on each other's doings.

Brian loved playing in the NBA. "The athletic ability of those guys is astounding," he says, "and the veterans are soo smart. In a crowd, where the refs can't see them, the vets use their hands like hatchets. They know when a little insignificant bump will knock you off the play. They're like karate masters. It was a great challenge, playing and learning."

But the flavor didn't last long enough. "Politics did me in," he says. "Let's see . . . it was in my third game with the Heat. We were getting waxed by the Bulls in Chicago, so Coach Madison emptied the bench. Rob, I had a great game. Seventeen points in fifteen minutes, seven-for-ten from the field, five dimes, four rebounds, two steals, no turnovers and I did a passable job against MJ. I thought I had it made, man. A contract for two mill, the NBA all-Star team, the Hall of Fame, here I come. I was so young and so dumb. Imagine my surprise when I didn't see any daylight for the next twelve games. That's right, three weeks of DNP's. What the hell? I was too intimidated to approach Madison, but I did talk to one of the assistants, Jimmy Lewis, a young brother from D.C. What he told me was this . . . some of the veterans were pissed off because I played so well, because I scored so much. I was a fucking threat to them, their playing time, their women, their money, their ink. So they complained to Madison and he benched me. I was too good for the Heat to just cut me, and besides, they didn't want me playing against them. So I sat for a year and a half. Believe me, Rob, I busted those suckers' asses in practice. But it didn't matter. So I said fuck this and I went for the guaranteed bucks overseas. Rob, it almost broke my heart. I mean it."

Italy, he went on, was enjoyable for a while . . . the wine, the women, the lira . . . "then everything started getting to me. The Italian coaches are incredibly ignorant and pigheaded. They think they know everything. The referees pamper the Italian players and call all kinds of crazy shit on the Americans. The Italian players really suck. And the ballgames began to bore me. Hey, I could score whenever I had to. Their defense was so bad I could get to the hoop against zones. But I was also getting soft and I didn't like my game anymore. Then the coach benched me because I missed a free throw that would've won a game. So I said to hell with it and came home. I'm ready, Rob. I've been working on my shot and my handle for three years and I know that the next time I get the call-up nobody's gonna be able to keep me on the bench."

Another reason why Brian returned to the CBL was because he thought I was still coaching in Peoria and that he'd be playing for me. "You used to let us play," he recalls. "Play hard and play smart. That's all we had to do. This Millhouse guy, all he does is play mind games. He hates going to practice. Everybody knows it. Sometimes he even has his assistant run practice while he's out playing golf or getting laid or who knows what. You know me, Rob. I like to practice and I need to shoot my two-hundred jays every day. But it's okay for this particular ballclub to miss an occasional practice at this point in the season. I mean, we always play real hard and we're a veteran team. You guys're the only team that plays the flex but we feel we can handle any situation on our own. So we don't mind the extra rest. But Millhouse always has to be fucking with us. Like on Friday. We get into town about two o'clock. 'Practice at three,' he says, so we get dressed right away and board the van. Then he gives the driver some directions and we end up at a playground out in the middle of nowhere. Half-moon metal backboards, an asphalt surface, the court's maybe eighty feet long, the sun's burning, the air's bad. Then he tells us that this is where the Stars have us scheduled to practice. He stomps around for a while and we go back to the hotel. Yesterday, too. We drive out to that weird-looking bubble? And he says, 'This is unacceptable.' And he stomps around again, talking about how Bo Lassner is deliberately fucking us over. Everybody knows what he's doing, but all the driving around, all the gearing up for practice, all that stuff gets us annoyed. And who're we gonna take it out on? You guys. Pretty smart. So we really haven't practiced since Thursday, which I think is way too long."

Brian is a meticulous eater, carefully buttering each pancake, then pouring an equal amount of maple syrup over each arc of the stack. Between mouthfuls, he rinses his tastebuds with an economical sip of water.

"All of this bullshit," he says, "it's insulting to me and it's insulting to you. Bo, I want to get back into The League so fucking bad that I'd fucking bleed for another chance."

Brian is also disillusioned with the "whole scene" in Capital City, widely renowned as the CBL's "model franchise." He says the fans are "snipers and front-runners." And Fishwick's ass-kissing antics disgust him. "There's no possible way you can beat us, Rob.

That gives me this series and the championship series, about two weeks to get called up. If it doesn't happen by then, *arrivederci,* CBL."

After I relate my own tribulations (138 ballgames won, 142 ballgames and one wife lost), we play basketball geography. Remember Emanuel Pacemaker? He's playing in New Zealand. What about Coffey Fredericks? Israel. Pico White? Turkey. Greece. Switzerland. Back home in Chocolate City. Spain, Venezuela. Selling insurance in St. Louis. Portugal. Belgium.

I pay the bill and the tip.

Time for a quick nap, then a shower and shave. I cut my chin and my neck in four places. Bad omens.

I hate afternoon ballgames. They mess with everybody's biological clock. Also, the TV people are scurrying all over the Coliseum— but I refuse to admit their cameras into my locker room.

The Cosmos haven't practiced since Thursday, eh? And maybe we need to do something uncharacteristic to get our hearts beating so early in the day. So we'll start the game with our diamond trap.

The mood in the locker room is somber, no taunts, no insults, no loud voices. Maybe it's because Kelly, our Clown Prince, is staining his drawers at the immediate prospect of testifying before the grand jury. "I didn't do nothing," he tells me. "I swear on my mother. I was just a backup, so nobody even asked me. Lots of other guys on the team were definitely shaving points. For sure. I saw the money. Guys who are playing in the NBA. But I didn't do nothing."

I advise him either to be totally forthright or else to lie and say he knows nothing about nothing. "You're right," Kelly says. "I'm gonna lie. I ain't no snitch bitch. That's good advice, Coach. I feel better already."

"DO IT!"

Herm has moved all those in attendance to the lower stands behind the Stars bench. With discreet camera angles, it'll look like a sellout. The referees are Pete Cantine and Stevie Stephenson.

Against my will, I am forced to wear a battery-pack tucked inside my jacket, also a mini-mike clipped to my necktie and a tiny speaker plugged into my right ear. "It's an innovation," says the technician who rigs me up. "During the game the announcers can ask you questions about strategy and stuff. The fans will love it. You'll be an overnight sensation."

Terrific.

The "Star-Spangled Banner" is boisterously sung by a church choir of black ladies. Nice touch, Herm. The Cosmos start James, Wagman, Hollander, Andrews and Henderson. On national TV, Cantine will handle the opening tip.

Henderson outjumps Cooper, then Sam forgets that we're springing our diamond trap and Hollander takes the ball for an uncontested layup. On the other end, Sam forces a shot before we can initiate our offense—James snatches the deep rebound and beats Kelly downcourt for another easy hoop. Simon Sez put your hands on your shoulders and call a twenty-second timeout.

"Wake up, Sam! We're in a fucking trap!"

"Oh, yeah," he says numbly. "My bad."

"We've got a 35 for Earl and a 40B for Nate. Let's get it right. Rebound! Rebound!"

"DO IT!"

Henderson receives the ball above the foul line and his savvy passes quickly dismember our trap. Then, three times running, Wagman and Henderson operate a pick-and-roll. Sam takes a wide detour around the 7'0", 260-pound Henderson, allowing Wagman to bag three jumpers.

Kelly plays his best game in weeks, even hitting a three-pointer; otherwise, the Cosmos completely defuse all of our offensive sets.

TIMEOUT.

I drape a towel over the lens of the camera that intrudes into our huddle. "Look. They're denying the post entry-pass on the flex. What we're supposed to do is go backdoor and replace with the wing. Right? And when they poach the post-to-post pass, the big men are supposed to dive. Right? Is this news to anybody? Okay. Let's come back to the flex later. Run our box set, Kelly. Double-X down. Y cross. And XB. Okay?"

"DO IT!"

Earl is fouled in the act of shooting by Hollander, and as he steps to the foul line, Millhouse yells out, "Patton. You're a fucking has-been. You're terrible." Earl misses the first free throw, then while he resets his feet, bounces the ball and tries to regain his composure, Stephenson calls a ten-second violation, the first I've ever seen.

Each free throw attempt shall be made within 10 seconds after the ball has been placed at the disposal of the free-thrower.

Rule No. 9–III

No lie. We're getting our fucking doors blown off.

My earplug suddenly begins to *beep* like a bomb about to explode. I tear all the mechanisms from my person and drop them into Magoo's lap.

Hollander is unstoppable, scoring from the paint and from beyond the pale. He surely looks like an NBA player to me. Henderson clobbers Cooper right in front of Stephenson but the ref won't make the call. "Mr. Ref," Cooper says to Stephenson, "how can you let him foul me like that?" Stephenson responds by zapping the rookie with a T.

Sam is as selfish as ever, and when he does start a modest run, Eric Mann enters the game to shut him down. Lem stinks up the court with his half-assed effort—and studiously avoids using his left hand. Josh plays well for five minutes, rebounding, blocking shots, even canning a long jumper, until he fizzles and begins pulling on the front of his shirt. Brent works hard, playing better defense on Wayne Toggins than I ever thought possible. Mitchell Miller comes off the bench to beat the living shit out of Nate. Earl plays valiantly but poorly, even dribbling the ball off his foot and out of bounds. Carl ignores our offense, keeping the ball on a string for twenty seconds, then unloading it to someone else, who must force a shot before the clock expires.

Just before the second quarter ends, Brian elbows Earl in the face as they both scuffle for a loose ball and Earl is sent crashing to the floor.

A player must be ejected for an elbow foul which makes contact above shoulder level.

Rule No. 12–VI–k(1)

But Stephenson takes the easy way out, calling a double foul.

At the half we trail 64–43.

Now, I could go berserk and throw furniture around the locker room. But I'll save that for another halftime, when going nutso might change the ballgame. So instead, I pacify them. The Cosmos have beaten us by twenty-one points over twenty-four minutes. We're certainly capable of turning the tables in the next twenty-four minutes. Ba ha. Ba ha. We're whipped, after the Oklahoma series, we're emotionally drained.

"Our passes aren't crisp," says Magoo.

I can only encourage them to play hard. "Anything can happen when you hustle."

"DO IT!"

I send them out, look briefly at the halftime stats, pee and wash my hands. The intermission clock reads 1:47 when I reach the bench and suddenly I am surrounded by the cheerleaders. Scanty uniforms, bulging tits, they all escort me to centercourt, singing, "Happy birthday to you."

Two of them (I don't know any of their names) hold a large rectangular cake in front of me. "Happy birthday to you." They help me blow out the candles. "Happy birthday, dear Coachie." Then they hand me a clutch of helium-filled balloons and the cake (which measures at least 3' X 2'). "Happy birthday to you." The cake has apparently been baked in a lopsided pan because one side is much thicker and heavier than the other.

A cameraman signals the girls to sing another chorus, and I stand there like a buffoon, holding the balloons in my right hand and balancing the cake in my left. "Happy birthday to you." The two refs stand facing me near the scorer's table, laughing. "Happy . . ." No ref has ever called a T on a balloon-holding, cake-juggling birthday fool of a coach on national TV. So I say to Stephenson, "That was a cowardly call, you fucking midget." But talking upsets my equilibrium and the cake slowly slips out of control . . . going, going, what the hell . . . before it's gone, I try to flip it forward into Stephenson's face. But the cake does a 1½ gainer and splatters onto the court, a mess of candles, icing and chocolate crumbs, all recorded for posterity. "Happy birthday, dear Coachie."

The mess is attended to, the game continues and the onslaught resumes. After six minutes I send in the subs. Josh plays like he's possessed, but Carl and Lem are horrendous.

The game clock mercifully winds down to 1:04 and the score is 127–100, when Millhouse suddenly institutes a full-court press! There's Mann and Smith converging on Carl in the backcourt, forcing a turnover and an easy score for Jerome. Fucking outrageous. Bush league. Just plain bad shit.

"Timeout."

I glare down at Millhouse but he turns his back on me. "Just sit tight," I tell my players. We have two timeouts left, plus our :20. The buzzer sounds and the Cosmos return to the floor. I instruct Cooper to stand inbounds and call another timeout. "Just sit there," I tell them again. Another buzzer and Cooper calls another timeout. Then my :20. Then even another timeout.

> Requests for timeout in excess of the authorized number shall be granted. However, a technical foul penalty shall be assessed. A team calling an excessive timeout is otherwise entitled to all regular timeout privileges.
>
> EXCEPTION: During the last two minutes of the fourth quarter and/or overtime(s), the offensive team shall not have the option of putting the ball into play at the midcourt line.
>
> Rule No. 12–II–a

The fans howl as Wagman converts the technical. I'm prepared to call illegal timeouts far into the night, but Cantine now approaches the bench, saying, "You've made your point, Coach. That's enough. Call another one and I'll run you."

The final score is 130–102.

The players are raging in the locker room. "That's humiliating," says Earl. "He treated us like dogs." Sam calls Millhouse "a cocksucker." Kelly calls him "a dickhead." Lem merely smiles at the ruckus, then I overhear him telling Brent, "If he doesn't start me tomorrow, I'm gone."

My postgame summation is brief: "Shootaround here at noon. Let's not forget what happened out there, guys. We owe that fucker one."

Herm storms into the room, claiming that I've embarrassed him, the league, the city, the fans and the game itself. "You're dead wrong, Herm," I say. "Millhouse is totally at fault here. Herm, think in terms of a football game. The Cosmos have the ball and they lead seventy-five to nothing. What Millhouse did was to run his two-minute offense, then kick a field goal as the gun went off. What Millhouse did was to spit in our faces, yours, mine, the team's and the city's. Go ahead. Talk to the players. See how they feel about it."

Herm refuses to see the light. "The media will have a field day with this," he huffs before leaving the room.

Yet Joe Patterson and Jim Packman seem more amused than antagonized, and they fail to question me about the timeouts. "The Cosmos are a good ballclub," I say for public consumption, "and they kicked us. But putting on a press like that was bush."

Joe Patterson reports what Millhouse told him about the full-court press: "The game was too easy for us. I needed to get a workout for my players. Some of them never broke a sweat."

In the hallway Fishwick is talking into Herm's ear. As I pass by, Fishwick looks my way and shakes his head in sad disapproval.

Brian is waiting for me outside the visitors' locker room. "That was bullshit," he says, "and I told the fucker that to his face. You know what he said? 'You get paid to play and I get paid to coach.' What an asshole." I invite Brian to dine at Wong's, but he has other plans. "Sam's hooking us up with some action," he says.

Chet has also lingered to commiserate with me and to reveal that Herm is taking Fishwick out to dinner. But Chad refuses to accompany me to Wong's, saying that he's "got a hot date" with a gymnast from the U. of Ga Ga.

I pause at a pay phone near the security gate. After my very first

COMMERCIAL BASKETBALL LEAGUE

Official Scorer's Report

Date **March 25, 1992** Game # **01** Arena **Coliseum** Attendance **2107**
Visitors **Capital City Cosmos** Home **Savannah Stars** Length of Game **2:17**

Visitors: Cosmos

No	Visitors	Min.	FG M	FG A	FT M	FT A	3Pt M	3Pt A	Pts	O	D	TOT	AST	PF	TO	BS	ST
12	James (G)	31	3	6	3	4	0	0	9	1	2	3	14	2	2	0	3
15	Smith	17	2	3	0	0	0	0	4	0	1	1	3	1	1	0	2
20	Mann	9	1	3	0	1	0	0	2	2	0	2	2	2	0	1	3
24	Henderson (c)	34	5	9	3	5	0	0	13	4	5	9	5	3	0	2	1
31	Wagman (G)	28	7	12	2	2	2	3	18	0	1	1	1	1	3	0	0
33	Hollander (F)	32	12	20	10	12	1	1	35	4	3	7	2	4	2	1	2
35	Jerome	5	1	4	0	0	0	0	2	0	0	0	0	1	1	1	0
42	Toggins	33	6	14	7	8	0	2	19	1	2	3	2	2	2	0	2
44	Andrews (F)	30	5	10	4	6	0	0	14	2	7	9	3	3	1	1	4
55	Miller	21	5	9	4	6	0	0	14	1	6	7	1	4	2	2	2
	TOTALS	240	47	90	33	44	3	6	130	15	27	42	33	23	14	8	19
	Pct.		50.2		75.0		50.0			Team 2				1			

Home: Stars

No	Home	Min	FG M	FG A	FT M	FT A	3Pt M	3Pt A	Pts	O	D	TOT	AST	PF	TO	BS	ST
6	Royal (G)	28	5	6	1	2	1	3	12	0	1	1	10	3	4	0	1
7	Franks (G)	37	7	23	2	2	2	5	18	1	2	3	0	1	3	0	0
8	Butler	20	2	9	3	4	0	1	7	0	0	0	0	2	5	0	1
10	Cooper (c)	28	4	8	3	4	0	0	11	3	6	9	2	4	2	1	1
11	Brusher	21	4	8	2	4	0	0	10	2	6	8	0	3	1	3	2
12	Kennison (F)	30	5	16	0	1	0	1	10	0	3	3	0	5	2	0	0
24	Jameson	22	2	7	1	1	0	0	5	1	3	4	0	4	4	0	0
32	Patton (F)	34	7	18	5	6	1	3	20	3	7	10	6	4	3	2	5
40	Springs	20	3	8	2	4	1	1	9	1	5	6	1	3	0	1	2
	TOTALS	240	39	97	19	28	5	14	102	11	33	44	19	29	24	7	12
	Pct.		40.2		67.9		35.7			Team 7				3			

Score By Quarters	1	2	3	4	OT	OT	OT	Final
V Cosmos	34	30	36	30				130
H Stars	21	22	24	35				102

Officials: Pete Cantine, Steve Stephenson

Technicals: Sav. 10 Cooper (Unsp.) 8:18 2nd Q
Sav. (Ill. def.) 5:37 2nd Q
Sav. (Ill. def.) 2:47 3rd Q
Sav. (Excess TO) 0:57 4th Q

— Miscellaneous Statistics —

Ties **0** Lead Changes **0**
Points off off rebounds (H) **6** (V) **9**
Points off steals (H) **4** (V) **15**
Offensive fouls (H) **1** (V) **0**

Remarks: 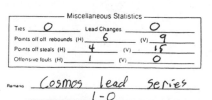 Cosmos lead series 1-0

week in Savannah I'd already memorized Wong's phone number and menu. Hot and sour soup. Shrimp toast. Spareribs in black bean sauce. War shu duck. To go. Fifteen minutes?

I eat in my cave, watching TV. Murder, mayhem, blonde-haired cherubs perishing from the disease-of-the-week. Sitcoms, a model for social behavior. Quiz shows, what color was George Washington's white horse? Old movies, talk shows, "Issues and Evasions." A boxing match, two brothers whaling on each other for the delectation of Massa. (A blowout like today is easy to forget. But I hate Barry Millhouse, now and forever.) Insufferable rap ditties on the tube, cornball country hymns. (What'll we do tomorrow without Kelly?) Rape, arson, fiery explosions, naked tits on HBO. (When I get fired I can go back to New York and collect unemployment checks.)

I fall asleep in front of the TV . . . "Oh, say, can y'all see . . . ?"

21

My PHONE RINGS at precisely 9:01 A.M. It's the girl at the front desk, a blonde who works the nine to five shift. "Excuse me, Coach," she says. "I'm just catching up with some paper work and there's this stoppage that y'all put on y'all's incoming calls? About ten days ago? March sixteenth at seven-thirty-five P.M., to be exact? Maybe y'all's forgot about it?"

Of course I've forgotten. No wonder nobody's called. "No, no. Keep it going. Just keep track of my messages."

She has "a scad" of messages already—from Rose and Smiley in the CBL office, from Patterson at the *Gazette* and Packman at Channel 17, from T-Bone, Chad, Herm, from Salvatore Giambalvo. "Some of these are a few days old," she says.

Ignoring the rest, I call Giambalvo's office, knowing that he won't be there for another hour. I tell his machine that Herm won't let me bring in Spencer. Thanks, anyway.

Long as I'm up, I might as well drive out to Savannah State to lift. There's someone else there already, a young student, 5'7" tall and weighing about 200 even. (Like a barker in a traveling carnival, basketball coaches can easily determine height and weight at first glance.) The youngster is working hard, pushing huge stacks of iron bars, grunting with the effort. But his form is atrocious. He's obviously more concerned with sheer mass than with quality. God bless America. With his awkward, herky-jerky movements, he's sure to injure his back.

"Hey," I say as friendly as possible, "I think you have too many plates on there. And if you keep your wrists straight you can isolate your biceps more effectively."

"Thanks," he says, then continues as before.

"You're welcome."

Without a warmup, I climb into the saddle of the quadriceps machine and get busy, exerting myself with all my might so that I'll nap long and sweet this afternoon. Pain as therapy, to sensitize myself from my heart out to my skin. Because the body is older and wiser than the mind.

I stop off at the Stars office to collect my check, my messages and my mail. My plan is to read them in the car and thereby avoid any unnecessary contact with my own species. But Mona signals Chet on the intercom to announce my arrival.

Naturally, Chet is brimming with bulletins . . . No, he didn't get laid last night but he thinks he's in love "for all time." Sam and Lem are in Herm's office making long-distance phone calls while Herm is out golfing with Fishwick. Rose called "again." He saw the game on TV and agrees with Herm that my behavior was "disgraceful."

I'm sick of hearing bad news from Chet. Has he ever heard about what the Spartans used to do with runners who brought back messages of battles lost?

Chet thinks I'm crazy all over again. What does Cy Rose have to do with the Michigan State football team?

I cash my check, park in the Coliseum lot and sort through my messages. T-Bone called, saying he's tried to reach me at the hotel several times. Why won't I call him back? Anyway, Millhouse is "a dang polecat" and T-Bone loved my "strategic use of timeouts."

Here's a letter from Nigeria, from a seventeen-year-old, 7'1" student who wants me to fly him to Savannah so he can learn how to play basketball and "learn how to become greatly rich." There are five letters from assorted agents, each containing a list of available players. Here's a letter from the SID of an NAIA college in South Carolina, recommending a 5'5½" point guard for the CBL draft. And here's a letter from the Oklahoma Rangers. It's from Mack

Cummings, a handwritten note and a brief newspaper clipping. "Maybe you missed this," the note reads. "Thought you might find it interesting."

Of course I missed it. I pride myself on not reading newspapers. People who believe what they read in newspapers are like dogs sniffing at a finger that points to the moon.

During the season, I won't even read the sports section. Lucky me, I get all the McNews I need from ESPN's Sports Center. Relevant info about trades and NBA cuts are thoughtfully relayed to me by compassionate agents, by T-Bone, by Chet.

The enclosed article is from the Associated Press, dateline Toronto . . .

HOOPS BEGIN AT 40

The third annual Not-So-Old-Timers Basketball Tournament will be held next week in Toronto, says spokesperson Billy McCue, an insurance salesman and self-styled basketball junkie. All the participants of this tourney must be 40 years old or older. Registration will be held on Friday, April 6, from 10–8 at the Toronto YMCA on Yonge Street. The fee is $100 per registrant and includes a reduced rate at a local hotel.

"I'll lock the door at eight o'clock," says McCue, the organizer of the event since its inception in 1989. "Then I'll divide the registrants into what I hope are equal teams based on age, size, experience and physical condition. Last year we had 78 players and 10 teams. In this tournament individuals are more important than teams. Like Dr. Naismith once said to Phog Allen, 'Basketball is just a game to play. You don't coach it.' The idea is to play as many games as possible over the weekend until nobody wants to play anymore. Your $100 buys you a place on a team and a T-shirt. There are no other prizes. For many of us, the highlight of the tournament is drinking beer and lying about what good players we used to be."

I stuff the article into my pants pocket and toss the other junk into the back seat.

The players are still fuming over yesterday's game and eager for revenge. Even Sam arrives five minutes before the deadline, his earliest appearance of the season. Am I the only one among us who doesn't believe we can defeat the Cosmos? After all, I've watched the tape of game one twice already and the Cosmos drilled us again and again. Especially without Kelly, how can the outcome be any different tonight? Let's see . . .

We jog, stretch, run a casual 3-on-2-on-1 drill before getting technical. There are several ways to defend the Cosmos pick-and-roll.

1) Jam-up the play by muscling the picker out beyond the three-point line. The Beast was especially adept at this tactic. But none of our surviving bigs have the bulk to move Henderson.
2) Go under the pick and allow the guard to shoot freely. But Wagman and Toggins would shoot the lights out.
3) Switch so that the big man chases the ball handler and the defensive guard follows the picker. Not a bad idea. But Wagman and/or Toggins would create terrific shots against any of our big men.
4) The defensive guard simply fights through the pick. This is the textbook solution, but not so simple to execute with Henderson in the way.
5) The defensive big man shows on the weak side of the pick, delaying the ball carrier and allowing the defensive guard time to recover. This is what we were allegedly doing yesterday. It's another good idea that's too sophisticated for our biggies to perform properly.
6) Double the ball, allowing Henderson to roll or fan. This is a "no-read" situation. Don't think. Just do. BINGO!

We review our defensive strategies for the Cosmos' other sets, and just as we start walking through their Under-out, Josh becomes unhinged at last. He jumps at me and grabs the ball out of my hands. Then he starts dunking the ball in a madcap frenzy. Slam! Bam! Dunking and redunking! Whenever the ball rolls away he dives on the floor to retrieve it, sliding and skidding headfirst like a baseball player stealing second base. Then he leaps to his feet and attacks the basket again. Smash! Crash! He pauses for only a moment, dripping sweat, his face cleaved by a madman's grin, his eyes wide and strangely dislocated. Then he commences to dunk again, silently, without a grunt or a grimace.

The players stand around, stunned, until Earl starts laughing. "I've seen him do this once before," Earl says, "in a free-agent camp in Milwaukee. It's like a seizure."

After a full three minutes, after at least fifty thunderous dunks and several belly-floppers, Josh suddenly gives out. He lies still as death on the floor for perhaps a dozen heartbeats, then slowly climbs to his feet and nods for me to continue.

So, we'll double every wing-pass off of James. Let James shoot jumpers, layups, whatever. Let's see if James can beat us.

As we shoot free throws, I approach Carl. "This is your chance," I say.

"Yeah. Until Kelly comes back."

"Tell you what. If we win tonight, you start on Wednesday."

"It's a bet."

After our communal prayer, Cooper walks up to Josh, asking, "Why did you do that?"

"Do what?" says Josh.

Instead of taking my usual nap, I drive out to Tybee Island for a walk on the beach. The summer homes are boarded up, the gulls are squawking, the white sand is coarse and crunchy beneath my sneakers. About a mile down from where I park, several bulldozers are shifting the beach into scientific configurations, hoping to delay erosion. It's almost chilly with the wind slanting in from the sea, smelling of salt, of eternal truths. An elderly couple walks hand in hand along the water's edge. Somebody's black cat chews on a dead bird. A jogger strides past, kicking up sand in his wake.

On the same impulse that brought me here, I also start to jog, then I run, faster and faster, until I'm running as hard as I can. My arms pumping, my heart thumping. Running, straining, raging. I want to scream. Faster and faster. Running where? Faster. If there was a hoop here, a basketball, if I could still dunk . . . faster. . . . I'd dunk with a vengeance. I'd kill the basket. I'd dunk so hard the ball would fracture the floorboards. Faster.

If,
inside the white lines,
    there is no transfiguration,
between the tip and the buzzer,
    no God,
then where do I go,
and what do I do with the rest of my life?

22

THERE'S A NEW trainer on duty in the locker room, a young blond kid with a frizzy moustache. Magoo is also there and he rushes over to grab my hand and greet me.

"I know I haven't been too much help to you," he says. "Obviously, this is a different level of competition than I'm used to. And the game has changed so much over the years. By golly, I don't think players like Bob Cousy or George Mikan could even make NBA squads these days. What I mean to say is this . . . I think you did a great job, Coach, with no help from anybody. And I just want to say thanks for putting up with me."

I appreciate his honesty and his good words. I never call him "Magoo" to his face. "George? You know how sometimes a ball-player can help his team without scoring a point? Well, I think the way you buoy everybody's spirits is worth at least fifteen points a game."

We shake hands and chuck each other on the shoulder. He'll undoubtedly be here next season and I won't.

The players file in, greet each other casually, then quietly prepare themselves for what might be their last home game of the season. There's Sam, munching on his pregame chili dog. Cooper earnestly prays, for what? No fouls? A Stars victory? World peace? Earl is stoic, as always. Carl seems fidgety. Josh is struggling to stay awake.

Nate comes over to me while I cover the blackboard with miracles. "I fucked up yesterday," he says. "But I'm ready today. Go to me."

After everybody is taped, the trainer informs me that Earl's finger is "definitely" broken. "Shh!" I whisper.

Everybody is attentive during my chalktalk. Carl even asks a germane question about a certain defensive switch in the early phase of Passing Game I.

Yes, they are focused, intense, and still angry. Angry enough to win?

"DO IT!"

There's a good crowd come to see us off, and during the introductions I am roundly booed. The refs are NBA vets Nick Sforza and Art Brennan, among the best the CBL ever gets. Obviously, an effort has been made to try and prevent any sinister fallout from yesterday's game.

Right away, Millhouse makes a mistake—he opens with a full-court press! We put Earl in the middle and get easy shots without having to establish our offense.

CC–8   STARS–12

The Cosmos are sloppy in the first quarter, their offense seems clumsy and incoherent. We're outworking them, getting loose balls and offensive rebounds we couldn't touch yesterday.

Cooper and Nate are neatly switching on their Passing Game II action. We're also sagging when James pops and conceding his jumper. Ploppers, bangers and rimmers. As planned, we're also doubling off James to cramp their isos.

The Cosmos are settling for the first available shots, mostly awkward springers by James. One of his shots clangs noisily off the backboard and flies out of bounds, prompting Sam to yell to his teammates, "Anybody get hurt?"

CC–19   STARS–24

The Cosmos want to run and have fun. They never imagined that yesterday's turkeys would offer any resistance. Hollander tries to rally his teammates, rebounding like a fiend, diving for loose balls, but nobody responds. As he inbounds the ball near our bench, Brian turns to me and says, "This is Millhouse's fault."

Nate is indeed ready, rebounding, defending, playing with unusual vigor. Sam is shooting well. Cooper sets vicious, distinctly non-Christ-like picks. Carl is alert and in total control. When the Cosmos deny the post entry pass, Carl waves Nate through the middle and summons Sam to replace him. When the Cosmos poach the post-to-post pass, Carl insists that Cooper dive to the hoop, taking James with him, and we get a layup.

CC–27   STARS–34

Josh provides effective defense in place of Nate, but he wanders through our offense like an amnesiac. Lem is obnoxious, screaming at the officials over ghostly fouls no one else can see. When Lem misses a layup, Henderson rebounds and the Cosmos are off to the races. But Lem remains in the backcourt, hacking at his right arm with his left arm and yelling at Sforza to "call the goddamned foul."

CC–33   STARS–41

Despite Earl's aggressive defense, Hollander keeps the Cosmos in the ballgame. When Toggins replaces Wagman, I send Brent in for Sam and the Cosmos offense remains stagnant. We overwhelm them on both boards, and Cooper has an easy time with our 50 and 50L, going one-on-one against the slower Henderson.

Carl continues to play with emotion and intelligence, rebounding over Toggins, taking a whiplash charge against Hollander. There's a battle for a loose rebound and the bodies are dropping like bowling pins, but Carl rescues the ball and passes ahead to Brent. James is slow getting to his feet, and as Carl catches up with the play he deliberately kicks James in the back of the head. Neither ref is witness to the deed.

Just before the half ends, Sam nails a stepback jumper near the Cosmos bench, then pauses to point a finger at Millhouse. "In your face, nigger!"

At the break, our lead is 53–46.

*   *   *

Everybody's roused in the locker room, but I only count seven players present. "George," I call to Magoo. "Where's Lem? See if he's in the shitter. Go find him. Please."

In the second half we will pick-and-roll them, something we haven't shown them before. The call is 4-Up, and we'll run it with Sam and Nate. Should the Cosmos double Sam, Nate will step back for the jumper. Sam is also cautioned that Nate intends to slip the pick should his defender cheat and show too soon.

Magoo reports that, even as we speak, Lem is in the hallway arguing with his girlfriend. Fuck him once and for all.

"DO IT!"

Our pick-and-roll confuses the Cosmos, and Nate drains every jumper he can find.

Hollander posts Earl on the right block, then takes one hard dribble into the lane with his left hand before spinning back to the baseline to uncork a turnaround jumper going right. Earl stays with him, leaping to block Brian's shot with his near hand, his left. Earl does tip the shot, then screams and slumps to the floor. I call a :20 and replace Earl with Brent. The young trainer inspects Earl's mangled finger and says, "It's broken, I told you it's broken." But Earl just shakes his head and says to the trainer, "Fuck you. You got X-ray vision? Just put some more fucking tape on it."

CC–67   STARS–72

Josh is so erratic that I want to strangle him. But I will not play Lem in any circumstance.

CC–72   STARS–75

Millhouse has been riding the refs all game long until finally, Sforza calls a T. Sam makes the foul shot, but the Cosmos get all the close calls until the game is tied at 80.

Here we go!

I think the refs are calling an exemplary game but I'm pushed into a corner. I need to get a T without antagonizing them. Hey, even the good refs can force a coach to be a prick.

There's a debatable charge-block call that goes against us, so I jump off the bench, flap my arms like a wounded flamingo and shout, "Jesus Christ!" Wham! Sforza T's me, and the calls even out again.

CC–82   STARS–86

Hollander is shooting the first of two free throws and Sforza stands near our bench. "Nick," I say. "Would you have given me the technical if I'd've said, Holy Moses?" He laughs.

Hollander and Toggins heat up, Nate and Cooper begin to tire, Kennedy and Mitchell start controlling the boards. The ballgame is up for grabs.

· CC–90   STARS–92

It's our ball, 0:54 left in the game, our timeout. We'll run something else the Cosmos haven't seen from us—posting Earl against Hollander, play #3 on the flex.

"DO IT!"

Earl catches on the left block, fakes to the middle and fakes again at the baseline. The Cosmos are too surprised to double the ball. Then Earl spins right and buries a jump hook.

CC–90   STARS–94

The clock reads 0:40 and Millhouse calls a timeout. What'll he do? An iso for Hollander has been the Cosmos' most effective play. Okay. Let's double that eventuality. Pick-and-roll for Wagman and Henderson? Let's double that, too. Brent's in for Sam (who scowls but says nothing). Josh for Nate.

"DO IT!"

The Cosmos surprise us by running a pick-and-roll for Wagman and Hollander. When Earl and Brent clamp Wagman, the ball is shuffled to Hollander, who hits a three-pointer. FUCK!

CC–93   STARS–94

Now there's 0:29 left and we burn our penultimate timeout. Sam back in for Brent. Nate for Josh. No, don't report now. Millhouse will see you and perhaps take measures. Wait until the huddle breaks. Okay. They won't be looking to foul because playing good defense will get them the ball, down by one, with sufficient time to get a good shot. Let's post Earl again. They'll double this time, so Nate will dive to the basket and Sam will replace him at the foul line. "Be ready, both of you," says Earl. "I'll get you the ball."

"DO IT!"

Yes! A perfect play. Earl is doubled quickly and he finds Nate near the basket, who dunks despite being fouled by Andrews. Then bango! Nate hits the free throw.

CC–93   STARS–97

There's 0:13 on the game clock and Millhouse wants his last timeout. Yes, Earl! Yes, Nate!

Our strategy is simple. "Don't foul. If they score and we can't get the ball inbounds immediately, call a timeout. Remember, there's only thirteen seconds left. Chances are, we won't have to advance the ball even if they do score."

But Wagman misses an off-balance three-pointer and Nate is deliberately fouled on the rebound. Nate makes two-for-two and Wagman finally hits a three-pointer at the buzzer.

As my old coach, Alexander Pope, used to say, "The race by vigor not by vaunts is won." And the vigorous win, 99–96.

We scream and yahoo in the locker room as though we've won the championship. We embrace each other and hop around the room until Nate calms us with a prayer of thanksgiving. "Amen."

I use a towel to erase the blackboard and draw this:

"*That's* what we have!" I say. "Big balls!"

Then Magoo distributes our itineraries—our flight leaves tomorrow at 7:04 A.M., the van leaves the hotel at 5:45 A.M. Magoo moves to admit the media, but I tell him to wait for another minute. Then I approach Lem's alcove, where he sits, still in his uniform, killing me with his red-rimmed stare.

"You're not making the trip," I tell him.

"What?"

"I'm suspending you."

He laughs. "Right. Like you suspended Sam."

"We'll see."

Lem stands up. He's two inches taller than I am and we both weigh 240. He has one healthy fist, I have two. "That's bullshit," he says. "And you're a bullshit mothafucker. I'll kick your fucking ass—"

"Hey, Lem," Cooper says. "C'mon. Cut it out."

I thrust my chest into Lem's and say, "You ain't kicking anybody's ass. And you know why? Because you're a pussy and everybody knows it. You want me? Come on. I'm right here, mothafucker."

"Fuck you," Lem says, grabbing his clothing and storming from the room.

Everybody's stunned. I enter the trainer's room and dial the CBL's after-hours transaction line. "This is Bo Lassner of the Savannah Stars. It's nine-forty-five P.M., March twenty-sixth. The Stars suspend Lem Jameson for conduct detrimental to the team."

Then I nod for Magoo to open the doors. Packman and Patterson rush in, desperate to know where Lem was going in his uniform. Why didn't he play in the second half?

He's been suspended for conduct detrimental to the team and I refuse to elaborate. No, it had nothing to do with drugs. "The game, fellas. What about the game?" But they're only interested in the latest scandal.

Herm dashes in like his pants are aflame, then he buttonholes me into the privacy of the trainer's room. "Lem told me y'all want to suspend him," Herm says sharply. "What is *this* one all about? Can't y'all control your damn players?"

I tell him my version of what happened, adding, "I had no choice."

Herm is thinking hard—the suspension probably won't make much of a difference unless we can win two-out-of-three in Capital City. Was tonight a fluke? Can we win the series with Lem? Can we win it without him? "Don't be too hasty," is all he says.

"I've already called it in. It's irrevocable. And I won't back down on this one. If you force me to take Lem back, I just won't play him."

Herm glares at me. Does the cleft on his chin flatten out? "I hope you realize what you're doing," he says.

"Yes. I'm trying to beat the Cosmos. What're you doing?"

Herm doesn't answer.

Later, as I *mange* a bag of shit from Bugger King and replay the game, the phone rings. How can that be? All of my incoming calls are supposed to be intercepted at the front desk. "Hello?"

It's Brian Hollander calling from down the hall. "I'm going up to the Cleveland Cavaliers! No shit! Millhouse told me after the game!"

That's great! Wonderful!

"The Cavs are already in Atlanta for a game tomorrow night. They've rented me a car and I'm out the door right now!"

Fantastic!

"Rob. Do me a favor? Beat that fucker till he cries."

> *Basketball Jones is in his heaven.*
> *All's right with the world.*
> —ROBERT BROWNING?

COMMERCIAL BASKETBALL LEAGUE
Official Scorer's Report

Date: **March 26, 1992** Game #: **02** Arena: **Coliseum** Attendance: **4893**

Visitors: **Capital City Cosmos** Home: **Savannah Stars** Length of Game: **2:19**

Visitors: Cosmos

No	Visitors: Cosmos	Min.	FG M	FG A	FT M	FT A	3Pt M	3Pt A	Pts.	O	D	TOT	AST	PF	TO	BS	ST
12	James (G)	36	4	13	0	0	0	0	8	0	1	1	8	2	2	0	2
15	Smith	3	0	2	0	0	0	0	0	0	0	0	1	1	0	0	1
20	Mann	DNP															
24	Henderson (c)	40	2	5	2	3	0	0	6	1	5	6	3	4	2	1	1
31	Wagman (G)	29	5	12	2	2	1	3	13	1	1	2	4	2	1	0	0
33	Hollander (F)	48	10	19	6	7	1	1	27	3	7	10	3	4	2	1	1
35	Jerome	DNP															
42	Toggins	20	8	15	3	3	0	2	19	0	2	2	0	2	3	0	2
44	Andrews (F)	36	3	7	1	2	0	0	7	2	8	10	0	3	1	2	0
55	Miller	28	6	14	4	4	0	0	16	2	7	9	2	3	3	1	0
	TOTALS	240	38	87	16	19	2	6	96	9	31	40	21	21	14	5	7
	Pct.		43.7		84.2		33.3			Team 2				3			

Home: Stars

No	Home: Stars	Min.	FG M	FG A	FT M	FT A	3Pt M	3Pt A	Pts.	O	D	TOT	AST	PF	TO	BS	ST
7	Franks (G)	40	10	19	4	6	1	2	25	1	1	2	1	3	2	0	1
8	Butler (G)	48	2	5	3	4	0	0	7	2	4	6	9	4	3	1	4
10	Cooper (c)	32	4	10	2	2	0	0	10	3	8	11	1	4	0	1	0
11	Brusher	17	2	5	0	1	0	0	4	4	5	9	0	0	0	3	0
12	Mennison (F)	41	9	15	8	9	0	0	26	2	6	8	1	2	2	0	0
24	Jameson	5	0	2	0	0	0	0	0	0	1	1	0	1	1	0	0
32	Patton (F)	42	7	13	6	7	2	3	22	1	9	10	5	3	2	1	3
40	Springs	15	2	8	1	1	0	0	5	0	4	4	2	2	0	1	2
	TOTALS	240	36	78	24	30	3	5	99	13	38	51	19	19	10	7	10
	Pct.		46.2		80.0		60.0			Team 6				4			

Score By Quarters

	1	2	3	4	OT	OT	OT	Final
V Cosmos	21	25	21	19				96
H Stars	26	27	19	27				99

Officials: Nick Sforza, Art Brennan

Technicals: CC – Millhouse (Unsp.) 10:48 4th
Sav. Lassner (Unsp.) 10:03 4th

Miscellaneous Statistics

Ties: **3** Lead Changes: **5**

Points off rebounds (H) **13** (V) **4**

Points off steals (H) **7** (V) **4**

Offensive fouls (H) **2** (V) **2**

Remarks: Stars even series 1-1

23

"Nothing but net!" Steve chants. "Around the rim and in! Count it! Book it!"

"Hey, man!" Nate shouts from the back of the van. "Shut the fuck up and keep your eyes on the road. Don't nobody but us listen to you anyways."

Steve nods and seems to quiet down, but from the shotgun seat I can hear him exhaling loudly into his cupped left hand, imitating the roar of the crowd and then mumbling with building excitement, "It's good! It's good! And the Stars win the championship . . ."

Once we reach the airport the players dump their bags at the American Airlines counter and hasten to the departure gate to secure the most sleepable spaces. Even Sam and Cooper are soon snoozing, the rookie having mastered the difficult (but dignified) hangman's technique. Earl's throbbing finger is once more packed in ice and he sits alone, awake and forlorn.

I drop heavily into the adjacent seat.

"Finger that bad?"

He sighs like an old man. "I can deal with the pain," he says. His eyes are dull, his face is gaunt. How much has he slept in the last week? "What bothers me is all those guys getting called up. Joseph. Hollander. I'm not saying they don't deserve it. Both of them are great players. Hey, Oz ate my lunch before he left. I guess it's Hollander that really sticks me. I'm not one for making excuses, but you've seen me play all year, Rob. You know that this finger is keeping me from playing at my best. *I know* I could stop Hollander if I was healthy. But the NBA scouts look at me and they don't want to hear dick about a broken finger. They just see that my game is outta whack. It sucks."

"Take some time off," I propose. "At least until the swelling goes down or the pain is more manageable. You look like an insomniac. Jeez, your health is more important than a ballgame."

A lie. In truth, I'm telling him what he wants to hear. I tell him to rest because I know he won't.

"Thanks, Rob. But the more games we can win, the better my chances of getting called up. The NBA guys are more likely to go with players who are still playing. I mean, look at Royce Ferguson. Even if anybody's interested in him, he's been sitting on his ass for almost a week now. How sharp can he be? So I'm much better off playing. And who's gonna pick up an injured player?"

He opens the zip-lock bag and pours some excess water into a console ashtray that stands beside his seat, then repositions the icebag around his finger.

"Rob? Remember that last practice before the Rangers series? Damn. It seems like a year ago."

"Sure do."

"Tripucka had just gotten hurt and I told you that I'd rather be in the playoffs with the Stars than sit on the bench and play out the string with the Hornets. Remember that?"

"Yes." He'd given me heart, making me feel that all the work I'd done, the tapes I'd studied, the plotting of Xs and Os, had been meaningful. Sure, I remember.

"Well, it was a lie. I'd rather be a janitor in the NBA than a superstar in the CBL."

The Cosmos are taking the same flight and they're all wearing ties and jackets. Millhouse is nowhere in sight. There are some free seats at the gate across from us and the Cosmos players bunch together, reading newspapers (sports sections?), eating breakfast McD's from several open paper bags provided by their trainer. Thomas James is even reading a book.

My path intersects with Charley Henderson as we both close in on a nearby water fountain. A good ol' boy with a wide face and narrow hillbilly eyes, Henderson has played for seven NBA teams during the nine years since he graduated from Ole Miss. Big white bodies who never complain are always at a premium in the NBA. We exchange polite salutations and I ask him where Millhouse is.

"Coach never travels with the team," he says. "He's always got some kind of business deal happening somewheres or other. I'm thinking he left Savannah last night. Come to think on it, he might be up to Hilton Head playing some golf. Y'all know he always takes his golf clubs on the road?"

"Yeah. Say, that's great about Brian, isn't it?"

"You bet," says the big man. "Coach says some guy name of Darwin Spencer is meeting us back in Cap City. Y'all know him? He any good?"

The shuttle to Atlanta is uneventful but we disembark to discover that a snowstorm in New England has temporarily closed the airport in Capital City. Our flight out is delayed by at least two hours.

Because I am so magnanimous, because I want to beat Millhouse so badly that my conscience has grown another face, I will nonetheless take the opportunity to try and make peace with Sam. I find him watching a soap opera in a bar near Gate B33.

"Sam."

"Shh," he says. "I gotta see this. I'll bet you Alexandra's gonna ditch him."

On the screen, a lovely blonde woman is telling a gray-smocked and slightly bloodsplattered young surgeon that she's "involved" with another man, a certain U.S. senator. She thanks the surgeon for putting her "face" and her "life back together." But her "heart has a life of its own."

The scene fades into a commercial for SPRUNT, a disposable douche. "Bitch," Sam says, sipping a coke. Then he turns to me, puckering his sweetheart smile. "What up, homey?"

"Straight up, Sam. We've got to resolve this problem between us. We don't even talk to each other any more. It's ridiculous."

"The problem," he says, "is all about respect."

"I do respect you, Sam. But I can't respect the way you waste your talent. I'm not gonna bullshit you. That little speech you delivered to us at the team meeting in Oklahoma was a fucking bad joke. How can I respect you when you don't respect anybody?"

"I know," he says, then he signals the waitress for another Coke and lifts his eyebrows to indicate this round's on him. According to Jewish folklore, drinking seltzer is good for the digestion, so I order club soda with a twist of lime.

"I should be in the NBA," Sam continues, "but I'm just another fuckup. Lookit, the CBL is full of fuckups like me. You wanna know something? I've actually been thinking about the NBA a lot lately, with the Beast going up. With Oz and Hollander too. I'm almost thirty, Rob, and at this point in my life maybe I'm afraid of the NBA. Maybe I really can't do it anymore at that level. Maybe I never could. Maybe it's good enough to be a big frog in a pisspond. I figure I could play three more top-caliber years here. Four or five if I'd take care of myself, which I know I won't. Lookit, I don't need to get up to The League and be embarrassed, you know? The CBL is safe. The CBL is easy. And I don't care what anybody says 'cause I been there . . . But the pussy in the CBL is just as good as NBA pussy. In fact, CBL pussy is younger, fresher, not as stretched out around the edges. You know what I'm saying?"

Yeah, sure. But what about the future? Playing in Europe? Money for his dotage?

"I played in France for a while," he says, "and I hated it. Nobody speaks English and you can't get a good meal. And lookit. I never told anybody this before . . . the toilet paper over there is like sandpaper. I had a rash on my ass all the time I was there. Fuck Europe. Everything's too strange over there."

"But we all need money, Sam. The meter's ticking."

"I'll worry about money later on. Who you talking to, man? There's always a way for a slick operator to fill his pockets. Lookit. Ballplayers travel all over the country, right? And nobody ever checks us out. I mean, nobody ever looks into our bags no matter what. Right?"

"Aw, shit, Sam . . . are you selling drugs? What're you saying?"

"I'm just talking about possibilities, man. Don't get a rupture.

Just be thinking about this, Rob. I've still got plenty of that red ketchup flowing in my million-dollar legs. Get me the ball and I can win it for you. I promise."

The waitress brings our drinks and clears the table. She's an old white woman and Sam gives her a five dollar tip for five dollars' worth of drinks.

"Rob," he says when she's gone, "I respect what you did to Lem. He had it coming. I also respect what you did to me. Maybe I had it coming too. Herm is a fucking wimp, we all know that. You? You're a stand-up guy. But in the CBL it's every man for himself."

I try to sleep on the long flight to Capital City, but the passenger sitting in front of me reclines his seat all the way back, pushing hard against my poor defenseless knees. The guy wears a brown business suit and a stiff gray crewcut. There's a porto-computer on his lap.

"Excuse me, sir? Do you think you could move your seat to the straight-back position? There's not much room back here for my legs as it is."

He ignores me and continues to peck at his machine.

"Excuse me? Sir? I'm six-foot-eight and your seat is crushing my knees."

His lap machine beeps and he pivots his head slightly, saying, "Look, bud. I paid good money for this seat. I can lean it back if I want to."

"Yeah. Well, I paid good money for my seat, too."

"Too bad, bud. Fly first-class next time."

I am surprised how quickly my blood is stirred. "You asshole," I say, then I bang the back of his seat with the heel of my hand. *Whump, whump*, like a jackhammer.

Finally, he summons a stewardess. Her solution is simple— moving me to a vacant seat in the first-class section.

We arrive in Capital City at 4:05 to find ten inches of fresh snow on the ground, and we don't reach the Highway House until 5:15. We'll watch the latest game-tape at 5:30 in my room. Don't be late.

Kelly Royal's flight from New York was due in at 1:45 this afternoon. But he's not at the motel and he's left no message.

I instruct the clerk at the front desk to notify me if/when Kelly shows, and to hold all other calls.

The motel is a dump, the worst in the league. There's not a highway within miles, just 200 rooms on two tiers, facing either the front or the rear parking lots, or else the parking lot of a White Castle stomach-burger emporium. There's also a pronto-service pizza palace across the street.

In my room there's a one-inch gap between the threshold and the bottom of the front door, large enough for the entrance to be soaking wet and dusted with snow. The heating system is almost too clangorous to use, the drab brown wallpaper is peeling, the showerhead leaks and the toilet gurgles.

The players invade my room, armed with cans of soda, bottles of juice, packets of cookies, popcorn, chips and candy bars (why are the brothers so inordinately fond of Snickers?). Nate and Earl bring a pizza. Sam has a sausage sandwich.

We watch the first and fourth quarters . . . Must we play angry to play well?

I stop the tape early in the fourth quarter to make what I think is an important observation. "Look who's on the floor for them . . . James, Wagman, Toggins, Andrews and Miller. I think this is the group Millhouse is going with tomorrow night. Toggins for Hollander and Miller for Henderson. I don't think Henderson's been as dominating as they thought he'd be. Josh and Coop are too quick for him to cover. Okay. This is a much quicker unit, not as big, not as strong, but quicker up and down the floor, and quicker to the ball. Look at what this unit runs . . . passing game II . . . and isos for Toggins . . . See? They also want to break. James and Toggins can both carry the ball. Which means what? What's the key element in tomorrow's game?"

"They can't run without the ball," Earl says. "We beat them if we control the boards."

"Exactly. Now let's look at this segment once more . . ."

Josh falls asleep in a chair and I anoint his cleanshaven, craggy head with several drops of Cooper's apple juice. Josh wakes up laughing.

When they leave, my room is strewn with wrappers, empty cups, unpopped kernels of corn, the residue of their movable feast. There are also two large tomato-sauce stains on the bed cover.

We are snowbound and the mall is out of reach. It's an evening for recuperation, for spiritual tranquility. I have my book, my tape, there's an acceptable Chinese restaurant several streets over that delivers ($10 minimum order) and the Atlanta–Cleveland game is on TBS.

Yes, yes. I love the snow, the pristine totality of it, infinite flakes in infinite shapes, falling on mansions and tenements, on flower beds and graveyards.

And I love the rhythm of the seasons, the deaths and the always miraculous rebirths. Another undeniable cycle to reaffirm the significance of all we do. Yes. I miss the wintertime. I wish there was a CBL franchise in Buffalo. And what the worthy habitants of Savannah really need is an occasional ten-inch snowfall to humble them.

I am fascinated by the Cleveland Cavaliers' offense. The spacing is a revelation—through all their picks and cuts, the players wind up at least fifteen feet apart from each other. That's why the Cavs' pivot play is so difficult to double. That's why there are ample lanes for dribble penetration and the passing angles are so wonderfully clean and acute. What great geometry! A good offense is a joy forever.

But, Brian doesn't play and I doze off in the middle of the fourth quarter.

There's a Charlie Chan movie playing when a rumbling snowplow awakens me. Staggering to my feet, I enter the bathroom and switch on the light. And there on the floor, scurrying wildly as though escaping from a death ray, is a congress of cockroaches. Most of them vanish through an aperture where the floor doesn't quite meet the base of the toilet bowl. One is caught inside the bowl, feasting on the crud that adheres to the porcelain just above the water line. I literally piss him off, then use him for target practice (The Omniscient Dick of God) before subjecting him to the Big Flush.

The roach will doubtless survive, likely to crawl out of the washbasin's faucet when I brush my teeth in the morning.

And the question arises ... which would *I* rather be? A cockroach that eats shit and survives for millennia? Or a butterfly that lives in gossamer beauty for a summer, then dies?

O to coach in the Cosmic Butterfly League.

For alas, in the Cockroach Basketball League we all eat shit and die anyway.

24

VAGUE DREAMS OF arctic tundra, of fucking an hospitable Eskimo's ice-cunted wife, and I wake up shivering, my blankets curled around my legs. I turn the heat on and the system clangs and coughs like the late Jack Benny's Maxwell. I call the front desk.

"Kelly Royal?" the clerk says cheerily. "Yes, he checked in at two o'clock this morning."

And there he is in the van, wearing a new set of sweats and a glistening short-haired fur coat (sealskin?) that's also brand-new. "I went from Brooklyn over to New York," he says, "to see all of my homeboys. Then the snow closed the airports so I just hung around New York and took a train up here last night. No big deal. A four-hour ride."

What happened with the grand jury?

"Not as bad as I expected," he says. "They went over everything about ten times trying to trip me up. It was a long, long session, about six hours. But it was easy to lie to them."

What about his new outfit?

"One of my boys owed me some money and I also cashed in the plane ticket."

The coat cost what? Two thousand?

"Nah, one of my boys hooked me up with some Mafia dudes at the airport. They had a rack of 'em, all stolen. Cost me three hundred."

Highly unlikely, but not worth a cross-examination.

*   *   *

The Cosmos home arena has long been a problem for the team's owner, Jason Duffy, a reclusive millionaire and native of Capital City. It's the Jefferson Street Armory, an enormous red-brick structure built prior to World War I, owned by the U.S. Army and used mostly for storage and also as a training center for reservists. The outside walls and the roof are faced with false turrets and battlements, giving a colossal, medieval quality to the building.

Inside, the basketball court is surrounded with backless bleacher seats, which can accommodate 2,800 spectators, and SRO crowds raise the total capacity to 3,500. The rest-room facilities may be primitive but the Armory is a cozy, idiosyncratic place to see a ballgame.

Since the Cosmos control all the game-time concessions (hot dogs, nachos, sodas, the usual empty snacks, plus at least $2,500 per game generated by the sale of beer), the ballclub certainly is capable of making money. Too bad there are no parking lots in the neighborhood. Also, the installation of cable-TV throughout the Capital City environs was completed two years ago and, since then, more and more erstwhile Cosmos fans have opted to stay home and watch NBA games for free. Last year, the franchise lost $375,000.

The most evident problem concerns the temperature level inside the building, and therein hangs a tale . . . The sale of beer is forbidden inside Capital City's high schools and the Armory was the only other suitable alternative when Jason Duffy purchased the rights to a CBL franchise in 1980. For a time, Duffy threatened to establish his franchise in a 7,000-seat civic auditorium in upstate Binghamton. But the good burghers of Capital City believed that a CBL team would mean black ink across the board, and a substantial amount of well-oiled political pressure forced the army to lease the Armory to the Cosmos.

In return for the inflated sum of $100,000 payable to the federal government, the U.S. Army Corps of Engineers was obligated to purchase and install a basketball court. For another $50,000, the army also arranged for the bleachers and the portable concession stands. The annual leasing fee was established at $75,000.

However, the day after the agreement was legally validated, Duffy contended that the army was also required to heat the premises during the Cosmos training camp, practice sessions and ballgames, a total of about sixty dates every season. The government stoutly maintained that the Cosmos were solely responsible for "temperature regulation." Apparently the relevant section of the leasing agreement was less than conclusive and extensive litigation was initiated before the Cosmos ever played a ballgame. Since it costs nearly $1,000 every time the heat switch is activated, the annual sum under dispute approaches $60,000, not including the playoffs.

Now, this Duffy character is a high roller who pays his basketball staff and his players more than any of their counterparts earn on any other CBL team. He has bucks to burn, but he will not let Uncle Sam bamboozle him. Until the lawsuits are finally resolved, the issue of whether or not there is to be heat in the building somehow depends upon a complicated mathematical formula that measures outside temperatures and degree days. The formula and its implementation are under the jurisdiction of a computer in the Pentagon and an anonymous retired general rumored to live in Albuquerque. The legal costs and the monies being held in escrow have long ago exceeded the two million mark. Duffy is a stubborn man.

What it all means to the Savannah Stars is that we can see our breath vaporizing inside the frigid Armory. When the weather is especially cold outside, visiting teams have been known to practice in hats and gloves. The Cosmos? They practice at a nearby high school.

As to the second problem, there are rumored to be tanks and live ammunition stored in the subbasement, but the basketball court is dangerous enough. The surface of the court is always slick as an ice-skating rink, the result of an improper oil-based compound used to seal the floorboards when they were first installed. To rectify the situation the court would have to be sanded down to raw wood, then repainted and resealed. The army will not swallow the $4,000 cost of the project and the governmental red tape also prohibits the involvement of a private contractor.

To make a bad situation even worse, the Armory's front and side entrances have been opened wide this morning to allow the arrival and storage of various military vehicles (mostly jeeps and armored troop-carriers). So, in addition to the intolerable temperature, we are being asked to conduct our gameday shootaround in the teeth of an Arctic headwind. Even the large proud banner suspended high above centercourt is flapping like a flag in a hurricane:

CAPITAL CITY COSMOS
1988–89
CBL CHAMPIONS OF THE WORLD

It's not worth the risk of pulled muscles and jammed fingers, so I send the rookie to find a phone and have the van fetch us back to the motel. Meanwhile, the rest of us huddle in a semi-sheltered angle beneath the bleachers.

Back at the motel my room is a sweat box and the heating apparatus sounds like an escaped convict trying to smash his leg chains with a sledgehammer. Shutting off the heat, I call the Chinese kitchen to order lunch and then try to nap while the room is still warm.

Just as I take the first tumble over the edge, the phone rings. It's Earl. "Tune to NWZ," he says. "Channel three. Quick."

Flicking the switch, I see an elongated human form seated in a swivel chair, his legs stretched and crossed, his hands clasped neatly in his lap and a large blue dot where his face should be. ". . . didn't do nothing," the figure says in an electronically altered but still familiar voice. "There were three guys on the team shaving points. For seven games they did it, but they weren't real good about doing it so we lost three of those seven games. Each guy got paid five thousand for a game. I saw the money. I heard the guys talking about it. I was there, man. But I didn't do nothing."

An announcer speaks in grave tones about "these astonishing accusations from a former player at Metropolitan University." The interview is billed as an NWZ exclusive.

"It's obviously Kelly," Earl says. "I'll bet they paid him to do it."

"I'll call him. Thanks, Earl. Get some rest."

The phone wakes Kelly and I must wait until he coughs, gasps and regains his senses. When I tell him about the NWZ interview he barely hesitates before saying, "I don't know nothing about no interview, Coach. I didn't do nothing. I swear on my mother."

Visiting teams always come to ballgames at the Armory dressed in their uniforms and warmups because the bathrooms and the showers are located down the hall, inside the public men's room. The locker room itself is miniscule, measuring perhaps 15' x 15'. One wall is lined with ancient, dented lockers so flaked with rust that the players will only stash their street shoes inside. Spare towels, overcoats and winter jackets are draped over the wire hangers which are hooked to a criss-crossed network of overhead pipes. The room is cold, dusty and smells faintly of decomposing mammals. There's one window at the far end so coated with gunk as to be opaque. And there's a solitary brick lying on the lower righthand corner of the windowsill. A brick? When I remove it I see a brick-sized gap in the window glass and a chill wind suddenly blasts through the room.

A tiny blackboard is mounted on the wall opposite the lockers. The only pieces of available chalk are the size of my smallest fingernail. In any case, the surface of the blackboard is much too greasy to retain any kind of chalk, crayon, pen or even painted markings. The surrounding walls are desperately scratched with sharp objects, as generations of visiting coaches have sought in vain to find a medium for their pregame messages.

Even though the basement locker room is cold, the players are in no rush to go upstairs and run around the court. It's cold up there too, the operational principle being, "the smaller the crowd, the colder the Armory."

Meanwhile, Earl has learned that Kelly received four Gs for the NWZ gig, most of which he's already spent on his new coat and on a high-flying party he threw for his New York friends on Monday night. Kelly's been boasting of caviar and champagne, of buying $180 Nikes for all of his hometown "pardners."

The locker room's doorway measures only 6'6" high, a constant menace. On his way back from the bathroom Josh conks his bare noggin when he forgets to duck. The contact is hard enough to draw a spot of blood and raise a welt. Josh doesn't even blink.

Upstairs, one of the baskets is notoriously crooked, mounted on a backboard that's at least ten degrees removed from being parallel to the baseline. Normally, I'd rather we played our second half defense at the basket in front of our bench. This way, in the most critical part of the game, I can easily call all the switches, traps and doubles we may need. Since the visiting team always has the choice of baskets, I tell captains Earl and Nate to reverse our usual procedure and start the game off by shooting at the far basket, the crooked one. It's a gamble, but we'll gain a significant psychological advantage, should we have the lead at halftime.

I review the Cosmos personnel and their plays. As before, we will attack them with our 4-up series, pick-and-roll plays for Nate and Sam. Otherwise, my instructions are cursory. "We have only eight players, so everybody plays and everybody has to be ready to play. The Cosmos think that Monday's game was an accident, that we're finished. But let's remember how we felt when they pressed us at the end of Sunday's game. The slate won't be clean until we win the series. Let's play hard and let's play smart."

"DO IT!"

The bad weather has limited our audience to less than 1,000 (the Cosmos will announce a capacity crowd). The county offices were closed today due to the snow and the beer-swilling young lawyers who regularly constitute the loudest group of Cosmos fans are noticeably absent. Still, someone yells at Kelly, "Hey, Royal . . . what's the point spread?" And a security guard must be sent for when another fan throws pennies on the floor as Kelly practices his free throws.

The visitors bench is composed of a dozen folding chairs, and as always, there's a fleet of wheelchairs parked too close behind us. Mostly unfortunates who have been otherwise immobilized by cerebral palsy, their steel-braced legs are pushed into the open backs of our chairs, which requires us to spend the game leaning forward and sitting/squatting on the front edges of our seats. Uncomfortable, distracting, yes, but how can one possibly complain and not be considered a monster?

The officials are Rennie Carson, a part-time NBAer who never calls illegal defenses, and Chad Gland, a CBL deadender who's too slow to run himself into the proper sightlines.

The Cosmos do indeed start Toggins in place of Hollander, but Henderson also starts and the reason is soon apparent. When we try our pick-and-roll sequences, Henderson always defends the picker (be he Nate or Cooper), using his superior strength to shove said picker beyond the three-point arc and thereby aborting the play. At the other end, Toggins is more mobile than Earl, and Carl is a step too slow in leaving James for the trap.

STARS–10   CC–16

They're outhustling us and playing us even on the boards. I call a :20 and change our approach. We'll go back to 40 and 40L, isolating Cooper against Henderson at the elbow. We'll also post Earl against the 6'3" Toggins.

Perfecto. Cooper forces Henderson out of the game with successive slashing moves that culminate in two layups and two fouls on the bigger man. Then, with Miller in for Henderson, our pick-and-roll options become functional.

Also, Carl begins to cheat off James to impair Toggins's creativity. And Earl easily overpowers Toggins in the lane. When the double comes, Earl always finds the open man.

STARS–25   CC–23

Toggins is instructed to front Earl in the pivot, so we move Nate to the high post and the lob pass becomes an easy option. For the time being, Millhouse has no answer for Earl in the box.

Carl doesn't miss a beat—his confidence is soaring and his shots are falling. Sam is mildly irritated because Earl is the focus of the offense, but Earl keeps him well supplied with easy jumpers.

STARS–38   CC–37

Offense is no problem for us tonight. Nor for them. With Henderson benched, the body contact is minimal and it's a wide-open ballgame, more finesse than power. Unless somebody steps up on defense, whoever has the last possession of the game will most likely win.

STARS–47   CC–49

Nate is shooting well but has no presence near the basket. Josh's shot-blocking heroics represent our only defense. Still, our offensive sets confuse Josh and his motto is, "When in doubt, air it out."

Kelly is miffed that Carl has supplanted him and shooting jumpers has become his misbegotten priority. Then James rips him twice and I must return Kelly to the bench. When Earl tires, Sam is delighted to resume his role as the Stars' top gunslinger.

STARS—58   CC—56

Sam cradles the ball, faking and head-jabbing at Wagman, who nervously tries to defend him. "I'm gonna hurt you, boy," Sam promises, then spins left and drops a twenty-footer. Not even the defensive ministrations of Eric Mann can control Sam. After banking another acrobatic jumper, Sam yells over to Millhouse, "You gotta kill me to stop me."

It's Wild West shoot 'em up basketball, and we lead at halftime, 68–62.

I remind them that the Cosmos must now attack the crooked basket, then I nag them about our lack of defense. "Doesn't anyone here want to play D? Does anyone here even know how to spell it? It's like a playground game out there. If we want to win we must work harder on defense!"

"DO IT!"

This is what I sound like on the bench:

"Three seconds! Get him outta there! . . . Get up, Nate! Rebound! . . . Box out! . . . Push it! . . . Run with him, Sam! . . . Twenty-two L! . . . What a terrible call, Chad! No, no! Don't try to sell it to me! It's not even your call! . . . Three seconds! . . . Four-up! . . . Double him, Carl! . . . Illegal! . . . Yo, Carl! Double-X down! . . . No, no, Sam! . . . Yes, Sam! . . . Switch! . . . Red! Shoot it! . . . Get back! . . . Make the goddamn call! He's getting killed in there! . . . Kelly! Thirty-five! . . . Are you serious? What game are you watching? . . . Illegal! . . . Buck up and play defense! . . . Illegal! They can't double-team a player who doesn't have the ball! . . . Josh! The other side! . . . Never mind the call, Coop! That was good D! . . . Forty B! . . . Illegal! They've got to move toward the area of intersection! . . . Box him out, Nate! . . . Don't guess! Call what you see! . . . Josh! Run the fucking play! . . . Ah, shit!"

STARS—96   CC—99

Sam now carries us and we begin to forge ahead. Snap, the net flips as he hits another three-pointer, then he carooms a sharp-angled jumper high off the glass and in. "The bank is open late tonight," he shouts. Sam hits threes like they were layups.

STARS–109   CC–103

Earl is wearing Toggins down, so, in desperation, Millhouse inserts Darwin Spencer into the small-forward slot. For a while Spencer's long arms and fresh legs override Earl's postup moves. But Sam's sharpshooting keeps our heads above the rim.

Then Carl snatches the dribble out of Spencer's hands. Cooper blocks Wagman's attempted layup. Earl takes a charge against Miller. And our defense has turned the game around.

Near the end, Sam has a breakaway. After his ram-slam-in-yo-mama's-eyes dunker, Sam hangs onto the rim with his left hand and points his free hand at Millhouse. "Eat outa my ass, sugar."

We win going away, 130–121.

Shrieking and laughing, we clamber down the stairs and dash into the locker room. "We got 'em," Sam yelps. "We got 'em." As before, we hug each other, we dance and hop about like kiddies on Christmas morning until the flush passes.

"We haven't won anything yet," I tell them. There'll be practice tomorrow. I'll leave a message about the time and place. For now, they're to towel off before venturing outside and boarding the van.

"Thank you, Father, for making all things possible. Amen!"

Afterward, bathed in the postgame glow, I buy the pizza and the beer for Earl and Nate and we watch TV in their room. Kelly's interview has been sold to all comers and is the leadoff story on the TV Sports Center.

"What a fool he is," Nate says. "What're you gonna do about it, Rob?"

"Nothing."

Eventually, we get silly drunk and tonight's subject turns out to be famous CBL brawls. Like the time Stanley Brooks (a CBL vet

COMMERCIAL BASKETBALL LEAGUE

Official Scorer's Report

Date March 28, 1442 Game # 03 Arena Jefferson Street Armory Attendance: 3479
Visitors: Savannah Stars Home Capitol City Cosmos Length of Game: 2:07

No.	Visitors: Stars	Min.	FG M	FG A	FT M	FT A	3Pt M	3Pt A	Pts.	Reb O	D	TOT	AST	PF	TO	BS	ST
6	Royal	8	1	5	1	1	0	1	3	0	0	0	0	3	2	0	0
7	Franks (G)	42	13	21	6	7	5	7	37	1	2	3	1	3	1	0	1
8	Butler (G)	40	6	10	4	5	0	0	16	2	3	5	11	4	2	1	3
10	Cooper (c)	38	8	16	4	5	0	0	20	3	9	12	1	5	2	3	1
11	Brusher	30	5	12	2	4	0	0	12	2	7	9	0	4	3	5	0
12	Hennison (F)	36	9	18	1	1	0	1	19	0	3	3	0	3	1	1	0
32	Patton (F)	40	8	14	6	9	0	2	22	4	7	11	6	5	2	1	2
40	Springs	6	0	5	1	1	0	0	1	0	2	2	1	2	0	1	1
	TOTALS	24	50	101	25	33	5	11	130	12	33	45	20	31	13	12	8
	Pct.		49.5		75.8		45.4			Team 7					4			

No.	Home: Cosmos	Min.	FG M	FG A	FT M	FT A	3Pt M	3Pt A	Pts.	Reb O	D	TOT	AST	PF	TO	BS	ST
12	James (G)	42	4	7	2	2	0	0	10	2	2	4	7	3	4	0	2
15	Smith	10	0	1	0	1	0	0	0	0	1	1	1	2	3	0	1
20	Mann	10	1	2	1	1	0	0	3	0	2	2	0	2	0	0	1
24	Henderson (c)	17	2	4	1	1	0	0	5	1	3	4	2	3	0	1	0
31	Wagman (G)	34	8	13	4	4	3	6	23	1	1	2	2	4	4	0	1
34	Spencer	10	2	4	1	1	0	0	5	1	3	4	0	1	1	1	0
35	Jerome	DNP															
42	Toggins (F)	45	10	21	7	9	2	4	29	2	4	6	1	4	2	0	1
44	Andrews (F)	35	9	14	7	11	0	0	25	2	11	13	3	3	2	2	0
55	Miller	27	8	18	5	7	0	0	21	1	8	9	2	4	3	1	1
	TOTALS	240	44	94	28	37	5	10	121	10	36	46	18	26	19	5	7
	Pct.		46.8		75.4		50.0			Team 2					6			

Score By Quarters	1	2	3	4	OT	OT	OT	Final
V: Stars	38	30	29	33				130
H: Cosmos	37	25	37	22				121

Officials: Rennie Carson, Chad Gland
Technicals:

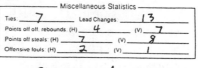

— Miscellaneous Statistics —
Ties: 7 Lead Changes 13
Points off off. rebounds (H) 4 (V) 7
Points off steals (H) 7 (V) 8
Offensive fouls (H) 2 (V) 1

Remarks: Stars lead series 2-1

239

who also played with the Knicks and the Bulls) stood at center-court during a timeout in a game at the Armory and challenged the entire crowd. "I can't even remember what started the whole shebang," says Earl, "but three drunks rushed him and he KO'd them one after another. Bap! Bap! Bap! The fans were throwing garbage and the refs were hiding out. Brooks was jumping around, beating on his chest like Hulk Hogan. This went on for about ten minutes. Every so often some fan would come out of the stands and make a little run at Brooks, then scoot back into the stands. If Brooks had ordered all of them to throw their wallets and watches onto the court and then leave, I swear they'd've done it. Finally, the riot cops came and Brooks was ready to fight them too. But they cuffed him and dragged him off the floor. I remember that we didn't get another call for the rest of the game and we lost in overtime."

. . . Or the time T-Bone Donaldson, a one-time Golden Glover, punched out Dave Scaley in the locker room. "Way I heard it," Nate says, "Scaley was the puncher and T-Bone was the punchee."

. . . Or the time three years ago when I was coaching in Peoria and I flew Red Lewison in from Los Angeles. "The trading dead-line was past," I say, "and my ballclub was getting too compla-cent. I needed something to shake them up, and Red was six-ten, two-sixty and meaner than a cat in a bag. I knew he had a big-time dope problem but I told him to come on out, be physical and we'd see what would happen. So Red takes the red-eye from L.A. and goes straight from the airport to the gym where we're practicing. He puts on his gear, jumps on the court and starts pounding everybody. Well, all my players are worried that maybe Red's here to replace them, right? So there's a battle royal out there. Elbows flying, punches thrown and I don't do a thing, don't even call a foul. We practiced for two hours and Red gets involved in three different fist-up fights with three different players. Mike Pressley, Freddie Harris and Duke Blanchard. Remember them? It's ba-sically ten guys against Red and he can't help but get the worst of it. Broken nose, cuts over both eyes, his lip split, his jaw swollen. After practice we take Red over to the hospital to get patched up. Then we give him a hundred bucks and put him right back on a plane for L.A. Right? And my team goes out and wins ten straight."

*   *   *

Several messages have been slipped under my door. They're all wet and blurred but I can guess who they are—Herm, Chet, T-Bone, the Savannah media muppets. Who else has any desire to speak to me? I promise myself to end my "sacred solitude" and return all the calls tomorrow, and tomorrow's a long time away from right now. Maybe I'll stay awake all night nurturing my mental orgasm as long as possible.

For now, I want to think only about THE WIN. THE W. THE DOUBLE-U.

Sufficient unto the day
is the DUB thereof.

25

JUST ONCE I'D like to be awakened by an act of God. The sunlight making my eyes blink. A rooster crowing outside my window. A tornado ripping off the roof. Even the natural pressure of a bursting bladder would be acceptable. Anything but the damn telephone, ringing this particular morning at 8:49 A.M.

"Rob? It's Points. Sam. You won't believe this . . . I just got a call from Millhouse. He said he's had enough of me showing him up during a ballgame. He said he's bringing two bodyguards to tomorrow's game. He called them glass-eaters. He said if I embarrassed him one more time, his bodyguards will kill me. That's the word he used, kill. He said they'll come right out on the court and twist my head off like the cap on a bottle of soda pop. He said he's not fooling around. I think he's stone crazy. The pressure's getting to him. He never thought we'd be ahead of them. I think he's just trying to scare me."

"Did it work? Are you scared?"

"I'll tell you this . . . He sure sounded desperate enough. But no, I'm not scared. Well, maybe a little."

"I'll take care of it, Sam."

"You can't do nothing, Rob. This is between me and him. What time's practice?"

"Don't know yet. You'll be the first to know."

"Later."

*   *   *

242

It's another instance of Millhouse illegally tampering with my players. What I should do is wait until the CBL office opens in Chicago, then call Smiley and nail the bastard.

In the meantime, Steve Collins is responsible for arranging practices on the road. I call his room but the line is busy. After attending to my morning ablutions I call again. BIZ. BIZ. BIZ. So I get dressed—gray sweats and scruffy sneax—and search out Steve's room.

According to my handy-dandy room list he's on the upper floor, 241, and there's an even bigger space under his door. I carefully case the area until I'm certain no one's around, then I drop to my knees and peep under the door.

I can see most of the room . . . His phone is off the hook and he's sitting in front of the TV watching a ballgame. His right hand is clenched in front of his face so that only his thumb protrudes. "He tries it from eighteen feet!" Steve tells his thumb. "And he has it . . . He tries it . . . He has it . . . I love it!"

I hear footsteps crunching in the snow so I struggle to my feet. The footsteps belong to a middle-aged black woman with a surly expression, apparently one of the Highway House's maids, and she glares at me as she passes. Then I knock on the door and Steve calls, "Entrez."

The floor is littered with clothing, pizza boxes, pizza crusts, empty beer bottles and disjointed newspapers. Steve looks up from his thumb and says, "And here he is, folks! The CBL's Coach of the Year! Tell our fans out there in fanland what it feels like to outcoach the legendary Barry Millhouse. Is this the greatest thrill in your life so far?" Then he points his thumb at me.

"Put that thing away," I tell him, and he goes through the motion of placing his thumb in a holster. "Is this what you do all day, Steve? In the airport, on planes, everywhere?"

"If you want to be a star," he says as though I were a recalcitrant child, "you have to pay your dues."

I tell him that I'd like a two-hour practice, preferably from 1:00 till 3:00, but under no circumstances starting later than 5:00. The Armory is not acceptable.

"I'll get right on it, chief," he says. "You know they can't beat you. You've got them psyched."

Yeah. Sure.

Back in my room, I phone the front desk to open my line to incoming calls. "By the way," I say, "could you tell me if there was a call to Sam Franks, that's Room 137, at about eight-thirty this morning?"

A nasal whine: "Sorry, sir. The computer is down. We have no record of incoming calls."

Computer in this dump? My ass.

I call the Cosmos office and ask the receptionist for Millhouse. "I'll connect you with the coach's office, sir. Whom shall I say is calling?"

"Red Auerbach."

"Just one moment, please."

Then Fishwick says, "Hello? Mr. Auerbach, sir? This is Dave Fishwick, the Cosmos Director of Player Personnel? I've always been a big fan of yours. How can I help you?"

"I need to speak to Millhouse."

"Hey, you're not Red Auerbach. You're Bo Lassner!"

"That's all right. Red and I go to the same shul. Now go get Millhouse."

"Coach Millhouse is busy watching films," Fishwick says stiffly. "He can't be disturbed."

"Listen, you imbecile, go get Millhouse or I'll come over there and rip your fucking wick off."

There's a fumbling, a mumbling, a clacking, then Millhouse says, "Coach, how are you? We haven't had much of a chance to speak, have we? You're doing a great job! It's a great series!"

"Tell me . . . Did you call Sam Franks at the motel earlier this morning? I wanted to ask you before I checked with the motel's switchboard."

"As a matter of fact, I did call to congratulate him. Me and Points go back a long way, you know? I tried to recruit him in the old days when I was at Southwest Florida. But I've never seen him play any better than he is now. You must be a great motivator, coach."

"Sam said you threatened to have some goons kill him if he fucked with you during the game."

"What? That's idiotic. Talking trash is part of the game. I do the same thing. Ask Patton. I've been around too long to let that kind of stuff bother me."

"Sam swears that you threatened him."

"He's lying," Millhouse says. "Maybe he had a bad dream. Maybe it's just someone he ate." When I refuse to laugh he continues: "Maybe Points is doing drugs again. That's been a concern for him ever since he was in high school. Anyway, I wouldn't worry about it. He's for sure not playing like he's stoned. Well, I do have to get back to work. There's a certain problem I have to solve. Like how the heck can we beat you two-for-two? So nice of you to call."

So I call Sam and relate Millhouse's version of their conversation. "That's bullshit," Sam says. "Why would I lie, Rob? What would I gain by lying?"

Who knows? A ready-made excuse, should he flub tomorrow's game? . . . "Millhouse said he recruited you out of high school."

"That's true. He offered me two hundred bucks a week. It was the lowest bid I got . . . what time's practice?"

"I still don't know."

"Get it together, man. Later."

Now I call Steve, who says that the Armory is the only court we can use. According to Fishwick, we can practice any time between 2:00 and 5:00.

Never mind. We'll look at the game tape in my room at 3:00. Steve will call the front desk and leave word for everybody.

Looks like I'm going to be on the wire all day. "T-Bone? It's Rob."

He's friendly as ever, offering profuse congratulations for our showing against the Cosmos. "Wasn't that Kelly on the news?" he asks. "Why would that boy do something so moronic? How'd he play last night?"

"Like shit. What's happening with your job?"

"No word yet."

"T-Bone, we've been friends for a long while and there's something I have to ask you. I heard that you called Herm several times last week. What's it all about?"

"Dang it, Rob! All's I'm trying to do with Herm is to save your job. What did you think I was up to? I'm just fiddling and diddling and talking him into rehiring you."

"And?"

"Rob. I can't get a read on him at all. He tells me the same stuff my owners tell me. That's he'll reevaluate every damn thing after the season. How can he not rehire you?"

So I tell him how Sam woofed at Rose and somehow I'm "responsible," how Fishwick gladly misconstrued the money that was wagered on the game between Sam and Earl. I explain the various suspensions and Herm's reactions. I tell him there's a TV sportscaster in Savannah who's after me because I won't let him practice with the team. But T-Bone still doesn't see any "legitimate" reason why I should be terminated.

"I'm a foreigner in Savannah. A funny-talking, highfaluting Jew from New Yawk. And Fishwick's been spelunking in Herm's ass."

"Watch that Fishwick. He's a nasty—whoops, there's my other line. Rob, I've got to take this call. Kick 'em. Bye."

Chet is next on my list. Herm is out playing golf, but Chet spoke to him earlier. "Everybody in Savannah saw the NWZ interview," says Chet, "and the phone's been ringing off the hook. Herm is freaked. He wants Kelly suspended, tarred-and-feathered, ridden out of town on a rail, hanged from a tree. Anything. He wants Kelly gone."

"Why?"

"So that nobody can say he's shaving points here."

"But he never did anything at Metro U. He just knows about it."

"Doesn't matter," Chet says. "People down here are naturally suspicious. Kelly's from New York, ain't he?"

"No. He just went to school there. Listen, if I suspend Kelly we're down to seven players."

"Exactly. That's why Herm also wants y'all to bring back Lem Jameson."

"That's absurd."

"Lem was on Packman's TV show last night, saying y'all're a terrible coach. Lem said you won't go to the outhouse without getting permission from Earl Patton. So Packman's conducting a call-in poll. Should the Stars hire you or fire you? I called the 'Hire' number twenty-five times. Y'all owe me lunch."

"But we're up two-to-one on the best team in the league!"

"Loyalty matters most here, Rob. Lem played in Savannah last season and you were in Peoria. But tell you what, win the damn championship and it'll blow over. Still and all, we had five calls into the office so far today wanting to cancel their season's tickets for next year if y'all're rehired. Herm doesn't know what to do. Got to go. Call Herm later and call me back."

I've got to get out, go for a walk. So I perambulate the State Avenue hill, Capital City's primary business district.

The plows have cleared the streets and the county offices are reopened for business. Near the curbs the snow is already black and crusty. The lawyers are out and about, their attaché cases tucked securely under their arms. Shoppers, businessmen, politicians, everybody stares at the sidewalk. Nowadays it may be dangerous to catch the eye of a passerby. After all, Capital City is the county seat where corruption is king, where everybody harbors a conspiracy or a grudge. And who knows? Maybe the guy you sneak a look at is a psychopath with a pistol in his pocket, a razor under his belt, an Uzi up his sleeve. Better to be safe than sorry.

An elderly woman in a shabby mink coat walks an elderly schnauzer. The dog pauses by the curb, sniffs in a slow circle, then squats and squeezes out two small, steaming Tootsie Rolls. The woman pulls a tissue from her purse, bends down and wipes her doggie's ass. The woman looks up and down the street to see if she's being observed—then she daintily kicks some loose snow over the tissue and the turds.

The Armory sits at the top of State Avenue, and when the front door swings open to admit the mailman, a cascade of familiar sounds escapes from within. Basketballs being dribbled. A shrill whistle. A loud, unintelligible voice shouting instructions. Son of a bitch! The heat is switched on and the Cosmos are practicing! I slide inside before the door shuts but a uniformed soldier bars my way and orders me back outside.

There's a public telephone down the street and I call the motel. Steve's line is busy, so I tell the clerk that it's a matter of life and/or death, then I wait while she hurries to knock on his door.

"Hello?" Steve says, a tremor in his voice.

"Relax. It's only me. Call Fishwick and tell him we've changed our minds, that we will practice in the Armory anytime we can. It's already past noon. Then call the players and get them up to speed."

I cruise back down the hill, grab a fish sandwich at Mickey D's and make my way to Steve's room. He reports that most of the players have gone to the mall and that the Armory is off-limits after two o'clock.

So it's back to Plan A, watching the latest flick in my room. "Tell the guys one more thing," I say to Steve. "Not to bring in any food or drinks."

Back inside my room, the phone rings. "Hello?"

"Hi, Rob. It's Joe Patterson from the *Gazette*. What's going on?"

"Nothing much. Just fielding some crank calls from the media."

Patterson wants to know about Kelly's testimony before the grand jury and the NWZ cameras. I know nothing. Then Patterson queries me about Lem's suspension and I take the opportunity to defend myself. "Lem didn't come into the locker room at halftime. Obviously, he doesn't want to be a part of the team."

It seems that Lem told Patterson that he was on his way to join his mates when he received word of an emergency phone call. Lem said that "his granny" was dying back in Baltimore and her last wish was to speak to her "favorite grandchild" before being permanently disconnected.

"He was out in the hall arguing with his squeeze," I say. "A dozen people saw them. Why don't you do your homework? And why are you guys so gullible?"

"If I'm so gullible," says Patterson, "then why should I believe you?"

"Believe who you want to believe," I say before hanging up.

Lord have mercy, the phone rings again—a writer from Sports Illustrated whose name I miss. He wants to know about Kelly. Baha. Baha. Then he says that Commissioner Rose is contemplating the immediate suspension of Kelly, pending a full investigation.

"Investigation of what?" I ask. "There are no charges, no indictments. Just somebody who may or may not be Kelly Royal talking about what some other guys may or may not have done."

"What if," the writer says, "Kelly told the grand jury one thing and told NWZ something completely contradictory."

"That's a lot of ifs."

"Hello?"

"Kelly, it's Rob. Did a writer from Sports Illustrated call you?"

"Yeah. I told him I didn't know nothing. Just like you said."

"Kelly. If that was you on NWZ, then you obviously do know something. Which means that you obviously lied to the grand jury. That you lied under oath. You could go to jail for that."

"Jail! But they told me nobody would ever know. I had new sweats on and everything. What do I do now?"

"Get a grip, Kelly. Do you have a lawyer?"

"Sort of. The school gave me one. His name is F.F. Scolari. He didn't have much to say. Here's his number . . ."

"Mr. Scolari, please."

"Speaking."

Uh oh. No secretary. Probably no office. Who is this guy? But I identify myself and prod him for information. Scolari reveals that Kelly was "uncooperative" before the grand jury and the Brooklyn DA was not satisfied with the witness' "blanket denials."

I warn Scolari of the CBL's intentions re Kelly. "If you want to protect Kelly," I add, "you might call Commissioner Rose and threaten to sue the CBL if they suspend the kid. Tell Rose you'll get an injunction and shut down the playoffs. There's been no crime committed, etcetera. You know what to say. You can bully Rose. Scare him. He'll back down."

"Okay," the lawyer says. "Thanks."

Herm calls on his cellular phone from the 14th tee and we go over the same turf once more. Herm mentions the possibility of "perjury." He's afraid of what Rose will do to Kelly to "protect the integrity of the league." Then Herm urges me to "swap" Kelly for

Lem. "Everybody will understand," he says. "That's the sentiment down here."

"Kelly may be dumb as a bag of rocks," I say, "but I'm not going to sacrifice him. What's wrong with you, Herm? Do you actually believe Lem's story?"

"No, but Savannah wants to believe it, and they don't want to believe you."

"What do you want to believe, Herm?"

"I want to believe that y'all'll do what's best for the team."

"Yeah, like winning the championship."

"We all want that. But it's your decision, Rob. It's up to y'all."

What a fucking coward. The candidate will always encourage someone else to crawl out on a limb as long as he holds the saw.

"Sorry, Herm. I won't throw Kelly away for no reason."

"I'm sorry, too. I think y'all's being loyal to the wrong people."

Even Salvatore Giambalvo calls. Once I "turned him down" he had to send Spencer to Capital City. They were the only team with an open roster spot, and Millhouse offered $500 a game, plus a free hotel room.

"I feel that I owed you an explanation," Sal says. "And what's with that stupid Royal kid? Why go on TV and make an issue of it? In case you're interested, I heard he was shaving points along with the rest of them."

By now the players are here and the tape is loaded, so I disconnect the phone. Carl is stinking drunk and Josh never shows. The others are too quiet, almost glum, as I lead them through the intricacies of game three, our finest performance of the season.

"What's up?" I ask them. "Why's everybody so down?"

"We're just tired," says Nate. "The long season catching up to us. We'll be ready tomorrow."

Suddenly, Carl bolts off the bed, runs into the bathroom and throws up.

I can only quote something appropriate from John Milton, ". . . Sabean odours from the spicy shore of Araby the Blest . . ." And send them away.

I do ask Earl to remain for a moment, then I call the front desk, requesting a maid to clean the bathroom.

"Earl. What the fuck?"

"They don't really believe we can win," he says. "It's enough that we've extended the Cosmos to five games. This team has no heart, Rob. There's nothing you can do."

"But we played so well last night! We're only one win away from playing for the championship!"

"It's like Wile E. Coyote chasing the Roadrunner off a cliff. He's running and chasing the little fucker in midair when all of a sudden he stops, looks down and falls. Rob, it's not your fault. You've taken them as far as they want to go."

"Great . . . and where's Josh?"

"In a holding pattern," Earl says, "about thirty thousand feet above Mars. Hey, I don't even know where he is when he's here."

Shortly thereafter, Herm calls from the 19th hole. "I just spoke to Kelly," he says, and I can hear icecubes tinkling in a glass. "He admits he was the guy on NWZ and he admits that he lied to the grand jury. He said y'all counseled him to perjure himself. Is this true?"

"Herm, I'm disgusted with all this. The kid told me he didn't know nothing from nothing and that's what I told him to say to the grand jury. How you want to twist that around is up to you—hold on, somebody's at the door, I'll call you later."

It's the same maid who caught me peeking under Steve's door. Before she enters the bathroom she sprays the area with a pine-scented deodorizer.

"It wasn't me who did it," I tell the maid. "It wasn't me."

After swabbing and mopping she leaves the room smelling sweet as a nursery. She also refuses a five-dollar tip.

I order twenty-dollars worth of Chinese food before asking the switchboard to kill all my calls. I've had enough. No more. Please.

Then I watch TV for several hours, until I realize that I have no idea what I've been watching. I try to read, but the words are crawling from line to line. So I do pushups and situps until I'm weary enough to sleep. Escape.

26

I'M GETTING A cold, a sinus infection, a strep throat. Which will collapse first, my mind or my body?

Josh remains AWOL when we board the bus for the shootaround. And the Armory is warm, almost too warm. I can feel my sinuses dehydrating. Kelly is (was) Josh's roommate, so while everybody stretches, I squat down beside him and ask, "When was the last time you saw Josh?"

"He was in the room when I got in from New York late on Monday. When I woke up in the morning, he was gone."

"Are his clothes still here?"

"Yes."

So I'm down to seven players—including one point guard who may be going to prison. The other point guard has rubber legs and his face is a brownish shade of green. Sam is all jittery, scratching his arms like a junkie at a prayer meeting. Cooper has apparently withdrawn from the turmoil, wearing his earphones and listening to Richard Burton rhapsodize about the Apocalypse. Of the others, Brent bristles with enthusiasm (I must find some more playing time for him), Nate seems drained and Earl is disgusted.

The shootaround is a waste of time. Sure, they sweat and when the script requires a fancy move they grunt and glide. They know their cues like worn-out hookers.

Can't say as I blame them. There are only two letters in my alphabet—Mr. X and Ms. O—and my strategical exegesis sounds stale even to me. Maybe we're all husbanding our energies until tonight.

Back at the motel, I can identify only three players who have retained the will to win—Earl, Cooper and Brent. Perhaps Kelly, if he feels he has something to prove. Sam? He sure looks shaky but he's probably more geeked than either Carl or Nate. That means Kelly at the point, Sam at #2, Brent out of position at #3, Earl out of position at #4, and Cooper in the middle. Well, maybe we can press and trap, play hugger-mugger hoops . . . Sure, with six sober players.

But anything's possible. I can fondly recall a game in my rookie season at Peoria when we trailed Kuback's Rangers by twenty-six points with only 6:21 left in the game. I used a small lineup, playing three guys out of position, and we won in regulation time on a buzzer-beating hoop by Brian Hollander . . . Or another game in Waco, where we lagged by six with :22 left and won in overtime . . . Or a ballgame in Madison . . .

Before I know it, I'm asleep.

Before I know it, I'm awake again, drowsier than ever, my throat raspy, my head clogged. I take a shave, but no shower, a perfect, bloodless shave.

The Cosmos locker room is just down the hall, several steps closer to the men's room. And there's Millhouse, promenading around with two hairless and neckless brothers walking beside him. Millhouse's henchmen both have the swollen, brutish bodies of lifetime steroid addicts. But they're stylish, too, with their bulging muscles stuffed into spiffy tuxedos. Even though the two goons may indeed sing soprano, I wouldn't be amazed to see them eat glass or nails, rocks or cannonballs. They growl when they see Sam, and my peerless scorer slinks into our locker room.

Still no sign of Josh. I never wanted him in the first place, but since the Waco Wildcats only demanded $500 and a seventh-round draft pick, Herm insisted that Josh was a bargain. "Josh may be certifiable," Herm said, "but he'll be boffo at the box office." Sure enough, our average home attendance was 2,917. Before Josh, soaring to 2,938 A.J.

Most of the players who are present and accounted for might as well be elsewhere for all the spunk they're showing. There's no chatter, no laughter. They're punching the clock. But I'm a stubborn cuss and I will not accept Earl's gloomy prognosis. That's why I dispense with the usual pregame scouting report and attempt to galvanize them with a frontal attack.

For openers, I slam my fist against the nearest locker, loosening a shower of rust flakes. "Hey," I shout, "you guys look like the living dead. Wake up. What's the problem here? You don't want to play any more? You're tired? Too fucking bad. Then don't cash your checks. Go steal somebody else's money. You guys are moping around like we're down two-to-nothing! Jesus. You don't think we can beat them again? Go get a heart transplant. If you're just gonna go through the motions, then get the fuck outta here. There's the door. Go on home. Get a nine-to-five at the A.-and-fucking-P. Take out the garbage. Fuck your own wife. Goddammit! I won't let you lie down!"

Then I grab the brick and hurl it against a vacant locker. In the close confines of the room the sound approximates an exploding hand grenade. "Go out there and show some pride. Play like men."

"DO IT!"

The referees are Stevie Stephenson and Danny Jones, one of my favorites, a dedicated weightlifter with a mild speech impediment. I hope Danny doesn't let Stephenson take over the game.

Millhouse's brace of goons is seated just behind the Cosmos bench. They stand during the National Anthem, but instead of gazing reverently at the huge flag hanging from one of the overhead girders, the two goons glare at Sam.

Henderson starts, but after he captures the tipoff, Miller takes his place. A ruthless move by Millhouse, relegating a seven-year NBA veteran to a flunky's role.

From the start Carl resembles a seasick sailor trying to sprint on the deck of a storm-tossed ship. The Cosmos open the game in a half-court trap and Carl misplays the ball the first two times he touches it. Only ninety-six seconds into the ballgame and we're already down 10–0. I call a :20 and try Kelly for Carl. No good. Kelly is so afraid to make a mistake that he overhandles the ball and our offense (the fluid, ball-popping flex of my dreams) has a seizure.

STARS–6   CC–19

Nate is a step behind every play. Sam can't spit in the ocean, but the more he misses, the more he shoots. I send Brent in for Sam and our intensity steps up.

STARS–11   CC–21

Then Darwin Spencer enters the game and proceeds to toss Earl around like the cowboy's made of straw.

STARS–15   CC–31

Nate for Earl. Carl for Kelly. I don't have much room to maneuver. But it doesn't matter. The Stars are in eclipse. We simply were not ready for the high-energy getaway that the Cosmos pressure created.

STARS–21   CC–43

Cooper is in early foul trouble, so Earl's bench-rest is abbreviated. But then Nate zeroes in on the basket and we make a feeble run at the ballgame.

STARS–29   CC–45

Stephenson calls a charge on Earl. I have a bad angle on the play but I scream at Stephenson anyway and the little man gives me another T. (Counting the playoffs, it's my twenty-seventh technical foul in sixty-five games, a total of $675 in fines so far.) During the next dead ball, Earl confesses that, yes, he did commit the charge.

The Cosmos lead at the half is 58–36.

I'm too depressed to hoot and holler. The locker room is gusty and cold until I replace the brick. Right now, our only realistic goal is to get through the rest of the ballgame with no physical, and minimal psychic, damage. The sun will rise tomorrow, resurrecting a new day and a new ballgame. Perhaps.

I resolve to have Carl play the full twenty-four minutes in the second half. Let him toss his cookies in the three-second lane.

STARS–53   CC–76

I am also moved to curtail Earl's suffering. Let me save his legs and his energy for game five. Brent is poised at the scorer's table, waiting only for the next whistle so he can replace Earl. But during a rebound melee, Earl dislocates the same damn finger. The Cosmos trainer has to snap it back in place and Earl nearly faints. Again he refuses an X-ray, and he sits on the bench, head covered with a towel, trying to ignore the rest of the ballgame.

When Cooper fouls out, the Savannah Stars are represented by Carl, Kelly, Sam, Brent and Nate. Our average size is slightly more than 6'3" and 190 pounds, a little smaller than a small high-school team.

The score is 112–79 with 1:17 on the game clock, when Millhouse orders his team into a full-court press.

Earl is fuming. "That cocksucker," he says. "Put me back in the game, Rob. Let me go hurt somebody."

I stand up and glower downcourt, where Millhouse likewise stands in front of his bench. "That's bullshit," I yell.

"Fuck you, chickenshit," is Millhouse's response. Then he waves his hands, challenging me, beckoning me to approach him. "Come over here and do something about it." Behind him the goons rise to their feet.

And I can't take any more! I lose it. *"YOU MOTHAFUCKER."*

Some last vestige of self-control snaps, leaving me wild and bellowing, a wounded beast turning on the hunters, charging downcourt, out of my mind with rage, intent on obliterating the smiling goons and killing Millhouse, who hides behind them, yes, killing him. Tearing open his throat with my teeth . . .

But Danny Jones grabs me in a bear hug from behind, swooping me off my feet. "It ain't wuth it, Bo," he says in my ear, pinning my arms. "Carm down. It ain't wuth it."

"It is, it is!"

Slowly, Danny increases the pressure on my chest so that I must gasp for breath. "It ain't wuth it." He carries me toward the baseline, where the desperate need to breathe, to inhale, to live, suddenly overrides my anger.

"I'm okay," I say. "Thanks, Danny. I'm okay. Let me down."

He releases me gently. "I have to cawl aynother T," he says, almost apologizing. "You're ejected."

"I understand. I'm okay."

So I walk slowly off the court, the fans uproarious behind me, above me, hurling abuse, paper cups, crumpled newspapers as I enter the tunnel which leads to the basement staircase, thinking, hoping, that this . . . this fiasco will maybe motivate my players for tomorrow. Then, just as I mount the top of the stairs, gathering my body for the rhythmic descent into the basement, a hand seizes my right forearm.

"What?"

It's a cop. About 5'8", a solid 170 pounds, wearing his play-hat with its shiny black brim, a badge on his hat, a badge on his chest. The nameplate above his right breast pocket says "G. Murray." His eyes are gray, almost colorless. There's an oversized six-shooter strapped to his waist.

Now his other hand also locks onto my forearm. "Let's go," he says. The force of his grip nearly tilts me headlong down the steps and he must yank me back to right my balance.

"I'm going," I say, then shake loose of him. "Get the fuck *off* me. This has nothing to do with you."

He clutches at me again. "Get the fuck *off*."

At the bottom of the stairs, he pushes the small of my back, propelling me toward the locker room. "Get away, leave me alone."

He shoves me into the locker room and slams the door behind me.

"Fuck you," I shout back at him through the closed door. Then I kick every dented, rusty locker from one end of the room to the other.

Right now, at this very moment, everything that's happened is someone else's fault. Herm's. Millhouse's. Murray the minicop's. I am the outraged innocent and the role is strangely gratifying.

But then, then I have to pee (whose fault is that?), so I venture into the hallway.

Evidently the game is over, because here comes Millhouse, bopping down the stairs, sans goons.

So I rush at him and suddenly we're face to face. I clench my right hand. But instead of moving to defend himself, he stares at me, speechless, apparently shocked at my riotous fury, his mouth twisted into a vacant grin. All at once I no longer want to hurt him, yet some red-eyed, swaggering compulsion moves my fist in a threatening arc. He never retreats as I swing weakly and miss his face by at least a foot.

Then there's something grabbing my neck from behind. My legs are pushed forward and I tumble to the floor. I find myself on my back, with the minicop jamming a forearm against my throat and a knee into my chest.

Then my players are there, shouting, gesticulating. "Get off him," I hear Nate say, and Earl shouts, "Let him up."

The cop backs away and I am helped to my feet. Then the cop is at me again, his left hand poking my chest, his right hand balled into a fist. There's a bright light shining on us from somewhere.

"If you didn't have a gun," I scream at the cop, "you'd be a doorstop."

"It's over," says Nate.

"Let him alone," says Earl. "We'll take him into the locker room."

The players slowly form a circle around me and Officer Murray. Large black men closing in behind him, cutting off his only avenue of escape. The cop's right hand moves slowly toward his gun, carefully unsnapping the strap on his holster.

"How many of us can you murder?" I say. "How many bullets do you have?"

Now the cop steps back, holding his hands open in front of his chest, allowing the players to hustle me into the locker room.

Inside, nobody quite knows what to do. So we move in an

aimless circle, waiting for the music to stop. They've all planned on showering back at the motel, but we have the feeling that we're under seige and none of us is eager to leave our sanctuary.

"I'm proud of you," Sam says. "You did what you had to do."

Nate agrees. "We let you down tonight, Rob. But you stood up for us anyway. We'll be ready to play tomorrow."

Could this be the communion I've been looking for all this time? A communion of martyrs? A sacrament under fire in a foxhole?

Then the door bursts opon and a dozen cops pour into the room. The biggest one—6'5", 240 pounds—the one with the angriest face, says to me, "Come outside, we want to ask you some questions."

"Ask them in here," I say.

"Come outside," he insists. Officer Jablonski.

"They're gonna bust you," Kelly says, and all the players surge forward to shield me. But the cops wave their night sticks and the players retreat. Then Jablonski grabs my lucky red-striped necktie, yanks me through the doorway and slams me face-first against the wall. My arms are pulled behind my back and my wrists are cuffed. And the peace officers are swarming around me, as the short one steps up close to club my legs and thighs. "You fucking cowards," I shout, and I want to say more but the handcuffs are pulled one notch tighter.

I'm pushed upstairs, outside and into the back seat of a squad car. A photographer flashes his gismo as the car door slams shut.

Officer Half-Pint drives while Jablonski rides shotgun. In the cramped back seat, my wrists tightly manacled, however I twist and angle my legs, some part of my body suffers. Jablonski recites my rights in rapid-fire delivery. I can't understand most of what he says but I don't dare ask for any clarification. My anger is forgotten. I'm a prisoner.

"What happens now?"

"You'll get booked," Murray says without a trace of hostility. Just doing his job. The law-abiding citizens of Capital City can rest easy tonight.

"What's the charge? Did Millhouse file charges?"

"No," says Murray. "We'll file the charges. Just cooperate and behave yourself."

"You know something?" I say to the driver. "You'd make a terrific referee."

The stationhouse is only a short jaunt from the Armory, and it resembles a smaller version of the latter, also built to withstand attack. Inside, everything's as neat and sanitized as a hospital. No crumbling walls here, no naked pipes, no bricks blocking broken windows. There's a massive oaken desk right inside the front door. The chairs and tables scattered about are made of gray plastic and the walls are painted the same glossy-colored gray. I am led through a bewildering maze of corridors and remanded to the custody of another uniformed officer. This one wears a brown cardigan sweater that hides his nameplate, also floppy slippers instead of shoes. He doesn't appear to be armed. It's Mr. Rogers' neighborhood.

"No funny stuff?" he asks.

"No. I'm done."

So he unlocks the cuffs and asks to see my driver's license. Both my wrists are pinched and bleeding. Does Mr. Rogers care? He takes my watch, wallet, belt, tie and my shoes and stashes them in a large canvas pouch. He hangs my jacket on a hook. He signs something, I sign something and I am handed a receipt.

All the while I try to be clinically curious about the proceedings. I'm put on a swivel stool for my mug shots, right and left profiles, then straight-faced. So help me, I can't help saying, "Cheese." Mr. Rogers holds my fingers firmly for the printing and it's all somehow reassuring. The photos will represent a true likeness, the fingerprints won't be smudged, and crime will never, ever pay.

Mr. Rogers tells me I've been charged with "simple" assault and also resisting arrest. In truth, I resisted being taken from the locker room to answer "some questions," but I never had the capability to resist arrest. In any event, my bail is $400, payable in cash or certified check only.

"I haven't got that kind of money on hand."

Do I want to make a phone call? No. The guys will be back for me when they've finished showering (and eating?).

*   *   *

So I pad down another carpeted corridor, bend through a door, and Mr. Rogers locks me into a cell. There's a sink and a crapper made of stainless steel. The walls are cinder blocks painted the same institutionalized gray as the main room. On top of a low cinder-block bed, there's a thin plastic mattress, also in gray. The floor is cold and bare. The ceiling is white and the only light is recessed overhead behind a wire grid.

I'm alone in a jail cell. No TV. No books. Not even tonight's stat sheet. My entire life has led me to this place, this moment. Shall I cry? Shall I pray? Lord, just get me out of this one and I'll be good forever?

Should I recite some poems from memory? "Whan that Aprille with his shoures soote..." Or should I fine-tune my excuses? Millhouse had no right to... Perhaps I should get my story straight. First he did that, then I did this...

How long have I been here? How long will I be here?

I'm alone. Totally. At least the ancient mariner had the sea to look at, the sky, the ship, the dead bodies sprawled on the deck. All I have for comfort, for distraction, is my own bottomless, wordless despair.

And, yes. I do weep. Because, in the clutch I cannot fool myself. "Vanity of vanities ... all is vanity," saith the Preacher, and his finger points at me. There are absolutely no extenuations that might excuse me. *Mea culpa.* I am utterly responsible for my own life.

That means a decision must be made.

Yes.

I'll reevaluate everything after the season is over.

After a while the door opens and Mr. Rogers returns my belongings and leads me to the front room, where Earl and Sam are waiting. Mr. Rogers tells me about my "plea" date. I must sign a few more documents, then I'm free to go.

"We chipped in for the bail," Earl says. His left hand is in a makeshift sling to keep his finger elevated. "Kelly had to kick in two hundred to make up the difference."

It also seems that Sam sweettalked the girl at the front desk into letting him have the keys to the motel's van, and all the guys have come along for the ride. When I curl into the shotgun seat, they all applaud and hoot and treat me like a hero.

"Ain't no thing," Sam says, behind the wheel. "Most brothers, if they live in a big city, have been in the joint some time or other. Me? Yep. I had a fight with some ofay in a bar. I stayed in jail overnight and the school got the charges dropped. Actually I didn't mind it 'cause I scored some pretty good weed." Then Sam hands me two McBuggers and a coke. "You're always hungry," he says, "when you're let outta jail."

"I been in jail too," Carl says. "I got caught drunk driving when I was in school and they also got them to drop the charges."

Who else? Kelly?

"No, siree. I ain't never been in jail."

"Not yet," says Sam, and we all laugh.

"I have," Nate volunteers. "I beat up some girl the year after I got out of school. She let me stay in jail for two days, then she dropped the charges. She was a good piece of ass, man. The day I got sprung, I moved in with her."

What about Brent?

"No, thank you. My momma would kill me if I even got me a parking ticket."

"Don't even bother asking the white guys," Sam says.

At the motel we laugh and hug. Would I join them for a quick beer? Sorry, no. And, hey, don't stay out too late. We've got a game tomorrow.

And I'm surprised at how peacefully I sleep.

27

A FURTIVE KNOCKING on the door is enough to wake me. The time is 9:17 A.M. "Mr. Lassner?" It's a young woman's voice, perhaps the young woman of my dreams. "There's an important phone call for you. Mr. Lassner?"

"Yeah. I hear you. Thanks."

No way I'm talking to anybody but my players today, so I lift the receiver from its cradle, then replace it. Long as I'm up I shuffle to the bathroom, pounding on the closed bathroom door to warn the cockroaches and give them time to retreat.

There's a sheaf of papers on the floor under the front door. Flash-paper messages to call everybody ASAP plus a bulging manila envelope from Steve Collins containing last night's game tape and the stat sheet. I drop the tape to the floor as though it were oozing blood.

The referees are obliged to "write me up," probably FAXing their versions of last night's misadventures to the CBL office this morning. But league policy requires that the commissioner view the tape before levying any penalties. So I should be safe until Monday.

The players seem rejuvenated at the shootaround, laughing and joking. "Your skin," Kelly says to Sam, "is the same color as dogshit that's been lying in the sun for about a year."

"What's those blotches on your neck?" Sam asks Kelly. "Nigger, you been into the Clorox again?"

COMMERCIAL BASKETBALL LEAGUE

Official Scorer's Report

Date **March 30, 1992** Game # **04** Arena **Jefferson Street Armory** Attendance: **3471**
Visitors **Savannah Stars** Home **Capitol City Cosmos** Length of Game **2:18**

Visitors: Stars

No	Visitors: Stars	Min	FG M	FG A	FT M	FT A	3Pt M	3Pt A	Pts	Reb O	Reb D	TOT	AST	PF	TO	BS	ST
6	Royal (G)	28	2	4	0	0	0	0	4	0	1	1	2	2	4	0	1
7	Franks (G)	46	6	19	4	6	2	5	18	0	2	2	1	2	3	0	0
8	Butler	30	3	6	0	0	0	0	6	1	1	2	2	3	6	0	0
10	Cooper (C)	37	5	11	5	7	0	0	15	4	7	11	1	6	3	2	1
12	Kennison (F)	47	8	17	1	1	0	0	17	1	5	6	1	4	3	1	0
32	Patton (F)	31	6	13	4	5	0	0	16	3	7	10	3	3	2	0	2
40	Springs	21	3	6	0	1	0	0	6	1	4	5	2	2	0	1	3
	TOTALS	240	33	76	14	20	2	5	82	10	27	37	12	22	21	4	7
	Pct.		43.4		70.0		40.0			Team 2					1		

Home: Cosmos

No	Home: Cosmos	Min	FG M	FG A	FT M	FT A	3Pt M	3Pt A	Pts	Reb O	Reb D	TOT	AST	PF	TO	BS	ST
12	James (G)	35	3	8	2	2	0	0	8	0	3	3	11	2	3	0	4
15	Smith	13	1	2	1	1	0	0	3	0	0	0	2	1	1	0	2
20	Mann	19	0	2	2	2	0	0	2	1	2	3	0	3	0	1	1
24	Henderson (C)	17	2	4	1	1	0	0	5	1	3	4	2	0	0	1	0
31	Wagman (G)	35	10	17	6	7	0	0	26	0	2	2	2	4	2	0	3
34	Spencer	20	4	8	3	4	0	0	11	3	5	8	0	2	2	2	0
35	Jerome	8	0	3	1	2	0	0	1	1	3	4	0	2	0	2	0
42	Toggins (F)	36	8	15	5	7	1	3	22	3	4	7	1	2	1	1	3
44	Andrews (F)	30	8	16	3	4	0	0	19	2	8	10	2	2	1	1	0
55	Miller	27	9	14	2	2	0	0	20	1	8	9	4	2	2	0	1
	TOTALS	240	45	89	26	32	1	3	117	12	38	50	24	20	12	8	16
	Pct.		50.6		81.5		33.3			Team 3					3		

Score By Quarters	1	2	3	4	OT	OT	OT	Final
V Stars	17	19	20	26				82
H Cosmos	31	27	27	32				117

Miscellaneous Statistics

Ties	0	Lead Changes	0
Points off off. rebounds (H)	8	(V)	3
Points off steals (H)	14	(V)	6
Offensive fouls (H)	2	(V)	3

Officials: **Steve Stephenson, Danny Jones**
Technicals: **Sav. Coach Lassner (UNSP) 11:24 2nd Q**
Sav. Coach Lassner (UNSP) 10:59 4th Q
– ejected

Remarks: **Cosmos even series 2-2**

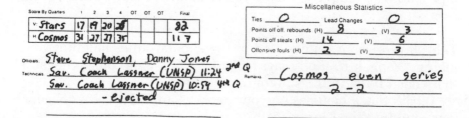

Even Carl appears to be sober. And, saints preserve us, Josh is there to meet us, not at the van, but in the Armory.

"Where have you been?" I ask him.

There's a small lump on his head and a smaller scab on the lump. Otherwise he looks about the same as ever. "Guess," he says, and one corner of his mouth starts to twitch.

"On a drug binge? Or was it booze?"

"Nope."

"Holed up with some girl?"

"Nope."

"You had to see your parole officer?"

"Nope."

"Josh. This is ridiculous."

"Keep guessing."

"Okay. You're an outpatient at a mental institution and you had to go get your prescriptions renewed."

"Nope."

"You were kidnapped by little green men and taken away in a flying saucer—"

"Little black men," he says.

"This has been fun, Josh, but I'll have to fine you."

"A fine is fine with me."

Just as we're underway, three strangers enter the playing area. A small slovenly man flashing a spiral-top notebook, a larger man lugging various components of a TV camera, and a slick-haired man in a sports jacket and tie. I summon a soldier and have them evicted.

"Did you see the papers?" Kelly says. "The Celtics got blown out last night and Oz Joseph got fourteen points. Sixteen minutes, six-for-eight, two-for-two. That boy got some junk in his trunk. Some shit in his kit."

"Has Brian Hollander played for the Cavs yet?"

"No. Hey, Rob. I also saw you on the TV this morning. Both of us are TV celebrities, huh? There was some footage of you and that little cop hassling outside the locker room. Then that guy, what's his name, Fishie Wishie? He gets interviewed and he said you're not fit to coach anywhere. He said you should be banned by the CBL for life. Ain't that a bitch? Now this may sound racist, Coach, but I'll say it, even though Coach Millhouse is a brother. Only black folks are gonna know that what you did was the right thing to do. The same thing with me. It's the white people gonna be self-righteous and crucify the both of us."

We work against the Cosmos half- and full-court pressure. With only eight players and one coach, we must use a folding chair to represent Kennedy Andrews. Then we play our spot-shooting game.

I am undeniably a white person and my impulse is to apologize to the team (my team), but they'd never understand.

I spend the afternoon reading, snoozing and daydreaming. I order three entrees, soup and an appetizer from the Chinese restaurant. The food is delivered by a small Chinese man of indeterminate age. He struggles with his English as he tries to tell me how much I must pay him. Finally, he gives up and hands me a copy of the bill.

I give him a generous tip, which he pockets. Then he points at me, smiles and says, "You!" Putting his dukes up, he shadowboxes until I slam the door.

The scoop at the Armory is that Commissioner Rose has nixed Millhouse's goons. According to the CBL bylaws, any "security personnel" can only be provided by the arena. Rose has decreed that Millhouse's personal bodyguards helped create an "inflammatory situation." For his folly, Millhouse has been fined fifty bucks.

I wonder if Millhouse would be willing to pay another fifty to scare the bejesus out of Sam again, virtually insuring that the Cosmos win the series.

Several reporters and camera crews have infiltrated the tiny locker room and, quietly and politely, I shoo them away.

My pregame harangue barely touches on tactical measures . . .

Spencer has a slow release. If we can ignore his head fakes, his turn-around-jumper is very blockable. Double hard of off James. Be ready for their pressure defenses.

Earl's finger is bound so tightly that the fingernail showing above the tape has turned blue. I will start Kelly, after exhorting him to trust his instincts and "just play." Nate will get short rotations of five or six minutes each to keep him fresh and alert.

The guys seem responsive and ready to play hard.

"DO IT!"

The refs are Brennan and Sforza, experienced and capable. Put away the K-Y, we won't get fucked tonight. And there's a cop sitting behind the bench—"G. Blackshaw," 6'1", 220—definitely not one of last night's assault troops.

As the game begins, Millhouse withholds his pressure defense and we jump out to an early lead. The Cosmos defense is physical, as always, and they're switching more than they've shown before. We are forced to take long shots against their belly-to-belly defense, but Sam, Earl and Nate are uncanny, filling the basket every which-way.

STARS–10   CC–7

Our own defense is feisty, but the Cosmos are patient and their Passing Game II produces good shots. Fortunately, most of their shots grow hair and slide off the rim.

STARS–17   CC–12

How long can we keep hitting the long ones? How long can the Cosmos keep missing the easies?

Cooper controls the boards and the refs let him play like a veteran. "I'm having *fun*," he says during a timeout.

STARS–23   CC–18

Whenever Nate exhibits the slightest physical or mental lapse, Josh comes off the bench to rebound and block shots. Strangely enough, Josh is also executing the offense as never before. Perhaps they also run the flex on Mars.

STARS–31   CC–27

Earl's game covers the entire court, assaulting loose balls, shooting long three-pointers, taking a sternum-smashing charge against Toggins. We double off James, who can't buy a hoop. When Spencer enters the game, we squelch his post-up dynamics by doubling him too. But nothing can keep Spencer from cleaning the offensive glass . . . Thanks, Herm. At least the "dance team" has new bras.

STARS–38   CC–33

Kelly moves the ball properly and Carl trips over the timeline. Brent is ferocious on defense but the calls go against him. It's my fault. I haven't played Brent enough all year for the refs to learn his game. In pro basketball, familiarity breeds free fouls.

All the while, the hecklers in the stands scream, "Jailbird!"

We're in front, 48–44, at the half, and the cop touches my arm as I leave the bench. What now?

"Let me give you a friendly piece of advice," Officer G. Blackshaw says. "Never say 'fuck you' to a cop."

The guys seem disgruntled, like we're down by twenty points instead of up by four. I can't berate them, so I'm supportive, even cheerful, but they won't be stimulated.

"We've come too far to let down now. We've been through too much not to dig a little deeper. C'mon, guys, let's keep it going. Just twenty-four minutes of hard work."

"DO IT!"

As he leaves the room, Earl turns to me, saying, "It's no good, Rob. They have nothing left."

Nobody else can hit a shot as we commence the second half, but Earl singlehandedly keeps us competitive. He plays like a demon on the block, he knocks down threes and he gets to the foul line.

STARS–58   CC–56

For a long stretch, our offense consists of three plays—30, 33 and 33L—all isos for Earl. We cling to the lead, but I feel like I'm sitting on a bomb.

STARS–66   CC–65

Carl shows some signs of life, ripping James and converting the layup. Sam hits two fancy jumpers. Then Earl bangs his finger on Toggins' head trying to block a shot.

STARS–79   CC–76

Sam cans a twisting twenty-footer. Maybe he can take us home. Nate is fouled on a drive and makes two-of-two. When Cooper hits a TAJ in the post, our lead is 85–80 with 2:07 remaining.

Then James misses an uncontested jumper when we double Toggins. Earl rebounds, dribbles wall-to-wall and misses a complicated layup. On the return trip, Wagman comes hard off a pick to sink an eighteen-footer.

STARS–85   CC–82

Sam rushes a jumper and misses. Miller posts Nate and beats him to the bucket. When Nate misses an easy fifteen-foot chippie, Spencer rebounds and Millhouse wants timeout.

STARS–85   CC–84

The clock says 1:10 when the Cosmos inbound. They show their Passing Game I set, then run a pick-and-roll with Andrews and Wagman. Cooper hesitates and Wagman clears the pick unguarded, lifting a nineteen-footer that goes halfway down before spinning out. But Nate is slow to react and Spencer dunks the rebound.

STARS–85   CC–86

It's our timeout with 0:49.7 left. We still have one timeout remaining, they have one full and one :20. Millhouse will no doubt replace Wagman with Eric Mann for defense. Nevertheless, we'll run a 21 Clear for Sam.

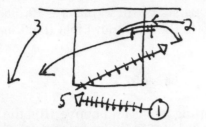

We need a good cut from Sam, a good pick from Nate and a good pass from Cooper. And the ballgame belongs to Sam.

Sam catches and Mann is suckered by the first fake. Sam ducks under the brunt of the contact and misses the fifteen-footer. The whistle blows and Sforza sends Sam to the line.

The first free throw veers to the left but Sam buckets the next one. Instead of a possible three-point play, we've barely managed a single point.

STARS–86   CC–86   0:38.8

Millhouse wants to preserve his last full timeout, so he lets Andrews inbound the ball to James, who dribbles nearly to mid-court before calling their 20-second timeout.

Millhouse immediately subs Wagman for Mann, thereby entitling me also to make a move off the bench—Carl for Kelly.

Okay. We're up by one. Right now there's 0:31.9 on the game clock, 0:17 on the shot clock, and the Cosmos haven't crossed the timeline, so they must inbound from their backcourt. This means they have 0:03 to cross midcourt. A major error by Millhouse. Okay. Let's try forcing them into a 10-second backcourt violation. We want fullcourt man-to-man pressure. Deny anybody in the frontcourt. Should they get the ball across in time, we'll be in our diamond 1-2-1-1 trap. Everybody to the boards.

"DO IT!"

The Cosmos are unaware that the :10 countdown is squeezing them. Another mistake compounding the first one. James blithely turns his back on Carl, advancing the ball much too slowly. Both James and Millhouse are startled when Sforza toots his tooter and gives us the ball.

STARS–86   CC–86   0:28.5

No need to extinguish our last timeout here—that would only allow Millhouse to send his defensive platoon into the game. We'll run XO-Cross, an iso for Earl.

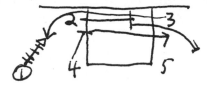

Holding the ball to consume every precious second, head-faking, looking for the double-team to rush him, Earl finally fires away with :06 on the shot clock and 0:10.7 left in the game. His stroke is compact, the release is smooth, the ball rides high, spinning tightly, then falling under the weight of so many hopes and fears, falling short. But Cooper is there, rising, flying, to nab the rebound. When he lands, the rookie is clobbered by Miller, and Brennan awards him a pair of free throws.

The diameter of the ball is ten inches, the inside diameter of the rim is eighteen inches. Easy does it, Coop.

Cooper crosses himself, and misses. The crowd screams.

"That's okay, Coop," I shout. "All we need is one!"

Bang. He has it. And Millhouse calls timeout.

STARS–87   CC–86   0:07.9

They have enough time to run a variety of plays. Okay. We'll switch every crossing, double the wings and double the post from the top. If they're destined to beat us, let's make them beat us from the perimeter. No fouls. Five to the glass.

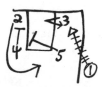

"DO IT!"

And then they run something they've never shown us before, a quick inbounds pass to Spencer on the right block. We're too befuddled to double-team, so Earl is left to defend Spencer one-on-one. Spencer fakes hard to the middle, then swings his right hand to the baseline. He fakes once, twice, Earl doesn't bite. Spencer shoots. Earl leaps at the ball, extending his near hand, his left, to block the shot. Then, at the last instant, Earl's left hand disobeys his brain and recoils just enough to let the shot pass, hit the inner edge of the side rim and tangle the net in celebration.

STARS–87   CC–88   0:04.1

I call a timeout. "Give it to me," Sam says. "I want it," says Earl. Okay. We'll run our special. Everybody remember it? My fingers are steady as they move the magnetic circles along my gameboard.

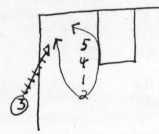

- Earl will inbound
- Sam cuts to the corner, using an outside or inside cut. This is our first option.
- Sam catches and goes

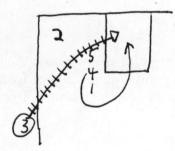

- If Sam is too tightly guarded
- Nate curls and goes to the hoop
- Earl looks to throw a lob pass to Nate

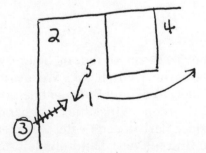

- If Sam and Nate are covered
- Kelly vacates
- Cooper steps up to receive Earl's pass

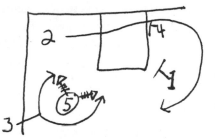

- Earl makes a sharp cut off of Cooper (either outside or inside), receives a return pass and goes
- Sam vacates and curls around staggered-pick
- If nothing else is there, Cooper goes

"DO IT!"

Sam runs an inside cut and loses Mann on the triple-pick. I know that Earl wants to wait for the last option, the pass and return with Cooper, but Sam is so open, so clean and so alone that Earl cannot shortcircuit his own instincts. Sam has the audacity to lick the fingers of his right hand just before he catches and shoots. Another whirling leather spheroid that spins into another dimension of dreams and nightmares, that also falls short.

Earl makes an heroic effort, running, leaping, tapping the ball with his left hand. The buzzer covers his shriek of agony, and the ball kicks out.

The hometown fans are jubilant as they rush onto the floor. The Cosmos leap about, jumping into each other's arms. Henderson and Andrews hoist Millhouse up onto their brawny shoulders. While the Savannah Stars and their scapegrace coach walk unnoticed to the visitors' locker room.

We shake hands and embrace. Earl and Nate are barely able to speak. Brent stares at his feet, Josh at the ceiling. Cooper is already plugged into his tape. Sam and Carl shake their heads in tandem. "You make some," Sam says, "and you miss some. What the fuck."

Across the narrow room Kelly is crying, his body shaking, his tears hidden under a towel. When I put my arm around Kelly's shoulder he leans his head into my chest, weeping louder than ever, dribbling his tears and his schnotz all over my not so lucky tie. Still holding Kelly, I deliver my eulogy for the dead season. (Was it murder? Or suicide?)

"We came a long way, guys, and we made a great effort tonight. I'm proud of all of you. You've proved to me that you all have the hearts of warriors. That you're all winners. I guess it just wasn't meant to be. Thanks for an interesting season. The van leaves the motel at seven, the plane leaves at eight."

Then we pile our hands for the last time and Nate leads us through The Lord's Prayer. "Our Father . . . Thy will be done . . . Forever and ever. Amen."

Earl, Nate and I find a backdoor bar on State Avenue. And we drink, not beer, but serious hootch. Vodka. Gin. What the hell do I know? They order, we drink and I pay the bill. We take turns saying, "What a fucking season."

Nate says he will retire. Earl will go overseas. Earl claims I will need a "disguise" to get back safely into Savannah. I agree, saying, "I'm definitely persona au gratin in Savannah."

We tell no funny stories about wild coaches we have known, about famous CBL squabbles. We just drink, hard and fast.

"This fucking finger," Earl says, displaying it on the bar. Swollen, crooked, black-blue-and-yellow. "It's so stupid."

A little guy in a blue blazer approaches us. He looks like a lawyer or an accountant. He also looks sloshed.

"You Bo Lassner?" he asks me. "Coach of the Savannah Stars?"

"Go 'way," says Earl.

"You don't look so tough to me," the little fellow says.

"Disappear," says Nate.

"You don't scare me," the little guy insists.

"Let's get outta here," I say. And we do.

I dread facing the consequences in Savannah. But I *am* glad the season's over.

Now it's time to make a decision.

COMMERCIAL BASKETBALL LEAGUE

Official Scorer's Report

Date: March 31, 1992   Game #: 05   Arena: Jefferson Street Armory   Attendance: 3486

Visitors: Savannah Stars   Home: Capitol City Cosmos   Length of Game: 2:05

NO	Visitors Stars	Min.	FG M	FG A	FT M	FT A	3Pt M	3Pt A	Pts.	Reb O	Reb D	Reb TOT	AST	PF	TO	BS	ST
6	Royal (G)	39	2	7	0	1	0	0	4	0	3	3	6	3	3	0	1
7	Franks (G)	44	8	12	2	3	0	2	18	1	3	4	2	2	3	0	0
8	Butler	9	1	2	0	0	0	0	2	0	1	1	1	2	1	0	1
10	Cooper (c)	42	7	14	2	3	0	0	16	3	10	13	0	3	1	1	0
11	Brusher	10	2	5	0	2	0	0	4	2	2	4	0	1	0	2	0
12	Kennison (F)	39	6	10	2	2	0	0	14	1	4	5	0	3	1	1	0
32	Patton (F)	46	9	18	7	8	4	7	29	2	7	9	8	4	2	1	4
40	Springs	11	0	1	0	2	0	0	0	0	1	1	2	4	1	0	2
	TOTALS	240	35	78	13	21	4	9	87	9	31	40	19	22	12	5	8
	Pct.		44.8		61.9		44.4			Team 3					0		

NO	Home Cosmos	Min.	FG M	FG A	FT M	FT A	3Pt M	3Pt A	Pts.	Reb O	Reb D	Reb TOT	AST	PF	TO	BS	ST
12	James (G)	39	2	4	1	2	0	0	5	1	1	2	9	2	3	0	3
15	Smith	9	0	1	0	0	0	0	0	0	0	0	2	1	0	0	2
20	Mann	18	0	2	0	2	0	0	0	0	2	2	0	2	0	1	2
24	Henderson (c)	10	1	3	0	0	0	0	2	0	1	1	0	1	0	1	0
31	Wayman (G)	35	7	12	4	4	0	2	18	1	2	3	3	2	2	0	0
34	Spencer	31	6	10	3	5	0	0	15	4	5	9	0	3	3	2	0
35	Jerome	DNP															
42	Toggins (F)	34	7	16	4	5	0	1	18	1	5	6	4	3	3	0	2
44	Andrews (F)	39	8	15	3	4	0	0	19	3	7	10	1	3	1	2	0
55	Miller	35	5	12	1	2	0	0	11	2	4	6	2	4	2	0	1
	TOTALS	240	36	80	16	24	0	3	88	12	27	39	21	21	14	6	10
	Pct.		45.0		75.0		0			Team 3					4		

Score By Quarters	1	2	3	4	OT	OT	OT	Final
V: Stars	23	25	19	20				87
H: Cosmos	19	25	21	23				88

Officials: Nick Sforza, Art Brennan

Technicals: _____

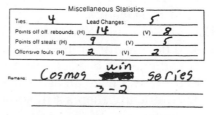

Miscellaneous Statistics

Ties: 4   Lead Changes: 5

Points off off. rebounds (H): 14   (V): 8

Points off steals (H): 9   (V): 5

Offensive fouls (H): 2   (V): 2

Remarks: Cosmos ~~win~~ series 3-2

28

WHAT'S LEFT OF my brain is numb, my ears are ringing out of tune. I'm not sure who I am or where it is I'm going. I just follow the crowd and wind up strapped into a seat on an airplane. My chin hits my chest, then I'm gone.

Dreaming of an immense, flying, vibrating, alien penisoid life-form that fucks volcanoes, abandoned mine shafts and floods the countryside with rivers of gism—

A stewardess wakes me, asking if I, "sir," want breakfast. My response is to gulp back the bile in my throat and, understandably, she quickly moves on to another customer.

My God, have I had a wet dream? Baad Mandrake. But it's not so. My dreams have not yet become my reality.

Okay. So I did a good job with the Stars, no question. Yes, I should have played Brent more. And I needed a better point guard, some-one with experience, stability, a jump shot. And last October dur-ing training camp, I could have traded Nate even-up for, say, Darwin Cook. But Nate's offense is perfectly suited for the flex, and I liked having him around. I also needed a drug-free scorer behind Earl and another bruiser behind the Beast.

Right now, I need an aspirin.

Theoretically, there's still some postseason work for me to do. In the past I've always held individual meetings with my players to discuss their plans for the future. I'd variously recommend that they return to the CBL ("Come Back Later"), go over the waters or get a real job. For some, I'd prescribe a summer program of weight-lifting or specific ballhandling drills. I've even taken bricklayers like Kelly and Brent into gyms and retooled their jump shots. But not this year.

I'm also expected to get the players out of town in proper order, making sure they have no outstanding bills at the Swedish Inn before releasing their plane tickets home. But Chet can handle the details.

There's a brief stopover in Atlanta and I pull on Earl's coat just before he dozes off. "Earl? My curiosity is killing me. Does anybody have any idea where Josh disappeared to? What do the guys say?"

"Nobody has a clue," Earl says. "If I was pushed, I'd say good drugs and a bad lady. But, like I told you, Josh is a crazy motherfucker. Don't even try to figure him out."

Even so, with Josh's bleeding fingertips and the crust of blood on his head, perhaps Josh Brusher is an imitation Messiah. He was gone three days. Resisting (or accepting) Satan's temptation on the mountaintop? Vacationing in hell? And surely he is risen, but not high enough.

Anyhow, Earl is going straight from the airport to the hospital, finally having his finger X-rayed and splinted. "I'd be really pissed," he says, "if this fucked up my golf game."

For the first time all season Magoo is not at the airport to welcome us. Patterson is there and Packman, with a cameraman. "Not right now, fellas," I tell them. "Let's do this . . . it's about twelve-thirty now. How's about coming out to the Swedish Inn at three o'clock? I'm in room one-o-one and I'll answer all your questions and give you all the time you need."

They are agreeable. April fool, suckers.

Back at the motel, the blonde on duty at the desk comes out to the van with "an important message." Herm has booked a team party for 7:00 tonight at the Red Lobster.

"Okay, guys. See you then."

In my room I pack my gear quickly, throwing armloads of dirty clothing into the trunk of the 1989 Honda. Where are those god-damn pants I was wearing last Monday when I stopped by the Stars office?

I remove my bankroll from under the mattress. How much money do I have? Five thousand? Ten? Twenty? I'll see how long it lasts. I leave my room key on top of the TV and abandon my cave forever.

Stopping at the front desk, I ask the blonde for a manila enve-lope, which I stuff with $400 worth of twenties. "This has to get to Earl Patton today," I tell her. "He'll be back about four." I hand her a twenty-dollar tip so she won't abscond with the funds. That's the theory, anyway.

Then I drive away, light of heart, heading to the Honda dealer-ship.

The boss's name is Huey Marlowe—6'7" and 300—a beefy man who never missed a home game. We chat about the season. When he wants to know what "really happened" in Capital City, I tell him the truth.

"Hot damn," he says. "Good for you. It'd've been me? I swear I might've kilt that nigra."

But bidness is bidness, so Huey puts on his game face and says, "Well, now. What can I do for you, Coach?"

I need to buy a used car and drive it away right now.

Impossible, says he. I'll need new license plates. Insurance. Besides, it's Sunday. These things take time.

What about the imported sardine can I've been using? Herm's tradeout? It has plates, insurance . . .

He'd like to help me but the same problems apply. Transferring plates, registration. Then he has a brainstorm. "Wait a minute,"

Huey says, and his jowly face brightens. "Tell you what, I can lease this here Japmobile to you for two hunnert a month. How's that?"

A deal. Here's $1200 for six months. All that cash bulges Huey's eyes. "Let me write up that leasing agreement," he says quickly before I can change my mind. "Won't take but a minute."

"Could I use your phone? A credit-card call."

"Sure."

So I dial the CBL's transaction line. "This is Bo Lassner of the Savannah Stars. It's Sunday, April first at two-fifteen P.M. The Stars waive Earl Patton, Sam Franks, Nate Kennison, Donald Cooper, Kelly Royal, Carl Butler, Brent Springs and Lem Jameson. The Stars also waive the rights to Benny Morrison. Thank you."

I feel like a renegade scientist sneaking into the experimental laboratory, opening all the cages and letting all the half-tortured animals go free. All except Josh.

I've never coached in the NBA and I never will. I've never coached college basketball and I never will.

After five years in the CBL, and two hours in jail, this is what I've come to understand . . .

That coaches are spectators, eunuchs at an orgy.

That the players are the only true communicants.

That the good doctor was right on—"Basketball is just a game to play. You don't coach it."

That's why I'm off to Toronto, to the YMCA on Yonge Street. I have a week to get there and get my game in shape.

DO IT!